SHE WAS JUST A MAIDEN ON THE
THRESHOLD OF A NEW LIFE . . . .

"Imagine to yourself, Madam, how my little coquette heart flutter'd with joy at the sight of a
white lute-string, flower'd with silver, scoured indeed, but passed on me for spick-and-span new,
a Brussels lace cap, braided shoes, and the rest in
proportion, all second-hand finery, and procured
instantly for the occasion, by the diligence and
industry of the good Mrs. Brown, who had already a chapman for me in the house, before
whom my charms were to pass in review; for he
had not only, in course, insisted on immediate
surrender to him, in case of his agreeing for me,
concluding very wisely that such a place as I was
in was of the hottest to trust the keeping of such a
perishable commodity in as a maidenhead."

AH, SWEET FANNY! HAD SHE BUT KNOWN
THE PLEASURES THAT LAY AHEAD . . . .

John Cleland's

MEMOIRS OF A
WOMAN OF PLEASURE

WITH AN INTRODUCTION
FOR MODERN READERS BY

Peter Quennell

A DELL/PUTNAM BOOK

Distributed by
Dell Publishing Co., Inc.
1 Dag Hammarskjold Plaza
New York, New York 10017

Dell ® TM 681510, Dell Publishing Co., Inc.

ISBN: 0-440-05555-5

Distributed by arrangement with G. P. Putnam's Sons

Printed in the United States of America

One previous edition
New edition
    First printing—July 1982

    Second printing—December 1984

Introduction

"Then Cleland; curious figure," wrote James Boswell in his London diary on October 14, 1769, as he listed some of the more memorable personages he had encountered during the course of a long and busy day. Addressing himself, an odd Boswellian habit, he recorded that he had "thought how 'twould have struck you some years ago." Boswell's second, and apparently his last, mention of this curious figure was made on March 31, 1772. "I called on Mr. Garrick," he wrote, "at his house in the Adelphi. I found him like a little minister of state, standing in the middle of a room . . . surrounded with several people, and among them old Cleland, in his youth the author of the *Woman of Pleasure*, that most licentious and inflaming book, and now the grave and prolix *Parlementarian* in the newspapers. He is the son of Will Honeycomb of the *Spectator*. He is a fine sly malcontent. Garrick was talking vainly of his being appointed executor of a clergyman by 'that great man, Lord Camden.' 'Not a very great man,' grumbled Cleland." After which, Boswell, feeling that his host was far too preoccupied to spare him all the attention that he deserved, bade a ceremonious farewell and went his way.

John Cleland, at the time, was a man of sixty-three, and the exciting narrative that Boswell remembered was over two decades old. He had been born in 1709, and, although the facts of his parentage are obscure, was probably the son of a certain William Cleland, a Scotsman who had held a modestly profitable public office, which he lost owing to a change of government, had frequented literary circles and been closely acquainted with Alexander Pope. The writer gave him his picture by Jervas and a copy of his translation of Homer, inscribed: *Mr. Cleland, who reads all other books, will please read this from his affectionate friend. . . .* John Cleland appears to have been proud of his father, and, in later life, is said to have kept his portrait hanging on his library wall. It seems doubtful whether William Cleland really provided hints for the character of Will Honeycomb; but presumably he was a respectable, well-liked citizen; and John was entered at Westminster School in the year 1722. We next hear of him as British Consul at Smyrna, where he spent the most formative period of his early manhood. By 1736, however, he had drifted eastwards to Bombay and joined the service of the British East India Company, an appointment that presently came to an abrupt and ignominious end. Having fallen out with his official superiors—how and why we cannot tell—he left Bombay "in a destitute condition," managed to reach Europe and, unsure perhaps of the welcome he would receive at home, elected to lead a wandering existence abroad. When he finally returned, his fears were justified. It proved difficult to secure a decent livelihood, and more than once he was thrown into a debtor's gaol.

Such was the battered, but resourceful, bohemian who, probably late in 1747 or in 1748, sold a manuscript to Ralph Griffiths. His fee was a mere twenty guineas; but starveling adventurers cannot be choosers; and, although Griffiths, a friend of Tom Davies, at whose shop Boswell first encountered Samuel Johnson, was an intelligent and cultivated man, he was also a shrewd commercialist and a stern, ungenerous taskmaster. Among his ill-paid employees was Oliver Goldsmith, whom he promised to furnish with bed and board and a diminutive pecuniary allowance if he would act as sub-editor on the *Monthly Review,* the original and influential publication that Griffiths founded in 1749. The publisher afterwards developed into a portly, impressive personage, "abounding (we are told) beyond most men in literary history and anecdote"; and he had an equally impressive literary wife, a large, capable, managing lady who wore a "neat and elevated wire-winged cap." Mrs. Griffiths shared her husband's concerns and presided over editorial meetings; and it would be interesting to know whether the manuscript of the *Memoirs* was ever permitted to fall beneath her eye.

Griffiths himself may perhaps have hesitated; a Welshman, who, before he moved to London and began to estab-

lish his fortune, had been a watchmaker in Staffordshire, he was once a member of the Presbyterian sect. But any doubts that his provincial upbringing inspired he evidently put behind him. The earliest known edition of Cleland's novel was advertised late in 1748 and published in 1749.*
According to the title page, these two volumes had been "printed for G. Fenton in the Strand"; but of Fenton nothing else is known—almost certainly he did not exist—and Griffiths, sheltering behind him, is thought to have been the actual publisher. Then, in 1750, under his own imprint, he brought out a bowdlerized version of the book, heralded by the *Monthly Review* with a eulogistic unsigned notice. The reviewer professed that he was quite at a loss to imagine why it had created so much official commotion: "as to the step lately taken to suppress this book, we are really at a loss to account for it. . . ." **

---

* From a bibliographical point of view, some mystery surrounds the publication of the book. It is impossible to establish which of the few surviving copies dated 1749 were really published that year Copies antedated 1749 were being printed as late as the 1770 For this, and for other interesting pieces of information I am indebted to my friend, the distinguished bibliographical authority Mr John Hayward, and to the courteous officials of the British Museum. For later editions, the most reliable authority i *Catena Librorum Tacendorum: Being Notes —on Curious and Uncommon Books,* by Pisanus Fraxi (H. S. Ashbee). London 1885 (Photolitho Offset Reprint, New York, 1962). which list translation into French, German, Italian, Portuguese nineteen English reprints before 1830 and one American edition printed in New York about 1845 Many of the later editions of the novel contained highly exaggerated illustrations and it is these various illustrations, not in any way a part of the novel. which are in good part responsible for many of the attempts to suppress the book. The most interesting twentieth-century edition is *L'Oeuvre de John Cleland,* a translation into French of the novel with an introduction and bibliographical essay by the distinguished poet Guillaume Apollinaire, who wrote of the book, "Le seul ouvrage qui garde de l'oubli le nom de John Cleland, c'est le roman de Fanny Hill, la soeur anglaise de Manon Lescaut, mais moins malheureuse, et le livre où elle parait à la saveur voluptueuse des récits que faisait Chéhérazade" (Bibliothèque des Curieux. 1914.) The various editions of Cleland's novel as listed in the *Catena* will be found in the Appendix.

** The Appendix includes this notice in its entirety.

The contemporary reading public needed no encouragement; Cleland's novel found a ready sale; and since 1749 it has remained in constant, though hitherto surreptitious, circulation. The subsequent history of the book is almost as peculiar as its origins. Purchased outright for twenty guineas—if not a particularly extravagant fee, certainly a respectable sum for the seventeen-fifties—it is reputed to have brought into Griffiths' coffers the handsome profit of ten thousand pounds. This dividend, with the earnings of the *Monthly Review,* enabled its virtuous publisher to set up as a gentleman. He kept two coaches, gave lavish dinner parties and built himself a dignified residence, Linden House, at the pretty suburban village of Turnham Green. He had remarried after the death of his literary consort, and on the wife of his middle age he begat a daughter Ann, who, in 1792, married Thomas Wainewright and, in 1794, became the mother of a son christened Thomas Griffiths. The boy grew up volatile, erratic and shifty, an amateur artist and draughtsman, for whom Linden House and the way of life that it symbolized were social ideals he must at any cost preserve. Alas, he had little ready money; and, to maintain his gentlemanly status, and live as a gentleman and a dilettante should, he embarked on a campaign of wholesale poisoning.

Just as strange, in a very different fashion, were the later vicissitudes of John Cleland's life. Despite a preliminary effort to suppress the book, neither he nor Ralph Griffiths suffered lasting inconvenience from the law, though in 1757 a bookseller named Drybutter was sentenced to the pillory for publishing an edition of the book, embellished with fresh inflammatory details.* True, the Bishop of London registered his protest; and Cleland, as the author of an allegedly obscene book, was summoned to appear before the Privy Council. But no action was taken against either Cleland or his novel; indeed Lord Granville, who had been present at the meeting, perhaps because he pitied a gifted writer in distress, perhaps because he sus-

---

* Drybutter seems to have added a scene in which Fanny witnessed a homosexual encounter between two young men. For further details, see the Appendix.

pected that Cleland's gifts might have political and journalistic uses, having stipulated that he must never repeat his offense procured him, in the good-humored eighteenth-century way, a pension of a hundred pounds a year.

Clearly, John Cleland was a born eccentric; the gifted amatory storyteller now became an impassioned student of philology, whose hobbyhorse was a universal language, "one discernibly elementary language of monosyllabic radicals," from which all modern languages were ultimately derived; and, besides producing some less successful novels—*Memories of a Coxcomb, Surprises of Love* and *The Man of Honour;* a series of tragedies and comedies—*Titus Vespasian, The Ladies' Subscription, Timbo-Chiqui, or the American Savage*—and contributing columns to the *Public Advertiser* under such pseudonyms as 'Modestus' or 'A Briton,' he hammered out a couple of imposing monographs in which he described and enlarged upon his favorite theory. 1766 saw the publication of a work characteristically and mysteriously entitled *The Way to Things by Words, and to Words by things; being a sketch of an Attempt at the Retrieval of the Ancient Celtic or primitive language of Europe; to which is added a succinct account of the Sanscrit, or the learned language of the Bramins; also two essays, the one on the origin of the Musical Waits at Christmas, the other on the real secret of the Freemasons.* It had been fortunate enough, Cleland announces, to meet with gratifying approbation "from several of the first rank in literature." He himself considered it a "much too crude essay"; and in 1768 he reverted to the same subject with his *Specimen of an Etymological Vocabulary, or Essay, by means of the Analytic Method, to retrieve the Ancient Celtic.*

Readers of *Memoirs of a Woman of Pleasure* may like to examine a passage, illustrating Cleland's more mature style, that occurs in the Preface, or "advertisment," of the *Etymological Vocabulary:*

I am very far from denying to other objects of the curiosity of antiquaries their just degree of utility, and consequently of merit. To grace a cabinet with the rare medals of a *Herennius,* a *Hostilian,* a *Balbinus,* a *Pupienus,* a

Pescennius Niger, an *Aquilia Severa,* wife of an *Heliogabalus* . . . or to supply the deficient, the elliptic, or obliterated letters on the monument of some Roman centurion . . . may all have, or rather doubtless have, their use; but surely an incomparably less one than that of but an attempt to discover the foundations of our present constitution of the church and state, in ages anterior to the invasion of this country by Julius Caesar. . . . *If* then, I repeat it, *if* I am not mistaken in this method of analysing words by an individuation of ideas, syllable by syllable, and through every particle that constitutes those ideas . . . by means of which the existence of things may be found in their natural records and repositories, words satisfactorily explained so as to convey undeniable truths by implication; if, I say, I am not mistaken in my application of this method . . . the reader will find, even in these imperfect sketches, some principal fixed points, attended with such a train of implicit accessories, as to form so many centrical lights; which diffusing clearness round them, at once illustrate objects actual, antecedent and subsequent . . . and lay open to their very foundations customs of great importance, prevalent at this moment, under all the ignorance or obscurity of their primigenial causes.

That passage, which Sterne would have loved to parody, may suffice the average twentieth-century reader; and it may help to explain why, as a philologist and scholarly essayist, Cleland never made his mark. The "fine sly malcontent" who questioned the eminence of Lord Camden, the celebrated lawyer and hero of the Wilkite troubles, remained as long as he lived a poor and hard-worked London journalist. During his latter years, the ingenious, cross-grained old man descended into deep obscurity. Almost an octogenarian, he died in Petty France, Westminster, on January 23, 1789.

Today his only solid memorial is the picturesque story he dashed off in his late thirties, anxious to earn the handful of guineas that may have saved him from a debtor's prison. Yet an author's best work is not necessarily the work on which he himself sets most value; and the *Memoirs* has literary qualities for which we look in vain among his serious writings. No other book of the same kind possesses so much elegance and energy; it is a genuine tale, told with considerable art, and gives us a graphic picture of its social age. The years 1748 and 1749 produced three important English novels: in 1748, Richardson completed *Clarissa: or, the History of a Young Lady*, which he had launched in 1747, and Smollett published *The Adventures of Roderick Random;* in 1749, Fielding gave us *Tom Jones*. Of these, only Richardson's story need concern us here. *Clarissa* must certainly have influenced Cleland, and its predecessor, *Pamela; or, Virtue Rewarded*, published in 1740, may also have affected him. Richardson's slightly mawkish, even faintly salacious, treatment of the subject of feminine innocence, though it drew floods of tears and fascinated innumerable readers, aroused some strongly controversial feelings. "Anti-Pamelas" were soon being put forth; and Fielding, in *Joseph Andrews*, covered the hero-ine with ridicule by turning the plot upside down and substituting for a high-flown maiden Pamela's chaste and sanctimonious brother. Other parodies or travesties in-cluded Fielding's *Apology for the Life of Mrs Shamela An-drews* and John Kelly's spurious sequel, *Pamela's Conduct in High Life*. Whether Cleland was provoked by *Pamela* or *Clarissa* or, at different times, by both novels, he, too, I think, may fairly be classed among the anti-Richardsonian writers. While Richardson's theme is unspotted female vir-tue, considered as its own reward, Cleland explains how a career of vice may reach a safe and happy ending. He shows Lust sanctified by the power of Love. Cleland, too, in his own fashion, is a romantic sentimentalist. If his story can be said to have a message, it is that, although the commerce of the sexes is usually enjoyable, and pleas-ure, for its own sake, almost always worth pursuing, the heights of enjoyment cannot be achieved until true affec-tion prepares the bed of passion. Love, Fanny announces, is "the Attic salt of enjoyment . . . for it is undoubtedly love alone that refines, ennobles and exalts it." Fanny never forgets her adored Charles, who first rescued her from an expensive London brothel; and, having inherited the for-tune of a good-natured old man, "a rational pleasurist," with whom she has set up house for eight months, she and that inimitable lover are at last permanently reunited. We are given to understand that she becomes an honest woman, enjoys an idyllic married life and brings up a family of blooming children.

Meanwhile, during her sexual apprenticeship, she has explored the devious bypaths of the London underworld. In 1749, Hogarth was fifty-two, "a strutting consequential little man," who had already accomplished many of his finest works, and whose incomparable *Harlot's Progress* had been issued seventeen years earlier. But *Memoirs of a Woman of Pleasure* has a decidedly Hogarthian background; and its heroine and the painter's famous Moll Hackabout—also a country girl ensnared by a clever London bawd—are personages of much the same stamp. They belong to a similar world, the world of masquerades and Covent Garden *bagnios* and the fashionable bawdy houses of the West End, where young women with panniered skirts, low-dressed ringleted coiffures and a single curl descending to the breast, meet dissipated gentlemen, fresh from the Court of the City, in full-skirted coats heavily laced and embroidered, long waistcoats, silk stockings and smart Parisian bag-wigs. Fanny Hill has an appreciative eye for clothes; and a delightful feature of the book is the vivid particularity with which she describes her characters. Fanny herself is invariably fresh and neat; she believes that her wardrobe should be simple and modest, however immodest may be her private conduct; and, having acquired her old friend's fortune, she has no difficulty in assuming "the new character of a young gentlewoman whose husband was gone to sea," and at once adopts "such lines of life and conduct as, leaving me a competent liberty to pursue my views . . . bounded me nevertheless strictly within the rules of decency and discretion."

Memoirs of a Woman of Pleasure, then, has an undoubted historical value, and gives a lively, though, no doubt, a somewhat highly colored picture of certain aspects of contemporary English life, at a time when Great Britain, after the long period of peaceful expansion presided over by Sir Robert Walpole, was yearly increasing in prosperity and power, and the thriving City of London was already

Europe's chief market. It also has a definite literary appeal; the narrator's characterization is often shrewd; and Cleland is at pains to establish the link between a man's temperament and outward appearance and the secret direction of his sexual interests. The flagellant, for example, has "a round, plump, fresh-coloured face" which "gave him greatly the look of a Bacchus, had not an air of austerity, not to say sternness . . . dash'd that character of joy. . . . As soon as Mrs. Cole was gone, he seated me near him, when now his face changed . . . into an expression of the most pleasing sweetness and good humour, the more remarkable for its sudden shift from the other extreme, which, I found afterwards, when I knew more of his character, was owing to a habitual state of conflict with, and dislike of himself, for being enslaved to so peculiar a gust. . . ." The effect, consequently, is far less monotonous, far less cloying and over-elaborate, than that of the ordinary erotic novel. Here and there, Cleland's descriptions of love-making are marred by what perhaps could be best described as his adherence to the "longitudinal fallacy"—the formidable bodily equipment of his most accomplished lovers is apt to be described with quite unnecessary relish; and he himself agrees that the recital of amatory exploits, if drawn out for a couple of hundred pages, may both overtax the novelist's ingenuity and impose a severe strain upon the reader's patience:

"If I have delayed the sequel of my history," she writes at the opening of her second Letter, "it has been purely to allow myself a little breathing time . . . I imagined, indeed, that you would have been cloy'd and tired with the uniformity of adventures and expressions, inseparable from a subject of this sort, whose bottom, or groundwork being, in the nature of things, eternally one and the same . . . there is no escaping a repetition of near the same images, the same figures, with this further inconvenience . . . that the words JOYS, ARDOURS, TRANSPORTS, EXTASIES, and the rest of those pathetic terms . . . flatten and lose much of their due spirit and energy by the frequency they indispensably recur with. . . ."

As for the moral aspect of the question, Cleland's book

seems to be far less subversive and demoralizing than not
a few of its twentieth-century counterparts, nowadays
openly sold and widely recommended by reviewers. It includes a dramatic flagellatory episode; but we escape the
nauseating modern mixture of sexual appetite and criminal
violence. To have been "beaten up" by a vagrant thug
would have outraged Fanny's finest instincts. Indeed, as she
remarks, after depicting a brothel orgy, "it is to be noted,
that, though all modesty and reserve were banished from
the transaction of those pleasures, good manners and
politeness were inviolably observed: here was no gross
ribaldry, no offensive or rude behaviour, or ungenerous
reproaches to the girls . . . On the contrary, nothing was
wanting, to soothe, encourage and soften the sense of their
condition . . ."

Memoirs of a Woman of Pleasure is the product of a
luxurious and licentious, but not a commercially degraded,
era. The Georgians prided themselves on their grace and
refinement; and although, in fact, they were sometimes
brutal and coarse, they aspired to an ideal elegance. Of
that elegance and the emotions it aroused, Cleland's heroine had her full share. For all its abounding improprieties,
his priapic novel is not a vulgar book. It treats of pleasure
as the aim and end of existence, and of sexual satisfaction
as the epitome of pleasure, but does so in a style that,
despite its inflammatory subject, never stoops to a gross or
unbecoming word. Fanny Hill would have shuddered at
Lady Chatterley. The actions described she would have
taken in good part—she might possibly have complained,
however, that Lawrence's sermon on the delights of sexual
love had a somewhat nonconformist twang; but the roughness and coarseness of the dialogue she would have found
unspeakably offensive. It includes the kind of phrases and
private amatory endearments that Mrs. Cole, "a gentlewoman born and bred," and her school of well-dressed,
well-disciplined young beauties would not have considered
fit for decent ears.

A Note on the American History of *Memoirs of a Woman of Pleasure*

Since acceptance of *Memoirs of a Woman of Pleasure* was quick and widespread in the author's native England, it is not surprising that copies of John Cleland's magnum opus soon found their way to the Colonies.

It is recorded that a new York bookseller, Benjamin Gomez, offered a copy of an illustrated edition of the *Memoirs* for sale in 1789, although whether the copy was imported from England or locally printed cannot now be ascertained. But there is strong evidence that sometime between 1786 and 1814 an edition of the book was published, probably surreptitiously, by one of the literary giants of the Federalist period, Isaiah Thomas of Worcester, Massachusetts, printer, historian, philanthropist and the author of the still-respected *History of Printing in America*. Thomas failed to mention Cleland's novel either in his history or in his published *Diary*. However, in a letter addressed to Thomas and dated July 29, 1786, Thomas Evans, a London bookseller, wrote of two trunks of books he was shipping Thomas and added: "I hope I did not omit anything necessary to be mentioned, except one, which I fear I did, it was, I think, the Memoirs of a W. of P." This letter is evidence Isaiah Thomas knew of the book; and since his personal library contained dozens of newspaper volumes bound in printed sheets of an edition of Cleland's novel which had first been marbled to make their use more aesthetically pleasing, it is safe to assume he also printed an edition.

In the early years of the nineteenth century the *Memoirs* figured in what is generally accepted as the first recorded suppression of a literary work on grounds of obscenity in the United States—two men, Peter Holmes of West Boylston, Massachusetts, and Stillman Howe of Holden were indicted "for publishing a lewd and obscene print, contained in a certain book entitled *Memoirs of a Woman of Pleasure*, and also for publishing the said book." * The significant fact here is the listing of the illustration before the book, for considering the sort of

* 17 Mass. 336 Commonwealth vs. Holmes, 1821.

illustrative exaggeration which has traditionally been appended to the *Memoirs*, it is not surprising that both the book and illustrations were suppressed, just as similarly illustrated copies of Boccaccio's *Decameron*, Balzac's *Droll Stories* or Chaucer's *Canterbury Tales* have been suppressed on numerous occasions. It is not recorded who first illustrated Cleland's novel, thus greatly degrading a most original work, but the *Catena Librorum Tacendorum*, that remarkable nineteenth-century bibiliography of "curious and uncommon books," lists the London edition of 1784 as containing "12 (?) engravings," thus making it probably the first illustrated edition to appear in English. Certainly the early copies imported into and printed in the United States were seemingly all abundantly and wickedly illustrated.

While names of printers and dates of editions are lacking, the *Memoirs* were certainly printed in this country, and both domestically printed and imported copies were circulated widely throughout the nineteenth century. A copy of the novel now in the New York Public Library, for example bears the inscription "Copy given N. Y. Public Library by Dr. I. W. Drummond of 436 W. 22nd Street on the 9th of May, 1927. Once the property of Governor Samuel J. Tilden for whom it had been bought by the late J. W. Bouton in London."

Most of the copies printed during the latter half of the eighteenth and early years of the nineteenth centuries were ill produced and shoddily bound. Some however were quite well produced and the fact that these latter are invariably inscribed as "limited" or "collectors'" editions indicates the *Memoirs* was a staple item in the limited-editions racket which flourished until fairly recently. Unscrupulous salesmen, often employees of standard publishing houses. would have a book set in type and run off as many copies of the work as they felt the traffic would currently bear (rarely over 350 to 500). Each copy would prominently bear some variation of the accepted legend:

> Privately printed for subscribers only. Edition strictly limited to 500 [or 350 or so] copies. Printed from type and type distributed.

and would carry a high price—often twenty to twenty-five dollars—as a limited edition. The salesman would then sell copies to such booksellers as he could at whatever price the traffic would bear, but normally at a relatively small fraction of the list price. The bookseller would then sell a "collectors' item" to a customer, occasionally giving a special discount, which he could well afford, as a mark of favor. When the edition was exhausted, the salesman normally waited a few years and then would have a new supply run from his plates. In addition to *Memoirs of a Woman of Pleasure*, such works as *The Memoirs of Jacques Casanova* were widely sold in this way.

David Loth writing in 1961 in his book *The Erotic in Literature*, while succumbing to several blatantly false ideas as to the publishing history of Cleland's novel as well as of the eroticism of the book (one doubts he ever read it), rightfully points out that the only legal penalty incurred by anyone within the author's lifetime was that inflicted on a bookseller named Drybutter who had issued an unauthorized, and considerably coarsened, edition of the work for which he was pilloried.

Loth also mentions a resurgence of interest in *Fanny Hill* in the U. S. about the middle of the nineteenth century, noting that many of the editions "added episodes and introduced into the text the old words for the sex organs and sex acts." Thus was the reputation of the work further tarnished.

The strengthening in 1857 of the Federal Statute of 1842 authorizing the customs to seize obscene pictures is credited in some circles with cutting down the importation of the work into the U. S., and with thereby increasing the quantities of the work printed in this country. However, since no authority can cite a single case of a specific seizure of copies of the book by the customs in the entire nineteenth century, this must be doubted. Nor is there recorded evidence of actual suppression or seizure of copies of the work during the legendary career of Anthony Comstock and his Committee for the Suppression of Vice in the years following 1872. Indeed, it has proven impossible to discover an actual suppression of the book by a lawful magistrate since the aforementioned case of Holmes and Howe.

Not that it has not been suppressed; almost certainly it has. But invariably because it has been relegated—either by undeserved repute or by fact of being obscenely bowdlerized or illustrated—to the literary underworld where it has been lumped with totally undistinguished works of no literary merit at all, it has been suppressed en masse with the other works without an opportunity to stand on its own considerable merits.

As the twentieth century has progressed, more and more critical attention has been paid to Cleland's novel. Ralph Thompson in 1935 published an article in *The Colophon** which dealt ably with the book's fascinating history, although at the same time denying it any claim to literary quality. Clifton Fadiman writing in *Holiday,*** while also taking an unenthusiastic view of the novel, compares its author not unfavorably with such modern literary practitioners as Ben Hecht, James Jones, J. P. Donleavy and William Faulkner.

Within recent years a number of American editors have been rediscovering the book and sections of it have appeared in various anthologies. A chapter appeared in *Banned #2 **** sandwiched between excerpts from Apuleius' *The Golden Ass* and Dostoevski's *The Dispossessed* and rather disparagingly heralded by critic Max Gartenberg's comment: "With the exception of the excerpts from John Cleland's *Memoirs of Fanny Hill*, each of the contents is by a writer whose importance is attested by a body of responsible criticism. *Fanny Hill* has its own value, as the portrait of a type of woman and as perhaps the most famous example of a literary genre whose vitality . . . remains undiminished."

Another excerpt appeared in *The Prostitute in Literature,* **** edited with Introduction and Commentary by Harold Greenwald and Aron Krich. In his Introduction Dr.

---

* "Deathless Lady," *The Colophon: A Quarterly for Bookmen.* Autumn 1935, Vol. 1, Number 2, pp. 207-220, New York, N.Y.

** "Party of One," *Holiday,* August, 1959.

*** 1962 Berkley Books.   **** 1960 Ballantine Books.

Greenwald paid ample and fitting testimony to the work of John Cleland's novel as a sociological document:

In these various "memoirs," John Cleland describes in very simple language the method of recruitment and training of a young woman in the London of 1749 for life as a "woman of pleasure." Fanny Hill's early experiences all are described with what seems like a fair degree of accuracy. It is fascinating, too, that he sees clearly the connection between homosexuality and prostitution which is so common to this day that many analysts of prostitution believe that it is the homosexuality alone, pure and simple, which drives women to choose prostitution as an occupation. Cleland, the author, says, for example, in describing Phoebe, who is assigned the task of arousing sexual desire in Fanny Hill, "Not that she hated men, or did not even prefer them to her own sex; but when she met with such occasions as this was, satiety of enjoyments in the common road, perhaps too a secret bias, inclined her to make the most of pleasure wherever she could find it without distinction of sexes."

Actually Cleland's explanation is more sophisticated than those of some modern analysts in that he recognizes that many of these women, being arrested at a very early stage of development, are indifferent as to the sex of the partner. This coincides with their fixation at an early stage of development, when the individual is not yet differentiated into full maleness or femaleness as far as his emotional attitudes are concerned. And this seems to be the case with the Phoebe he describes in the book, as well as in Lucian's dialogues.

In his widely read *An Unhurried View of Erotica*[*] Ralph Ginzburg points out that a dozen translations into French are known as well as ten into German, and, as have others before him, comments on the amount of undeserved notoriety bowdlerized versions and unrelated works usurping "both *Fanny Hill's* title and Cleland's byline" have brought to the novel.

Psychologist Dr. Albert Ellis, in an Introduction to a bowdlerized version of the *Memoirs*,[**] stated the case for

[*] 1958 The Helmsman Press.
[**] *EROS*, Autumn, 1962. Volume 1, Number 3.

the free circulation of Cleland's novel in America extremely well, noting the literary worth of the book—"Cleland's book is unusually well written. . . . [he] was a true master of the English tongue," and going on to comment that in our day, "it is difficult to see how American mores would actually be undermined by the perusal of this book. . . ." Ellis further points out that the *Memoirs* is "psychologically perspicacious," and emphasizes Cleland's insistence on the pleasures, even the joys, of heterosexual relations.

In this connection an interesting thought about the source of Cleland's curiously modern view of the enjoyments of sex can be found in the Introduction by W. G. Archer, perhaps the outstanding living Western authority on Indian culture, to a recent edition of the classic Indian treatise on the science and art of sex and love, The Kama Sutra of Vatsyayana. Wrote Archer of "that eighteenth-century classic, *The Memoirs of Fanny Hill*": "John Cleland, its author, had lived in India and it can hardly be coincidence that in relating his heroine's adventures, he should stress what Vatsyayana himself would have stressed—the supreme delights of sex in all its forms."

Almost immediately after the publication of the hardcover edition of the *Memoirs* by G. P. Putnam's Sons—the first open publication of the novel in two centuries—the Corporation Counsel of New York, together with the five District Attorneys of the five counties that make up New York City, sought to suppress its publication. The legal action, if successful, would result in an injunction against the publisher and the seizure and destruction of all copies of the book. The City and the District Attorneys were represented by Seymour Quel of the Corporation Counsel's office. The publisher, and the book, were defended by Charles Rembar.

Prior to the trial, on the affidavits of the Corporation Counsel and the District Attorneys to the effect that the book was obscene, the City obtained a preliminary injunction which would remain effective while the litigation was pending.

The trial lasted two days. Witnesses for the defense, in

addition to Walter J. Minton, the president of the publishing company, were literary critics and scholars: Louis Untermeyer, J. Donald Adams, Eric Bentley, John Hollander, Gerald Willen and Eliot Fremont-Smith. Witnesses called by the City were three clergymen and a social worker: the Rev. Dr. William F. Rosenblum, the Rev. Edward Soares, Mr. Julius Nierow and the Rev. Canon William S. Van Meter. Certain of the witnesses appearing for the City gave testimony, on Mr. Rembar's cross-examination, which aided in the defense of the book.

After the trial, Supreme Court Justice Arthur G. Klein held that the publication of the book was protected by the First Amendment to the Constitution. He terminated the preliminary injunction and dismissed the action. Mr. Justice Klein's opinion follows:

The Corporation Counsel of the City of New York, together with the District Attorneys of the five counties comprising said City, seeks, pursuant to Section 22-a of the Code of Criminal Procedure, to enjoin the publishing, acquiring, selling or distributing of a certain book entitled "John Cleland's Memoirs of a Woman of Pleasure" (commonly known as Fanny Hill) (plaintiffs' exhibit #1 in evidence) hereinafter referred to as "Memoirs," or "the book." The book in question (Library of Congress catalog card #63-9656) is published by defendant G. P. Putnam's Sons, conceded by plaintiffs to be an old established, reputable publishing firm. Both sides have waived findings of fact and conclusions of law. The action has been discontinued without costs as against the other defendants (S.M., p. 3).

Section 22-a, Code of Criminal Procedure, provides, in part, that the District Attorney of any county may maintain an action to enjoin the sale, distribution, etc. of any book, magazine, etc. "of an indecent character, which is obscene, lewd, lascivious, filthy, indecent or disgusting. . . ." Subdivision 2 of said section provides: "The person, firm or corporation sought to be enjoined shall be entitled to a trial of the issues within one day after joinder of issue and a decision shall be rendered by the court within two days of the conclusion of the trial."

Pending the present trial, a temporary injunction was

granted by this court (Marks, J., 7/24/63). The granting
of the injunction pendente lite served, as does every temporary stay, only to hold the matter in status quo pending a
determination on the merits and the granting of the temporary injunction can in no wise be considered an adjudica-
tion on the merits. "The issues must be tried to the same
extent as though no temporary injunction had been applied
for. . . ." (Walker Memorial Baptist Church v. Sanders,
285 N.Y. 462).

The publication of "Memoirs" is herein sought to be
suppressed on the ground of its alleged obscenity. Since
no two books are exactly alike, each book must be sepa-
rately judged and from an examination of the leading cases
on the subject, it is apparent that there exists no auto-
matically controlling precedent.

The United States Supreme Court has set up several
standards by which a book is to be judged, and it is well
settled that a book must fail these standards before it may
be suppressed.

Two of these tests were announced in Roth v. United
States, 354 U.S. 476, and a third in Manual Enterprises
Inc. et al v. Day, 370 U.S. 478. Still another test was for-
mulated by our Court of Appeals in People v. Richmond
County News Inc., 9 N.Y. 2d 578.

The tests are as follows:

1) The "social value" test. The core of the opinion in the
leading case is found in the following language:

> "All ideas having even the slightest redeeming social
> importance—unorthodox ideas, controversial ideas, even
> ideas hateful to the prevailing climate of opinion—have
> the full protection of the guaranties, unless excludable
> because they encroach upon the limited area of more im-
> portant interests. But implicit in the history of the First
> Amendment is the rejection of obscenity as utterly with-
> out redeeming social importance." (Roth v. U.S., 354
> U.S. 476)

2) The "prurient interest" test.

> "However, sex and obscenity are not synonymous.
> Obscene material is material which deals with sex in a

manner appealing to prurient interest. The portrayal of sex, e.g. in art, literature and scientific works, is not itself sufficient reason to deny material the constitutional protection of freedom of speech and press. Sex, a great and mysterious motive force in human life, has indisputably been a subject of absorbing interest to mankind through the ages; it is one of the vital problems of human interest and public concern."

" '***A thing is obscene if, considered as a whole, its predominant appeal is to prurient interest, i.e., a shameful or morbid interest in nudity, sex, or excretion, and if it goes substantially beyond customary limits of candor in description or representations of such matters.'***" (Roth v. U.S., supra)

3) The "patently offensive" test.

"These magazines cannot be deemed so offensive on their face as to affront current community standards of decency—a quality that we shall hereafter refer to as 'patent offensiveness' or 'indecency'. Lacking that quality, the magazines cannot be deemed legally 'obscene', and we need not consider the question of the proper 'audience' by which their 'prurient interest' appeal should be judged." (Manual Enterprises, Inc. et al v. Day, 370 U.S. 478)

4) The "hard core pornography" test.

"***The inquiry for the court, therefore, is whether the publication is so entirely obscene as to amount to 'hard-core pornography' (not necessarily dealing with deviate sex relations since while there is a pornography of perversion, 'pornography' is not limited to the depiction of unnatural acts)." (People v. Richmond County News Inc., 9 N Y 2d 578)

While the standards or tests are clearly defined, their application presents considerable difficulty, witness, for example, the case involving Henry Miller's "Tropic of Cancer". This book has been held obscene in the 9th Circuit Federal Court, (Besig v. U.S., 208 F., 2d 142), in the State of Connecticut, (State v. Huntington, 1962 #24657,

Superior Court, Hartford County) and in the State of
Pennsylvania (Commonwealth v. Robin, #3177, 1962, Ct.
of Common Pleas, Phila. County), while at the same time
it has been held to be not obscene by the courts of Massachusetts, Wisconsin and Illinois. (Atty. Gen. v. Book named
Tropic of Cancer, 344 Mass. —, McCauley v. Tropic of
Cancer — Wis. —, Haiman v. Marris, S 19718, Superior
Court, Cook County, Illinois.) On July 2, 1963, the highest
court of the State of California declared the book not
obscene (Zeitlin et ano v. Arnebergh — Cal. —) yet
within 10 days after the seven members of that Court had
unanimously rendered their judgment, the highest court of
our State in a four to three decision (People v. Fritch, —
N Y 2d —,) declared the book to be obscene.

So zealously is the constitutional right to freedom of
expression guarded that the section under which the present
action has been brought (22-a, Code of Criminal Procedure, supra), contains two unique provisions not to be
found in any other statute—(1) that the party sought to be
enjoined shall be entitled to a trial of the issues within one
day after joinder of issue, and (2) that a decision shall be
rendered within two days after the conclusion of the trial.

The book, though undeniably containing numerous descriptions of the sex act and certain aberrations thereof as
its central theme, contains not one single obscene word.
While it is undoubtedly true that obscenity is not rendered
less obscene by virtue of the fact that it has been well
written—nor for that matter must a writing necessarily
appear exclusively on the walls of men's public lavatories
to be considered pornographic—there is present herein an
additional factor, not normally encountered in cases where
books are sought to be suppressed and that is the high literary quality of the book. With respect to the literary
quality of the book, defendant produced several expert
literary figures as witnesses who testified at some length.

The witnesses, all highly qualified and eminent in their
field, included J. Donald Adams, writer, publisher, presently a contributing editor to the New York SUNDAY
TIMES BOOK REVIEW, with which he has been asso-
ciated for forty years, eighteen of which were as editor of

said BOOK REVIEW: John Hollander, Poet, Assistant Professor of English Literature at Yale University, book reviewer for many literary quarterlies, The New York TIMES, New York HERALD TRIBUNE, London GUARDIAN and London SUNDAY TIMES; Louis Untermeyer, well known writer, poet and literary critic; Gerald Willen, formerly Chairman of the Department of English, Fairleigh Dickinson University, and presently Assistant Professor of English at Hunter College and Eric Bentley, teacher of dramatic literature and chairman of the Program of the Arts at Columbia University.

These witnesses were of the unanimous opinion that the book had great literary merit. Their testimony characterized the book as an historical novel (to a limited extent), containing passages not normally included in a book written solely to arouse passions, and their praises ranged from "extremely interesting" to "skillful". In addition, Mr. Untermeyer testified that the book contained the three great attributes of a good novel: (1) treatment of the subject matter with grace and beauty; (2) skillful and eloquent charm of writing; and (3) characters coming to life. He characterized the book as a "work of art." Plaintiffs did not produce a single literary expert to rebut the foregoing testimony.

Although the instant action is brought pursuant to the Code of Criminal Procedure, it nevertheless is in the nature of a civil proceeding. While plaintiffs need not, therefore, establish their allegations beyond a reasonable doubt, in order to prevail herein, they must, as in every civil action, nevertheless establish their case by a fair preponderance of the evidence. The burden is therefore upon them to establish by such preponderance of evidence that the defendant has caused to be published, distributed, etc., a book not encompassed within the orbit of constitutional protection. In applying these recognized standards, it is the Court's opinion that the plaintiffs have failed to sustain that burden of proof sufficient to entitle them to judgment in this case.

Under the "social value" test referred to in Roth v. United States, 354 U.S. 476, the expert testimony adduced at the trial indicates, and the Court so finds, that the book herein sought to be suppressed is an historical novel of literary value. While each book must necessarily be evaluated on its own individual worth, of interest, nevertheless, is the opinion of defendant's witness, Eliot Fremont-Smith, an editor of the Book Review Section of the New York Sunday Times, who testified that with respect to the depiction of the act of sex, the book involved in this action does not exceed the limits of candor which have been established by the publication and acceptance of books sold through reputable book stores and reviewed in reputable publications during the past several years (SM 152, 155). In addition, the Court takes judicial notice of the fact that many books in circulation today contain much offensive language.

With respect to the "prurient interest" test enunciated in Roth v. United States (supra), taking the book as a whole and not just those portions thereof which appeal to the salacious page turner, plaintiffs, here, too, have failed to sustain the burden of proof.

Under Manual Enterprises v. Day, 370 U.S. 478, in addition to the "prurient interest" test, to warrant a suppression of the book, plaintiffs must establish that the challenged material is "patently offensive" to current community standards of decency.

If the standards of the community are to be gauged by what it is permitted to read in its daily newspapers, then Fanny Hill's experiences contain little more than what the community has already encountered on the front pages of many of its newspapers in the reporting of the recent "Profumo" and other sensational cases involving sex.

If the standards are to be measured by what the public has of late been permitted to view in the so-called "foreign art" movies, and indeed, some of our domestic products, then it is equally clear that "Memoirs" does these standards no violence whatsoever. "The Community cannot, where liberty of speech and press are at issue, condemn that which it generally tolerates" (Smith v. Calif, 361 U. S. 147 [171]).

The book can in no manner whatsoever be characterized as "patently offensive" when examined in the light of *current* community standards.

In a case involving a violation of section 1141 of the

Penal Law (sale, etc., of obscene literature, etc.) the Court of Appeals held such section applicable only to material which may properly be termed "hard core pornography" (People v. Richmond County News, Inc., 9 N.Y. 2d 578). In the two hundred and fourteen years that have elapsed since "Memoirs" was first published in 1749, the book has been in constant, though for the most part surreptitious, circulation and has been translated into every major European language. Copies of the novel are to be found in the British Museum and Library of Congress. Benjamin Franklin is reputed to have had a copy in his library. The New York Public Library's copy of the novel indicates in its inscription that same once belonged to Governor Samuel J. Tilden. Of the author and the book it has been said: "***While Dr. Johnson lived in Gough Square, while Edward Gibbon was yet a boy, long before William Wordsworth was born, an obscure and harassed Englishman turned out a book which, to judge from the fascination it still holds for a great variety of readers, is more nearly immortal than anything these and the other great men of the time ever wrote" (Ralph Thompson, "Deathless Lady", The Colophon: A Quarterly for Bookmen, 1935, Vol. I) (pltf's exh. I, p. 27). Were the book "hard core pornography", "dirt for dirt's sake" or "dirt for money's sake", it is extremely doubtful that it would have existed these many years under the aforementioned circumstances. Here, too, then, the plaintiffs have failed to establish their case by a fair preponderance of the evidence.

In view of all of the foregoing and upon a careful reading of the book, it is the Court's view that same is not of such a nature as to warrant the drastic relief sought herein.

While parents would not like the book to be read by their young children, this hardly constitutes a legally sufficient ground upon which to predicate a constitutional judgment that the book is not entitled to the protection of the 1st Amendment. As was pointed out by Mr. Justice Frankfurter on behalf of a unanimous court in Butler v. Michigan, 352 U.S. 380,

"It is clear on the record that appellant was convicted because Michigan by Section 343 made it an offense for him to make available for the general reading public (and he in fact sold to a police officer) a book that the trial judge found to have a potentially deleterious influence upon youth. The State insists that, by thus guaranteeing the general public against books not too rugged for grown men and women in order to shield juvenile innocence, it is exercising its power to promote the general welfare. Surely, this is to burn the house to roast the pig. °°°The incidence of this enactment is to reduce the adult population of Michigan to reading only what is fit for children. It thereby arbitrarily curtails one of those liberties of the individual now enshrined in the Due Process Clause of the Fourteenth Amendment, that history has attested as the indispensable conditions for the maintenance and progress of a free society." (352 U.S. 380, 383, 384)

While the saga of Fanny Hill will undoubtedly never replace "Little Red Riding Hood" as a popular bedtime story, it is quite possible that were Fanny to be transposed from her mid eighteenth century Georgian surroundings to our present day society, she might conceivably encounter many things which would cause her to blush.

The complaint is dismissed, the temporary injunction is vacated, and judgment is directed for the defendant.

The foregoing constitutes the decision of the Court pursuant to section 440 of the Civil Practice Act. Settle judgment.   Dated: August 23, 1963

A considerable effort has been made to present this edition of John Cleland's novel as close to the way he wrote it as possible, a task made more difficult by the fact that it has proven impossible to discover a copy that can be authenticated as the original edition. It is known, for example, that copies dated 1749 were printed as much as forty years later, and that some of these bore alterations in the text. However, in the interests of consistency some alterations of spelling and punctuation have been made to conform to modern usage and to eliminate inconsistencies that may or may not have been the author's fault.

                                        THE PUBLISHER

MEMOIRS OF
A WOMAN OF PLEASURE

Letter the First

MADAM,

I sit down to give you an undeniable proof of my considering your desires as indispensable orders. Ungracious then as the task may be, I shall recall to view those scandalous stages of my life, out of which I emerg'd, at length, to the enjoyment of every blessing in the power of love, health, and fortune to bestow; whilst yet in the flower of youth, and not too late to employ the leisure afforded me by great ease and affluence, to cultivate an understanding, naturally not a despicable one, and which had, even amidst the whirl of loose pleasures I had been tost in, exerted more observation on the characters and manners of the world than what is common to those of my unhappy profession, who looking on all thought or reflection as their capital enemy, keep it at as great a distance as they can, or destroy it without mercy.

Hating, as I mortally do, all long unnecessary preface, I shall give you good quarter in this, and use no farther apology, than to prepare you for seeing the loose part of my life, wrote with the same liberty that I led it.

Truth! stark, naked truth, is the word; and I will not so much as take the pains to bestow the strip of a gauze wrapper on it, but paint situations such as they actually rose to me in nature, careless of violating those laws of decency that were never made for such unreserved intimacies as ours; and you have too much sense, too much knowledge of the ORIGINALS themselves, to sniff prudishly and out of character at the PICTURES of them. The greatest men, those of the first and most leading taste, will not scruple adorning their private closets with nudities, though, in compliance with vulgar prejudices, they may not think them decent decorations of the staircase, or salon.

This, and enough, premised, I go souse into my personal history. My maiden name was *Frances Hill*. I was born at a small village near *Liverpool*, in *Lancashire*, of parents extremely poor, and, I piously believe, extremely honest.

My father, who had received a maim on his limbs that disabled him from following the more laborious branches of country-drudgery, got, by making of nets, a scanty subsistence, which was not much enlarg'd by my mother's keeping a little day-school for the girls in her neighbourhood. They had had several children; but none lived to any age except myself, who had received from nature a constitution perfectly healthy.

My education, till past fourteen, was no better than very vulgar; reading, or rather spelling, an illegible scrawl, and a little ordinary plain work composed the whole system of it; and then all my foundation in virtue was no other than a total ignorance of vice, and the shy timidity general to our sex, in the tender stage of life when objects alarm or frighten more by their novelty than anything else. But then, this is a fear too often cured at the expence of innocence, when Miss, by degrees, begins no longer to look on a man as a creature of prey that will eat her.

My poor mother had divided her time so entirely between her scholars and her little domestic cares, that she had spared very little of it to my instruction, having, from her own innocence from all ill, no hint or thought of guarding me against any.

I was now entering on my fifteenth year, when the worst of ills befell me in the loss of my tender fond parents, who were both carried off by the small-pox, within a few days of each other; my father dying first, and thereby hastening the death of my mother: so that I was now left an unhappy friendless orphan (for my father's coming to settle there was accidental, he being originally a *Kentishman*). That cruel distemper which had proved so fatal to them, had indeed seized me, but with such mild and favourable symptoms, that I was presently out of danger, and, what I then did not know the value of, was entirely unmark'd. I skip over here an account of the natural grief and affliction which I felt on this melancholy occasion. A little time, and the giddiness of that age dissipated, too soon, my reflections on that irreparable loss; but nothing contributed more to reconcile me to it, than the notions that were immediately put into my head, of going to *London*, and looking out for a service, in which I was promised all assistance and advice from one *Esther Davis*, a young woman that had been down to see her friends, and who, after the stay of a few days, was to return to her place.

As I had now nobody left alive in the village who had concern enough about what should become of me to start any objections to this scheme, and the woman who took care of me after my parents' death rather encouraged me to pursue it, I soon came to a resolution of making this launch into the wide world, by repairing to *London*, in order to SEEK MY FORTUNE, a phrase which, by the bye, has ruined more adventurers of both sexes, from the country, than ever it made or advanced.

Nor did Esther Davis a little comfort and inspirit me to venture with her, by piquing my childish curiosity with the fine sights that were to be seen in *London*: the Tombs, the Lions, the King, the Royal Family, the fine Plays and Operas, and, in short, all the diversions which fell within her sphere of life to come at; the detail of all which perfectly turn'd the little head of me.

Nor can I remember, without laughing, the innocent admiration, not without a spice of envy, with which we poor girls, whose church-going clothes did not rise above dowlass shifts and stuff gowns, beheld Esther's scowered satin gowns, caps border'd with an inch of lace, taudry ribbons, and shoes belaced with silver: all which we imagined grew in London, and entered for a great deal into my determination of trying to come in for my share of them.

The idea however of having the company of a townswoman with her, was the trivial, and all the motives that engaged Esther to take charge of me during my journey to town, where she told me, after her manner and style, "as how several maids out of the country had made them-

selves and all their kin for ever: that by preserving their
VIRTUE, some had taken so with their masters, that they
had married them, and kept them coaches, and lived
vastly grand and happy; and some, may-hap, came to be
Duchesses; luck was all, and why not I, as well as another?"; with other almanacs to this purpose, which set
me a tip-toe to begin this promising journey, and to leave
a place which, though my native one, contained no relations that I had reason to regret, and was grown insupportable to me, from the change of the tenderest usage
into a cold air of charity, with which I was entertain'd
even at the only friend's house that I had the least expectation of care and protection from. She was, however,
so just to me, as to manage the turning into money of the
little matters that remained to me after the debts and
burial charges were accounted for, and, at my departure,
put my whole fortune into my hands; which consisted of
a very slender wardrobe, pack'd up in a very portable box,
and eight guineas, with seventeen shillings in silver;
stowed up in a spring-pouch, which was a greater treasure
than ever I had yet seen together, and which I could not
conceive there was a possibility of running out; and indeed, I was so entirely taken up with the joy of seeing myself mistress of such an immense sum, that I gave very
little attention to a world of good advice which was given
me with it.

Places, then, being taken for Esther and me in the London waggon, I pass over a very immaterial scene of leave-
taking, at which I dropt a few tears betwixt grief and
joy; and, for the same reasons of insignificance, skip over
all that happened to me on the road, such as the waggon-
er's looking liquorish on me, the schemes laid for me by
some of the passengers, which were defeated by the vigilance of my guardian Esther; who, to do her justice, took
a motherly care of me, at the same time that she taxed me
for her protection by making me bear all travelling
charges, which I defrayed with the utmost cheerfulness,
and thought myself much obliged to her into the bargain.

She took indeed great care that we were not over-rated,

or imposed on, as well as of managing as frugally as possible; expensiveness was not her vice.

It was pretty late in a summer evening when we reached London-town, in our slow conveyance, though drawn by six at length. As we passed through the greatest streets that led to our inn, the noise of the coaches, the hurry, the crowds of foot passengers, in short, the new scenery of the shops and houses, at once pleased and amazed me.

But guess at my mortification and surprize when we came to the inn, and our things were landed and deliver'd to us, when my fellow traveller and protectress, Esther Davis, who had used me with the utmost tenderness during the journey, and prepared me by no preceding signs for the stunning blow I was to receive, when I say, my only dependence and friend, in this strange place, all of a sudden assumed a strange and cool air towards me, as if she dreaded my becoming a burden to her.

Instead, then, of proffering me the continuance of her assistance and good offices, which I relied upon, and never more wanted, she thought herself, it seems, abundantly acquitted of her engagements to me, by having brought me safe to my journey's end; and seeing nothing in her procedure towards me but what was natural and in order, began to embrace me by way of taking leave, whilst I was so confounded, so struck, that I had not spirit or sense enough so much as to mention my hopes or expectations from her experience, and knowledge of the place she had brought me to.

Whilst I stood thus stupid and mute, which she doubtless attributed to nothing more than a concern at parting, this idea procured me perhaps a slight alleviation of it, in the following harangue: That now we were got safe to London, and that she was obliged to go to her place, she advised me by all means to get into one as soon as possible; that I need not fear getting one; there were more places than parish-churches; that she advised me to go to an intelligence office; that if she heard of any thing stirring, she would find me out and let me know; that in the meantime, I should take a private lodging, and acquaint

her where to send to me; that she wish'd me good luck,
and hoped I should always have the grace to keep myself
honest, and not bring a disgrace on my parentage. With
this, she took her leave of me, and left me, as it were, on
my own hands, full as lightly as I had been put into hers.

Left thus alone, absolutely destitute and friendless, I
began then to feel most bitterly the severity of this separation, the scene of which had passed in a little room in the
inn; and no sooner was her back turned, but the affliction
I felt at my helpless strange circumstances burst out into
a flood of tears, which infinitely relieved the oppression
of my heart; though I still remained stupefied, and most
perfectly perplex'd how to dispose of myself.

One of the waiters coming in, added yet more to my
uncertainty by asking me, in a short way, if I called for
anything? to which I replied innocently: "No." But I
wished him to tell me where I might get a lodging for
that night. He said he would go and speak to his mistress,
who accordingly came, and told me drily, without entering in the least into the distress she saw me in, that I might
have a bed for a shilling, and that, as she supposed I had
some friends in town (here I fetched a deep sigh in vain!)
I might provide for myself in the morning.

'Tis incredible what trifling consolations the human
mind will seize in its greatest afflictions. The assurance
of nothing more than a bed to lie on that night, calmed
my agonies; and being asham'd to acquaint the mistress
of the inn that I had no friends to apply to in town, I
proposed to myself to proceed, the very next morning,
to an intelligence office, to which I was furnish'd with
written directions on the back of a ballad Esther had given
me. There I counted on getting information of any place
that such a country girl as I might be fit for, and where I
could get into any sort of being, before my little stock
should be consumed; and as to a character, Esther had
often repeated to me that I might depend on her managing
me one; nor, however affected I was at her leaving me
thus, did I entirely cease to rely on her, as I began to
think, good-naturedly, that her procedure was all in course,

and that it was only my ignorance of life that had made me take it in the light I at first did.

Accordingly, the next morning I dress'd myself as clean and as neat as my rustic wardrobe would permit me; and having left my box, with special recommendation, with the landlady, I ventured out by myself, and without any more difficulty than can be supposed of a young country girl, barely fifteen, and to whom every sign or shop was a gazing trap, I got to the wish'd-for intelligence office.

It was kept by an elderly woman, who sat at the receipt of custom, with a book before her in great form and order, and several scrolls, ready made out, of directions for places.

I made up then to this important personage, without lifting up my eyes or observing any of the people round me, who were attending there on the same errand as myself, and dropping her curtsies nine-deep, just made a shift to stammer out my business to her.

Madam having heard me out, with all the gravity and brow of a petty minister of State, and seeing at one glance over my figure what I was, made me no answer, but to ask me the preliminary shilling, on receipt of which she told me places for women were exceedingly scarce, especially as I seemed too slight built for hard work; but that she would look over her book, and see what was to be done for me, desiring me to stay a little till she had dispatched some other customers.

On this I drew back a little, most heartily mortified at a declaration which carried with it a killing uncertainty that my circumstances could not well endure.

Presently, assuming more courage, and seeking some diversion from my uneasy thoughts, I ventured to lift up my head a little, and sent my eyes on a course round the room, wherein they met full tilt with those of a lady (for such my extreme innocence pronounc'd her) sitting in a corner of the room, dress'd in a velvet mantle (*nota bene*, in the midst of summer), with her bonnet off; squab-fat, red-faced, and at least fifty.

She look'd as if she would devour me with her eyes, staring at me from head to foot, without the least regard

to the confusion and blushes her eyeing me so fixedly put
me to, and which were to her, no doubt, the strongest
recommendation and marks of my being fit for her purpose. After a little time, in which my air, person and whole
figure had undergone a strict examination, which I had,
on my part, tried to render favourable to me, by prim-
ming, drawing up my neck, and setting my best looks, she
advanced and spoke to me with the greatest demureness:

"Sweet-heart, do you want a place?"

"Yes, and please you" (with a curtsy down to the
ground).

Upon this she acquainted me that she was actually come
to the office herself to look out for a servant; that she believed I might do, with a little of her instructions; that she
could take my very looks for a sufficient character; that
London was a very wicked, vile place; that she hoped I
would be tractable, and keep out of bad company; in short,
she said all to me that an old experienced practitioner in
town could think of, and which was much more than was
necessary to take in an artless inexperienced country-
maid, who was even afraid of becoming a wanderer about
the streets, and therefore gladly jump'd at the first offer
of a shelter, especially from so grave and matron-like a
lady, for such my flattering fancy assured me this new
mistress of mine was; I being actually hired under the nose
of the good woman that kept the office, whose shrewd
smiles and shrugs I could not help observing, and innocently interpreted them as marks of her being pleased at
my getting into place so soon: but, as I afterwards came to
know, these BELDAMS understood one another very well,
and this was a market where *Mrs. Brown*, my mistress,
frequently attended, on the watch for any fresh goods that
might offer there, for the use of her customers, and her
own profit.

Madam was, however, so well pleased with her bargain, that fearing, I presume, lest better advice or some accident might occasion my slipping through her fingers, she
would officiously take me in a coach to my inn, where, calling herself for my box, it was, I being present, delivered

without the least scruple or explanation as to where I was going.

This being over, she bid the coachman drive to a shop in St. Paul's Churchyard, where she bought a pair of gloves, which she gave me, and thence renewed her directions to the coachman to drive to her house in *** street, who accordingly landed us at her door, after I had been cheer'd up and entertain'd by the way with the most plausible flams, without one syllable from which I could conclude anything but that I was, by the greatest good luck, fallen into the hands of the kindest mistress, not to say friend, that the *varsal* world could afford; and accordingly I enter'd her doors with most compleat confidence and exultation, promising myself that, as soon as I should be a little settled, I would acquaint Esther Davis with my rare good fortune.

You may be sure the good opinion of my place was not lessen'd by the appearance of a very handsome back parlour, into which I was led and which seemed to me magnificently furnished, who had never seen better rooms than the ordinary ones in inns upon the road. There were two gilt pierglasses, and a buffet, on which a few pieces of plates, set out to the most shew, dazzled, and altogether persuaded me that I must be got into a very reputable family.

Here my mistress first began her part, with telling me that I must have good spirits, and learn to be free with her; that she had not taken me to be a common servant, to do domestic drudgery, but to be a kind of companion to her; and that if I would be a good girl, she would do more than twenty mothers for me; to all which I answered only by the profoundest and the awkwardest curtsies, and a few monosyllables, such as "yes! no! to be sure!"

Presently my mistress touch'd the bell, and in came a strapping maid-servant, who had let us in. "Here, Martha," said Mrs. Brown—"I have just hir'd this young woman to look after my linen; so step up and shew her her chamber; and I charge you to use her with as much respect as you would myself, for I have taken a prodigious liking to her, and I do not know what I shall do for her."

Martha, who was an arch-jade, and, being used to this decoy, had her cue perfect, made me a kind of half curtsy, and asked me to walk up with her; and accordingly shew'd me a neat room, two pair of stairs backwards, in which there was a handsome bed, where Martha told me I was to lie with a young gentlewoman, a cousin of my mistress's, who she was sure would be vastly good to me. Then she ran out into such affected encomiums on her good mistress! her sweet mistress! and how happy I was to light upon her! that I could not have bespoke a better; with other the like gross stuff, such as would itself have started suspicions in any but such an unpractised simpleton, who was perfectly new to life, and who took every word she said in the very sense she laid out for me to take it; but she readily saw what a penetration she had to deal with, and measured me very rightly in her manner of whistling to me, so as to make me pleased with my cage, and blind to the wires.

In the midst of these false explanations of the nature of my future service, we were rung for down again, and I was reintroduced into the same parlour, where there was a table laid with three covers; and my mistress had now got with her one of her favourite girls, a notable manager of her house, and whose business it was to prepare and break such young fillies as I was to the mounting-block; and she was accordingly, in that view, allotted me for a bed-fellow; and, to give her the more authority, she had the title of cousin conferr'd on her by the venerable president of this college.

Here I underwent a second survey, which ended in the full approbation of *Mrs. Phœbe Ayres*, the name of my tutoress elect, to whose care and instructions I was affectionately recommended.

Dinner was now set on table, and in pursuance of treating me as a companion, *Mrs. Brown*, with a tone to cut off all dispute, soon over-rul'd my most humble and most confused protestations against sitting down with her Lady-ship, which my very short breeding just suggested to me could not be right, or in the order of things.

At table, the conversation was chiefly kept up by the

two madams, and carried on in double-meaning expressions, interrupted every now and then by kind assurance to me, all tending to confirm and fix my satisfaction with my present condition: augment it they could not, so very a novice was I then.

It was here agreed that I should keep myself up and out of sight for a few days, till such cloaths could be procured for me as were fit for the character I was to appear in, of my mistress's companion, observing withal, that on the first impressions of my figure much might depend; and, as they well judged, the prospect of exchanging my country cloaths for London finery, made the clause of confinement digest perfectly well with me. But the truth was, Mrs. Brown did not care that I should be seen or talked to by any, either of her customers, or her DOES (as they call'd the girls provided for them), till she had secured a good market for my maidenhead, which I had at least all the appearances of having brought into her LADYSHIP'S service.

To slip over minutes of no importance to the main of my story, I pass the interval to bed-time, in which I was more and more pleas'd with the views that opened to me, of an easy service under these good people; and after supper being shew'd up to bed, Miss Phœbe, who observed a kind of reluctance in me to strip and go to bed, in my shift, before her, now the maid was withdrawn, came up to me, and beginning with unpinning my handkerchief and gown, soon encouraged me to go on with undressing myself; and, still blushing at now seeing myself naked to my shift, I hurried to get under the bedcloaths out of sight. Phœbe laugh'd and was not long before she placed herself by my side. She was about five and twenty, by her most suspicious account, in which, according to all appearances, she must have sunk at least ten good years: allowance, too, being made for the havoc which a long course of hackneyship and hot waters must have made of her constitution, and which had already brought on, upon the spur, that stale stage in which those of her profession are reduced to think of SHOWING company, instead of SEEING it.

No sooner then was this precious substitute of my mistress'd laid down, but she, who was never out of her way when any occasion of lewdness presented itself, turned to me, embraced and kiss'd me with great eagerness. This was new, this was odd; but imputing it to nothing but pure kindness, which, for aught I knew, it might be the London way to express in that manner, I was determin'd not to be behind-hand with her, and returned her the kiss and embrace, with all the fervour that perfect innocence knew.

Encouraged by this, her hands became extremely free, and wander'd over my whole body, with touches, squeezes, pressures, that rather warm'd and surpriz'd me with their novelty, than they either shock'd or alarm'd me.

The flattering praises she intermingled with these invasions, contributed also not a little to bribe my passiveness; and, knowing no ill, I feared none, especially from one who had prevented all doubt of her womanhood by conducting my hands to a pair of breasts that hung loosely down, in a size and volume that full sufficiently distinguished her sex, to me at least, who had never made any other comparison . . .

I lay then all tame and passive as she could wish, whilst her freedom raised no other emotions but those of a strange, and, till then, unfelt pleasure. Every part of me was open and exposed to the licentious courses of her hands, which, like a lambent fire, ran over my whole body, and thaw'd all coldness as they went.

My breasts, if it is not too bold a figure to call so two hard, firm, rising hillocks, that just began to shew themselves, or signify anything to the touch, employ'd and amus'd her hands a-while, till, slipping down lower, over a smooth track, she could just feel the soft silky down that had but a few months before put forth and garnish'd the mount-pleasant of those parts, and promised to spread a grateful shelter over the seat of the most exquisite sensation, and which had been, till that instant, the seat of the most insensible innocence. Her fingers play'd and strove to twine in the young tendrils of that moss, which nature has contrived at once for use and ornament.

But, not contented with these outer posts, she now attempts the main spot, and began to twitch, to insinuate, and at length to force an introduction of a finger into the quick itself, in such a manner, that she had not proceeded by insensible gradations that inflamed me beyond the power of modesty to oppose its resistance to their progress, I should have jump'd out of bed and cried for help against such strange assaults.

Instead of which, her lascivious touches had lighted up a new fire that wanton'd through all my veins, but fix'd with violence in that center appointed them by nature, where the first strange hands were now busied in feeling, squeezing, compressing the lips, then opening them again, with a finger between, till an "Oh!" express'd her hurting me, where the narrowness of the unbroken passage refused it entrance to any depth.

In the meantime, the extension of my limbs, languid stretchings, sighs, short heavings, all conspired to assure that experienced wanton that I was more pleased than offended at her proceedings, which she seasoned with repeated kisses and exclamations, such as "Oh! what a charming creature thou art! . . . What a happy man will he be that first makes a woman of you! . . . Oh! that I were a man for your sake! . . ." with the like broken expressions, interrupted by kisses as fierce and fervent as ever I received from the other sex.

For my part, I was transported, confused, and out of myself; feelings so new were too much for me. My heated and alarm'd senses were in a tumult that robbed me of all liberty of thought; tears of pleasure gush'd from my eyes, and somewhat assuaged the fire that rag'd all over me.

Phœbe, herself, the hackney'd, thorough-bred Phœbe, to whom all modes and devices of pleasure were known and familiar, found, it seems, in this exercise of her art to break young girls, the gratification of one of those arbitrary tastes, for which there is no accounting. Not that she hated men, or did not even prefer them to her own sex; but when she met with such occasions as this was, a satiety of enjoyments in the common road, perhaps too, a secret bias, inclined her to make the most of pleasure, wherever she could find it, without distinction of sexes. In this view, now well assured that she had, by her touches, sufficiently inflamed me for her purpose, she roll'd down the bed-cloaths gently, and I saw myself stretched nak'd, my shift being turned up to my neck, whilst I had no power or sense to oppose it. Even my glowing blushes expressed more desire than modesty, whilst the candle, left (to be sure not undesignedly) burning, threw a full light on my whole body.

"No!" says Phœbe, "you must not, my sweet girl, think to hide all these treasures from me. My sight must be feasted as well as my touch . . . I must devour with my eyes this springing BOSOM . . . Suffer me to kiss it . . . I have not seen it enough . . . Let me kiss it once more . . . What firm, smooth, white flesh is here! . . . How delicately shaped! . . . Then this delicious down! Oh! let me view the small, dear, tender cleft! . . . This is too much, I cannot bear it! . . . I must . . . I must . . ." Here she took my hand, and in a transport carried it where you will easily guess. But what a difference in the state of the same thing! . . . A spreading thicket of bushy curls marked the full-grown, complete woman. Then the cavity to which she guided my hand easily received it; and as soon as she felt it within her, she moved herself to and fro, with so rapid a friction that I presently withdrew it, wet and clammy, when instantly Phœbe grew more composed, after two or three sighs, and heart-fetched Oh's! and giving me a kiss that seemed to exhale her soul through her lips, she replaced the bed-cloaths over us. What pleasure she had found I will not say; but this I know, that the first sparks of kindling nature, the first ideas of pollution, were caught by me that night; and that the acquaintance and communication with the bad of our own sex, is often as fatal to innocence as all the seductions of the other. But to go on. When Phœbe was restor'd to that calm, which I was far from the enjoyment of myself, she artfully sounded me on all the points necessary to govern the designs of my virtuous mistress on me, and by my answers, drawn from pure undissembled nature, she had no reason but to promise herself all imaginable success, so far as it depended on my ignorance, easiness, and warmth of constitution.

After a sufficient length of dialogue, my bedfellow left me to my rest, and I fell asleep, through pure weariness from the violent emotions I had been led into, when nature (which had been too warmly stir'd and fermented to subside without allaying by some means or other) relieved me by one of those luscious dreams, the transports of which are scarce inferior to those of waking real action.

In the morning I awoke about ten, perfectly gay and refreshed. Phœbe was up before me, and asked me in the kindest manner how I did, how I had rested, and if I was ready for breakfast, carefully, at the same time, avoiding to increase the confusion she saw I was in, at looking her in the face, by any hint of the night's bed scene. I told her if she pleased I would get up, and begin any work she would be pleased to set me about. She smil'd; presently the maid brought in the tea-equipage, and I had just huddled my cloaths on, when in waddled my mistress. I expected no less than to be told of, if not chid for, my late rising, when I was agreeably disappointed by her compliments on my pure and fresh looks. I was "a bud of beauty" (this was her style), "and how vastly all the fine men would admire me!" to all which my answers did not, I can assure you, wrong my breeding; they were as simple and silly as they could wish, and, no doubt, flattered them infinitely more than had they proved me enlightened by education and a knowledge of the world.

We breakfasted, and the tea things were scarce removed, when in were brought two bundles of linen and wearing apparel: in short, all the necessaries for *rigging me out*, as they termed it, completely.

Imagine to yourself, Madam, how my little coquette heart flutter'd with joy at the sight of a white lute-string, flower'd with silver, scoured indeed, but passed on me for spick-and-span new, a *Brussels* lace cap, braided shoes, and the rest in proportion, all second-hand finery, and procured instantly for the occasion, by the diligence and

industry of the good Mrs. Brown, who had already a
chapman for me in the house, before whom my charms
were to pass in review; for he had not only, in course, insisted on a previous sight of the premises, but also on immediate surrender to him, in case of his agreeing for me;
concluding very wisely that such a place as I was in was
of the hottest to trust the keeping of such a perishable
commodity in as a maidenhead.

The care of dressing, and tricking me out for the market, was then left to Phœbe, who acquitted herself, if
not well, at least perfectly to the satisfaction of every
thing but my impatience of seeing myself dress'd. When
it was over, and I view'd myself in the glass, I was, no
doubt, too natural, too artless, to hide my childish joy at
the change: a change, in the real truth, for much the
worse, since I must have much better become the neat
easy simplicity of my rustic dress than the awkward, untoward, taudry finery that I could not conceal my strange-
ness to.

Phœbe's compliments, however, in which her own
share in dressing me was not forgot, did not a little confirm me in the first notions I had ever entertained concerning my person; which, be it said without vanity, was
then tolerable to justify a taste for me, and of which it
may not be out of place here to sketch you an unflatter'd
picture.

I was tall, yet not too tall for my age, which, as I before
remark'd, was barely turned of fifteen; my shape perfectly
straight, thin waisted, and light and free, without owing
any thing to stays; my hair was a glossy auburn, and as
soft as silk, flowing down my neck in natural buckles, and
did not a little set off the whiteness of a smooth skin; my
face was rather too ruddy, though its features were delicate, and the shape a roundish oval, except where a pit
on my chin had far from a disagreeable effect; my eyes
were as black as can be imagin'd, and rather languishing
than sparkling, except on certain occasions, when I have
been told they struck fire fast enough; my teeth, which
I ever carefully preserv'd, were small, even and white;
my bosom was finely rais'd, and one might then discern

rather the promise, than the actual growth, of the round, firm breasts, that in a little time made that promise good. In short, all the points of beauty that are most universally in request, I had, or at least my vanity forbade me to appeal from the decision of our sovereign judges the men, who all, that I ever knew at least, gave it thus highly in my favour; and I met with, even in my own sex, some that were above denying me that justice, whilst others praised me yet more unsuspectedly, by endeavouring to detract from me, in points of person and figure that I obviously excelled in. This is, I own, too strong of self praise; but should I not be ungrateful to nature, and to a form to which I owe such singular blessings of pleasure and fortune, were I to suppress, through an affectation of modesty, the mention of such valuable gifts?

Well then, dress'd I was, and little did it then enter into my head that all this gay attire was no more than decking the victim out for sacrifice, whilst I innocently attributed all to mere friendship and kindness in the sweet good Mrs. Brown; who, I was forgetting to mention, had, under pretence of keeping my money safe, got from me, without the least hesitation, the driblet (so I now call it) which remained to me after the expences of my journey.

After some little time most agreeably spent before the glass, in scarce self-admiration, since my new dress had by much the greatest share in it, I was sent for down to the parlour, where the old lady saluted me, and wished me joy of my new cloaths, which she was not asham'd to say, fitted me as if I had worn nothing but the finest all my life-time; but what was it she could not see me silly enough to swallow? At the same time, she presented me to another cousin of her own creation, an elderly gentleman, who got up, at my entry into the room, and on my dropping a curtsy to him, saluted me, and seemed a little affronted that I had only presented my cheek to him: a mistake, which, if one, he immediately corrected, by glewing his lips to mine, with an ardour which his figure had not at all disposed me to thank him for: his figure, I say, than which nothing could be more shocking or detestable:

for ugly, and disagreeable, were terms too gentle to convey a just idea of it.

Imagine to yourself a man rather past threescore, short and ill-made, with a yellow cadaverous hue, great goggling eyes that stared as if he was strangled; an outmouth from two more properly tusks than teeth, livid lips, and breath like a jake's: then he had a peculiar ghastliness in his grin that made him perfectly frightful, if not dangerous to women with child; yet, made as he was thus in mock of man, he was so blind to his own staring deformities as to think himself born for pleasing, and that no woman could see him with impunity: in consequence of which idea, he had lavish'd great sums on such wretches as could gain upon themselves to pretend love to his person, whilst to those who had not art or patience to dissemble the horror it inspir'd, he behaved even brutally. Impotence, more than necessity, made him seek in variety the provocative that was wanting to raise him to the pitch of enjoyment, which too he often saw himself baulked of, by the failure of his powers: and this always threw him into a fit of rage, which he wreak'd, as far as he durst, on the innocent objects of his fit of momentary desire.

This then was the monster to which my conscientious benefactress, who had long been his purveyor in this way, had doom'd me, and sent for me down purposely for his examination. Accordingly she made me stand up before him, turn'd me round, unpinn'd my handkerchief, remark'd to him the rise and fall, the turn and whiteness of a bosom just beginning to fill; then made me walk, and took even a handle from the rusticity of my gait, to inflame the inventory of my charms: in short, she omitted no point of jockeyship; to which he only answer'd by gracious nods of approbation, whilst he look'd goats and monkies at me: for I sometimes stole a corner glance at him, and encountering his fiery, eager stare, looked another way from pure horror and affright, which he, doubtless in character, attributed to nothing more than maiden modesty, or at least the affectation of it.

However, I was soon dismiss'd, and reconducted to my room by Phœbe, who stuck close to me; not leaving me alone and at leisure to make such reflections as might naturally rise to any one, not an idiot, on such a scene as I had just gone through; but to my shame be it confess'd, such was my invincible stupidity, or rather portentous innocence, that I did not yet open my eyes to Mrs. Brown's designs, and saw nothing in this titular cousin of hers but a shocking hideous person which did not at all concern me, unless that my gratitude for my benefactress made me extend my respect to all her cousinhood.

Phœbe, however, began to sift the state and pulses of my heart towards this monster, asking me how I should approve of such a fine gentleman for a husband? (fine gentleman, I suppose she called him, from his being daubed with lace). I answered her very naturally, that I had no thoughts of a husband, but that if I was to choose one, it should be among my own degree, sure! So much had my aversion to that wretch's hideous figure indisposed me to all "fine gentlemen," and confounded my ideas, as if those of that rank had been necessarily cast in the same mould that he was! But Phœbe was not to be beat off so, but went on with her endeavours to melt and soften me for the purposes of my reception into that hospitable house: and whilst she talked of the sex in general, she had no reason to despair of a compliance, which more than one reason shewed her would be easily enough obtained of me; but then she had too much experience not to discover that my particular fix'd aversion to that frightful cousin would be a block not so readily to be removed, as suited the consummation of their bargain, and sale of me.

Mother Brown had in the mean time agreed the terms with this liquorish old goat, which I afterwards understood were to be fifty guineas peremptory for the liberty of attempting me, and a hundred more at the compleat gratification of his desires, in the triumph over my virginity: and as for me, I was to be left entirely at the discretion of his liking and generosity. This unrighteous contract being thus settled, he was so eager to be put in possession, that he insisted on being introduc'd to drink tea with me that afternoon, when we were to be left alone;

nor would he hearken to the procuress's remonstrances, that I was not sufficiently prepared and ripened for such an attack; that I was too green and untam'd, having been scarce twenty-four hours in the house: it is the character of lust to be impatient, and his vanity arming him against any supposition of other than the common resistance of a maid on those occasions, made him reject all proposals of a delay, and my dreadful trial was thus fix'd, unknown to me, for that very evening.

At dinner, Mrs. Brown and Phœbe did nothing but run riot in praises of this wonderful cousin, and how happy that woman would be that he would favour with his addresses; in short my two gossips exhausted all their rhetoric to persuade me to accept them: "that the gentleman was violently smitten with me at first sight . . . that he would make my fortune if I would be a good girl and not stand in my own light . . . that I should trust his honour . . . that I should be made for ever, and have a chariot to go abroad in . . . ," with all such stuff as was fit to turn the head of such a silly ignorant girl as I then was: but luckily here my aversion had taken already such deep root in me, my heart was so strongly defended from him by my senses, that wanting the art to mask my sentiments, I gave them no hopes of their employer's succeeding, at least very easily, with me. The glass too march'd pretty quick, with a view, I suppose, to make a friend of the warmth of my constitution, in the minutes of the imminent attack.

Thus they kept me pretty long at table, and about six in the evening, after I was retired to my own apartment, and the tea board was set, enters my venerable mistress follow'd close by that satyr, who came in grinning in a way peculiar to him, and by his odious presence confirm'd me in all the sentiments of detestation which his first appearance had given birth to.

He sat down fronting me, and all tea time kept ogling me in a manner that gave me the utmost pain and confusion, all the marks of which he still explained to be my bashfulness, and not being used to see company.

Tea over, the commoding old lady pleaded urgent business (which indeed was true) to go out, and earnestly desir'd me to entertain her cousin kindly till she came back, both for my own sake and her's; and then with a "Pray, sir, be very good, be very tender of the sweet child," she went out of the room, leaving me staring, with my mouth open, and unprepar'd, by the suddenness of her departure, to oppose it.

We were now alone; and on that idea a sudden fit of trembling seiz'd me. I was so afraid, without a precise notion of why, and what I had to fear, that I sat on the settee, by the fire-side, motionless, and petrified, without life or spirit, not knowing how to look or how to stir.

But long I was not suffered to remain in this state of stupefaction: the monster squatted down by me on the settee, and without farther ceremony or preamble, flings his arms about my neck, and drawing me pretty forcibly towards him, oblig'd me to receive, in spite of my struggles to disengage from him, his pestilential kisses, which quite overcame me. Finding me then next to senseless, and unresisting, he tears off my neck handkerchief, and laid all open there to his eyes and hands: still I endur'd all without flinching, till embolden'd by my sufferance and silence, for I had not the power to speak or cry out, he attempted to lay me down on the settee, and I felt his hand on the lower part of my naked thighs, which were cross'd, and which he endeavoured to unlock . . . Oh then! I was roused out of my passive endurance, and springing from him with an activity he was not prepar'd for, threw myself at his feet, and begg'd him, in the most moving tone, not to be rude, and that he would not hurt me:—"Hurt you, my dear?" says the brute; "I intend you no harm . . . has not the old lady told you that I love you? . . . that I shall do handsomely by you?" "She has indeed, sir," said I; "but I cannot love you, indeed I cannot! . . . pray let me alone . . . yes! I will love you dearly if you will let me alone, and go away . . ." But I was talking to the wind; for whether my tears, my attitude, or the disorder of my dress prov'd fresh incentives, or whether he was now under the dominion of desires he could not bridle, but snorting and foaming with lust and rage, he renews his attack, seizes me, and again attempts to extend and fix me on the settee: in which he succeeded so far as to lay me along, and even to toss my petticoats over my head, and lay my thighs bare, which I obstinately kept close, nor could he, though he attempted with his knee to force them open, effect it so as to stand fair for being master of the main avenue; he was unbuttoned, both waistcoat and breeches, yet I only felt the weight of his body upon me, whilst I lay struggling with indignation, and dying with terrors; but he stopped all of a sudden, and got off, panting, blowing, cursing, and repeating "old and ugly!" for so I had very naturally called him in the heat of my defence.

The brute had, it seems, as I afterwards understood, brought on, by his eagerness and struggle, the ultimate period of his hot fit of lust, which his power was too short-liv'd to carry him through the full execution of; of which my thighs and linen received the effusion.

When it was over he bid me, with a tone of displeasure, get up, saying that he would not do me the honour to think of me any more . . . that the old bitch might look out for another cully . . . that he would not be fool'd so by e'er a country mock modesty in England . . . that he supposed I had left my maidenhead with some hobnail in the country, and was come to dispose of my skim-milk in town, with a volley of the like abuse; which I listened to with more pleasure than ever fond woman did to protestations of love from her darling minion: for, incapable as I was of receiving any addition to my perfect hatred and aversion to him, I look'd on this railing as my security against his renewing his most odious caresses.

Yet, plain as Mrs. Brown's views were now come out, I had not the heart or spirit to open my eyes to them: still I could not part with my dependence on that beldam, so much did I think myself her's, soul and body: or rather, I sought to deceive myself with the continuation of my good opinion of her, and chose to wait the worst at her hands sooner than be turn'd out to starve in the streets, without a penny of money or a friend to apply to: these fears were my folly.

Whilst this confusion of ideas was passing in my head,

and I sat pensive by the fire, with my eyes brimming with tears, my neck still bare, and my cap fall'n off in the struggle, so that my hair was in the disorder you may guess, the villain's lust began, I suppose, to be again in flow, at the sight of all that bloom of youth which presented itself to his view, a bloom yet unenjoy'd, and of course not yet indifferent to him.

After some pause, he ask'd me, with a tone of voice mightily softened, whether I would make it up with him before the old lady returned and all should be well; he would restore me his affections, at the same time offering to kiss me and feel my breasts. But now my extreme aversion, my fears, my indignation, all acting upon me, gave me a spirit not natural to me, so that breaking loose from him, I ran to the bell and rang it, before he was aware, with such violence and effect as brought up the maid to know what was the matter, or whether the gentleman wanted any thing; and before he could proceed to greater extremities, she bounc'd into the room, and seeing me stretch'd on the floor, my hair all dishevell'd, my nose gushing out blood, which did not a little tragedize the scene, and my odious persecutor still intent of pushing his brutal point, unmoved by all my cries and distress, she was herself confounded and did not know what to say.

As much, however, as Martha might be prepared and hardened to transactions of this sort, all womanhood must have been out of her heart, could she have seen this unmov'd. Besides that, on the face of things, she imagined that matters had gone greater lengths than they really had, and that the courtesy of the house had been actually consummated on me, and flung me into the condition I was in: in this notion she instantly took my part, and advis'd the gentleman to go down and leave me to recover myself, and "that all would be soon over with me . . . that when Mrs. Brown and Phœbe, who were gone out, were return'd, they would take order for every thing to his satisfaction . . . that nothing would be lost by a little patience with the poor tender thing . . . that for her part she was frighten'd . . . she could not tell what to say to such doings . . . . but that she would stay by me till my mistress came home." As the wench said all this in a resolute tone, and the monster himself began to perceive that things would not mend by his staying, he took his hat and went out of the room, murmuring, and pleating his brows like an old ape, so that I was delivered from the horrors of his detestable presence.

As soon as he was gone, Martha very tenderly offered me her assistance in any thing, and would have got me some hartshorn drops, and put me to bed; which last, I at first positively refused, in the fear that the monster might return and take me at that advantage. However, with much persuasion, and assurances that I should not be molested that night, she prevailed on me to lie down; and indeed I was so weakened by my struggles, so dejected by my fearful apprehensions, so terror-struck, that I had not power to sit up, or hardly to give answers to the questions with which the curious Martha ply'd and perplex'd me.

Such too, and so cruel was my fate, that I dreaded the sight of Mrs. Brown, as if I had been the criminal and she the person injur'd; a mistake which you will not think so strange, on distinguishing that neither virtue nor principles had the least share in the defence I had made, but only the particular aversion I had conceiv'd against the first brutal and frightful invader of my tender innocence.

I pass'd then the time till Mrs. Brown's return home, under all the agitations of fear and despair that may easily be guessed.

About eleven at night my two ladies came home, and having receiv'd rather a favourable account from Martha, who had run down to let them in, for *Mr. Crofts* (that was the name of my brute) was gone out of the house, after waiting till he had tired his patience for Mrs. Brown's return, they came thundering up-stairs, and seeing me pale, my face bloody, and all the marks of the most thorough dejection, they employed themselves more to comfort and re-inspirit me, than in making me the reproaches I was weak enough to fear, I who had so many juster and stronger to retort upon them.

Mrs. Brown withdrawn, Phœbe came presently to bed

to me, and what with the answers she drew from me, what with her own method of *palpably* satisfying herself, she soon discovered that I had been more frighted than hurt; upon which I suppose, being herself seiz'd with sleep, and reserving her lectures and instructions till the next morning, she left me, properly speaking, to my unrest; for, after tossing and turning the greatest part of the night, and tormenting myself with the falsest notions and apprehensions of things, I fell, through mere fatigue, into a kind of delirious doze, out of which I waked late in the morning, in a violent fever: a circumstance which was extremely critical to reprieve me, at least for a time, from the attacks of a wretch infinitely more terrible to me than death itself.

The interested care that was taken of me during my illness, in order to restore me to a condition of making good the bawd's engagements, or of enduring further trials, had however such an effect on my grateful disposition, that I even thought myself oblig'd to my undoers for their attention to promote my recovery; and, above all, for the keeping out of my sight of that brutal ravisher, the author of my disorder, on their finding I was too strongly mov'd at the bare mention of his name.

Youth is soon raised, and a few days were sufficient to conquer the fury of my fever: but, what contributed most to my perfect recovery and to my reconciliation with life, was the timely news that *Mr. Crofts*, who was a merchant of considerable dealings, was arrested at the King's suit, for nearly forty thousand pounds, on account of his driving a certain contraband trade, and that his affairs were so desperate that even were it in his inclination, it would not be in his power to renew his designs upon me: for he was instantly thrown into a prison, which it was not likely he would get out of in haste.

Mrs. Brown, who had touched his fifty guineas, advanc'd to so little purpose, and lost all hopes of the remaining hundred, began to look upon my treatment of him with a more favourable eye; and as they had observ'd my temper to be perfectly tractable and conformable to their views, all the girls that compos'd her flock were suffered to visit me, and had their cue to dispose me, by their conversation, to a perfect resignation of myself to Mrs. Brown's direction.

Accordingly they were let in upon me, and all that frolic and thoughtless gaiety in which those giddy creatures consume their leisure made me envy a condition of which I only saw the fair side; insomuch, that the being one of them became even my ambition: a disposition which they all carefully cultivated; and I wanted now nothing but to restore my health, that I might be able to undergo the ceremony of the initiation.

Conversation, example, all, in short, contributed, in that house, to corrupt my native purity, which had taken no root in education; whilst now the inflammable principal of pleasure, so easily fired at my age, made strange work within me, and all the modesty I was brought up in the habit, not the instruction of, began to melt away like dew before the sun's heat; not to mention that I made a vice of necessity, from the constant fears I had of being turn'd out to starve.

I was soon pretty well recover'd, and at certain hours allow'd to range all over the house, but cautiously kept from seeing any company till the arrival of *Lord B . . . ,* from *Bath,* to whom Mrs. Brown, in respect to his experienced generosity on such occasions, proposed to offer the perusal of that trinket of mine, which bears so great an imaginary value; and his lordship being expected in town in less than a fortnight, Mrs. Brown judged I would be entirely renewed in beauty and freshness by that time, and afford her the chance of a better bargain than she had driven with Mr. Crofts.

In the meantime, I was so thoroughly, as they call it, brought over, so tame to their whistle, that, had my cage door been set open, I had no idea that I ought to fly anywhere, sooner than stay where I was; nor had I the least sense of regretting my condition, but waited very quietly for whatever Mrs. Brown should order concerning me; who on her side, by herself and her agents, took more than the necessary precautions to lull and lay asleep all just reflections on my destination.

Preachments of morality over the left shoulder; a life

of joy painted in the gayest colours; caresses, promises, indulgent treatment: nothing, in short, was wanting to domesticate me entirely and to prevent my going out anywhere to get better advice. Alas! I dream'd of no such thing.

Hitherto I had been indebted only to the girls of the house for the corruption of my innocence: their luscious talk, in which modesty was far from respected, their description of their engagements with men, had given me a tolerable insight into the nature and mysteries of their profession, at the same time that they highly provok'd an itch of florid warm-spirited blood through every vein: but above all, my bed-fellow Phœbe, whose pupil I more immediately was, exerted her talents in giving me the first tinctures of pleasure: whilst nature, now warm'd and wantoned with discoveries so interesting, piqu'd a curiosity which Phœbe artfully whetted, and leading me from question to question of her own suggestion, explain'd to me all the mysteries of Venus. But I could not long remain in such a house as that, without being an eye-witness of more than I could conceive from her descriptions.

One day, about twelve at noon, being thoroughly recover'd of my fever, I happen'd to be in Mrs. Brown's dark closet, where I had not been half an hour, resting upon the maid's settle-bed, before I heard a rustling in the bed-chamber, separated from the closet only by two sash-doors, before the glasses of which were drawn two yellow damask curtains, but not so close as to exclude the full view of the room from any person in the closet.

I instantly crept softly, and posted myself so, that seeing every thing minutely, I could not myself be seen; and who should come in but the venerable mother Abbess herself! handed in by a tall, brawny young Horse-grenadier, moulded in the *Hercules* style: *in fine,* the choice of the most experienced dame, in those *affairs,* in all London.

Oh! how still and hush did I keep at my stand, lest any noise should baulk my curiosity, or bring Madam into the closet!

But I had not much reason to fear either, for she was so

entirely taken up with her present great concern, that she had no sense of attention to spare to any thing else.

Droll was it to see that clumsy fat figure of hers flop down on the foot of the bed, opposite to the closet-door, so that I had a full front-view of all her charms.

Her paramour sat down by her: he seemed to be a man of very few words, and a great stomach; for proceeding instantly to essentials, he gave her some hearty smacks, and thrusting his hands into her breasts, disengag'd them from her stays, in scorn of whose confinement they broke loose, and swagged down, navel-low at least. A more enormous pair did my eyes never behold, nor of a worse colour, flagging-soft, and most lovingly contiguous: yet such as they were, this neck-beef eater seem'd to paw them with a most uninvitable gust, seeking in vain to confine or cover one of them with a hand scarce less than a shoulder of mutton. After toying with them thus some time, as if they had been worth it, he laid her down pretty briskly, and canting up her petticoats, made barely a mask of them to her broad red face, that blush'd with nothing but brandy.

As he stood on one side, for a minute or so, unbuttoning his waist-coat and breeches, her fat, brawny thighs hung down, and the whole greasy landscape lay fairly open to my view; a wide open-mouth'd gap, overshaded with a grizzly bush, seemed held out like a beggar's wallet for its provision.

But I soon had my eyes called off by a more striking object, that entirely engross'd them.

Her sturdy stallion had now unbutton'd, and produced naked, stiff, and erect, that wonderful machine, which I had never seen before, and which, for the interest my own seat of pleasure began to take furiously in it, I star'd at with all the eyes I had: however, my senses were too much flurried, too much concenter'd in that now burning spot of mine, to observe any thing more than in general the make and turn of that instrument, from which the instinct of nature, yet more than all I had heard of it, now strongly informed me I was to expect that supreme pleasure which she had placed in the meeting of those parts so admirably fitted for each other.

Long, however, the young spark did not remain before giving it two or three shakes, by way of brandishing it; he threw himself upon her, and his back being now towards me, I could only take his being ingulph'd for granted, by the directions he mov'd in, and the impossibility of missing so staring a mark; and now the bed shook, the curtains rattled so, that I could scarce hear the sighs and murmurs, the heaves and pantings that accompanied the action, from the beginning to the end; the sound and sight of which thrill'd to the very soul of me, and made every vein of my body circulate liquid fires: the emotion grew so violent that it almost intercepted my respiration.

Prepared then, and disposed as I was by the discourse of my companions, and Phœbe's minute detail of everything, no wonder that such a sight gave the last dying blow to my native innocence.

Whilst they were in the heat of the action, guided by nature only, I stole my hand up my petticoats, and with fingers all on fire, seized, and yet more inflamed that center of all my senses: my heart palpitated, as if it would force its way through my bosom; I breath'd with pain; I twisted my thighs, squeezed, and compressed the lips of that virgin slit, and following mechanically the example of Phœbe's manual operation on it, as far as I could find admission, brought on at last the critical extasy, the melting flow, into which nature, spent with excess of pleasure, dissolves and dies away.

After which, my senses recover'd coolness enough to observe the rest of the transaction between this happy pair.

The young fellow had just dismounted, when the old lady immediately sprung up, with all the vigour of youth, derived, no doubt, from her late refreshment; and making him sit down, began in her turn to kiss him, to pat and pinch his cheeks, and play with his hair: all which he receiv'd with an air of indifference and coolness, that shew'd him to me much altered from what he was when he first went on to the breach.

My pious governess, however, not being above calling in auxiliaries, unlocks a little case of cordials that stood near the bed, and made him pledge her in a very plentiful dram: after which, and a little amorous parley, Madam sat herself down upon the same place, at the bed's foot; and the young fellow standing sideway by her, she, with the greatest effrontery imaginable, unbuttons his breeches, and removing his shirt, draws out his affair, so shrunk and diminish'd, that I could not but remember the difference, now crestfallen, or just faintly lifting its head: but our experienc'd matron very soon, by chafing it with her hands, brought it to swell to that size and erection I had before seen it up to.

I admired then, upon a fresh account, and with a nicer survey, the texture of that capital part of man: the flaming red head as it stood uncapt, the whiteness of the shaft, and the shrub growth of curling hair that embrowned the roots of it, the roundish bag that dangled down from it, all exacted my eager attention, and renewed my flame. But, as the main affair was now at the point the industrious dame had laboured to bring it to, she was not in the humour to put off the payment of her pains, but laying herself down, drew him gently upon her, and thus they finish'd, in the same manner as before, the old last act.

This over, they both went out lovingly together, the old lady having first made him a present, as near as I could observe, of three or four pieces; he being not only her particular favourite on account of his performances, but a retainer to the house; from whose sight she had taken great care hitherto to secrete me, lest he might not have had patience to wait for my lord's arrival, but have insisted on being his taster, which the old lady was under too much subjection to him to dare dispute with him; for every girl of the house fell to him in course, and the old lady only now and then got her turn, in consideration of the maintenance he had, and which he could scarce be accused of not earning from her.

As soon as I heard them go down-stairs, I stole up softly to my own room, out of which I had luckily not been miss'd; there I began to breathe freer, and to give a loose

to those warm emotions which the sight of such an encounter had raised in me. I laid me down on the bed,
stretched myself out, joining and ardently wishing, and
requiring any means to divert or allay the rekindled rage
and tumult of my desires, which all pointed strongly to
their pole: man. I felt about the bed as if I sought
for something that I grasp'd in my waking dream, and not
finding it, could have cry'd for vexation; every part of me
glowing with stimulating fires. At length, I resorted to the
only present remedy, that of vain attempts at digitation,
where the smallness of the theatre did not yet afford room
enough for action, and where the pain my fingers gave
me, in striving for admission, tho' they procured me a slight
satisfaction for the present, started an apprehension, which
I could not be easy till I had communicated to Phœbe, and
received her explanations upon it.

The opportunity, however, did not offer till next morning, for Phœbe did not come to bed till long after I was
gone to sleep. As soon then as we were both awake, it was
but in course to bring our ly-a-bed chat to land on the subject of my uneasiness: to which a recital of the love scene
I had thus, by chance, been spectatress of, serv'd for a
preface.

Phœbe could not hear it to the end without more than
one interruption by peals of laughter, and my ingenuous
way of relating matters did not a little heighten the joke
to her.

But, on her sounding me how the sight had affected
me, without mincing or hiding the pleasurable emotions it
had inspir'd me with, I told her at the same time that one
remark had perplex'd me, and that very considerably.—
"Aye!" says she, "what was that?"—"Why," replied I,
"having very curiously and attentively compared the size
of that enormous machine, which did not appear, at least
to my fearful imagination, less than my wrist, and at least
three of my handfuls long, to that of the tender small part
of me which was framed to receive it, I can not conceive
its being possible to afford it entrance without dying, perhaps in the greatest pain, since you well know that even
a finger thrust in there hurts me beyond bearing . . . As

to my mistress's and yours, I can plainly distinguish the different dimensions of them from mine, palpable to the touch, and visible to the eye; so that, in short, great as the promis'd pleasure may be, I am afraid of the pain of the experiment."

Phœbe at this redoubled her laugh, and whilst I expected a very serious solution of my doubts and apprehensions in this matter, only told me that she never heard of a mortal wound being given in those parts by that terrible weapon, and that some she knew younger, and as delicately made as myself, had outlived the operation; that she believed, at the worst, I should take a great deal of killing; that true it was, there was a great diversity of sizes in those parts, owing to nature, child-bearing, frequent over-stretching with unmerciful machines, but that at a certain age and habit of body, even the most experienc'd in those affairs could not well distinguish between the maid and the woman, supposing too an absence of all artifice, and things in their natural situation: but that since chance had thrown in my way one sight of that sort, she would procure me another, that should feast my eyes more delicately, and go a great way in the cure of my fears from that imaginary disproportion.

On this she asked me if I knew *Polly Philips.* "Undoubtedly," says I, "the fair girl which was so tender of me when I was sick, and has been, as you told me, but two months in the house." "The same," says Phœbe. "You must know then, she is kept by a young Genœse merchant, whom his uncle, who is immensely rich, and whose darling he is, sent over here with an English merchant, his friend, on a pretext of settling some accounts, but in reality to humour his inclinations for travelling, and seeing the world. He met casually with this *Polly* once in company, and taking a liking to her, makes it worth her while to keep entirely to him. He comes to her here twice or thrice a week, and she receives him in her light closet up one pair of stairs, where he enjoys her in a taste, I suppose, peculiar to the heat, or perhaps the caprices of his own country. I say no more, but to-morrow being his day, you shall see what passes between them, from a place only known to your mistress and myself."

You may be sure, in the ply I was now taking, I had no objection to the proposal, and was rather a tip-toe for its accomplishment.

At five in the evening, next day, Phœbe, punctual to her promise, came to me as I sat alone in my own room, and beckon'd me to follow her.

We went down the back-stairs very softly, and opening the door of a dark closet, where there was some old furniture kept, and some cases of liquor, she drew me in after her, and fastening the door upon us, we had no light but what came through a long crevice in the partition between ours and the light closet, where the scene of action lay; so that sitting on those low cases, we could, with the greatest ease, as well as clearness, see all objects (ourselves unseen), only by applying our eyes close to the crevice, where the moulding of a panel had warped, or started a little on the other side.

The young gentleman was the first person I saw, with his back directly towards me, looking at a print. Polly was not yet come: in less than a minute tho', the door opened, and she came in; and at the noise the door made he turned about, and came to meet her, with an air of the greatest tenderness and satisfaction.

After saluting her, he led her to a couch that fronted us, where they both sat down, and the young Genœse help'd her to a glass of wine, with some Naples bisket on a salver.

Presently, when they had exchanged a few kisses, and questions in broken English on one side, he began to unbutton, and, in fine, stript to his shirt.

As if this had been the signal agreed on for pulling off all their cloaths, a scheme which the heat of the season perfectly favoured, Polly began to draw her pins, and as she had no stays to unlace, she was in a trice, with her gallant's officious assistance, undress'd to all but her shift.

When he saw this, his breeches were immediately loosen'd, waist and knee bands, and slipped over his ankles, clean off; his shirt collar was unbuttoned too: then, first giving Polly an encouraging kiss, he stole, as it were, the shift off the girl, who being, I suppose, broke and familiariz'd to this humour, blush'd indeed, but less than I did at the apparition of her, now standing stark-naked, just as she came out of the hands of pure nature, with her black hair loose and a-float down her dazzling white neck and shoulders, whilst the deepen'd carnation of her cheeks went off gradually into the hue of glaz'd snow: for such were the blended tints and polish of her skin.

This girl could not be above eighteen: her face regular and sweet-featur'd, her shape exquisite; nor could I help envying her two ripe enchanting breasts, finely plump'd out in flesh, but withal so round, so firm, that they sustain'd themselves, in scorn of any stay: then their nipples, pointing different ways, mark'd their pleasing separation; beneath them lay the delicious tract of the belly, which terminated in a parting or rift scarce discernible, that modestly seem'd to retire downwards, and seek shelter between two plump fleshy thighs: the curling hair that overspread its delightful front, cloathed it with the richest sable fur in the universe: in short, she was evidently a subject for the painters to court her sitting to them for a pattern of female beauty, in all the true pride and pomp of nakedness.

The young Italian (still in his shirt) stood gazing and transported at the sight of beauties that might have fir'd a dying hermit; his eager eyes devour'd her, as she shifted attitudes at his discretion: neither were his hands excluded their share of the high feast, but wander'd, on the hunt of pleasure, over every part and inch of her body, so qualified to afford the most exquisite sense of it.

In the mean time, one could not help observing the swell of his shirt before, that bolster'd out, and shewed the condition of things behind the curtain: but he soon remov'd it, by slipping his shirt over his head; and now, as to nakedness, they had nothing to reproach one another.

The young gentleman, by Phœbe's guess, was about two and twenty; tall and well limb'd. His body was finely form'd, and of a most vigorous make, square-shoulder'd, and broad-chested: his face was not remarkable in any way, but for a nose inclining to the *Roman*, eyes large, black, and sparkling, and a ruddiness in his cheeks that was the more a grace, for his complexion was of the brownest, not of that dusky dun colour which excludes the idea of freshness, but of that clear, olive gloss which, glowing with life, dazzles perhaps less than fairness, and yet pleases more, when it pleases at all. His hair, being too short to tie, fell no lower than his neck, in short easy curls; and he had a few sprigs about his paps, that garnish'd his chest in a style of strength and manliness. Then his grand movement, which seem'd to rise out of a thicket of curling hair that spread from the root all round thighs and belly up to the navel, stood stiff and upright, but of a size to frighten me, by sympathy, for the small tender part which was the object of its fury, and which now lay expos'd to my fairest view; for he had, immediately on stripping off his shirt, gently push'd her down on the couch, which stood conveniently to break her willing fall. Her thighs were spread out to their utmost extension, and discovered between them the mark of the sex, the red-center'd cleft of flesh, whose lips, vermilioning inwards, exprest a small rubid line in sweet miniature, such as *Guido's* touch of colouring could never attain to the life or delicacy of.

Phœbe, at this, gave me a gentle jog, to prepare me for a whispered question: whether I thought my little maidenhead was much less? But my attention was too much engross'd, too much enwrapp'd with all I saw, to be able to give her any answer.

By this time the young gentleman had changed her posture from lying breadth to length-wise on the couch: but her thighs were still spread, and the mark lay fair for him, who now kneeling between them, display'd to us a side-view of that fierce erect machine of his, which threaten'd no less than splitting the tender victim, who lay smiling at the uplifted stroke, nor seem'd to decline it. He looked upon his weapon himself with some pleasure, and guiding it with his hand to the inviting slit, drew aside the lips, and lodg'd it (after some thrusts, which Polly seem'd even to assist) about half way; but there it stuck, I suppose from its growing thickness: he draws it again, and just wetting

it with spittle, re-enters, and with ease sheath'd it now up
to the hilt, at which Polly gave a deep sigh, which was
quite another tone than one of pain; he thrusts, she heaves,
at first gently, and in a regular cadence; but presently the
transport began to be too violent to observe any order or
measure; their motions were too rapid, their kisses too
fierce and fervent for nature to support such fury long:
both seem'd to me out of themselves: their eyes darted
fires: "Oh! . . . oh! . . . I can't bear it . . . It is too
much . . . I die . . . I am going . . ." were Polly's expressions of extasy: his joys were more silent; but soon
broken murmurs, sighs heart-fetch'd, and at length a dis-
patching thrust, as if he would have forced himself up her
body, and then motionless languor of all his limbs, all
shewed that the die-away moment was come upon him;
which she gave signs of joining with, by the wild throwing of her hands about, closing her eyes, and giving a deep
sob, in which she seemed to expire in an agony of bliss.

When he had finish'd his stroke, and got from off her,
she lay still without the least motion, breathless, as it
should seem, with pleasure. He replaced her again
breadth-wise on the couch, unable to sit up, with her
thighs open, between which I could observe a kind of
white liquid, like froth, hanging about the outward lips
of that recently opened wound, which now glowed with
a deeper red. Presently she gets up, and throwing her arms
round him, seemed far from undelighted with the trial he
had put her to, to judge at least by the fondness with
which she ey'd and hung upon him.

For my part, I will not pretend to describe what I felt all
over me during this scene; but from that instant, adieu
all fears of what man could do unto me; they were now
changed into such ardent desires, such ungovernable longings, that I could have pull'd the first of that sex
that should present himself, by the sleeve, and offered him
the bauble, which I now imagined the loss of would be a
gain I could not too soon procure myself.

Phœbe, who had more experience, and to whom such
sights were not so new, could not however be unmoved
at so warm a scene; and drawing me away softly from the

peep-hole, for fear of being over-heard, guided me as near the door as possible, all passive and obedient to her least signals.

Here was no room either to sit or lie, but making me stand with my back towards the door, she lifted up my petticoats, and with her busy fingers fell to visit and explore that part of me where now the heat and irritations were so violent that I was perfectly sick and ready to die with desire; that the bare touch of her finger, in that critical place, had the effect of a fire to a train, and her hand instantly made her sensible to what a pitch I was wound up, and melted by the sight she had thus procured me. Satisfied then with her success in allaying a heat that would have made me impatient of seeing the continuation of the transactions between our amorous couple, she brought me again to the crevice so favourable to our curiosity.

We had certainly been but a few instants away from it, and yet on our return we saw every thing in good forwardness for recommencing the tender hostilities.

The young foreigner was sitting down, fronting us, on the couch, with Polly upon one knee, who had her arms round his neck, whilst the extreme whiteness of her skin was not undelightfully contrasted by the smooth glossy brown of her lover's.

But who could count the fierce, unnumber'd kisses given and taken? in which I could often discover their exchanging the velvet thrust, when both their mouths were double tongued, and seemed to favour the mutual insertion with the greatest gust and delight.

In the mean time, his red-headed champion, that has so lately fled the pit, quell'd and abash'd, was now recover'd to the top of his condition, perk'd and crested up between Polly's thighs, who was not wanting, on her part, to coax and keep it in good humour, stroking it, with her head down, and received even its velvet tip between the lips of not its proper mouth: whether she did this out of any particular pleasure, or whether it was to render it more glib and easy of entrance, I could not tell; but it had such an effect, that the young gentleman seem'd by his eyes, that sparkled with more excited lustre, and his inflamed countenance, to receive increase of pleasure. He got up, and taking Polly in his arms, embraced her, and said something too softly for me to hear, leading her withal to the foot of the couch, and taking delight to slap her thighs and posteriors with that stiff sinew of his, which hit them with a spring that he gave it with his hand, and made them resound again, but hurt her about as much as he meant to hurt her, for she seemed to have as frolic a taste as himself.

But guess my surprise, when I saw the lazy young rogue lie down on his back, and gently pull down Polly upon him, who giving way to his humour, straddled, and with her hands conducted her blind favourite to the right place; and following her impulse, ran directly upon the flaming point of this weapon of pleasure, which she stak'd herself upon, up pierc'd, and infix'd to the extremest hair-breadth of it: thus she sat on him a few instants, enjoying and relishing her situation, whilst he toyed with her provoking breasts. Sometimes she would stoop to meet his kiss: but presently the sting of pleasure spur'd them up to fiercer action; then began the storm of heaves, which, from the undermost combatant, were thrusts at the same time, he crossing his hands over her, and drawing her home to him with a sweet violence: the inverted strokes of anvil over hammer soon brought on the critical period, in which all the signs of a close conspiring extasy informed us of the *point* they were at.

For me, I could bear to see no more; I was so overcome, so inflamed at the second part of the same play, that, mad to an intolerable degree, I hugg'd, I clasped Phœbe, as if she had wherewithal to relieve me. Pleased however with, and pitying the taking she could feel me in, she drew me towards the door, and opening it as softly as she could, we both got off undiscover'd, and she reconducted me to my own room, where, unable to keep my legs, in the agitation I was in, I instantly threw myself down on the bed, where I lay transported, though asham'd at what I felt.

Phœbe lay down by me, and ask'd me archly if, now

that I had seen the enemy, and fully considered him, I was still afraid of him? or did I think I could venture to come to a close engagement with him? To all which, not a word on my side; I sigh'd, and could scarce breathe. She takes hold of my hand, and having roll'd up her own petticoats, forced it half strivingly towards those parts, where, now grown more knowing, I miss'd the main object of my wishes; and finding not even the shadow of what I wanted, where every thing was so flat, or so hollow, in the vexation I was in at it, I should have withdrawn my hand but for fear of disobliging her. Abandoning it then entirely to her management, she made use of it as she thought proper, to procure herself rather the shadow than the substance of any pleasure. For my part, I now pin'd for more solid food, and promis'd tacitly to myself that I would not be put off much longer with this foolery from woman to woman, if Mrs. Brown did not soon provide me with the essential specific. In short, I had all the air of not being able to wait the arrival of my lord B . . . tho' he was now expected in a very few days: nor did I wait for him, for love itself took charge of the disposal of me, in spite of interest, or gross lust.

It was now two days after the closet-scene, that I got up about six in the morning, and leaving my bed-fellow fast asleep, stole down, with no other thought than of taking a little fresh air in a small garden, which our back-parlour open'd into, and from which my confinement debarr'd me at the times company came to the house; but now sleep and silence reign'd all over it.

I open'd the parlour door, and well surpriz'd was I at seeing, by the side of a fire half-out, a young gentleman in the old lady's elbow chair, with his legs laid upon another, fast asleep, and left there by his thoughtless companions, who had drank him down, and then went off with every one his mistress, whilst he stay'd behind by the courtesy of the old matron, who would not disturb or turn him out in that condition, at one in the morning; and beds, it is more than probable, there were none to spare. On the table still remain'd the punch bowl and glasses, strew'd about in their usual disorder after a drunken revel.

But when I drew nearer, to view the sleeping one, heavens! what a sight! No! no term of years, no turn of fortune could ever erase the lightning-like impression his form made on me . . . Yes! dearest object of my earliest passion, I command for ever the remembrance of thy first appearance to my ravish'd eyes . . . it calls thee up, present; and I see thee now!

Figure to yourself, Madam, a fair stripling, between eighteen and nineteen, with his head reclin'd on one of the sides of the chair, his hair in disorder'd curls, irregularly shading a face on which all the roseate bloom of youth and all the manly graces conspired to fix my eyes and heart. Even the languor and paleness of his face, in which the momentary triumph of the lily over the rose was owing to the excess of the night, gave an inexpressible sweetness to the finest features imaginable: his eyes, closed in sleep, displayed the meeting edges of their lids beautifully bordered with long eyelashes; over which no pencil could have described two more regular arches than those that grac'd his forehead, which was high, perfectly white and smooth. Then a pair of vermilion lips, pouting and swelling to the touch, as if a bee had freshly stung them, seem'd to challenge me to get the gloves off this lovely sleeper, had not the modesty and respect, which in both sexes are inseparable from a true passion, check'd my impulses.

But on seeing his shirt-collar unbutton'd, and a bosom whiter than a drift of snow, the pleasure of considering it could not bribe me to lengthen it, at the hazard of a health that began to be my life's concern. Love, that made me timid, taught me to be tender too. With a trembling hand I took hold of one of his, and waking him as gently as possible, he started, and looking, at first a little wildly, said with a voice that sent its harmonious sound to my heart: "Pray, child, what o'clock is it?" I told him, and added that he might catch cold if he slept longer with his breast open in the cool of the morning air. On this he thanked me with a sweetness perfectly agreeing with that of his features and eyes; the last now broad open, and eagerly surveying me, carried the sprightly fires they sparkled with directly to my heart.

It seems that having drank too freely before he came upon the rake with some of his young companions, he had put himself out of a condition to go through all the weapons with them, and crown the night with getting a mistress; so that seeing me in a loose undress, he did not doubt but I was one of the misses of the house, sent in to repair his loss of time; but though he seiz'd that notion, and a very obvious one it was, without hesitation, yet, whether my figure made a more than ordinary impression on him, or whether it was natural politeness, he address'd me in a manner far from rude, tho' still on the foot of one of the house pliers, come to amuse him; and giving me the first kiss that I ever relish'd from man in my life, ask'd me if I could favour him with my company, assuring me that he would make it worth my while: but had not even new-born love, that true refiner of lust, oppos'd so sudden a surrender, the fear of being surpriz'd by the house was a sufficient bar to my compliance.

I told him then, in a tone set me by love itself, that for reasons I had not time to explain to him, I could not stay with him, and might not even ever see him again: with a sigh at these last words, which broke from the bottom of my heart. My conqueror, who, as he afterwards told me, had been struck with my appearance, and lik'd me as much as he could think of liking any one in my suppos'd way of life, ask'd me briskly at once if I would be kept by him, and that he would take a lodging for me directly, and relieve me from any engagements he presum'd I might be under to the house. Rash, sudden, undigested, and even dangerous as this offer might be from a perfect stranger, and that stranger a giddy boy, the prodigious love I was struck with for him had put a charm into his voice there was no resisting, and blinded me to every objection; I could, at that instant, have died for him: think if I could resist an invitation to live with him! Thus my heart, beating strong to the proposal, dictated my answer, after scarce a minute's pause, that I would accept of his offer, and make my escape to him in what way he pleased, and that I would be entirely at his disposal, let it be good or bad. I have often since wondered that so great an easiness did not disgust him, or make me too cheap in his eyes, but my fate had so appointed it, that in his fears of the hazard of the town, he had been some time looking out for a girl to take into keeping, and my person happening to hit his fancy, it was by one of those miracles reserved to love that we struck the bargain in the instant, which we sealed by an exchange of kisses, that the hopes of a more uninterrupted enjoyment engaged him to content himself with.

Never, however, did dear youth carry in his person, more wherewith to justify the turning of a girl's head, and making her set all consequences at defiance for the sake of following a gallant.

For, besides all the perfections of manly beauty which were assembled in his form, he had an air of neatness and gentility, a certain smartness in the carriage and port of his head, that yet more distinguish'd him; his eyes were sprightly and full of meaning; his looks had in them something at once sweet and commanding. His complexion outbloom'd the lovely-colour'd rose, whilst its inimitable tender vivid glow clearly sav'd it from the reproach of wanting life, of raw and dough-like, which is commonly made to those so extremely fair as he was.

Our little plan was that I should get out about seven the next morning (which I could *readily* promise, as I knew where to get the key of the street-door), and he would wait at the end of the street with a coach to convey me safe off; after which, he would send, and clear any debt incurr'd by my stay at Mrs. Brown's, who, he only judged, in gross, might not care to part with one he thought so fit to draw custom to the house.

I then just hinted to him not to mention in the house his having seen such a person as me, for reasons I would explain to him more at leisure. And then, for fear of miscarrying, by being seen together, I tore myself from him with a bleeding heart, and stole up softly to my room, where I found Phœbe still fast asleep, and hurrying off my few cloaths, lay down by her, with a mixture of joy and anxiety that may be easier conceived than express'd.

The risks of Mrs. Brown's discovering my purpose, of disappointments, misery, ruin, all vanish'd before this new-

kindl'd flame. The seeing, the touching, the being, if but
for a night, with this idol of my fond virgin-heart, appeared
to me a happiness above the purchase of my liberty or
life. He might use me ill, let him! he was the master; happy, too happy, even to receive death at so dear a
hand.

To this purpose were the reflections of the whole day,
of which every minute seem'd to me a little eternity. How
often did I visit the clock! nay, was tempted to advance
the tedious hand, as if that would have advanc'd the time
with it! Had those of the house made the least observations
on me, they must have remark'd something extraordinary
from the discomposure I could not help betraying; especially when at dinner mention was made of the charm-
ingest youth having been there, and stay'd breakfast. "Oh!
he was such a beauty! . . . I should have died for him!
. . . they would pull caps for him! . . ." and the like
fooleries, which, however, was throwing oil on a fire I was
sorely put to it to smother the blaze of.

The fluctuations of my mind, the whole day, produc'd
one good effect: which was, that, through mere fatigue,
I slept tolerably well till five in the morning, when I got
up, and having dress'd myself, waited, under the double
tortures of fear and impatience, for the appointed hour.
It came at last, the dear, critical, dangerous hour came;
and now, supported only by the courage love lent me, I
ventured, a tip-toe, down-stairs, leaving my box behind,
for fear of being surpriz'd with it in going out.

I got to the street-door, the key whereof was always
laid on the chair by our bed-side, in trust with Phœbe, who
having not the least suspicion of my entertaining any design to go from them (nor indeed had I but the day before), made no reserve or concealment of it from me. I
open'd the door with great ease; love, that embolden'd,
protected me too: and now, got safe into the street, I saw
my new guardian-angel waiting at a coach-door, ready
open. How I got to him I know not: I suppose I flew; but
I was in the coach in a trice, and he by the side of me, with
his arms clasp'd round me, and giving me the kiss of welcome. The coachman had his orders, and drove to them.

My eyes were instantly fill'd with tears, but tears of the most delicious delight; to find myself in the arms of that beauteous youth was a rapture that my little heart swam in. Past or future were equally out of the question with me. The present was as much as all my powers of life were sufficient to bear the transport of, without fainting. Nor were the most tender embraces, the most soothing expressions wanting on his side, to assure me of his love, and of never giving me cause to repent the bold step I had taken, in throwing myself thus entirely upon his honour and generosity. But, alas! this was no merit in me, for I was drove to it by a passion too impetuous for me to resist, and I did what I did because I could not help it.

In an instant, for time was now annihilated with me, we landed at a public house in *Chelsea*, hospitably commodious for the reception of duet-parties of pleasure, where a breakfast of chocolate was prepared for us.

An old jolly stager, who kept it, and understood life perfectly well, breakfasted with us, and leering archly at me, gave us both joy, and said we were well paired, i' faith! that a great many gentlemen and ladies used his house, but he had never seen a handsomer couple . . . he was sure I was a fresh piece . . . I look'd so country, so innocent! well my spouse was a lucky man! . . . all which common landlord's cant not only pleas'd and sooth'd me, but help'd to divert my confusion at being with my new sovereign, whom, now the minute approach'd, I began to fear to be alone with: a timidity which true love had a greater share in than even maiden bashfulness.

I wish'd, I doted, I could have died for him; and yet, I know not how, or why, I dreaded the point which had been the object of my fiercest wishes; my pulses beat fears, amidst a flush of the warmest desires. This struggle of the passions, however, this conflict betwixt modesty and lovesick longings, made me burst again into tears; which he took, as he had done before, only for the remains of concern and emotion at the suddenness of my change of condition, in committing myself to his care; and, in consequence of that idea, did and said all that he thought would most comfort and re-inspirit me.

After breakfast, *Charles* (the dear familiar name I must take the liberty henceforward to distinguish my *Adonis* by), with a smile full of meaning, took me gently by the hand, and said: "Come, my dear, I will show you a room that commands a fine prospect over some gardens"; and without waiting for an answer, in which he relieved me extremely, he led me up into a chamber, airy and light-some, where all seeing of prospects was out of the question, except that of a bed, which had all the air of having recommended the room to him.

Charles had just slipp'd the bolt of the door, and running, caught me in his arms, and lifting me from the ground, with his lips glew'd to mine, bore me, trembling, panting, dying, with soft fears and tender wishes, to the bed; where his impatience would not suffer him to undress me, more than just unpinning my handkerchief and gown, and unlacing my stays.

My bosom was now bare, and rising in the warmest throbs, presented to his sight and feeling the firm hard swell of a pair of young breasts, such as may be imagin'd of a girl not sixteen, fresh out of the country, and never before handled; but even their pride, whiteness, fashion, pleasing resistance to the touch, could not bribe his rest-less hands from roving; but, giving them the loose, my petticoats and shift were soon taken up, and their stronger center of attraction laid open to their tender invasion. My fears, however, made me mechanically close my thighs; but the very touch of his hand insinuated between them, disclosed them and opened a way for the main attack.

In the mean time, I lay fairly exposed to the examina-tion of his eyes and hands, quiet and unresisting; which confirm'd him the opinion he proceeded so cavalierly upon, that I was no novice in these matters, since he had taken me out of a common bawdy-house, nor had I said one thing to prepossess him of my virginity; and if I had, he would sooner have believ'd that I took him for a cully that would swallow such an improbability, than that I was still mis-tress of that darling treasure, that hidden mine, so eagerly sought after by the men, and which they never dig for, but to destroy.

Being now too high wound up to bear a delay, he un-button'd, and drawing out the engine of love-assaults, drove it currently, as at a ready-made breach . . . Then! then! for the first time, did I feel that stiff horn-hard gristle, battering against the tender part; but imagine to yourself his surprize when he found, after several vigorous pushes which hurt me extremely, that he made not the least impression.

I complain'd but tenderly complain'd that I could not bear it . . . indeed he hurt me! . . . Still he thought no more than that being so young, the largeness of his machine (for few men could dispute size with him) made all the difficulty; and that possibly I had not been enjoy'd by any so advantageously made in that part as himself: for still, that my virgin flower was yet uncrop'd, never enter'd into his head, and he would have thought it idling with time and words to have question'd me upon it.

He tries again, still no admittance, still no penetration; but he had hurt me yet more, whilst my extreme love made me bear extreme pain, almost without a groan. At length, after repeated fruitless trials, he lay down panting by me, kiss'd my falling tears, and ask'd me tenderly what was the meaning of so much complaining? and if I had not borne it better from others than I did from him? I answered, with a simplicity fram'd to persuade, that he was the first man that ever serv'd me so. Truth is powerful, and it is not always that we do not believe what we eagerly wish.

Charles, already dispos'd by the evidence of his senses to think my pretences to virginity not entirely apocryphal, smothers me with kisses, begs me, in the name of love, to have a little patience, and that he will be as tender of hurting me as he would be of himself.

Alas! it was enough I knew his pleasure to submit joyfully to him, whatever pain I foresaw it would cost me.

He now resumes his attempts in more form: first, he put one of the pillows under me, to give the blank of his aim a more favourable elevation, and another under my head, in ease of it; then spreading my thighs, and placing himself standing between them, made them rest upon his hips;

applying then the point of his machine to the slit, into
which he sought entrance: it was so small, he could scarce
assure himself of its being rightly pointed. He looks, he
feels, and satisfies himself: the driving forward with fury,
its prodigious stiffness, thus impacted, wedgelike, breaks
the union of those parts, and gain'd him just the insertion
of the tip of it, lip-deep; which being sensible of, he improved his advantage, and following well his stroke, in a
straight line, forcibly deepens his penetration; but put me
to such intolerable pain, from the separation of the sides of
that soft passage by a hard thick body, I could have
scream'd out; but, as I was unwilling to alarm the house, I
held in my breath, and cramm'd my petticoat, which was
turn'd up over my face, into my mouth, and bit it through
in the agony. At length, the tender texture of that tract
giving way to such fierce tearing and rending, he pierc'd
something further into me: and now, outrageous and no
longer his own master, but borne headlong away by the
fury and over-mettle of that member, now exerting itself
with a kind of native rage, he breaks in, carries all before
him, and one violent merciless lunge sent it, imbrew'd, and
reeking with virgin blood, up to the very hilt in me . . .
Then! then all my resolution deserted me: I scream'd out,
and fainted away with the sharpness of the pain; and, as he
told me afterwards, on his drawing out, when emission was
over with him, my thighs were instantly all in a stream of
blood that flow'd from the wounded torn passage.

When I recover'd my senses, I found myself undress'd,
and a-bed, in the arms of the sweet relenting murderer of
my virginity, who hung mourning tenderly over me, and
holding in his hand a cordial, which, coming from the
still dear author of so much pain, I could not refuse; my
eyes, however, moisten'd with tears, and languishingly
turn'd upon him, seemed to reproach him with his cruelty,
and ask him if such were the rewards of love. But Charles,
to whom I was now infinitely endear'd by this complete
triumph over a maidenhead, where he so little expected to
find one, in tenderness to that pain which he had put me
to, in procuring himself the height of pleasure, smother'd
his exultation, and employ'd himself with so much sweet-

ness, so much warmth, to sooth, to caress, and comfort me in my soft complainings, which breath'd, indeed, more love than resentment, that I presently drown'd all sense of pain in the pleasure of seeing him, of thinking that I belong'd to him: he who was now the absolute disposer of my happiness, and, in one word, my fate.

The sore was, however, too tender, the wound too bleeding fresh, for Charles's good-nature to put my patience presently to another trial; but as I could not stir, or walk across the room, he order'd the dinner to be brought to the bed-side, where it could not be otherwise than my getting down the wing of a fowl, and two or three glasses of wine, since it was my ador'd youth who both serv'd, and urged them on me, with that sweet irresistible authority with which love had invested him over me.

After dinner, and as everything but the wine was taken away, Charles very impudently asks a leave, he might read the grant of in my eyes, to come to bed to me, and accordingly falls to undressing; which I could not see the progress of without strange emotions of fear and pleasure.

He is now in bed with me the first time, and in broad day; but when thrusting up his own shirt and my shift, he laid his naked glowing body to mine . . . oh! insupportable delight! oh! superhuman rapture! what pain could stand before a pleasure so transporting? I felt no more the smart of my wounds below; but, curling round him like the tendril of a vine, as if I fear'd any part of him should be untouch'd or unpress'd by me, I return'd his strenuous embraces and kisses with a fervour and gust only known to true love, and which mere lust could never rise to.

Yes, even at this time, when all the tyranny of the passions is fully over and my veins roll no longer but a cold tranquil stream, the remembrance of those passages that most affected me in my youth, still cheers and refreshes me. Let me proceed then. My beauteous youth was now glew'd to me in all the folds and twists that we could make our bodies meet in; when, no longer able to rein in the fierceness of refresh'd desires, he gives his steed the head and gently insinuating his thighs between mine, stopping my mouth with kisses of humid fire, makes a fresh irruption, and renewing his thrusts, pierces, tears, and forces his way up the torn tender folds that yielded him admission with a smart little less severe than when the breach was first made. I stifled, however, my cries, and bore him with the passive fortitude of a heroine; soon his thrusts, more and more furious, cheeks flush'd with a deeper scarlet, his eyes turn'd up in the fervent fit, some dying sighs, and an agonizing shudder, announced the approaches of that extatic pleasure, I was yet in too much pain to come in for my share of it.

Nor was it till after a few enjoyments had numb'd and blunted the sense of the smart, and given me to feel the titillating inspersion of balsamic sweets, drew from me the delicious return, and brought down all my passion, that I arrived at excess of pleasure through excess of pain. But, when successive engagements had broke and inur'd me, I began to enter into the true unallay'd relish of that pleasure of pleasures, when the warm gush darts through all the ravish'd inwards; what floods of bliss! what melting transports! what agonies of delight! too fierce, too mighty for nature to sustain; well has she therefore, no doubt, provided the relief of a delicious momentary dissolution, the approaches of which are intimated by a dear delirium, a sweet thrill on the point of emitting those liquid sweets, in which enjoyment itself is drown'd, when one gives the languishing stretch-out, and dies at the discharge.

How often, when the rage and tumult of my senses had subsided after the melting flow, have I, in a tender meditation ask'd myself coolly the question, if it was in nature for any of its creatures to be so happy as I was? Or, what were all fears of the consequence, put in the scale of one night's enjoyment of any thing so transcendently the taste of my eyes and heart, as that delicious, fond, matchless youth?

Thus we spent the whole afternoon till supper time in a continued circle of love delights, kissing, turtle-billing, toying, and all the rest of the feast. At length, supper was serv'd in, before which Charles had, for I do not know what reason, slipt his cloaths on; and sitting down by the bed-side, we made table and table-cloth of the bed and sheets, whilst he suffer'd nobody to attend or serve but himself. He ate with a very good appetite, and seem'd charm'd to see me eat. For my part, I was so enchanted with my fortune, so transported with the comparison of the delights I now swam in, with the insipidity of all my past scenes of life, that I thought them sufficiently cheap at even the price of my ruin, or the risk of their not lasting. The present possession was all my little head could find room for.

We lay together that night, when, after playing repeated prizes of pleasure, nature, overspent and satisfy'd, gave us up to the arms of sleep: those of my dear youth encircled me, the consciousness of which made even that sleep more delicious.

Late in the morning I wak'd first; and observing my lover slept profoundly softly disengag'd myself from his arms, scarcely daring to breathe for fear of shortening his repose; my cap, my hair, my shift, were all in disorder from the rufflings I had undergone; and I took this opportunity to adjust and set them as well as I could: whilst, every now and then, looking at the sleeping youth with inconceivable fondness and delight, and reflecting on all the pain he had put me to tacitly own'd that the pleasure had overpaid me for my sufferings.

It was then broad day. I was sitting up in the bed, the cloaths of which were all tossed, or rolled off, by the unquietness of our motions, from the sultry heat of the weather; nor could I refuse myself a pleasure that solicited me so irresistibly, as this fair occasion of feasting my sight with all those treasures of youthful beauty I had enjoy'd, and which lay now almost entirely naked, his shirt being truss'd up in a perfect wisp, which the warmth of the room and season made me easy about the consequence of. I hung over him enamour'd indeed! and devoured all his naked charms with only two eyes, when I could have wish'd them at least a hundred, for the fuller enjoyment of the gaze.

Oh! could I paint his figure, as I see it now, still present to my transported imagination! a whole length of an all-perfect, manly beauty in full view. Think of a face without a fault, glowing with all the opening bloom and vernal freshness of an age in which beauty is of either sex, and which the first down over his upper lip scarce began to distinguish.

The parting of the double ruby pout of his lips seem'd to exhale an air sweeter and purer than what it drew in: ah! what violence did it not cost me to refrain the so tempted kiss!

Then a neck exquisitely turn'd, grac'd behind and on the sides with his hair, playing freely in natural ringlets, connected his head to a body of the most perfect form, and of the most vigorous contexture, in which all the strength of manhood was conceal'd and soften'd to appearance by the delicacy of his complexion, the smoothness of his skin, and the plumpness of his flesh.

The platform of his snow-white bosom, that was laid out in a manly proportion, presented, on the vermilion summit of each pap, the idea of a rose about to blow.

Nor did his shirt hinder me from observing that symmetry of his limbs, that exactness of shape, in the fall of it towards the loins, where the waist ends and the rounding swell of the hips commences; where the skin, sleek, smooth, and dazzling white, burnishes on the stretch over firm, plump ripe flesh, that crimp'd and ran into dimples at the least pressure, or that the touch could not rest upon, but slid over as on the surface of the most polished ivory.

His thighs, finely fashioned, and with a florid glossy roundness, gradually tapering away to the knees, seem'd pillars worthy to support that beauteous frame; at the bottom of which I could not, without some remains of terror, some tender emotions too, fix my eyes on that terrible machine, which had, not long before, with such fury broke into, torn, and almost ruin'd those soft, tender parts of mine that had not yet done smarting with the effects of its rage; but behold it now! crest fall'n, reclining its half-capt vermilion head over one of his thighs, quiet, pliant, and to all appearance incapable of the mischiefs and cruelty it had committed. Then the beautiful growth of the hair, in short and soft curls round its root, its whiteness, branch'd veins, the supple softness of the shaft, as it lay foreshorten'd, roll'd and shrunk up into a squab thickness, languid, and borne up from between his thighs by its globular appendage, that wondrous treasure-bag of nature's sweets, which, rivell'd round, and purs'd up in the only wrinkles that are known to please, perfected the prospect, and all together formed the most interesting moving picture in nature, and surely infinitely superior to those nudities furnish'd by the painters, statuaries, or any art, which are purchas'd at immense prices; whilst the sight of them in actual life is scarce sovereignly tasted by any but the few whom nature has endowed with a fire of imagination, warmly pointed by a truth of judgment to the spring-head, the originals of beauty, of nature's unequall'd composition, above all the imitation of art, or the reach of wealth to pay their price.

But every thing must have an end. A motion made by this angelic youth, in the listlessness of going off sleep, replac'd his shirt and the bed-cloaths in a posture that shut up that treasure from longer view.

I lay down then, and carrying my hands to that part of me in which the objects just seen had begun to raise a mutiny that prevail'd over the smart of them, my fingers now open'd themselves an easy passage; but long I had not time to consider the wide difference *there,* between the maid and the now finish'd woman, before Charles wak'd, and turning towards me, kindly enquir'd how I had rested? and, scarce giving me time to answer, imprinted on my lips one of his burning rapture-kisses, which darted a flame to my heart, that from thence radiated to every part of me; and presently, as if he had proudly meant revenge for the survey I had smuggled of all his naked beauties, he spurns off the bed-cloaths, and trussing up my shift as high as it would go, took his turn to feast his eyes on all the gifts nature had bestow'd on my person; his busy hands, too, rang'd intemperately over every part of me. The delicious austerity and hardness of my yet unripe budding breasts, the whiteness and firmness of my flesh, the freshness and regularity of my features, the harmony of my limbs, all seem'd to confirm him in his satisfaction with his bargain; but when curious to explore the havoc he had made in the centre of his over-fierce attack, he not only directed his hands there, but with a pillow put under, placed me favourably for his wanton purpose of inspection. Then, who can express the fire his eyes glisten'd, his hands glow'd with! whilst sighs of pleasure, and tender broken exclamations, were all the praises he could utter. By this time his machine, stiffly risen at me, gave me to see it in its highest state and bravery. He feels it himself, seems pleas'd at its condition, and, smiling loves and graces, seizes one of my hands, and carries it, with a gentle compulsion, to his pride of nature, and its richest masterpiece.

I, struggling faintly, could not help feeling what I could not grasp, a column of the whitest ivory, beautifully streak'd with blue veins, and carrying, fully uncapt, a head of the liveliest vermilion: no horn could be harder or stiffer; yet no velvet more smooth or delicious to the touch. Presently he guided my hand lower, to that part in which nature and pleasure keep their stores in concert, so aptly fasten'd and hung on to the root of their first instrument and minister, that not improperly he might be styl'd their purse-bearer too: there he made me feel distinctly, through their soft cover, the contents, a pair of roundish balls, that seem'd to play within, and elude all pressure but the tenderest, from without.

But now this visit of my soft warm hand in those so sensible parts had put every thing into such ungovernable fury that, disdaining all further preluding, and taking advantage of my commodious posture, he made the storm fall where I scarce patiently expected, and where he was sure to lay it: presently, then, I felt the stiff insertion between the yielding, divided lips of the wound, now open for life; where the narrowness no longer put me to intolerable pain, and afforded my lover no more difficulty than what heighten'd his pleasure, in the strict embrace of that tender, warm sheath, round the instrument it was so delicately adjusted to, and which, now cased home, so gorged me with pleasure that it perfectly suffocated me and took away my breath; then the killing thrusts! the unnumber'd kisses! every one of which was a joy inexpressible; and that joy lost in a crowd of yet greater blisses! But this was a disorder too violent in nature to last long: the vessels, so stirr'd and intensely heated, soon boil'd over, and for that time put out the fire; meanwhile all this dalliance and disport had so far consum'd the morning, that it became a kind of necessity to lay breakfast and dinner into one.

In our calmer intervals Charles gave the following account of himself, every word of which was true. He was the only son of a father who, having a small post in the revenue, rather over-liv'd his income, and had given this young gentleman a very slender education: no profession had he bred him up to, but design'd to provide for him in the army, by purchasing him an ensign's commission, that is to say, provided he could raise the money, or procure it by interest, either of which clauses was rather to be wish'd than hoped for by him. On no better a plan, however, had this improvident father suffer'd this youth, a youth of great promise, to run up to the age of manhood, or near it at least, in next to idleness; and had, besides, taken no sort of pains to give him even the common premonitions against the vices of the town, and the dangers of all sorts which wait the unexperienc'd and unwary in it. He liv'd at home, and at discretion, with his father, who himself kept a mistress; and for the rest, provided Charles did not ask him for money, he was indolently kind to him: he might lie out when he pleas'd; any excuse would serve, and even his reprimands were so slight that they carried with them rather an air of connivance at the fault than any serious control or constraint. But, to supply his calls for money, Charles, whose mother was dead, had, by her side, a grandmother who doted upon him. She had a considerable annuity to live on, and very regularly parted with every shilling she could spare to this darling of hers, to the no little heartburn of his father; who was vex'd, not that she by this means fed his son's extravagance, but that she preferr'd Charles to himself; and we shall too soon see what a fatal turn such a mercenary jealousy could operate in the breast of a father.

Charles was, however, by the means of his grandmother's lavish fondness, very sufficiently enabled to keep a mistress so easily contented as my love made me; and my good fortune, for such I must ever call it, threw me in his way, in the manner above related, just as he was on the look-out for one.

As to temper, the even sweetness of it made him seem born for domestic happiness: tender, naturally polite, and gentle-manner'd; it could never be his fault if ever jars or animosities ruffled a calm he was so qualified in every way to maintain or restore. Without those great or shining qualities that constitute a genius, or are fit to make a noise in the world, he had all those humble ones that compose the softer social merit: plain common sense, set off with every grace of modesty and good nature, made him, if not admir'd, what is much happier, universally belov'd and esteem'd. But, as nothing but the beauties of his person had at first attracted my regard and fix'd my passion, neither was I then a judge of that internal merit, which I had afterward full occasion to discover, and which perhaps, in that season of giddiness and levity, would have touch'd my heart very little, had it been lodg'd in a person less the delight of my eyes and idol of my senses. But to return to our situation.

After dinner, which we ate a-bed in a most voluptuous disorder, Charles got up, and taking a passionate leave of me for a few hours, he went to town where, concerting matters with a young sharp lawyer, they went together to my late venerable mistress's, from whence I had, but the day before, made my elopement, and with whom he was determin'd to settle accounts in a manner that should cut off all after reckonings from that quarter.

Accordingly they went; but on the way, the Templar, his friend, on thinking over Charles's information, saw reason to give their visit another turn, and, instead of offering satisfaction, to demand it.

On being let in, the girls of the house flock'd round Charles, whom they knew, and from the earliness of my escape, and their perfect ignorance of his ever having so much as seen me, not having the least suspicion of his being accessory to my flight, they were, in their way, *making up* to him; and as to his companion, they took him probably for a fresh cully. But the Templar soon wardness, by enquiring for the old lady, , he said, with a grave judge-like countenance, had some business to settle.

Madam was immediately sent down for, and the ladies being desir'd to clear the room, the lawyer ask'd her, severely, if she did know, or had not decoy'd, under pretence of hiring a a servant, a young girl, just come out of the country, called FRANCES or FANNY HILL, describing me withal as particularly as he could from Charles's description.

It is peculiar to vice to tremble at the enquiries of justice; and Mrs. Brown, whose conscience was not entirely clear upon my account, as knowing as she was of the town, as hackney'd as she was in bluffing through all the dangers of her vocation, could not help being alarm'd at the question, especially when he went on to talk of a Justice of peace, *Newgate*, the *Old Bailey*, indictments for keeping a disorderly house, pillory, carting, and the whole process of that nature. She, who, it is likely, imagin'd I had lodg'd an information against her house, look'd extremely blank, and began to make a thousand protestations and excuses. However, to abridge, they brought away triumphantly my box of things, which, had she not been under an awe, she might have disputed with them; and not only that, but a clearance and discharge of any demands on the house, at the expense of no more than a bowl of arrackpunch, the reat of which, together with the choice of the house conveniences, was offer'd and not accepted. Charles all the time acted the chance-companion of the lawyer, who had brought him there, as he knew the house, and appear'd in no wise interested in the issue; but he had the collateral pleasure of hearing all that I had told him verified, so far as the bawd's fears would give her leave to enter into my history, which, if one may guess by the composition she so readily came into, were not small.

Phœbe, my kind tutoress Phœbe, was at that time gone out, perhaps in search of me, or their cook'd-up story had not, it is probable, pass'd so smoothly.

This negotiation had, however, taken up some time, which would have appear'd much longer to me, left, as I

was, in a strange house, if the landlady, a motherly sort of a
woman, to whom Charles had liberally recommended me,
had not come up and borne me company. We drank tea,
and her chat help'd to pass away the time very agreeably,
since he was our theme; but as the evening deepened,
and the hour set for his return was elaps'd, I could not dis-
pel the gloom of impatience and tender fears which gathered upon me, and which our timid sex are apt to feel in
proportion to their love.

Long, however, I did not suffer: the sight of him overpaid me; and the soft reproach I had prepar'd for him ex-
pired before it reach'd my lips.

I was still a-bed, yet unable to use my legs otherwise
than aukwardly, and Charles flew to me, catched me in
his arms, rais'd and extending mine to meet his dear embrace, and gives me an account, interrupted by many a
sweet parenthesis of kisses, of the success of his measures.

I could not help laughing at the fright the old woman
had been put into, which my ignorance, and indeed my
want of innocence, had far from prepar'd me for bespeaking. She had, it seems, apprehended that I fled for shelter
to some relation I had recollected in town, on my dislike
of their ways and proceeding towards me, and that this
application came from thence; for, as Charles had rightly
judg'd, not one neighbour had, at that still hour, seen
the circumstance of my escape into the coach, or, at least,
notic'd him; neither had any in the house the least hint or
clue of suspicion of my having spoke to him, much less
of my having clapt up such a sudden bargain with a perfect stranger: thus the greatest improbability is not always what we should most mistrust.

We supped with all the gaiety of two young giddy creatures at the top of their desires; and as I had most joyfully
given up to Charles the whole charge of my future happiness, I thought of nothing beyond the exquisite pleasure
of possessing him.

He came to bed in due time; and this second night, the
pain being pretty well over, I tasted, in full draughts, all
the transports of perfect enjoyment: I swam, I bathed
in bliss, till both fell fast asleep, through the natural con-

sequences of satisfied desires, and appeas'd flames; nor
did we wake but to renew'd raptures.

Thus, making the most of love and life, did we stay
in this lodging in Chelsea about ten days; in which
time Charles took care to give his excursions from home a
favourable gloss, and to keep his footing with his fond indulgent grandmother, from whom he drew constant and
sufficient supplies for the charge I was to him, and which
was very trifling, in comparison with his former less regular
course of pleasures.

Charles remov'd me then to a private ready furnish'd
lodging in D . . . *street, St. James's,* where he paid half
a guinea a week for two rooms and a closet on the second
floor, which he had been some time looking out for, and
was more convenient for the frequency of his visits than
where he had at first plac'd me, in a house which I cannot
say but I left with regret, as it was infinitely endear'd to
me by the first possession of my Charles, and the circumstance of losing, there, that jewel which can never be twice
lost. The landlord, however, had no reason to complain of
any thing, but of a procedure in Charles too liberal not to
make him regret the loss of us.

Arrived at our new lodgings, I remember I thought
them extremely fine, though ordinary enough, even at
that price; but, had it been a dungeon that Charles had
brought me to, his presence would have made it a little
Versailles.

The landlady, *Mrs. Jones,* waited on us to our apartment, and with great volubility of tongue explain'd to us
all its conveniences—that her own maid should wait on
us . . . that the best of quality had lodg'd at her house
. . . that her first floor was let to a foreign secretary of
an embassy, and his lady . . . that I looked like a very
good-natur'd lady. . . . At the word lady, I blush'd out
of flatter'd vanity: this was too strong for a girl of my condition; for though Charles had had the precaution of dressing me in a less tawdry flaunting style than were the
cloaths I escap'd to him in, and of passing me for his wife,
that he had secretly married, and kept private (the old
story) on account of his friends, I dare swear this appear'd

extremely apocryphal to a woman who knew the town so well as she did; but that was the least of her concern. It was impossible to be less scruple-ridden than she was; and the advantage of letting her rooms being her sole object, the truth itself would have far from scandaliz'd her, or broke her bargain.

A sketch of her picture, and personal history, will dispose you to account for the part she is to act in my concerns.

She was about forty-six years old, tall, meagre, red-hair'd, with one of those trivial ordinary faces you meet with everywhere, and go about unheeded and unmentioned. In her youth she had been kept by a gentleman who, dying, left her forty pounds a year during her life, in consideration of a daughter he had by her; which daughter, at the age of seventeen, she sold, for not a very considerable sum neither, to a gentleman who was going on *Envoy* abroad, and took his purchase with him, where he us'd her with the utmost tenderness, and it is thought, was secretly married to her: but had constantly made a point of her not keeping up the least correspondence with a mother base enough to make a market of her own flesh and blood. However, as she had no nature, nor, indeed, any passion but that of money, this gave her no further uneasiness, than, as she thereby lost a handle of squeezing presents, or other after-advantages, out of the bargain. Indifferent then, by nature of constitution, to every other pleasure but that of increasing the lump by any means whatever, she commenc'd a kind of private procuress, for which she was not amiss fitted, by her grave decent appearance, and sometimes did a job in the matchmaking way; in short, there was nothing that appear'd to her under the shape of gain that she would not have undertaken. She knew most of the ways of the town, having not only herself been upon, but kept up constant intelligences in it, dealing, besides her practice in promoting a harmony between the two sexes, in private pawn-broking and other profitable secrets. She rented the house she liv'd in, and made the most of it by letting it out in lodgings; though she was worth, at least, near three or four thousand pounds, she would not allow herself even the necessaries of life, and pinn'd her subsistence entirely on what she could squeeze out of her lodgers.

When she saw such a young pair come under her roof, her immediate notions, doubtless, were how she should make the most money of us, by every means that money might be made, and which, she rightly judged, our situation and inexperience would soon beget her occasions of.

In this hopeful sanctuary, and under the clutches of this harpy, did we pitch our residence. It will not be mighty material to you, or very pleasant to me, to enter into a detail of all the petty cut-throat ways and means with which she used to fleece us; all which Charles indolently chose to bear with, rather than take the trouble of removing, the difference of expense being scarce attended to by a young gentleman who had no ideas of stint, or even of economy, and a raw country girl who knew nothing of the matter.

Here, however, under the wings of my sovereignly belov'd, did I flow the most delicious hours of my life; my Charles I had, and, in him, everything my fond heart could wish or desire. He carried me to plays, operas, masquerades, and every diversion of the town; all of which pleas'd me indeed, but pleas'd me infinitely the more for his being with me, and explaining everything to me, and enjoying, perhaps, the natural impressions of surprize and admiration, which such sights, at the first, never fail to excite in a *country girl*, new to the delights of them; but to me, they sensibly prov'd the power and full dominion of the sole passion of my heart over me, a passion in which soul and body were concentre'd, and left me no room for any other relish of life but love.

As to the men I saw at those places, or at any other, they suffer'd so much in the comparison my eyes made of them with my all-perfect Adonis, that I had not the infidelity even of one wandering thought to reproach myself with upon his account. He was the universe to me, and all that was not him was nothing to me.

My love, in fine, was so excessive, that it arriv'd at annihilating every suggestion or kindling spark of jealousy;

for, one idea only tending that way, gave me such exquisite torment that my self-love, and dread of worse than death, made me for ever renounce and defy it: nor had I, indeed, occasion; for, were I to enter here on the recital of several instances wherein Charles sacrific'd to me women of greater importance than I dare hint (which, considering his form, was no such wonder), I might, indeed, give you full proof of his unshaken constancy to me; but would not you accuse me of warming up again a feast that my vanity ought long ago to have been satisfy'd with?

In our cessations from active pleasure, Charles fram'd himself one, in instructing me, as far as his own lights reach'd, in a great many points of life that I was, in consequence of my no-education, perfectly ignorant of: nor did I suffer one word to fall in vain from the mouth of my lovely teacher: I hung on every syllable he utter'd, and receiv'd, as oracles, all he said; whilst kisses were all the interruption I could not refuse myself the pleasure of admitting, from lips that breath'd more than Arabian sweetness.

I was in a little time enabled, by the progress I had made, to prove the deep regard I had paid to all that he had said to me: repeating it to him almost word for word; and to shew that I was not entirely the parrot, but that I reflected upon, that I enter'd into it, I join'd my own comments, and ask'd him questions of explanation.

My country accent, and the rusticity of my gait, manners, and deportment, began now sensibly to wear off, so quick was my observation, and so efficacious my desire of growing every day worthier of his heart.

As to money, though he brought me constantly all he receiv'd, it was with difficulty he even got me to give it room in my bureau; and what clothes I had, he could prevail on me to accept of on no other foot than that of pleasing him by the greater neatness in my dress, beyond which I had no ambition. I could have made a pleasure of the greatest toil, and worked my fingers to the bone, with joy, to have supported him: guess, then, if I could harbour any idea of being burdensome to him, and this disinterested turn in me was so unaffected, so much the dictate of my heart, that Charles could not but feel it: and if he did not love me as much as I did him (which was the constant and only matter of sweet contention between us), he manag'd so, at least, as to give me the satisfaction of believing it impossible for man to be more tender, more true, more faithful than he was.

Our landlady, Mrs. Jones, came frequently up to my apartment, from whence I never stirr'd on any pretext without Charles; nor was it long before she worm'd out, without much art, the secret of our having cheated the church of a ceremony, and, in course, of the terms we liv'd together upon; a circumstance which far from displeas'd her, considering the designs she had upon me, and which, alas! she will, too soon, have room to carry into execution. But in the mean time, her own experience of life let her see that any attempt, however indirect or disguis'd to divert or break, at least presently, so strong a cement of hearts as ours was, could only end in losing two lodgers, of whom she made very competent advantages, if either of us came to smoke her commission; for a commission she had from one of her customers, either to debauch, or get me away from my keeper at any rate.

But the barbarity of my fate soon sav'd her the task of disuniting us. I had now been eleven months with this life of my life, which had passed in one continu'd rapid stream of delight: but nothing so violent was ever made to last. I was about three months gone with child by him, a circumstance which would have added to his tenderness had he ever left me room to believe it could receive an addition, when the mortal, the unexpected blow of separation fell upon us. I shall gallop post over the particulars, which I shudder yet to think of, and cannot to this instant reconcile myself how, or by what means, I could out-live it.

Two life-long days had I linger'd through without hearing from him, I who breath'd, who existed but in him, and had never yet seen twenty-four hours pass without seeing or hearing from him. The third day my impatience was so strong, my alarms had been so severe, that I perfectly sicken'd with them; and being unable to support the shock longer, I sunk upon the bed and ringing for Mrs. Jones, who had far from comforted me under my anxieties, she came up. I had scarce breath and spirit enough to find words to beg of her, if she would save my life, to fall upon some means of finding out, instantly, what was become of its only prop and comfort. She pity'd me in a way that rather sharpen'd my affliction than suspended it, and went out upon this commission.

Far she had not to go: Charles's father lived but at an easy distance, in one of the streets that run into *Covent Garden*. There she went into a publick house, and from thence sent for a maid-servant, whose name I had given her, as the properest to inform her.

The maid readily came, and as readily, when Mrs. Jones enquir'd of her what was become of Mr. Charles, or whether he was gone out of town, acquainted her with the disposal of her master's son, which, the very day after, was no secret to the servants. Such sure measures had he taken, for the most cruel punishment of his child for having more interest with his grandmother than he had, though he made use of a pretense, plausible enough, to get rid of him in this secret and abrupt manner, for fear her fondness should have interpos'd a bar to his leaving England, and proceeding on a voyage he had concerted for him; which pretext was, that it was indispensably necessary to secure a considerable inheritance that devolv'd to him by the death of a rich merchant (his own brother) at one of the factories in the South-Seas, of which he had lately receiv'd advice, together with a copy of the will.

In consequence of which resolution to send away his son, he had, unknown to him, made the necessary preparations for fitting him out, struck a bargain with the captain of a ship, whose punctual execution of his orders he had secured, by his interest with his principal owner and patron; and, in short, concerted his measures so secretly and effectually that whilst his son thought he was going down the river for a few hours, he was stopt on board of a ship, debar'd from writing, and more strictly watch'd than a State criminal.

Thus was the idol of my soul torn from me, and forc'd

on a long voyage, without taking of one friend, or receiving one line of comfort, except a dry explanation and instructions, from his father, how to proceed when he should arrive his destin'd port, enclosing, withal, some letters of recommendation to a factor there: all these particulars I did not learn minutely till some time after.

The maid, at the same time, added that she was sure this usage of her sweet young master would be the death of his grand-mama, as indeed it prov'd true; for the old lady, on hearing it, did not survive the news a whole month; and as her fortune consisted in an annuity, out of which she had laid up no reserves, she left nothing worth mentioning to her so fatally envied darling, but absolutely refus'd to see his father before she died.

When Mrs. Jones return'd and I observ'd her looks, they seem'd so unconcern'd, and even near to pleas'd, that I half flatter'd myself she was going to set my tortur'd heart at ease by bringing me good news; but this, indeed, was a cruel delusion of hope: the barbarian, with all the coolness imaginable, stab'd me to the heart, in telling me, succinctly, that he was sent away at least on a four years' voyage (here she stretch'd maliciously), and that I could not expect, in reason, ever to see him again: and all this with such pregnant circumstances that I could not help giving them credit, as in general they were, indeed, too true!

She had hardly finish'd her report before I fainted away and after several successive fits, all the while wild and senseless, I miscarried of the dear pledge of my Charles's love: but the wretched never die when it is fittest they should die, and women are hard-liv'd to a proverb.

The cruel and interested care taken to recover me sav'd an odious life: which, instead of the happiness and joys it had overflow'd in, all of a sudden presented no view before me of any thing but the depth of misery, horror, and the sharpest affliction.

Thus I lay six weeks, in the struggles of youth and constitution, against the friendly efforts of death, which I constantly invoked to my relief and deliverance, but which proving too weak for my wish, I recovered at length, tho' into a state of stupefaction and despair that threatened me with the loss of my senses, and a madhouse.

Time, however, that great comforter in ordinary, began to assuage the violence of my sufferings, and to numb my feeling of them. My health return'd to me, though I still retain'd an air of grief, dejection, and languor, which taking off the ruddiness of my country complexion, render'd it rather more delicate and affecting.

The landlady had all this while officiously provided, and taken care that I wanted for nothing: and as soon as she saw me retriev'd into a condition of answering her purpose, one day, after we had dined together, she congratulated me on my recovery, the merit of which she took entirely to herself, and all this by way of introduction to a most terrible and scurvy epilogue: "You are now," says she, "Miss Fanny, tolerably well, and you are very welcome to stay in the lodgings as long as you please; you see I have ask'd you for nothing this long time, but truly I have a call to make up a sum of money, which must be answer'd." And, with that, presents me with a bill of arrears for rent, diet, apothecary's charges, nurse, etc., sum total twenty-three pounds, seventeen and sixpence: towards discharging of which, I had not in the world (which she well knew) more than seven guineas, left by chance, of my dear Charles's common stock with me. At the same time, she desir'd me to tell her what course I would take for payment. I burst out into a flood of tears and told her my condition; adding that I would sell what few cloaths I had, and that, for the rest, I would pay her as soon as possible. But my distress, being favourable to her views, only stiffen'd her the more.

She told me, very coolly, that "she was indeed sorry for my misfortunes, but that she must do herself justice, though it would go to the very heart of her to send such a tender young creature to prison . . ." At the word "prison!" every drop of my blood chill'd, and my fright acted so strongly upon me, that, turning as pale and faint as a criminal at the first sight of his place of execution, I was on the point of swooning. My landlady, who wanted only to terrify me to a certain point, and not to throw me into a state of body inconsistent with her designs upon it, began to soothe me again, and told me, in a tone compos'd to more pity and gentleness, that it would be my own fault, if she was forc'd to proceed to such extremities; but she believ'd there was a friend to be found in the world who would make up matters to both our satisfactions, and that she would bring him to drink tea with us that very afternoon, when she hoped we would come to a right understanding in our affairs. To all this, not a word of answer; I sat mute, confounded, terrify'd.

Mrs. Jones however, judging rightly that it was time to strike while the impressions were so strong upon me, left me to myself and to all the terrors of an imagination, wounded to death by the idea of going to a prison, and, from a principle of self-preservation, snatching at every glimpse of redemption from it.

In this situation I sat near half an hour, swallow'd up in grief and despair, when my landlady came in, and observing a death-like dejection in my countenance and still in pursuance of her plan, put on a false pity, and bidding me be of a good heart: Things, she said, would not be so bad as I imagined if I would be but my own friend; and closed with telling me she had brought a very honourable gentleman to drink tea with me, who would give me the best advice how to get rid of all my troubles. Upon which, without waiting for a reply, she goes out, and returns with this very honourable gentleman, whose very honourable procuress she had been, on this as well as other occasions.

The gentleman, on his entering the room, made me a very civil bow, which I had scarce strength, or presence of mind enough to return a curtsy to; when the landlady, taking upon her to do all the honours of the first interview (for I had never, that I remember'd, seen the gentleman before), sets a chair for him, and another for herself. All this while not a word on either side; a stupid stare was all the face I could put on this strange visit.

The tea was made, and the landlady, unwilling, I suppose, to lose any time, observing my silence and shyness before this entire stranger: "Come, Miss Fanny," says she, in a coarse familiar style, and tone of authority, "hold up your head, child, and do not let sorrow spoil that pretty face of yours. What! sorrows are only for a time; come, be free, here is a worthy gentleman who has heard of your misfortunes and is willing to serve you; you must be better acquainted with him; do not you now stand upon your punctilio's, and this and that, but make your market while you may."

At this so delicate and eloquent harangue, the gentleman, who saw I look'd frighted and amaz'd, and indeed, incapable of answering, took her up for breaking things in so abrupt a manner, as rather to shock than incline me to an acceptance of the good he intended me; then, addressing himself to me, told me he was perfectly acquainted with my whole story and every circumstance of my distress, which he own'd was a cruel plunge for one of my youth and beauty to fall into; that he had long taken a liking to my person, for which he appeal'd to Mrs. Jones, there present, but finding me so absolutely engag'd to another, he had lost all hopes of succeeding till he had heard the sudden reverse of fortune that had happen'd to me, on which he had given particular orders to my landlady to see that I should want for nothing; and that, had he not been forc'd abroad to The Hague, on affairs he could not refuse himself to, he would himself have attended me during my sickness; that on his return, which was but the day before, he had, on learning my recovery, desir'd my landlady's good offices to introduce him to me, and was as angry, at least, as I was shock'd, at the manner in which she had conducted herself towards obtaining him that happiness; but, that to shew me how much he disown'd her procedure, and how far he was from taking any ungenerous advantage of my situation, and from exacting any security for my gratitude, he would before my face, that instant, discharge my debt entirely to my landlady and give me her receipt in full; after which I should be at liberty either to reject or grant his suit, as he was much above putting any force upon my inclinations.

Whilst he was exposing his sentiments to me, I ventur'd just to look up to him, and observed his figure, which was that of a very sightly gentleman, well made, about forty, drest in a suit of plain cloaths, with a large diamond ring on one of his fingers, the lustre of which play'd in my eyes as he wav'd his hand in talking, and rais'd my notions of his importance. In short, he might pass for what is commonly call'd a comely black man, with an air of distinction natural to his birth and condition.

To all his speeches, however, I answer'd only in tears that flow'd plentifully to my relief, and choking up my voice, excus'd me from speaking, very luckily, for I should not have known what to say.

The sight, however, mov'd him, as he afterwards told me, irresistibly, and by way of giving me some reason to be less powerfully afflicted, he drew out his purse, and calling for pen and ink, which the landlady was prepar'd for, paid her every farthing of her demand, independent of a liberal gratification which was to follow unknown to me; and taking a receipt in full, very tenderly forc'd me to secure it, by guiding my hand, which he had thrust it into, so as to make me passively put it into my pocket.

Still I continued in a state of stupidity, or melancholy despair, as my spirits could not yet recover from the violent shocks they had receiv'd; and the accommodating landlady had actually left the room, and me alone with this strange gentleman, before I observ'd it, and then I observ'd it without alarm, for I was now lifeless and indifferent to everything.

The gentleman, however, no novice in affairs of this sort, drew near me; and under the pretence of comforting me, first with his handkerchief dried my tears as they ran down my cheeks: presently he ventur'd to kiss me: on my part, neither resistance nor compliance. I sat stock-still; and now looking on myself as bought by the payment that had been transacted before me, I did not care what became of my wretched body: and wanting life, spirits, or courage to oppose the least struggle, even that of the modesty of my sex, I suffer'd, tamely, whatever the gentleman pleased; who proceeding insensibly from freedom to freedom, insinuated his hand between my handkerchief and bosom, which he handled at discretion: finding thus no repulse, and that every thing favour'd, beyond expectation, the completion of his desires, he took me in his arms, and bore me, without life or motion, to the bed, on which laying me gently down, and having me at what advantage he pleas'd, I did not so much as know what he was about, till recovering from a trance of lifeless insensibility, I found him buried in me, whilst I lay passive and innocent of the least sensation of pleasure: a death-cold corpse could scarce have less life or sense in it. As soon as he had thus pacified a passion which had too little respected the condition I was in, he got off, and after recomposing the disorder of my cloaths, employ'd himself with the utmost tenderness to calm the transports of remorse and madness at myself with which I was seized, too late, I confess, for having suffer'd on that bed the embraces of an utter stranger. I tore my hair, wrung my hands, and beat my breast like a madwoman. But when my new master, for in that light I then view'd him, applied himself to appease me, as my whole rage was levell'd at myself, no part of which I thought myself permitted to aim at him, I begged of him, with more submission than anger, to leave me alone that I might, at least, enjoy my affliction in quiet. This he positively refused, for fear, as he pretended, I should do myself a mischief.

Violent passions seldom last long, and those of women least of any. A dead still calm succeeded this storm, which ended in a profuse shower of tears.

Had any one, but a few instants before, told me that I should have ever known any man but Charles, I would have spit in his face; or had I been offer'd infinitely a greater sum of money than that I saw paid for me, I had spurn'd the proposal in cold blood. But our virtues and our vices depend too much on our circumstances; unexpectedly beset as I was, betray'd by a mind weakened by a long severe affliction, and stunn'd with the terrors of a jail, my defeat will appear the more excusable, since I certainly was not present at, or a party in any sense, to it. However, as the first enjoyment is decisive, and he was now over the bar, I thought I had no longer a right to refuse the caresses of one that had got that advantage over me, no matter how obtain'd; conforming myself then to this maxim, I consider'd myself as so much in his power that I endur'd his kisses and embraces without affecting struggles or anger; not that they, as yet, gave me any pleasure, or prevail'd over the aversion of my soul to give myself up to any sensation of that sort; what I suffer'd, I suffer'd out of a kind of gratitude, and as a matter of course after what had pass'd.

He was, however, so regardful as not to attempt the renewal of those extremities which had thrown me, just before, into such violent agitations; but, now secure of possession, contented himself with bringing me to temper by degrees, and waiting at the hand of time for those fruits of generosity and courtship which he since often reproach'd himself with having gather'd much too green, when, yielding to the invitations of my inability to resist him, and overborne by desires, he had wreak'd his passion on a mere lifeless, spiritless body dead to all purposes of joy, since, taking none, it ought to be suppos'd incapable of giving any. This is, however, certain; my heart never thoroughly forgave him the manner in which I had fallen to him, although, in point of interest, I had reason to be pleas'd that he found, in my person, wherewithal to keep him from leaving me as easily as he had gained me.

The evening was, in the mean time, so far advanc'd, that the maid came in to lay the cloth for supper, when I understood, with joy, that my landlady, whose sight was present poison to me, was not to be with us.

Presently a neat and elegant supper was introduc'd, and a bottle of Burgundy, with the other necessaries, were set on a dumb-waiter.

The maid quitting the room, the gentleman insisted, with a tender warmth, that I should sit up in the elbow chair by the fire, and see him eat if I could not be prevailed on to eat myself. I obey'd with a heart full of affliction, at the comparison it made between those delicious *tête-à-têtes* with my ever dear youth, and this forc'd situation, this new aukward scene, impos'd and obtruded on me by cruel necessity.

At supper, after a great many arguments used to comfort and reconcile me to my fate, he told me that his name was H. . . , brother to the Earl of L. . . and that having, by the suggestions of my landlady, been led to see me, he had found me perfectly to his taste and given her a commission to procure me at any rate, and that he had at length succeeded, as much to his satisfaction as he passionately wished it might be to mine; adding, withal, some flattering assurances that I should have no cause to repent my knowledge of him.

I had now got down at most half a partridge, and three or four glasses of wine, which he compelled me to drink by way of restoring nature; but whether there was anything extraordinary put into the wine, or whether there wanted no more to revive the natural warmth of my constitution and give fire to the old train, I began no longer to look with that constraint, not to say disgust, on Mr. H. . . , which I had hitherto done; but, withal, there was not the least grain of love mix'd with this softening of my sentiments: any other man would have been just the same to me as Mr. H. . . , that stood in the same circumstances and had done for me, and with me, what he had done.

There are not, on earth at least, eternal griefs; mine were, if not at an end, at least suspended: my heart, which had been so long overloaded with anguish and vexation, began to dilate and open to the least gleam of diversion or amusement. I wept a little, and my tears reliev'd me; I sigh'd, and my sighs seem'd to lighten me of a load that oppress'd me; my countenance grew, if not cheerful, at least more compos'd and free.

Mr. H. . . , who had watched, perhaps brought on this change, knew too well not to seize it: he thrust the table imperceptibly from between us, and bringing his chair to face me, he soon began, after preparing me by all the endearments of assurances and protestations, to lay hold of my hands, to kiss me, and once more to make free with my bosom, which, being at full liberty from the disorder of a loose dishabille, now panted and throbb'd, less with indignation than with fear and bashfulness at being used so familiarly by still a stranger. But he soon gave me greater occasion to exclaim, by stooping down and slipping his hand above my garters: thence he strove to regain the pass, which he had before found so open, and unguarded: but now he could not unlock the twist of my thighs; I gently complained, and begg'd him to let me alone; told him I was not well. However, as he saw there was more form and ceremony in my resistance than good earnest, he made his conditions for desisting from pursuing his point that I should be put instantly to bed, whilst he gave certain orders to the landlady, and that he would return in an hour, when he hoped to find me more reconcil'd to his passion for me than I seem'd at present. I neither assented nor deny'd, but my air and manner of receiving this proposal gave him to see that I did not think myself enough my own mistress to refuse it.

Accordingly he went out and left me, when, a minute or two after, before I could recover myself into any composure for thinking, the maid came in with her mistress's service, and a small silver porringer of what she called a bridal posset, and desir'd me to eat it as I went to bed, which consequently I did, and felt immediately a heat, a fire run like a hue-and-cry thro' every part of my body; I burnt, I glow'd, and wanted even little of wishing for any man.

The maid, as soon as I was lain down, took the candle away, and wishing me a good night, went out of the room and shut the door after her.

She had hardly time to get down-stairs before Mr. H. . . open'd my room-door softly, and came in, now undress'd in his night-gown and cap, with two lighted wax candles, and bolting the door, gave me, tho' I expected him, some sort of alarm. He came a tip-toe to the bed-side, and said with a gentle whisper: "Pray, my dear, do not be startled . . . I will be very tender and kind to you." He then hurry'd off his cloaths, and leap'd into bed, having given me openings enough, whilst he was stripping, to observe his brawny structure, strong-made limbs, and rough shaggy breast.

The bed shook again when it receiv'd this new load. He lay on the outside, where he kept the candles burning, no doubt for the satisfaction of ev'ry sense; for as soon as he had kiss'd me, he rolled down the bed-cloaths, and seemed transported with the view of all my person at full length, which he cover'd with a profusion of kisses, sparing no part of me. Then, being on his knees between my legs, he drew up his shirt and bared all his hairy thighs, and stiff staring truncheon, red-topt and rooted into a thicket of curls, which covered his belly to the navel and gave it the air of a flesh brush; and soon I felt it joining close to mine, when he had drove the nail up to the head, and left no partition but the intermediate hair on both sides.

I had it now, I felt it now, and, beginning to drive, he soon gave nature such a powerful summons down to her favourite quarters, that she could no longer refuse repairing thither; all my animal spirits then rush'd mechanically to that center of attraction, and presently, inly warmed, and stirr'd as I was beyond bearing, I lost all restraint, and yielding to the force of the emotion, gave down, as mere woman, those effusions of pleasure, which, in the strictness of still faithful love, I could have wished to have held up.

Yet oh! what an immense difference did I feel between this impression of a pleasure merely animal, and struck out of the collision of the sexes by a passive bodily effect, from that sweet fury, that rage of active delight which crowns the enjoyments of a mutual love-passion, where two hearts, tenderly and truly united, club to exalt the joy, and give it a spirit and soul that bids defiance to that end which mere momentary desires generally terminate in, when they die of a surfeit of satisfaction!

Mr. H . . . , whom no distinctions of that sort seemed to disturb, scarce gave himself or me breathing time from the last encounter, but, as if he had task'd himself to prove that the appearances of his vigour were not signs hung out in vain, in a few minutes he was in a condition for renewing the onset; to which, preluding with a storm of kisses, he drove the same course as before, with unbated fervour; and thus, in repeated engagements, kept me constantly in exercise till dawn of morning; in all which time he made me fully sensible of the virtues of his firm texture of limbs, his square shoulders, broad chest, compact hard muscles, in short a system of manliness that might pass for no bad image of our ancient sturdy barons, when they wielded the battle-ax: whose race is now so thoroughly refin'd and frittered away into the more delicate and modern-built frame of our pap-nerv'd softlings, who are as pale, as pretty, and almost as masculine as their sisters.

Mr. H . . . , content, however, with having the day break upon his triumphs, delivered me up to the refreshment of a rest we both wanted, and we soon dropped into a profound sleep.

Tho' he was some time awake before me, yet did he not offer to disturb a repose he had given me so much occasion for; but on my first stirring, which was not till past ten o'clock, I was oblig'd to endure one more trial of his manhood.

About eleven, in came Mrs. Jones, with two basins of the richest soup, which her experience in these matters had mov'd her to prepare. I pass over the fulsome compliments, the cant of the decent procuress, with which she saluted us both; but tho' my blood rose at the sight of her, I supprest my emotions, and gave all my concern to reflections on what would be the consequence of this new engagement.

But Mr. H . . . , who penetrated my uneasiness, did not long suffer me to languish under it. He acquainted me that, having taken a solid sincere affection to me, he would begin by giving me one leading mark of it by removing me out of a house which must, for many reasons, be irksome and disagreeable to me, into convenient lodgings, where he would take all imaginable care of me; and desiring me not to have any explanations with my landlady, or be impatient till he returned, he dress'd and went out, having left me a purse with two and twenty guineas in it, being all he had about him, as he expresst it, to keep my pocket till further supplies.

As soon as he was gone, I felt the usual consequence of the first launch into vice (for my love-attachment to Charles never appear'd to me in that light). I was instantly borne away down the stream, without making back to the shore. My dreadful necessities, my gratitude, and above all, to say the plain truth, the dissipation and diversion I began to find, in this new acquaintance, from the black corroding thoughts my heart had been a prey to ever since the absence of my dear Charles, concurr'd to stun all contrary reflections. If I now thought of my first, my only charmer, it was still with the tenderness and regret of the fondest love, embitter'd with the consciousness that I was no longer worthy of him. I could have begg'd my bread with him all over the world, but wretch that I was, I had neither the virtue nor courage requisite not to outlive my separation from him!

Yet, had not my heart been thus pre-ingaged, Mr. H. . . might probably have been the sole master of it; but the place was full, and the force of conjunctures alone had made him the possessor of my person; the charms of which had, by the bye, been his sole object and passion, and were, of course, no foundation for a love either very delicate or very durable.

He did not return till six in the evening to take me away to my new lodgings; and my moveables being soon pack'd, and convey'd into a hackney-coach, it cost me but little regret to take my leave of a landlady whom I thought I had so much reason not to be overpleas'd with; and as for her part, she made no other difference to my staying or going, but what that of the profit created.

We soon got to the house appointed for me, which was that of a plain tradesman who, on the score of interest, was entirely at Mr. H. . .'s devotion, and who let him the first floor, very genteelly furnish'd, for two guineas a week, of which I was instated mistress, with a maid to attend me.

He stayed with me that evening, and we had a supper from a neighbouring tavern, after which, and a gay glass or two, the maid put me to bed. Mr. H. . . soon follow'd, and notwithstanding the fatigues of the preceding night, I found no quarter nor remission from him: he piqued himself, as he told me, on doing the honours of my new apartment.

The morning being pretty well advanc'd, we got to breakfast; and the ice now broke, my heart, no longer engross'd by love, began to take ease, and to please itself with such trifles as Mr. H. . .'s liberal liking led him to make his court to the usual vanity of our sex. Silks, laces, ear-rings, pearl-necklace, gold watch, in short, all the trinkets and articles of dress were lavishly heap'd upon me; the sense of which, if it did not create returns of love, forc'd a kind of grateful fondness something like love; a distinction it would be spoiling the pleasure of nine tenths of the keepers in the town to make, and is, I suppose, the very good reason why so few of them ever do make it.

I was now establish'd the kept mistress in form, well lodg'd, with a very sufficient allowance, and lighted up with all the lustre of dress.

Mr. H . . . continu'd kind and tender to me; yet, with all this, I was far from happy; for, besides my regret for my dear youth, which, though often suspended or diverted, still return'd upon me in certain melancholic moments with redoubled violences, I wanted more society, more dissipation.

As to Mr. H . . . , he was so much my superior in every sense, that I felt it too much to the disadvantage of the gratitude I ow'd him. Thus he gain'd my esteem, though he could not raise my taste; I was qualify'd for no sort of conversation with him except one sort, and that is a satisfaction which leaves tiresome intervals, if not fill'd up by love, or other amusements.

Mr. H . . . , so experienc'd, so learned in the ways of women, numbers of whom had passed through his hands, doubtless soon perceiv'd this uneasiness, and without approving or liking me the better for it, had the complaisance to indulge me.

He made suppers at my lodgings, where he brought several companions of his pleasures, with their mistresses; and by this means I got into a circle of acquaintance that soon strip'd me of all the remains of bashfulness and modesty which might be yet left of my country education, and were, to a just taste, perhaps the greatest of my charms.

We visited one another in form, and mimic'd, as near as we could, all the miseries, the follies, and impertinences of the women of quality, in the round of which they trifle away their time, without its ever entering into their little heads that on earth there cannot subsist any thing more silly, more flat, more insipid and worthless, than, generally consider'd, their system of life is: they ought to treat the men as their tyrants, indeed! were they to condemn them to it.

But tho', amongst the kept mistresses (and I was now acquainted with a good many, besides some useful matrons, who live by their connexions with them), I hardly knew one that did not perfectly detest her keeper, and, of course, made little or no scruple of any infidelity she could safely accomplish, I had still no notion of wronging mine: for, besides that no mark of jealousy on his side induced in me the desire or gave me the provocation to play him a trick of that sort, and that his constant generosity, politeness, and tender attentions to please me forc'd a regard to him, that without affecting my heart, insur'd him my fidelity, no object had yet presented that could overcome the habitual liking I had contracted for him; and I was on the eve of obtaining, from the movements of his own voluntary generosity, a modest provision for life, when an accident happen'd which broke all the measures he had resolv'd upon in my favour.

I had now liv'd near seven months with Mr. H . . . , when one day returning to my lodgings from a visit in the neighbourhood, where I us'd to stay longer, I found the street door open, and the maid of the house standing at it, talking with some of her acquaintances, so that I came in without knocking; and, as I passed by, she told me Mr. H . . . was above. I step up-stairs into my own bed-chamber, with no other thought than of pulling off my hat, etc., and then to wait upon him in the dining room, into which my bed-chamber had a door, as is common enough. Whilst I was untying my hat-strings, I fancied I heard my maid *Hannah's* voice and a sort of tussle, which raising my curiosity, I stole softly to the door, where a knot in the wood had been slipt out and afforded a very commanding peep-hole to the scene then in agitation, the actors of which had been too earnestly employ'd to hear my opening my own door, from the landing-place of the stairs, into my bed-chamber.

The first sight that struck me was Mr. H . . . pulling

and hauling this coarse country strammel towards a couch
that stood in a corner of the dining room; to which the
girl made only a sort of aukward hoidening resistance,
crying out so loud, that I, who listened at the door, could
scarce hear her: "Pray sir, don't . . . , let me alone . . .
I am not for your turn . . . You cannot, sure, demean
yourself with such a poor body as I . . . Lord! Sir, my
mistress may come home . . . I must not indeed . . . I
will cry out . . ." All of which did not hinder her from insensibly suffering herself to be brought to the foot of the
couch, upon which a push of no mighty violence serv'd to
give her a very easy fall, and my gentleman having got up
his hands to the strong-hold of her VIRTUE, she, no doubt,
thought it was time to give up the argument, and that all
further defense would be vain: and he, throwing her petticoats over her face, which was now as red as scarlet, discover'd a pair of stout, plump, substantial thighs, and tolerably white; he mounted them round his hips, and
coming out with his drawn weapon, stuck it in the cloven
spot, where he seem'd to find a less difficult entrance than
perhaps he had flatter'd himself with (for, by the way, this
blouze had left her place in the country, for a bastard),
and, indeed, all his motions shew'd he was lodg'd pretty
much at large. After he had done, his DEAREE gets up,
drops her petticoats down, and smooths her apron and
handkerchief. Mr. H . . . look'd a little silly, and taking
out some money, gave it her, with an air indifferent enough,
bidding her be a good girl, and say nothing.

Had I lov'd this man, it was not in nature for me to have
had patience to see the whole scene through: I should
have broke in and play'd the jealous princess with a vengeance. But that was not the case, my pride alone was hurt,
my heart not, and I could easier win upon myself to see
how far he would go, till I had no uncertainty upon my
conscience.

The least delicate of all affairs of this sort being now
over, I retir'd softly into my closet, where I began to consider what I should do. My first scheme, naturally, was to
rush in and upbraid them; this, indeed, flatter'd my present
emotions and vexations, as it would have given immediate

vent to them; but, on second thoughts, not being so clear as
to the consequences to be apprehended from such a step,
I began to doubt whether it was not better to dissemble my
discovery till a safer season, when Mr. H . . . should
have perfected the settlement he had made overtures to
me of, and which I was not to think such a violent explanation, as I was indeed not equal to the management of,
could possibly forward, and might destroy. On the other
hand, the provocation seem'd too gross, too flagrant, not to
give me some thoughts of revenge; the very start of which
idea restor'd me to perfect composure; and delighted as I
was with the confus'd plan of it in my head, I was easily
mistress enough of myself to support the part of ignorance
I had prescrib'd to myself; and as all this circle of reflections was instantly over, I stole a tip-toe to the passage
door, and opening it with a noise, pass'd for having that
moment come home; and after a short pause, as if to pull
off my things, I opened the door into the dining room,
where I found the dowdy blowing the fire, and my faithful shepherd walking about the room and whistling, as
cool and unconcern'd as if nothing had happened. I think,
however, he had not much to brag of having out-dis-
sembled me: for I kept up, nobly, the character of our sex
for art, and went up to him with the same open air of frankness as I had ever receiv'd him. He stayed but a little
while, made some excuse for not being able to stay the
evening with me, and went out.

As for the wench, she was now spoil'd, at least for my
servant; and scarce eight and forty hours were gone round,
before her insolence, on what had pass'd between Mr.
H . . . and her, gave me so fair an occasion to turn her
away, at a minute's warning, that not to have done it would
have been the wonder: so that he could neither disapprove
it nor find in it the least reason to suspect my original motive. What became of her afterwards, I know not; but
generous as Mr. H . . . was, he undoubtedly made her
amends; though, I dare answer, that he kept up no farther
commerce with her of that sort; as his stooping to such a
coarse morsel was only a sudden sally of lust, on seeing a
wholesome-looking, buxom country-wench, and no more

strange than hunger, or even a whimsical appetite's making a fling meal of neck-beef, for change of diet.

Had I consider'd this escapade of Mr. H . . . in no more than that light and contented myself with turning away the wench, I had thought and acted right; but, flush'd as I was with imaginary wrongs, I should have held Mr. H . . . to have been cheaply off, if I had not push'd my revenge farther, and repaid him, as exactly as I could for the soul of me, in the same coin.

Nor was this worthy act of justice long delay'd: I had it too much at heart. Mr. H . . . had, about a fortnight before, taken into his service a tenant's son, just come out of the country, a very handsome young lad scarce turn'd of nineteen, fresh as a rose, well shap'd and clever limb'd: in short, a very good excuse for any woman's liking, even tho' revenge had been out of the question; any woman, I say, who was disprejudic'd, and had wit and spirit enough to prefer a point of pleasure to a point of pride.

Mr. H . . . had clap'd a livery upon him; and his chief employ was, after being shewn my lodgings, to bring and carry letters or messages between his master and me; and as the situation of all kept ladies is not the fittest to inspire respect, even to the meanest of mankind, and, perhaps, less of it from the most ignorant, I could not help observing that this lad, who was, I suppose, acquainted with my relation to his master by his fellow-servants, used to eye me in that bashful confus'd way, more expressive, more moving and readier catch'd at by our sex, than any other declarations whatever: my figure had, it seems, struck him, and modest and innocent as he was, he did not himself know that the pleasure he took in looking at me was love, or desire; but his eyes, naturally wanton, and now enflam'd with passion, spoke a great deal more than he durst have imagin'd they did. Hitherto, indeed, I had only taken notice of the comeliness of the youth, but without the least design: my pride alone would have guarded me from a thought that way, had not Mr. H . . .'s condescension with my maid, where there was not half the temptation in point of person, set me a dangerous example; but now I began to look on this stripling as every way a delicious instrument of my design'd retaliation upon Mr. H . . . of an obligation for which I should have made a conscience to die in his debt.

In order then to pave the way for the accomplishment of my scheme, for two or three times that the young fellow came to me with messages, I manag'd so, as without affectation to have him admitted to my bed-side, or brought to me at my toilet, where I was dressing; and by carelessly shewing or letting him see, as if without meaning or design, sometimes my bosom rather more bare than it should be; sometimes my hair, of which I had a very fine head, in the natural flow of it while combing; sometimes a neat leg, that had unfortunately slipt its garter, which I made no scruple of tying before him, easily gave him the impressions favourable to my purpose, which I could perceive to sparkle in his eyes, and glow in his cheeks: then certain slight squeezes by the hand, as I took letters from him, did his business compleatly.

When I saw him thus mov'd, and fired for my purpose, I inflam'd him yet more, by asking him several leading questions, such as had he a mistress? . . . was she prettier than me? . . . could he love such a one as I was? . . . and the like; to all which the blushing simpleton answer'd to my wish, in a strain of perfect nature, perfect undebauch'd innocence, but with all the aukwardness and simplicity of country-breeding.

When I thought I had sufficiently ripen'd him for the laudable point I had in view, one day that I expected him at a particular hour, I took care to have the coast clear for the reception I design'd him; and, as I laid it, he came to the dining-room door, tapped at it, and, on my bidding him come in, he did so, and shut the door after him. I desir'd him, then, to bolt it on the inside, pretending it would not otherwise keep shut.

I was then lying at length upon that very couch, the scene of Mr. H . . .'s polite joys, in an undress which was with all the art of negligence flowing loose, and in a most tempting disorder: no stays, no hoop . . . no incumbrance whatever. On the other hand, he stood at a little distance, that gave me a full view of a fine featur'd, shapely, healthy country lad, breathing the sweets of fresh blooming youth; his hair, which was of a perfect shining black, play'd to his face in natural side-curls, and was set out with a smart tuck-up behind; new buckskin breeches, that, clipping close, shew'd the shape of a plump, well made thigh; white stockings, garter-lac'd livery, shoulder knot, altogether compos'd a figure in which the beauties of pure flesh and blood appeared under no disgrace from the lowness of a dress, to which a certain spruce neatness seems peculiarly fitted.

I bid him come towards me and give me his letter, at the same time throwing down, carelessly, a book I had in my hands. He colour'd, and came within reach of delivering me the letter, which he held out, aukwardly enough, for me to take, with his eyes riveted on my bosom, which was, through the design'd disorder of my handkerchief, sufficiently bare, and rather shaded than hid.

I, smiling in his face, took the letter, and immediately catching gently hold of his shirt sleeve, drew him towards me, blushing, and almost trembling; for surely his extreme bashfulness, and utter inexperience, call'd for, at least, all the advances to encourage him: his body was now conveniently inclin'd towards me, and just softly chucking his smooth beardless chin, I asked him if he was afraid of a lady? . . . , and with that took, and carrying his hand to my breasts, I prest it tenderly to them. They were now finely furnish'd, and rais'd in flesh, so that, panting with desire, they rose and fell, in quick heaves, under his touch: at this, the boy's eyes began to lighten with all the fires of inflam'd nature, and his cheeks flush'd with a deep scarlet: tongue-tied with joy, rapture, and bashfulness, he could not speak, but then his looks, his emotion, sufficiently satisfy'd me that my train had taken, and that I had no disappointment to fear.

My lips, which I threw in his way, so as that he could not escape kissing them, fix'd, fired, and embolden'd him: and now, glancing my eyes towards that part of his dress which cover'd the essential object of enjoyment, I plainly discover'd the swell and commotion there; and as I was now too far advanc'd to stop in so fair a way, and was indeed no longer able to contain myself, or wait the slower progress of his maiden bashfulness (for such it seem'd, and really was), I stole my hand upon his thighs, down one of which I could both see and feel a stiff hard body, confin'd by his breeches, that my fingers could discover no end to. Curious then, and eager to unfold so alarming a mystery, playing, as it were, with his buttons, which were bursting ripe from the active force within, those of his waistband and fore-flap flew open at a touch, when out rr started; and now, disengag'd from the shirt, I saw, with wonder and surprise, what? not the play-thing of a boy, not the weapon of a man, but a maypole of so enormous a standard, that had proportions been observ'd, it must have belong'd to a young giant. Its prodigious size made me shrink again; yet I could not, without pleasure, behold, and even ventur'd to feel, such a length, such a breadth of animated ivory! perfectly well turn'd and fashion'd, the proud stiffness of which distended its skin, whose smooth polish and velvet softness might vie with that of the most delicate of our sex, and whose exquisite whiteness was not a little set off by a sprout of black curling hair round the root, through the jetty sprigs of which the fair skin shew'd as in a fine evening you may have remark'd the clear light æther through the branchwork of distant trees over-topping the summit of a hill: then the broad and blueish-casted incarnate of the head, and blue serpentines of its veins, altogether compos'd the most striking assemblage of figure and colours in nature. In short, it stood an object of terror and delight.

But what was yet more surprising, the owner of this natural curiosity, through the want of occasions in the strictness of his home-breeding, and the little time he had been in town not having afforded him one, with hitherto an absolute stranger, in practice at least, to the use of all that manhood he was no nobly stock'd with; and it now fell to my lot to stand this first trial of it, if I could resolve to run the risks of its disproportion to that tender part of me, which such an oversiz'd machine was very fit to lay in ruins.

But it was now of the latest to deliberate; for, by this

time, the young fellow, overheated with the present objects, and too high mettled to be longer curb'd in by that modesty and awe which had hitherto restrain'd him, ventur'd, under the stronger impulse and instructive promptership of nature alone, to slip his hands, trembling with eager impetuous desires, under my petticoats; and seeing, I suppose, nothing extremely severe in my looks to stop or dash him, he feels out, and seizes, gently, the center-spot of his ardours. Oh then! the fiery touch of his fingers determines me, and my fears melting away before the glowing intolerable heat, my thighs disclose of themselves, and yield all liberty to his hand: and now, a favourable movement giving my petticoats a toss, the avenue lay too fair, too open to be miss'd. He is now upon me; I had placed myself with a jet under him, as commodious and open as possible to his attempts, which were untoward enough, for his machine, meeting with no inlet, bore and batter'd stiffly against me in random pushes, now above, now below, now beside his point; till, burning with impatience from its irritating touches, I guided gently, with my hand, this furious engine to where my young novice was now to be taught his first lesson of pleasure. Thus he nick'd, at length, the warm and insufficient orifice; but he was made to find no breach impracticable, and mine, tho' so often enter'd, was still far from wide enough to take him easily in.

By my direction, however, the head of his unwieldy machine was so critically pointed that, feeling him fore-right against the tender opening, a favourable motion from me met his timely thrust, by which the lips of it, strenuously dilated, gave way to his thus assisted impetuosity, so that we might both feel that he had gain'd a lodgment. Pursuing then his point, he soon, by violent, and, to me, most painful piercing thrusts, wedges himself at length so far in, as to be now tolerably secure of his entrance: here he stuck, and I now felt such a mixture of pleasure and pain, as there is no giving a definition of. I dreaded alike his splitting me farther up, or his withdrawing; I could not bear either to keep or part with him. The sense of pain however prevailing, from his prodigious size and stiffness, acting upon me in those continued rapid thrusts, with which he furiously pursu'd his penetration, made me cry out gently: "Oh! my dear you hurt me!" This was enough to check the tender respectful boy even in his mid-career; and he immediately drew out the sweet cause of my complaint, whilst his eyes eloquently express'd, at once, his grief for hurting me, and his reluctance at dislodging from quarters of which the warmth and closeness had given him a gust of pleasure that he was now desire-mad to satisfy, and yet too much a novice not to be afraid of my withholding his relief, on account of the pain he had put me to.

But I was, myself, far from being pleas'd with his having too much regarded my tender exclaims; for now, more and more fired with the object before me, as it still stood with the fiercest erection, unbonnetted, and displaying its broad vermilion head, I first gave the youth a re-encouraging kiss, which he repaid me with a fervour that seem'd at once to thank me, and bribe my farther compliance; and soon replac'd myself in a posture to receive, at all risks, the renew'd invasion, which he did not delay an instant: for, being presently remounted, I once more felt the smooth hard gristle forcing an entrance, which he achiev'd rather easier than before. Pain'd, however, as I was, with his efforts of gaining a complete admission, which he was so regardful as to manage by gentle degrees, I took care not to complain. In the meantime, the soft strait passage gradually loosens, yields, and stretch'd to its utmost bearing, by the stiff, thick, indriven engine, sensible, at once, to the ravishing pleasure of the *feel* and the pain of the distension, let him in about half way, when all the most nervous activity he now exerted, to further his penetration, gain'd him not an inch of his purpose: for, whilst he hesitated there, the crisis of pleasure overtook him, and the close compressure of the warm surrounding fold drew from him the extatic gush, even before mine was ready to meet it, kept up by the pain I had endur'd in the course of the engagement, from the insufferable size of his weapon, tho' it was not as yet in above half its length.

I expected then, but without wishing it, that he would draw, but was pleasantly disappointed: for he was not to be let off so. The well breath'd youth, hot-mettled, and flush with genial juices, was now fairly in for making me know my driver. As soon, then, as he had made a short pause, waking, as it were, out of the trance of pleasure (in which every sense seem'd lost for a while, whilst, with his eyes shut, and short quick breathing, he had yielded down his maiden tribute), he still kept his post, yet unsated with enjoyment, and solacing in these so new delights; till his stiffness, which had scarce perceptibly remitted, being thoroughly recovered to him, who had not once unsheath'd, he proceeded afresh to cleave and open to himself an entire entry into me, which was not a little made easy to him by the balsamic injection with which he had just plentifully moisten'd the whole internals of the passage. Redoubling, then, the active energy of his thrusts, favoured by the fervid appetite of my motions, the soft oiled wards can no longer stand so effectual a pick-lock, but yield, and open him an entrance. And now, with conspiring nature, and my industry, strong to aid him, he pierces, penetrates, and at length, winning his way inch by inch, gets entirely in, and finally mighty thrust sheaths it up to the guard: on the information of which, from the close jointure of our bodies (insomuch that the hair on both sides perfectly interweav'd and incircl'd together), the eyes of the transported youth sparkl'd with more joyous fires, and all his looks and motions acknowledged excess of pleasure, which I now began to share, for I felt him in my very vitals! I was quite sick with delight! stir'd beyond bearing with its furious agitations within me, and gorged and cramm'd, even to surfeit. Thus I lay gasping, panting under him, till his broken breathings, faltering accents, eyes twinkling with humid fires, lunges more furious, and an increased stiffness, gave me to hail the approaches of the second period: it came . . . and the sweet youth, overpower'd with the extasy, died away in my arms, melting in a flood that shot in genial warmth into the innermost recesses of my body; every conduit of which, dedicated to that pleasure, was on flow to mix with it. Thus we continued for some instants, lost, breathless, senseless of every thing, and in every part but those favourite ones of nature, in which all that we enjoyed of life and sensation was now totally concentre'd.

When our mutual trance was a little over, and the young fellow had withdrawn that delicious stretcher, with which he had most plentifully drowned all thoughts of revenge in the sense of actual pleasure, the widen'd wounded passage refunded a stream of pearly liquids, which flowed down my thighs, mixed with streaks of blood, the marks of the ravage of that monstrous machine of his, which had now triumph'd over a kind of second maidenhead. I stole, however, my handkerchief to those parts, and wip'd them as dry as I could, whilst he was re-adjusting and buttoning up.

I made him now sit down by me, and as he had gather'd courage from such extreme intimacy, he gave me an aftercourse of pleasure, in a natural burst of tender gratitude and joy, at the new scenes of bliss I had opened to him: scenes positively new, as he had never before had the least acquaintance with that mysterious mark, the cloven stamp of female distinction, tho' nobody better qualify'd than he to penetrate into its deepest recesses, or do it nobler justice. But when, by certain motions, certain unquietnesses of his hands, that wandered not without design, I found he languish'd for satisfying a curiosity, natural enough, to view and handle those parts which attract and concentre the warmest force of imagination, charmed as I was to have any occasion of obliging and humouring his young desires, I suffer'd him to proceed as he pleased, without check or control, to the satisfaction of them.

Easily, then, reading in my eyes the full permission of myself to all his wishes, he scarce pleased himself more than me when, having insinuated his hand under my petticoat and shift, he presently removed those bars to the sight by slyly lifting them upwards, under favour of a thousand kisses, which he thought, perhaps, necessary to divert my attention from what he was about. All my drapery being now roll'd up to my waist, I threw myself into such a posture upon the couch, as gave up to him, in full view, the whole region of delight, and all the luxurious landscape round it. The transported youth devour'd every thing with his eyes, and try'd, with his fingers, to lay more open to his sight the secrets of that dark and delicious deep: he opens the folding lips, the softness of which, yielding entry to any thing of a hard body, close round it, and oppose the sight: and feeling further, meets with, and wonders at, a soft fleshy excrescence, which, limber and relaxed after the late enjoyment, now grew, under the touch and examination of his fiery fingers, more and more stiff and considerable, till the titillating ardours of that so sensible part made me sigh, as if he had hurt me; on which he withdrew his curious probing fingers, asking me pardon, as it were, in a kiss that rather increased flame *there*.

Novelty ever makes the strongest impressions, and in pleasures, especially; no wonder, then, that he was swallowed up in raptures of admiration of things so interesting by their nature, and now seen and handled for the first time. On my part, I was richly overpaid for the pleasure I gave him, in that of examining the power of those objects thus abandon'd to him, naked and free to his loosest wish, over the artless, natural stripling: his eyes streaming fire, his cheeks glowing with a florid red, his fervid frequent sighs, whilst his hands convulsively squeez'd, opened, pressed together again the lips and sides of that deep flesh wound, or gently twitched the overgrowing moss; and all proclaimed the excess, the riot of joys, in having his wantonness thus humour'd. But he did not long abuse my patience, for the objects before him had now put him by all his, and, coming out with that formidable machine of his, he lets the fury loose, and pointing it directly to the pouting-lipt mouth, that bid him sweet defiance in dumb-shew, squeezes in the head, and, driving with refreshed rage, breaks in, and plugs up the whole passage of that soft pleasure-conduit, where he makes all shake again, and put, once more, all within me into such an uproar, as nothing could still but a fresh inundation from the very engine of those flames, as well as from all the springs with which nature floats that reservoir of joy, when risen to its flood-mark.

I was now so bruised, so batter'd, so spent with this over-match, that I could hardly stir, or raise myself, but lay palpitating, till the ferment of my sense subsiding by degrees, and the hour striking at which I was oblig'd to dispatch my young man, I tenderly advised him of the necessity there was for parting; which I felt as much displeasure at as he could do, who seemed eagerly disposed to keep the field, and to enter on a fresh action. But the danger was too great, and after some hearty kisses of leave, and recommendations of secrecy and discretion, I forc'd myself to send him away, not without assurances of seeing him again, to the same purpose, as soon as possible, and thrust a guinea into his hands: not more, lest, being too flush of money, a suspicion or discovery might arise from thence, having everything to fear from the dangerous indiscretion of that age in which young fellows would be too irresistible, too charming, if we had not that terrible fault to guard against.

Giddy and intoxicated as I was with such satiating draughts of pleasure, I still lay on the couch, supinely stretched out, in a delicious languor diffus'd over all my limbs, hugging myself for being thus revenged to my heart's content, and that in a manner so precisely alike, and on the identical spot in which I had received the supposed injury. No reflections on the consequences ever once perplex'd me, nor did I make myself one single reproach for having, by this step, completely entered myself of a profession more decry'd than disused. I should have held it ingratitude to the pleasure I had received to have repented of it; and since I was now over the bar, I thought, by plunging over head and ears into the stream I was hurried away by, to drown all sense of shame or reflection.

Whilst I was thus making these laudable dispositions, and whispering to myself a kind of tacit vow of incontinency, enters Mr. H . . . The consciousness of what I had been doing deepen'd yet the glowing of my cheeks, flushed with the warmth of the late action, which, joined to the piquant air of my dishabille, drew from Mr. H . . . a compliment on my looks, which he was proceeding to back the sincerity of with proofs, and that with so brisk an action as made me tremble for fear of a discovery from the condition of those parts were left in from their late severe handling: the orifice dilated and inflamed, the lips swollen with their uncommon distension, the ringlets pressed down, crushed and uncurl'd with the over-flowing moisture that had wet every thing round it; in short, the different feel and state of things would hardly have passed upon one of Mr. H . . .'s nicety and experience unaccounted for but by the real cause. But here the woman saved me: I pretended a violent disorder of my head, and a feverish heat, that indispos'd me too much to receive his embraces. He gave in to this, and good-naturedly desisted. Soon after, an old lady coming in made a third, very *à-propos* for the confusion I was in, and Mr. H . . . , after bidding me take care of myself, and recommending me to my repose, left me much at ease and reliev'd by his absence.

In the close of the evening, I took care to have prepar'd for me a warm bath of aromatick and sweet herbs; in which having fully laved and solaced myself, I came out voluptuously refresh'd in body and spirit.

The next morning, waking pretty early, after a night's perfect rest and composure, it was not without some dread and uneasiness that I thought of what innovation that tender, soft system of mine might have sustained from the shock of a machine so sized for its destruction.

Struck with this apprehension, I scarce dared to carry my hand thither, to inform myself of the state and posture of things.

But I was soon agreeably cur'd of my fears.

The silky hair that covered round the borders, now smooth'd and re-pruned, had resumed its wonted curl and trimness; the fleshy pouting lips that had stood the brunt of the engagement, were no longer swollen or moisture-drenched; and neither they, nor the passage into which they opened, that suffered so great a dilatation, betray'd any the least alteration, outward or inwardly, to the most curious research, notwithstanding also the laxity that naturally follows the warm bath.

This continuation of that grateful stricture which is in us, to the men, the very jet of their pleasure, I ow'd, it seems, to a happy habit of body, juicy, plump and furnished towards the texture of those parts, with a fullness of soft springy flesh, that yielding sufficiently, as it does, to almost any distension soon recovers itself so as to retighten that strict compression of its mantlings and folds, which form the sides of the passage, wherewith it so tenderly embraces and closely clips any foreign body introduc'd into it, such as my exploring finger then was.

Finding then every thing in due tone and order, I remember'd my fears, only to make a jest of them to myself. And now, palpably mistress of any size of man, and triumphing in my double achievement of pleasure and revenge, I abandon'd myself entirely to the ideas of all the delight I had swam in. I lay stretching out, glowingly alive all over, and tossing with burning impatience for the renewal of joys that had sinned but in a sweet excess; nor did I loose my longing, for about ten in the morning, according to expectation, *Will*, my new humble sweetheart, came with a message from his master, Mr. H . . . , to know how I did. I had taken care to send my maid on an errand into the city, that I was sure would take up time enough; and, from the people of the house, I had nothing to fear, as they were plain good sort of folks, and wise enough to mind no more other people's business than they could well help.

All dispositions then made, not forgetting that of lying in bed to receive him, when he was entered the door of my bed-chamber, a latch, that I governed by a wire, descended and secur'd it.

I could not but observe that my young minion was as much spruced out as could be expected from one in his condition: a desire of pleasing that could not be indifferent to me, since it prov'd that I pleased him; which, I assure you, was now a point I was not above having in view.

His hair trimly dressed, clean linen, and, above all, a hale, ruddy, wholesome country look, made him out as pretty a piece of woman's meat as you could see, and I should have thought any one much out of taste that could not have made a hearty meal of such a morsel as nature seemed to have design'd for the highest diet of pleasure.

And why should I here suppress the delight I received from this amiable creature, in remarking each artless look, each motion of pure undissembled nature, betrayed by his wanton eyes; or shewing, transparently, the glow and suffusion of blood through his fresh, clear skin, whilst even his sturdy rustic pressures wanted not their peculiar charm? Oh! but, say you, this was a young fellow of too low a rank of life to deserve so great a display. May be so: but was my condition, strictly consider'd one jot more exalted? or, had I really been much above him, did not his capacity of giving such exquisite pleasure sufficiently raise and ennoble him, to *me*, at least? Let who would, for me, cherish, respect, and reward the painter's, the statuary's, the musician's arts, in proportion to delight taken in them: but at my age, and with my taste for pleasure, a taste strongly constitutional to me, the talent of pleasing, with which nature has endowed a handsome person, form'd to me the greatest of all merits; compared to which, the vulgar prejudices in favour of titles, dignities, honours, and the like, held a very low rank indeed. Nor perhaps would the beauties of the body be so much affected to be held cheap, were they, in their nature, to be bought and delivered. But for me, whose natural philosophy all resided in the favourite center of sense, and who was rul'd by its powerful instinct in taking pleasure by its right handle, I could scarce have made a choice more to my purpose.

Mr. H . . .'s loftier qualifications of birth, fortune and sense laid me under a sort of subjection and constraint that were far from making harmony in the concert of love; nor had he, perhaps, thought me worth softening that superiority to; but, with this lad, I was more on that level which love delights in.

We may say what we please, but those we can be the easiest and freest with are ever those we like, not to say love, the best.

With this stripling, all whose art of love was the action

of it, I could, without check of awe or restraint, give a
loose to joy, and execute every scheme of dalliance my
fond fancy might put me on, in which he was, in every
sense, a most exquisite companion. And now my great
pleasure lay in humouring all the petulances, all the wanton frolic of a raw novice just fleshed, and keen on the
burning scent of his game, but unbroken to the sport:
and, to carry on the figure, who could better THREAD THE
WOOD than he, or stand fairer for the HEART OF THE
HUNT?

He advanc'd then to my bed-side, and whilst he fal-
tered out his message, I could observe his colour rise, and
his eyes lighten with joy, in seeing me in a situation as
favourable to his loosest wishes as if he had bespoke the
play.

I smiled, and put out my hand towards him, which he
kneeled down to (a politeness taught him by love alone,
that great master of it) and greedily kiss'd. After exchanging a few confused questions and answers, I ask'd him if
he would come to bed to me, for the little time I could
venture to detain him. This was just asking a person, dying with hunger, to feast upon the dish on earth the most
to his palate. Accordingly, without further reflection, his
cloaths were off in an instant; when, blushing still more
at his new liberty, he got under the bed-cloaths I held up
to receive him, and was now in bed with a woman for the
first time in his life.

Here began the usual tender preliminaries, as delicious,
perhaps, as the crowning act of enjoyment itself; which
they often beget an impatience of, that makes pleasure
destructive of itself, by hurrying on the final period, and
closing that scene of bliss, in which the actors are generally too well pleas'd with their parts not to wish them an
eternity of duration.

When we had sufficiently graduated our advances towards the main point, by toying, kissing, clipping, feeling
my breasts, now round and plump, feeling that part of
me I might call a furnace-mouth, from the prodigious
intense heat his fiery touches had rekindled there, my
young sportsman, embolden'd by every freedom he could
wish, wantonly takes my hand, and carries it to that enor-

mous machine of his, that stood with a stiffness! a hardness! an upward bent of erection! and which, together
with its bottom dependence, the inestimable bulge of
lady's jewels, formed a grand show out of goods indeed!
Then its dimensions, mocking either grasp or span, almost
renew'd my terrors.

I could not conceive how, or by what means I could
take, or put such a bulk out of sight. I stroked it gently, on
which the mutinous rogue seemed to swell, and gather a
new degree of fierceness and insolence; so that finding it
grew not to be trifled with any longer, I prepar'd for rub-
bers in good earnest.

Slipping then a pillow under me, that I might give him
the fairest play, I guided officiously with my hand this
furious battering ram, whose ruby head, presenting nearest the resemblance of a heart, I applied to its proper
mark, which lay as finely elevated as we could wish; my
hips being borne up, and my thighs at their utmost extension, the gleamy warmth that shot from it made him
feel that he was at the mouth of the indraught, and driving foreright, the powerfully divided lips of that pleasure-
thirsty channel receiv'd him. He hesitated a little; then,
settled well in the passage, he makes his way up the straits
of it, with a difficulty nothing more than pleasing, widen-
ing as he went, so as to distend and smooth each soft furrow: our pleasure increasing deliciously, in proportion as
our points of mutual touch increas'd in that so vital part
of me in which I had now taken him, all indriven, and
completely sheathed; and which, crammed as it was,
stretched, splitting ripe, gave it so gratefully strait an
accommodation! so strick a fold! a suction so fierce! that
gave and took unutterable delight. We had now reach'd
the closest point of union; but when he backened to
come on the fiercer, as if I had been actuated by a fear
of losing him, in the height of my fury I twisted my legs
round his naked loins, the flesh of which, so firm, so
springy to the touch, quiver'd again under the pressure;
and now I had him every way encircled and begirt; and
having drawn him home to me, I kept him fast there, as
if I had sought to unite bodies with him at that point. This
bred a pause of action, a pleasure stop, whilst that delicate

glutton, my nethermouth, as full as it could hold, kept palating, with exquisite relish, the morsel that so deliciously ingorged it. But nature could not long endure a pleasure that so highly provoked without satisfying it: pursuing then its darling end, the battery recommenc'd with redoubled exertion; nor lay I inactive on my side, but encountering him with all the impetuosity of motion I was mistress of. The downy cloth of our meeting mounts was now of real use to break the violence of the tilt; and soon, too soon indeed! the highwrought agitation, the sweet urgency of this to-and-fro friction, raised the titillation on me to its height; so that finding myself on the point of going, and loath to leave the tender partner of my joys behind me, I employed all the forwarding motions and arts my experience suggested to me, to promote his keeping me company to our journey's end. I not only then tighten'd the pleasure-girth round my restless inmate by a secret spring of friction and compression that obeys the will in those parts, but stole my hand softly to that store bag of nature's prime sweets, which is so pleasingly attach'd to its conduit pipe, from which we receive them; there feeling, and most gently indeed, squeezing those tender globular reservoirs; the magic touch took instant effect, quicken'd, and brought on upon the spur the symptoms of that sweet agony, the melting moment of dissolution, when pleasure dies by pleasure, and the mysterious engine of it overcomes the titillation it has rais'd in those parts, by plying them with the stream of a warm liquid that is itself the highest of all titillations, and which they thirstily express and draw in like the hot-natured leach, which to cool itself, tenaciously attracts all the moisture within its sphere of exsuction. Chiming then to me, with exquisite consent, as I melted away, his oily balsamic injection, mixing deliciously with the sluices in flow from me, sheath'd and blunted all the stings of pleasure, it flung us into an extasy that extended us fainting, breathless, entranced. Thus we lay, whilst a voluptuous languor possest, and still maintain'd us motionless and fast locked in one another's arms. Alas! that these delights should be no longer-lived! for now the point of pleasure, unedged by enjoyment, and all the brisk sensations flatten'd upon us, resigned us up to the cool cares of insipid life. Disengaging myself then from his embrace, I made him sensible of the reasons there were for his present leaving me; on which, though reluctantly, he put on his cloaths with as little expedition, however, as he could help, wantonly interrupting himself, between whiles, with kisses, touches and embraces I could not refuse myself to. Yet he happily return'd to his master before he was missed; but, at taking leave, I forc'd him (for he had sentiments enough to refuse it) to receive money enough to buy a silver watch, that great article of subaltern finery, which he at length accepted of, as a remembrance he was carefully to preserve of my affections.

And here, Madam, I ought, perhaps, to make you an apology for this minute detail of things, that dwelt so strongly upon my memory, after so *deep* an impression: but, besides that this intrigue bred one great revolution in my life, which historical truth requires I should not sink from you, may I not presume that so exalted a pleasure ought not to be ungratefully forgotten, or suppress'd by me, because I found it in a character in low life; where, by the bye, it is oftener met with, purer, and more unsophisticate, that among the false, ridiculous refinements with which the great suffer themselves to be so grossly cheated by their pride: the great! than whom there exist few amongst those they call the vulgar, who are more ignorant of, or who cultivate less, the art of living than they do; they, I say, who for ever mistake things the most foreign of the nature of pleasure itself; whose capital favourite object is enjoyment of beauty, wherever that rare invaluable gift is found, without distinction of birth, or station.

As love never had, so now revenge had no longer any share in my commerce with this handsome youth. The sole pleasures of enjoyment were now the link I held to him by: for though nature had done such great matters for him in his outward form, and especially in that superb piece of furniture she had so liberally enrich'd him with; though he was thus qualify'd to give the senses their richest feast, still there was something more wanting to create in me, and constitute the passion of love. Yet Will had very good qualities too; gentle, tractable, and, above all, grateful; close, and secret, even to a fault: he spoke, at any time, very little, but made it up emphatically with action; and, to do him justice, he never gave me the least reason to complain, either of any tendency to encroach upon me for the liberties I allow'd him, or of his indiscretion in blabbing them. There is, then, a fatality in love, or have loved him I must; for he was really a treasure, a bit for the BONNE BOUCHE of a duchess; and, to say the truth, my liking for him was so extreme, that it was distinguishing very nicely to deny that I loved him.

My happiness, however, with him did not last long, but found an end from my own imprudent neglect. After having taken even superfluous precautions against a discovery, our success in repeated meetings embolden'd me to omit the barely necessary ones. About a month after our first intercourse, one fatal morning (the season Mr. H . . . rarely or never visited me in) I was in my closet, where my toilet stood, in nothing but my shift, a bed gown and under-petticoat. Will was with me, and both ever too well disposed to baulk an opportunity. For my part, a warm whim, a wanton toy had just taken me, and I had challeng'd my man to execute it on the spot, who hesitated not to comply with my humour: I was set in the arm-chair, my shift and petticoat up, my thighs wide spread and mounted over the arms of the chair, presenting the fairest mark to Will's drawn weapon, which he stood in act to plunge into me; when, having neglected to secure the chamber door, and that of the closet standing a-jar, Mr. H . . . stole in upon us before either of us was aware, and saw us precisely in these convicting attitudes.

I gave a great scream, and drop'd my petticoat: the thunder-struck lad stood trembling and pale, waiting his sentence of death. Mr. H . . . looked sometimes at one, sometimes at the other, with a mixture of indignation and scorn; and, without saying a word, turn'd upon his heel and went out.

As confused as I was, I heard him very distinctly turn the key, and lock the chamber-door upon us, so that there was no escape but through the dining-room, where he himself was walking about with distempered strides, stamping in a great chafe, and doubtless debating what he would do with us.

In the mean time, poor William was frightened out of his senses, and, as much need as I had of spirits to support myself, I was obliged to employ them all to keep his a little up. The misfortune I had now brought upon him, endear'd him the more to me, and I could have joyfully suffered any punishment he had not shared in. I water'd, plentifully, with my tears, the face of the frightened youth, who sat, not having strength to stand, as cold and as lifeless as a statue.

Presently Mr. H . . . comes in to us again, and made us go before him into the dining-room, trembling and dreading the issue. Mr. H . . . sat down on a chair whilst we stood like criminals under examination; and, beginning with me, ask'd me, with an even firm tone of voice, neither soft nor severe, but cruelly indifferent, what I could say for myself, for having abused him in so unworthy a manner, with his own servant too, and how he had deserv'd this of me?

Without adding to the guilt of my infidelity that of an audacious defence of it, in the old style of a common kept Miss, my answer was modest, and often interrupted by my tears, in substance as follows: that I never had a single thought of wronging him (which was true), till I had seen him taking the last liberties with my servant-wench (here he colour'd prodigiously), and that my resentment at that, which I was over-awed from giving vent to by complaints, or explanations with him, had driven me to a course that I did not pretend to justify; but that as to the young man, he was entirely faultless; for that, in the view of making him the instrument of my revenge, I had down-right seduced him to what he had done; and therefore hoped, whatever he determined about me, he would distinguish between the guilty and the innocent; and that, for the rest, I was entirely at his mercy.

Mr. H . . . , on hearing what I said, hung his head a little; but instantly recovering himself, he said to me, as near as I can retain, to the following purpose:

"Madam, I owe shame to myself, and confess you have

fairly turn'd the tables upon me. It is not with one of your cast of breeding and sentiments that I should enter into a discussion of the very great difference of the provocations: be it sufficient that I allow you so much reason on your side, as to have changed my resolutions, in consideration of what you reproach me with; and I own, too, that your clearing that rascal there, is fair and honest in you. Renew with you I cannot: the affront is too gross. I give you a week's warning to go out of these lodgings; whatever I have given you, remains to you; and as I never intend to see you more, the landlord will pay you fifty pieces on my account, with which, and every debt paid, I hope you will own I do not leave you in a worse condition than what I took you up in, or than you deserve of me. Blame yourself only that it is no better."

Then, without giving me time to reply, he address'd himself to the young fellow:

"For you, spark, I shall, for your father's sake, take care of you: the town is no place for such an easy fool as thou art; and to-morrow you shall set out, under the charge of one of my men, well recommended, in my name, to your father, not to let you return and be spoil'd here."

At these words he went out, after my vainly attempting to stop him by throwing myself at his feet. He shook me off, though he seemed greatly mov'd too, and took Will away with him, who, I dare swear, thought himself very cheaply off.

I was now once more a-drift, and left upon my own hands, by a gentleman whom I certainly did not deserve. And all the letters, arts, friends' entreaties that I employed within the week of grace in my lodging, could never win on him so much as to see me again. He had irrevocably pronounc'd my doom, and submission to it was my only part. Soon after he married a lady of birth and fortune, to whom, I have heard, he prov'd an irreproachable husband.

As for poor Will, he was immediately sent down to the country to his father, who was an easy farmer, where he was not four months before an inn-keeper's buxom young widow, with a very good stock, both in money and trade, fancy'd, and perhaps pre-acquainted with his secret excellencies, marry'd him: and I am sure there was, at least, one good foundation for their living happily together.

Though I should have been charm'd to see him before he went, such measures were taken, by Mr. H . . .'s orders, that it was impossible; otherwise I should certainly have endeavour'd to detain him in town, and would have spared neither offers nor expence to have procured myself the satisfaction of keeping him with me. He had such powerful holds upon my inclinations as were not easily to be shaken off, or replaced; as to my heart, it was quite out of the question: glad, however, I was from my soul, that nothing worse, and as things turn'd out, probably nothing better could have happened to him.

As to Mr. H . . . , though views of conveniency made me, at first, exert myself to regain his affection, I was giddy and thoughtless enough to be much easier reconcil'd to my failure than I ought to have been; but as I never had lov'd him, and his leaving me gave me a sort of liberty that I had often long'd for, I was soon comforted; and flattering myself that the stock of youth and beauty I was going into trade with could hardly fail of procuring me a maintenance, I saw myself under a necessity of trying my fortune with them, rather, with pleasure and gaiety, than with the least idea of despondency.

In the mean time, several of my acquaintances among the sisterhood, who had soon got wind of my misfortune, flocked to insult me with their malicious consolations. Most of them had long envied me the affluence and splendour I had been maintain'd in; and though there was scarce one of them that did not at least deserve to be in my case, and would probably, sooner or later, come to it, it was equally easy to remark, even in their affected pity, their secret pleasure at seeing me thus disgrac'd and discarded, and their secret grief that it was no worse with me. Unaccountable malice of the human heart! and which is not confin'd to the class of life they were of.

But as the time approached for me to come to some resolution how to dispose of myself, and I was considering round where to shift my quarters to, *Mrs. Cole*, a middle-aged discreet sort of woman, who had been brought into my acquaintance by one of the Misses that visited me, upon learning my situation, came to offer her cordial advice and service to me; and as I had always taken to her more than to any of my female acquaintances, I listened the easier to her proposals. And, as it happened, I could not have put myself into worse, or into better hands in all London: into worse, because keeping a house of conveniency, there were no lengths in lewdness she would not advise me to go, in compliance with her customers; no schemes of pleasure, or even unbounded debauchery, she did not take even a delight in promoting: into a better, because nobody having had more experience of the wicked part of the town than she had, was fitter to advise and guard one against the worst dangers of our profession; and what was rare to be met with in those of her's, she contented herself with a moderate living profit upon her industry and good offices, and had nothing of their greedy rapacious turn. She was really too a gentlewoman born and bred, but through a train of accidents reduc'd to this course, which she pursued, partly through necessity, partly through choice, as never woman delighted more in encouraging a brisk circulation of trade for the sake of the trade itself, or better understood all the mysteries and refinements of it, than she did; so that she was consummately at the top of her profession, and dealt only with customers of distinction: to answer the demands of whom she kept a competent number of her daughters in constant recruit (so she call'd those whom their youth and personal charms recommended to her adoption and management: several of whom by her means, and through her tuition and instructions, succeeded very well in the world).

This useful gentlewoman upon whose protection I now threw myself, having her reasons of state, respecting Mr. H . . . , for not appearing too much in the thing herself, sent a friend of her's, on the day appointed for my removal, to conduct me to my new lodgings at a brushmaker's in R*** *street, Covent Garden*, the very next door to her own house, where she had no conveniences to lodge me herself: lodgings that, by having been for several successions tenanted by ladies of pleasure, the landlord of them was familiarized to their ways; and provided the rent was duly paid, every thing else was as easy and commodious as one could desire.

The fifty guineas promis'd me by Mr. H . . . , at his parting with me, having been duly paid me, all my cloaths and moveables chested up, which were at least of two hundred pounds' value, I had them convey'd into a coach, where I soon followed them, after taking a civil leave of the landlord and his family, with whom I had never liv'd in a degree of familiarity enough to regret the removal; but still, the very circumstance of its being a removal drew tears from me. I left, too, a letter of thanks for Mr. H . . . , from whom I concluded myself, as I really was, irretrievably separated.

My maid I had discharged the day before, not only because I had her of Mr. H . . . , but that I suspected her of having some how or other been the occasion of his discovering me, in revenge, perhaps, for my not having trusted her with him.

We soon got to my lodgings, which, though not so handsomely furnish'd nor so showy as those I left, were to the full as convenient, and at half price, though on the first floor. My trunks were safely landed, and stow'd in my apartments, where my neighbour, and now *gouvernante*, Mrs. Cole, was ready with my landlord to receive me, to whom she took care to set me out in the most favourable light, that of one from whom there was the clearest reason to expect the regular payment of his rent: all the cardinal virtues attributed to me would not have had half the weight of that recommendation alone.

I was now settled in lodgings of my own, abandon'd to my own conduct, and turned loose upon the town, to sink or swim, as I could manage with the current of it; and what were the consequences, together with the number of adventures which befell me in the exercise of my new profession, will compose the matter of another letter: for surely it is high time to put a period to this.

I am,

MADAM,

Yours, etc., etc., etc.

THE END OF THE FIRST LETTER

there exist as slender motives of attachment that, gathering force from habit and liking, have proved often more solid and durable than those founded on much stronger reasons; but this I know, that tho' I had no other acquaintance with her than seeing her at my lodgings when I lived with Mr. H . . . , where she had made errands to sell me some millinery ware, she had by degrees insinuated herself so far into my confidence that I threw myself blindly into her hands, and came, at length, to regard, love, and obey her implicitly; and, to do her justice, I never experienc'd at her hands other than a sincerity of tenderness, and care for my interest, hardly heard of in those of her profession. We parted that night, after having settled a perfect unreserv'd agreement; and the next morning Mrs. Cole came, and took me with her to her house for the first time.

Here, at the first sight of things, I found everything breath'd an air of decency, modesty and order.

In the outer parlour, or rather shop, sat three young women, very demurely employ'd on millinery work, which was the cover of a traffic in more precious commodities; but three beautifuller creatures could hardly be seen. Two of them were extremely fair, the eldest not above nineteen; and the third, much about that age, was a piquant brunette, whose black sparkling eyes, and perfect harmony of features and shape, left her nothing to envy in her fairer companions. Their dress too had the more design in it, the less it appeared to have, being in a taste of uniform correct neatness, and elegant simplicity. These were the girls that composed the small domestick flock, which my governess train'd up with surprising order and management, considering the giddy wildness of young girls once got upon the loose. But then she never continued any in her house, whom, after a due novitiate, she found untractable, or unwilling to comply with the rules of it. Thus had she insensibly formed a little family of love, in which the members found so sensibly their account, in a rare alliance of pleasure with interest, and of a necessary outward decency with unbounded secret liberty, that Mrs. Cole, who had pick'd them as much for

their temper as their beauty, govern'd them with ease to
herself and them too.

To these pupils then of hers, whom she had prepar'd,
she presented me as a new boarder, and one that was to
be immediately admitted to all the intimacies of the
house; upon which these charming girls gave me all the
marks of a welcome reception, and indeed of being perfectly pleased with my figure, that I could possibly expect
from any of my own sex: but they had been effectually
brought to sacrifice all jealousy, or competition of charms,
to a common interest, and consider'd me a partner that
was bringing no despicable stock of goods into the trade
of the house. They gathered round me, view'd me on all
sides; and as my admission into this joyous troop made
a little holiday the shew of work was laid aside; and Mrs.
Cole giving me up, with special recommendation, to their
caresses and entertainment, went about her ordinary business of the house.

The sameness of our sex, age, profession, and views
soon created as unreserv'd a freedom and intimacy as if
we had been for years acquainted. They took and shew'd
me the house their respective apartments, which were
furnished with every article of conveniency and luxury;
and above all, a spacious drawing-room, where a select
revelling band usually met, in general parties of pleasure;
the girls supping with their sparks, and acting their wanton pranks with unbounded licentiousness; whilst a defiance of awe, modesty or jealousy were their standing
rules by which, according to the principles of their society, whatever pleasure was lost on the side of sentiment
was abundantly made up to the senses in the poignancy
of variety and the charms of ease and luxury. The au-
thors and supporters of this secret institution would, in
the height of their humours style themselves the restor-
ers of the golden age and its simplicity of pleasures, before
their innocence became so injustly branded with the
names of guilt and shame.

As soon then as the evening began, and the shew of a
shop was shut, the academy open'd; the mask of mock-
modesty was completely taken off, and all the girls de-

liver'd over to their respective calls of pleasure or interest with their men; and none of that sex was promiscuously admitted, but only such as Mrs. Cole was previously satisfied with their character and discretion. In short, this was the safest, politest, and, at the same time, the most thorough house of accommodation in town: every thing being conducted so that decency made no intrenchment upon the most libertine pleasures, in the practice of which too, the choice familiars of the house had found the secret so rare and difficult, of reconciling even all the refinements of taste and delicacy with the most gross and determinate gratifications of sensuality.

After having consum'd the morning in the endearments and instructions of my new acquaintance, we went to dinner, when Mrs. Cole, presiding at the head of her club, gave me the first idea of her management and address, in inspiring these girls with so sensible a love and respect for her. There was no stiffness, no reserve, no airs of pique, or little jealousies, but all was unaffectedly gay, cheerful and easy.

After dinner, Mrs. Cole, seconded by the young ladies, acquainted me that there was a chapter to be held that night in form, for the ceremony of my reception into the sisterhood; and in which, with all due reserve to my maidenhead that was to be occasionally cook'd up for the first proper chapman, I was to undergo a ceremonial of initation they were sure I should not be displeased with.

Embark'd as I was, and moreover captivated with the charms of my new companions, I was too much prejudic'd in favour of any proposal they could make, to much as hesitate an assent; which, therefore, readily giving in the style of a *carte blanche*, I receiv'd fresh kisses of compliment from them all, in approval of my docility and good nature. Now I was "a sweet girl . . ." I came into things with a "good grace . . ." I was not "affectedly coy . . ." I should be "the pride of the house . . ." and the like.

This point thus adjusted, the young women left Mrs. Cole to talk and concert matters with me: she explained to me that I should be introduc'd, that very evening, to four of her best friends, one of whom she had, according

to the custom of the house, favoured with the preference
of engaging me in the first party of pleasure; assuring me,
at the same time, that they were all young gentlemen
agreeable in their persons, and unexceptionable in every
respect; that united, and holding together by the band of
common pleasures, they composed the chief support of
her house, and made very liberal presents to the girls that
pleas'd and humour'd them, so that they were, properly
speaking, the founders and patrons of this little seraglio.
Not but that she had, at proper seasons, other customers
to deal with, whom she stood less upon punctilio with
than with these; for instance, it was not on one of them
she could attempt to pass me for a maid; they were not
only too knowing, too much town-bred to bite at such a
bait, but they were such generous benefactors to her that
it would be unpardonable to think of it.

Amidst all the flutter and emotion which this promise
of pleasure, for such I conceiv'd it, stirr'd up in me, I preserved so much of the woman as to feign just reluctance
enough to make some merit of sacrificing it to the influence of my patroness, whom I likewise, still in character,
reminded of it perhaps being right for me to go home and
dress, in favour of my first impressions.

But Mrs. Cole, in opposition to this, assured me that
the gentlemen I should be presented to were, by their
rank and taste of things, infinitely superior to the being
touched with any glare of dress or ornaments, such as silly
women rather confound and overlay than set off their
beauty with; that these veteran voluptuaries knew better
than not to hold them in the highest contempt: they with
whom the pure native charms alone could pass current,
and who would at any time leave a sallow, washy, painted
duchess on her own hands, for a ruddy, healthy, firm-
flesh'd country maid; and as for my part, that nature had
done enough for me, to set me above owing the least
favour to art; concluding withal, that for the instant occasion, there was no dress like an undress.

I thought my governess too good a judge of these matters not to be easily over-ruled by her: after which she
went on preaching very pathetically the doctrine of pas-

sive obedience and non-resistance to all those arbitrary tastes of pleasure, which are by some styl'd the refinements, and by others the depravations of it; between whom it was not the business of a simple girl, who was to profit by pleasing, to decide, but to conform to. Whilst I was edifying by these wholesome lessons, tea was brought in, and the young ladies, returning, joined company with us.

After a great deal of mix'd chat, frolic and humour, one of them, observing that there would be a good deal of time on hand before the assembly-hour, proposed that each girl should entertain the company with that critical period of her personal history in which she first exchanged the maiden state for womanhood. The proposal was approv'd, with only one restriction of Mrs. Cole, that she, on account of her age, and I, on account of my titular maidenhead, should be excused, at least till I had undergone the forms of the house. This obtain'd me a dispensation, and the promotress of this amusement was desired to begin.

Her name was *Emily;* a girl fair to excess, and whose limbs were, if possible, too well made, since their plump fulness was rather to the prejudice of that delicate slimness requir'd by the nicer judges of beauty; her eyes were blue, and streamed inexpressible sweetness, and nothing could be prettier than her mouth and lips, which clos'd over a range of the evenest and whitest teeth. Thus she began:

"Neither my extraction, nor the most critical adventure of my life, is sublime enough to impeach me of any vanity in the advancement of the proposal you have approv'd of. My father and mother were, and for aught I know, are still, farmers in the country, not above forty miles from town: their barbarity to me, in favour of a son, on whom only they vouchsafed to bestow their tenderness, had a thousand times determined me to fly their house, and throw myself on the wide world; but, at length, an accident forc'd me on this desperate attempt at the age of fifteen. I had broken a china-bowl, the pride and idol of both their hearts; and as an unmerciful beating was the least

I had to depend on at their hands, in the silliness of those
tender years I left the house, and, at all adventures, took
the road to London. How my loss was resented I do not
know, for till this instant I have not heard a syllable about
them. My whole stock was two broad pieces of my god-
mother's, a few shillings, silver shoe-buckles and a silver
thimble. Thus equipp'd, with no more cloaths than the
ordinary ones I had on my back, and frighten'd at every
foot or noise I heard behind me, I hurried on; and I dare
swear, walked a dozen miles before I stopped, through
mere weariness and fatigue. At length I sat down on a
stile, wept bitterly, and yet was still rather under increased
impressions of fear on the account of my escape; which
made me dread, worse than death, the going back to face
my unnatural parents. Refresh'd by this little repose, and
relieved by my tears, I was proceeding onward, when I
was overtaken by a sturdy country lad who was going to
London to see what he could do for himself there, and,
like me, had given his friends the slip. He could not be
above seventeen, was ruddy, well featur'd enough, with
uncomb'd flaxen hair, a little flapp'd hat, kersey frock,
yearn stockings, in short, a perfect ploughboy. I saw
him come whistling behind me, with a bundle tied to the
end of a stick, his travelling equipage. We walk'd by one
another for some time without speaking; at length we
joined company, and agreed to keep together till we got
to our journey's end. What his designs or ideas were, I
know not: the innocence of mine I can solemnly protest.

"As night drew on, it became us to look out for some
inn or shelter; to which perplexity another was added,
and that was, what we should say for ourselves, if we were
question'd. After some puzzle, the young fellow started a
proposal, which I thought the finest that could be; and
what was that? why, that we should pass for husband and
wife: I never once dream'd of consequences. We came
presently, after having agreed on this notable expedient,
to one of those hedge-accommodations for foot passengers, at the door of which stood an old crazy beldam,
who seeing us trudge by, invited us to lodge there. Glad
of any cover, we went in, and my fellow traveller, taking

all upon him, call'd for what the house afforded, and we supped together as man and wife; which, considering our figures and ages, could not have passed on any one but such as any thing could pass on. But when bedtime came on, we had neither of us the courage to contradict our first account of ourselves; and what was extremely pleasant, the young lad seem'd as perplex'd as I was, how to evade lying together, which was so natural for the state we had pretended to. Whilst we were in this quandary, the landlady takes the candle and lights us to our apartment, through a long yard, at the end of which it stood, separate from the body of the house. Thus we suffer'd ourselves to be conducted, without saying a word in opposition to it; and there, in a wretched room, with a bed answerable, we were left to pass the night together, as a thing quite of course. For my part, I was so incredibly innocent as not even then to think much more harm of going into bed with the young man than with one of our dairy-wenches; nor had he, perhaps, any other notions than those of innocence, till such a fair occasion put them into his head.

"Before either of us undressed, however, he put out the candle; and the bitterness of the weather made it a kind of necessity for me to go into bed: slipping then my cloaths off, I crept under the bed-cloaths, where I found the young stripling already nestled, and the touch of his warm flesh rather pleas'd than alarm'd me. I was indeed too much disturbed with the novelty of my condition to be able to sleep; but then I had not the least thought of harm. But, oh! how powerful are the instincts of nature! how little is there wanting to set them in action! The young man, sliding his arm under my body, drew me gently towards him, as if to keep himself and me warmer; and the heat I felt from joining our breasts, kindled another that I had hitherto never felt, and was, even then, a stranger to the nature of. Emboldened, I suppose, by my easiness, he ventur'd to kiss me, and I insensibly returned it, without knowing the consequence of returning it: for, on this encouragement, he slipped his hand all down from my breast to that part of me where the sense of feeling is so exquisitely critical, as I then experienc'd by its instant taking fire upon the touch, and glowing with a strange tickling heat: there he pleas'd himself and me, by feeling, till, growing a little too bold, he hurt me, and made me complain. Then he took my hand, which he guided, not unwillingly on my side, between the twist of his closed thighs, which were extremely warm; there he lodged and pressed it, till raising it by degrees, he made me feel the proud distinction of his sex from mine. I was frighten'd at the novelty, and drew back my hand; yet, pressed and spurred on by sensations of a strange pleasure, I could not help asking him what that was for? He told me he would show me if I would let him; and, without waiting for my answer, which he prevented by stopping my mouth with kisses I was far from disrelishing, he got upon me, and inserting one of his thighs between mine, opened them so as to make way for himself, and fixed me to his purpose; whilst I was so much out of my usual sense, so subdu'd by the present power of a new one, that, between fear and desire, I lay utterly passive, till the piercing pain rous'd and made me cry out. But it was too late: he was too firm fix'd in the saddle for me to compass flinging him, with all the struggles I could use, some of which only served to further his point, and at length an irresistible thrust murdered at once my maidenhead, and almost me. I now lay a bleeding witness of the necessity impos'd on our sex, to gather the first honey off the thorns.

"But the pleasure rising as the pain subsided, I was soon reconciled to fresh trials, and before morning, nothing on earth could be dearer to me than this rifler of my virgin sweets: he was every thing to me now. How we agreed to join fortunes; how we came up to town together, where we lived some time, till necessity parted us, and drove me into this course of life, in which I had been long ago battered and torn to pieces before I came to this age, as much through my easiness, as through my inclination, had it not been for my finding refuge in this house: these are all circumstances which pass the mark I proposed, so that here my narrative ends."

In the order of our sitting, it was *Harriet's* turn to go on. Amongst all the beauties of our sex that I had before or have since seen, few indeed were the forms that could dispute excellence with her's; it was not delicate, but delicacy itself incarnate, such was the symmetry of her small but exactly fashion'd limbs. Her complexion, fair as it was, appeared yet more fair from the effect of two black eyes, the brilliancy of which gave her face more vivacity than belonged to the colour of it, which was only defended from paleness by a sweetly pleasing blush in her cheeks, that grew fainter and fainter, till at length it died away insensibly into the overbearing white. Then her miniature features join'd to finish the extreme sweetness of it, which was not belied by that of temper turned to indolence, languor, and the pleasures of love. Press'd to subscribe her contingent, she smiled, blushed a little, and thus complied with our desires:

"My father was neither better nor worse than a miller near the city of *York;* and both he and my mother dying whilst I was an infant, I fell under the care of a widow and childless aunt, housekeeper to my lord N . . . , at his seat in the county of . . . , where she brought me up with all imaginable tenderness. I was not seventeen, as I am not now eighteen, before I had, on account of my person purely (for fortune I had notoriously none), several advantageous proposals; but whether nature was slow in making me sensible in her favourite passion, or that I had not seen any of the other sex who had stirr'd up the least emotion or curiosity to be better acquainted with it, I had, till that age, preserv'd a perfect innocence, even of thought: whilst my fears of I did not well know what, made me no more desirous of marrying than of dying. My aunt, good woman, favoured my timorousness, which she look'd on as childish affection, that her own experience might probably assure her would wear off in time, and gave my suitors proper answers for me.

"The family had not been down at that seat for years, so that it was neglected, and committed entirely to my aunt, and two old domestics to take care of it. Thus I had the full range of a spacious lonely house and gardens, situate at about half a mile distance from any other habitation, except, perhaps, a straggling cottage or so.

"Here, in tranquillity and innocence, I grew up without any memorable accident, till one fatal day I had, as I had often done before, left my aunt fast asleep, and secure for some hours, after dinner; and resorting to a kind of ancient summer-house, at some distance from the house, I carried my work with me, and sat over a rivulet, which its door and window fac'd upon. Here I fell into a gentle breathing slumber, which stole upon my senses, as they fainted under the excessive heat of the season at that hour; a cane couch, with my work-basket for a pillow, were all the conveniences of my short repose; for I was soon awaked and alarmed by a flounce, and noise of splashing in the water. I got up to see what was the matter; and what indeed should it be but the son of a neighbouring gentleman, as I afterwards found (for I had never seen him before), who had strayed that way with his gun, and heated by his sport, and the sultriness of the day, had been tempted by the freshness of the clear stream; so that presently stripping, he jump'd into it on the other side, which bordered on a wood, some trees whereof, inclined down to the water, form'd a pleasing shady recess, commodious to undress and leave his clothes under.

"My first emotions at the sight of this youth, naked in the water, were, with all imaginable respect to truth, those of surprise and fear; and, in course, I should immediately have run out, had not my modesty, fatally for itself, interposed the objection of the door and window being so situated that it was scarce possible to get out, and make my way along the bank to the house, without his seeing me: which I could not bear the thought of, so much ashamed and confounded was I at having seen him. Condemn'd then to stay till his departure should release me, I was greatly embarrassed how to dispose of myself: I kept some time betwixt terror and modesty, even from looking through the window, which being an old-fashion'd casement, without any light behind me, could hardly betray any one's being there to him from within; then the door was so secure, that without violence, or my own consent, there was no opening it from without.

"But now, by my own experience, I found it too true that objects which affright us, when we cannot get from them, draw our eyes as forcibly as those that please us. I could not long withstand that nameless impulse, which, without any desire of this novel sight, compelled me towards it; embloden'd too by my certainty of being at once unseen and safe, I ventur'd by degrees to cast my eyes on an object so terrible and alarming to my virgin modesty as a naked man. But as I snatched a look, the first gleam that struck me was in general the dewy lustre of the whitest skin imaginable, which the sun playing upon made the reflection of it perfectly beamy. His face, in the confusion I was in, I could not well distinguish the lineaments of, any farther than that there was a great deal of youth and freshness in it. The frolic and various play of all his polish'd limbs, as they appeared above the surface, in the course of his swimming or wantoning with the water, amus'd and insensibly delighted me: sometimes he lay motionless, on his back, waterborne, and dragging after him a f‍‍ head of hair, that, floating, swept the stream in a bush urls. Then the overflowing water would make een his breast and glossy white belly; I could not escape observing lack mossy tuft, out softish, limber, with ever the l but that part tracted, deta the power o from it; and ance, I ins they gave and I m long lai made his p with

to effe
as mine,
few moments
green borders
round for the young
and concern sunk me
have lasted me some time;
till I was rous'd out of it by
me to the young
circumstance of finding myself not on
this very same young gentleman I had bee

not have been cast, whilst his floating locks played over
a neck and shoulders whose whiteness they delightfully
set off. Then the luxuriant swell of flesh that rose from
the small of his back, and terminated its double cope at
where the thighs are sent off, perfectly dazzled one with
its watery glistening gloss.

"By this time I was so affected by this inward involu-
tion of sentiments, so soften'd by this sight, that now,
betrayed into a sudden transition from extreme fears to
extreme desires, I found these last so strong upon me, the
heat of the weather too perhaps conspiring to exalt their
rage, that nature almost fainted under them. Not that I so
much as knew precisely what was wanting to me: my
only thought was that so sweet a creature as this youth
seemed to me could only make me happy; but then, the
little likelihood there was of compassing an acquaintance
with him, or perhaps of ever seeing him again, dash'd my
desires, and turn'd them into torments. I was still gazing,
with all the powers of my sight, on this bewitching object,
when, in an instant, down he went. I had heard of such
things as a cramp seizing on even the best swimmers, and
occasioning their being drowned; and imagining this so
sudden eclipse to be owing to it, the inconceivable fondness this unknown lad had given birth to distracted me
with the most killing terrors; insomuch, that my concern
giving the wings, I flew to the door, open'd it, ran down
to the canal, guided thither by the madness of my fears
for him, and the intense desire of being an instrument
save him, though I was ignorant how, or by what means
it: but was it for fears, and a passion so sudden
reason? All this took up scarce the space of a
I had then just life enough to reach the
the waterpiece, where wildly looking
an, and missing him still, my fright
in a deep swoon, which must
for I did not come to myself
nse of pain that pierced
the most surprising
in the arms of
so solicitous

to save, but taken at such an advantage in my unresisting
condition that he had actually completed his entrance
into me so far, that weakened as I was by all the preceding
conflicts of mind I had suffer'd, and struck dumb by the
violence of my surprise, I had neither the power to cry
out, nor the strength to disengage myself from his strenuous embraces, before, urging his point, he had forced
his way and completely triumphed over my virginity, as
he might now as well see by the streams of blood that
follow'd his drawing out, as he had felt by the difficulties
he had met with consummating his penetration. But the
sight of the blood, and the sense of my condition, had (as
he told me afterwards), since the ungovernable rage of
his passion was somewhat appeas'd, now wrought so far
on him that at all risks, even of the worst consequences,
he could not find in his heart to leave me, and make off,
which he might easily have done. I still lay all discompos'd
in bleeding ruin, palpitating, speechless, unable to get
off, and frightened, and fluttering like a poor wounded
partridge, and ready to faint away again at the sense of
what had befallen me. The young gentleman was by me,
kneeling, kissing my hand, and with tears in his eyes beseeching me to forgive him, and offering all the reparation
in his power. It is certain that could I, at the instant of
regaining my senses, have called out, or taken the blood-
iest revenge, I would not have stuck at it: the violation
was attended too with such aggravating circumstances,
though he was ignorant of them, since it was to my concern for the preservation of his life that I owed my ruin.

"But how quick is the shift of passions from one extreme to another! and how little are they acquainted with
the human heart who dispute it! I could not see this amiable criminal, so suddenly the first object of my love,
and as suddenly of my just hate, on his knees, bedewing
my hand with his tears, without relenting. He was still
stark-naked, but my modesty had been already too much
wounded, in essentials, to be so much shocked as I should
have otherwise been with appearances only; in short, my
anger ebbed so fast, and the tide of love return'd so strong
upon me, that I felt it a point of my own happiness to

forgive him. The reproaches I made him were murmur'd
in so soft a tone, my eyes met his with such glances, expressing more languor than resentment, that he could not
but presume his forgiveness was at no desperate distance;
but still he would not quit his posture of submission, till
I had pronounced his pardon in form; which after the
most fervent entreaties, protestations, and promises, I had
not the power to withhold. On which, with the utmost
marks of a fear of again offending, he ventured to kiss my
lips, which I neither declined nor resented: but on my
mild expostulations with him upon the barbarity of his
treatment, he explain'd the mystery of my ruin, if not
entirely to the clearance, at least much to the alleviation
of his guilt, in the eyes of a judge so partial in his favour
as I was grown.

"It seems that the circumstance of his going down, or
sinking, which in my extreme ignorance I had mistaken
for something very fatal, was no other than a trick of div-
ing which I had not ever heard, or at least attended to,
the mention of: and he was so long-breath'd at it, that in
the few moments in which I ran out to save him, he had
not yet emerged, before I fell into the swoon, in which,
as he rose, seeing me extended on the bank, his first idea
was that some young woman was upon some design of
frolic or diversion with him, for he knew I could not have
fallen a-sleep there without his having seen me before:
agreeably to which notion he had ventured to approach,
and finding me without sign of life, and still perplex'd
as he was what to think of the adventure, he took me in
his arms at all hazards, and carried me into the summer-
house, of which he observed the door open: there he laid
me down on the couch, and tried, as he protested in good
faith, by several means to bring me to myself again, till
fired, as he said, beyond all bearing by the sight and
touch of several parts of me which were unguardedly
exposed to him, he could no longer govern his passion;
and the less, as he was not quite sure that his first idea
of this swoon being a feint was not the very truth of the
case: seduced then by this flattering notion, and overcome
by the present, as he styled them, superhuman tempta-

tions, combined with the solitude and seeming security of the attempt, he was not enough his own master not to make it. Leaving me then just only whilst he fastened the door, he returned with redoubled eagerness to his prey: when, finding me still entranced, he ventured to place me as he pleased, whilst I felt, no more than the dead, what he was about, till the pain he put me to roused me just in time enough to be witness of a triumph I was not able to defeat, and now scarce regretted: for as he talked, the tone of his voice sounded, methought, so sweetly in my ears, the sensible nearness of so new and interesting an object to me wrought so powerfully upon me, that, in the rising perception of things in a new and pleasing light, I lost all sense of the past injury. The young gentleman soon discern'd the symptoms of a reconciliation in my softened looks, and hastening to receive the seal of it from my lips, press'd them tenderly to pass his pardon in the return of a kiss so melting fiery, that the impression of it being carried to my heart, and thence to my new-discover'd sphere of Venus, I was melted into a softness that could refuse him nothing. When now he managed his caresses and endearments so artfully as to insinuate the most soothing consolations for the past pain and the most pleasing expectations of future pleasure, but whilst mere modesty kept my eyes' from seeing his and rather declined them, I had a glimpse of that instrument of the mischief which was now, obviously even to me, who had scarce had snatches of a comparative observation of it, resuming its capacity to renew it, and grew greatly alarming with its increase of size, as he bore it no doubt designedly, hard and stiff against one of my hands carelessly dropt; but then he employ'd such tender prefacing, such winning progressions, that my returning passion of desire being now so strongly prompted by the engaging circumstances of the sight and incendiary touch of his naked glowing beauties, I yielded at length at the force of the present impressions, and he obtained of my tacit blushing consent all the gratifications of pleasure left in the power of my poor person to bestow, after he had cropt its richest flower, during my suspension of life and abilities to guard it.

"Here, according to the rule laid down, I should stop; but I am so much in motion, that I could not if I would. I shall only add, however, that I got home without the least discovery, or suspicion of what had happened. I met my young ravisher several times after, whom I now passionately lov'd and who, tho' not of age to claim a small but independent fortune, would have married me; but as the accidents that prevented it, and their consequences which threw me on the publick, contain matters too moving and serious to introduce at present, I cut short here."

Louisa, the brunette whom I mentioned at first, now took her turn to treat the company with her history. I have already hinted to you the graces of her person, than which nothing could be more exquisitely touching; I repeat touching, as a just distinction from striking, which is ever a less lasting effect, and more generally belongs to the fair complexions: but leaving that decision to every one's taste, I proceed to give you Louisa's narrative as follows:

"According to practical maxims of life, I ought to boast of my birth, since I owe it to pure love, without marriage; but this I know, it was scarce possible to inherit a stronger propensity to that cause of my being than I did. I was the rare production of the first essay of a journeyman cabinetmaker on his master's maid: the consequence of which was a big belly, and the loss of a place. He was not in circumstances to do much for her; and yet, after all this blemish, she found means, after she had dropt her burthen and disposed of me to a poor relation's in the country, to repair it by marrying a pastry-cook here in London, in thriving business; on whom she soon, under favour of the complete ascendant he had given her over him, passed me for a child she had by her first husband. I had, on that footing, been taken home, and was not six years old when this step-father died and left my mother in tolerable circumstances, and without any children by him. As to my natural father, he had betaken himself to the sea; where, when the truth of things came

out, I was told that he died, not immensely rich you may
think, since he was no more than a common sailor. As I
grew up, under the eyes of my mother, who kept on the
business, I could not but see, in her severe watchfulness,
the marks of a slip which she did not care should be hered-
itary, but we no more choose our passions than our features or complexion, and the bent of mine was so strong
to the forbidden pleasure, that it got the better, at length,
of all her care and precaution. I was scarce twelve years
old before that part which she wanted so much to keep
out of harm's way made me feel its impatience to be taken
notice of, and come into play: already had it put forth the
signs of forwardness in the sprout of a soft down over it,
which had often flatter'd, and I might also say, grown
under my constant touch and visitation, so pleas'd was I
with what I took to be a kind of title to womanhood, that
state I pin'd to be entr'd of, for the pleasures I conceiv'd
were annexed to it; and now the growing importance of
that part to me, and the new sensations in it, demolish'd
at once all my girlish playthings and amusements. Nature
now pointed me strongly to more solid diversions, while
all the stings of desire settled so fiercely in that little centre of them, that I could not mistake the spot I wanted a
playfellow in.

"I now shunn'd all company in which there was no
hopes of coming at the object of my longings, and used
to shut myself up, to indulge in solitude some tender
meditation on the pleasures I strongly perceiv'd the overture of, in feeling and examining what nature assur'd me
must be the chosen avenue, the gates for unknown bliss
to enter at, that I panted after.

"But these meditations only increas'd my disorder, and
blew the fire that consumed me. I was yet worse when,
yielding at length to the insupportable irritations of the
little fairy charm that tormented me, I seiz'd it with my
fingers, teasing it to no end. Sometimes, in the furious
excitations of desire, I threw myself on the bed, spread
my thighs abroad, and lay as it were expecting the longed-
for relief, till finding my illusion, I shut and squeez'd
them together again, burning and fretting. In short, this

dev'lish thing, with its impetuous girds and itching fires, led me such a life that I could neither night nor day be at peace with it or myself. In time, however, I thought I had gained a prodigious prize, when figuring to myself that my fingers were some thing of the shape of what I pined for, I worked my way in for one of them with great agitation and delight; yet not without pain too did I deflower myself as far as it could reach; proceeding with such a fury of passion, in this solitary and last shift of pleasure, as extended me at length breathless on the bed in an amorous melting trance.

"But frequency of use dulling the sensation, I soon began to perceive that this work was but a paltry shallow expedient that went but a little way to relieve me, and rather rais'd more flame than its dry and insignificant titillation could rightly appease.

"Man alone, I almost instinctively knew, as well as by what I had industriously picked up at weddings and christenings, was possess'd of the only remedy that could reduce this rebellious disorder; but watch'd and overlook'd as I was, how to come at it was the point, and that, to all appearance, an invincible one; not that I did not rack my brains and invention how at once to elude my mother's vigilance, and procure myself the satisfaction of my impetuous curiosity and longings for this mighty and untasted pleasure. At length, however, a singular chance did at once the work of a long course of alertness. One day that we had dined at an acquaintance's over the way, together with a gentlewoman-lodger that occupied the first floor of our house, there started an indispensable necessity for my mother's going down to *Greenwich* to accompany her: the party was settled, when I do not know what genius whispered me to plead a headache, which I certainly had not, against my being included in a jaunt that I had not the least relish for. The pretext however passed, and my mother, with much reluctance, prevailed with herself to go without me; but took particular care to see me safe home, where she consign'd me into the hands of an old trusty maid-servant, who served in the shop, for we had not a male creature in the house.

"As soon as she was gone, I told the maid I would go up and lie down on our lodger's bed, mine not being made, with a charge to her at the same time not to disturb me, as it was only rest I wanted. This injunction probably prov'd of eminent service to me. As soon as I was got into the bed-chamber, I unlaced my stays, and threw myself on the outside of the bed-cloaths, in all the loosest undress. Here I gave myself up to the old insipid privy shifts of my self-viewing, self-touching, self-enjoying, *in fine*, to all the means of *self-knowledge* I could devise, in search of the pleasure that fled before me, and tantalized with that unknown something that was out of my reach; thus all only serv'd to enflame myself, and to provoke violently my desires, whilst the one thing needful to their satisfaction was not at hand, and I could have bit my fingers, for representing it so ill. After then wearying and fatiguing myself with grasping shadows, whilst that most sensible part of me disdain'd to content itself with less than realities, the strong yearnings, the urgent struggles of nature towards the melting relief, and the extreme self-agitations I had used to come at it, had wearied and thrown me into a kind of unquiet sleep: for, if I tossed and threw about my limbs in proportion to the distraction of my dreams, as I had reason to believe I did, a bystander could not have help'd seeing all for love. And one there was it seems; for waking out of my very short slumber, I found my hand lock'd in that of a young man, who was kneeling at my bed-side, and begging my pardon for his boldness: but that being a son to the lady to whom this bed-chamber, he knew, belonged, he had slipp'd by the servant of the shop, as he supposed, unperceiv'd, when finding me asleep, his first ideas were to withdraw; but that he had been fix'd and detain'd there by a power he could better account for than resist.

"What shall I say? my emotions of fear and surprize were instantly subdued by those of the pleasure I bespoke in great presence of mind from the turn this adventure might take. He seem'd to me no other than a pitying angel, dropt out of the clouds: for he was young and perfectly handsome, which was more than even I had asked

for; *man*, in general, being all that my utmost desires had
pointed at. I thought then I could not put too much encouragement into my eyes and voice; I regretted no
leading advances; no matter for his after-opinion of my
forwardness, so it might bring him to the point of answering my pressing demands of present case; it was not now
with his thoughts, but his actions, that my business immediately lay. I rais'd then my head, and told him, in a soft
tone that tended to prescribe the same key to him, that
his mamma was gone out and would not return till late at
night: which I thought no bad hint; but as it prov'd, I
had nothing of a novice to deal with. The impressions I
had made on him from the discoveries I had betrayed of
my person in the disordered motions of it, during his view
of me asleep, had, as he afterwards told me, so fix'd and
charmingly prepar'd him, that, had I known his dispositions, I had more to hope from his violence than to fear
from his respect; and even less than the extreme tenderness which I threw into my voice and eyes, would have
served to encourage him to make the most of the opportunity. Finding then that his kisses, imprinted on my hand,
were taken as tamely as he could wish, he rose to my lips;
and glewing his to them, made me so faint with over-com-
ing joy and pleasure that I fell back, and he with me, in
course, on the bed, upon which I had, by insensibly shift-
ing from the side to near the middle, invitingly made
room for him. He is now lain down by me, and the minutes being too precious to consume in untimely ceremony,
or dalliance, my youth proceeds immediately to those
extremities, which all my looks, flushing and palpitations
had assured him he might attempt without the fear of
repulse: those rogues, the men, read us admirably on these
occasions. I lay then at length panting for the imminent
attack, with wishes far beyond my fears, and for which it
was scarce possible for a girl, barely thirteen, but all and
well grown, to have better dispositions. He threw up my
petticoat and shift, whilst my thighs were, by an instinct
of nature, unfolded to their best; and my desires had so
thoroughly destroy'd all modesty in me, that even their
being now naked and all laid open to him, was part of the

prelude that pleasure deepen'd my blushes at, more than
shame. But when his hand, and touches, naturally attracted to their centre, made me feel all their wantonness
and warmth in, and round it, oh! how immensely different
a sense of things did I perceive there, than when under
my own insipid handling! And now his waistcoat was
unbuttoned, and the confinement of the breeches burst
through, when out started to view the amazing, pleasing
object of all my wishes, all my dreams, all my love, the
king member indeed! I gaz'd at, I devoured it, at length
and breadth, with my eyes intently directed to it, till his
getting upon me, and placing it between my thighs, took
from me the enjoyment of its sight, to give me a far more
grateful one in its touch, in that part where its touch is so
exquisitely affecting. Applying it then to the minute opening, for such at that age it certainly was, I met with too
much good in, I felt with too great a rapture of pleasure
the first insertion of it, to heed much the pain that followed: I thought nothing too dear to pay for this the richest treat of the senses; so that, split up, torn, bleeding,
mangled, I was still superiourly pleas'd, and hugg'd the
author of all this delicious ruin. But when, soon after, he
made his second attack, sore as every thing was, the smart
was soon put away by the sovereign cordial; all my soft
complainings were silenc'd, and the pain melting fast away
into pleasure. I abandon'd myself over to all its transports,
and gave it the full possession of my whole body and soul;
for now all thought was at an end with me; I lived but in
what I felt only. And who could describe those feelings,
those agitations, yet exalted by the charm of their novelty
and surprize? when that part of me which had so long
hunger'd for the dear morsel that now so delightfully
crammed it, forc'd all my vital sensations to fix their home
there, during the stay of my beloved guest; who too soon
paid me for his hearty welcome in a dissolvent, richer far
than that I have heard of some queen treating her paramour with, in liquify'd pearl, and ravishingly pour'd into
me, where, now myself too much melted to give it a dry
reception, I hail'd it with the warmest confluence on my
side, amidst all those extatic raptures, not unfamiliar I

presume to this good company! Thus, however, I arrived at the very top of all my wishes, by an accident unexpected indeed, but not so wonderful; for this young gentleman was just arriv'd in town from college, and came familiarly to his mother at her apartment, where he had once before been, though by mere chance. I had not seen him: so that we knew one another by hear-say only; and finding me stretched on his mother's bed, he readily concluded, from her description who it was. The rest you know.

"This affair had however no ruinous consequences, the young gentleman escaping then, and many more times undiscover'd. But the warmth of my constitution, that made the pleasures of love a kind of necessary of life to me, having betray'd me into indiscretions fatal to my private fortune, I fell at length to the publick; from which, it is probable, I might have met with the worst of ruin if my better fate had not thrown me into this safe and agreeable refuge."

Here Louisa ended; and these little histories having brought the time for the girls to retire, and to prepare for the revels of the evening, I staid with Mrs. Cole till Emily came and told us the company was met, and waited for us.

Mrs. Cole on this, taking me by the hand, with a smile of encouragement, led me up-stairs, preceded by Louisa, who was come to hasten us, and lighted us with two candles, one in each hand.

On the landing-place of the first pair of stairs, we were met by a young gentleman, extremely well dress'd, and a very pretty figure, to whom I was to be indebted for the first essay of the pleasures of the house. He saluted me with great gallantry, and handed me into the drawing room, the floor of which was overspread with a Turkey carpet, and all its furniture voluptuously adapted to every demand of the most study'd luxury; now too it was, by means of a profuse illumination, enliven'd by a light scarce inferior, and perhaps more favourable to joy, more tenderly pleasing, than that of broad sun-shine.

On my entrance into the room, I had the satisfaction

to hear a buzz of approbation run through the whole company which now consisted of four gentlemen, including my particular (this was the cant-term of the house for one's gallant for the time), the three young women, in a neat flowing dishabille, the mistress of the academy, and myself. I was welcomed and saluted by a kiss all round, in which, however, it was easy to discover, in the superior warmth of that of the men, the distinction of the sexes.

Aw'd and confounded as I was at seeing myself surrounded, caress'd, and made court to by so many strangers, I could not immediately familiarize myself to all that air of gaiety and joy which dictated their compliments, and animated their caresses.

They assur'd me that I was so perfectly to their taste as to have but one fault against me, which I might easily be cur'd of, and that was my modesty: this, they observ'd, might pass for a beauty the more with those who wanted it for a heightener; but their maxim was, that it was an impertinent mixture, and dash'd the cup so as to spoil the sincere draught of pleasure; they consider'd it accordingly as their mortal enemy, and gave it no quarter wherever they met with it. This was a prologue not unworthy of the revels that ensu'd.

In the midst of all the frolic and wantonnesses, which this joyous band had presently, and all naturally, run into, an elegant supper was serv'd in, and we sat down to it, my spark-elect placing himself next to me, and the other couples without order or ceremony. The delicate cheer and good wine soon banish'd all reserve; the conversation grew as lively as could be wished, without taking too loose a turn: these professors of pleasure knew too well, to stale impressions of it, or evaporate the imagination in words, before the time of action. Kisses however were snatch'd at times, or where a handkerchief round the neck interpos'd its feeble barrier, it was not extremely respected: the hands of the men went to work with their usual petulance, till the provocations on both sides rose to such a pitch that my particular's proposal for beginning the country-dances was received with instant assent: for, as he laughingly added, he fancied the instruments were in tune. This was a signal for preparation, that the complaisant Mrs. Cole, who understood life, took for her cue of disappearing; no longer so fit for personal service herself, and content with having settled the order of battle, she left us the field, to fight it out at discretion.

As soon as she was gone, the table was remov'd from the middle, and became a side-board; a couch was brought into its place, of which when I whisperingly inquired the reason, of my particular, he told me that as it was chiefly on my account that this convention was met, the parties intended at once to humour their taste of variety in pleasures, and by an open publick enjoyment, to see me broke of any taint of reserve or modesty, which they look'd on as the poison of joy; that though they occasionally preached pleasure, and lived up to the text, they did not enthusiastically set up for missionaries, and only indulg'd themselves in the delights of a practical instruction of all the pretty women they lik'd well enough to bestow it upon, and who fell properly in the way of it; but that as such a proposal might be too violent, too shocking for a young beginner, the old standers were to set an example, which he hoped I would not be averse to follow, since it was to him I was devolv'd in favour of the first experiment; but that still I was perfectly at my liberty to refuse the party, which being in its nature one of pleasure, suppos'd an exclusion of all force of constraint.

My countenance expressed, no doubt, my surprise as my silence did my acquiescence. I was now embarked, and thoroughly determined on any voyage the company would take me on.

The first that stood up, to open the ball, were a cornet of horse, and that sweetest of olive-beauties, the soft and amorous Louisa. He led her to the couch "nothing loth," on which he gave her the fall, and extended her at her length with an air of roughness and vigour, relishing high of amorous eagerness and impatience. The girl, spreading herself to the best advantage, with her head upon the pillow, was so concentred in what she was about, that our presence seemed the least of her care and concern.

Her petticoats, thrown up with her shift, discovered to the company the finest turn'd legs and thighs that could be imagined, and in broad display, that gave us a full view of that delicious cleft of flesh into which the pleasing hair-grown mount over it, parted and presented a most inviting entrance between two close-hedges, delicately soft and pouting. Her gallant was now ready, having disencumber'd himself from his cloaths, overloaded with lace, and presently, his shirt removed, shew'd us his forces in high plight, bandied and ready for action. But giving us no time to consider the dimensions, he threw himself instantly over his charming antagonist, who receiv'd him as he pushed at once dead at mark like a heroine, without flinching; for surely never was girl constitutionally truer to the taste of joy, or sincerer in the expressions of its sensations, than she was: we could observe pleasure lighten in her eyes, as she introduc'd his plenipotentiary instrument into her; till, at length, having indulg'd her to its utmost reach, its irritations grew so violent, and gave her the spurs so furiously, that collected within herself, and lost to everything but the enjoyment of her favourite feelings, she retorted his thrusts with a just concert of springy heaves, keeping time so exactly with the most pathetic sighs, that one might have number'd the strokes in agitation by their distinct murmurs, whilst her active limbs kept wreathing and intertwisting with his, in convulsive folds: then the turtle-billing kisses, and the poignant painless love-bites, which they both exchang'd in a rage of delight, all conspiring towards the melting period. It soon came on when Louisa, in the ravings of her pleasure-frenzy, impotent of all restraint, cried out: "Oh Sir! . . . Good Sir! . . . pray do not spare me! ah! ah! . . ." All her accents now faltering into heart-fetched sighs, she clos'd her eyes in the sweet death, in the instant of which she was embalm'd by an injection, of which we could easily see the signs in the quiet, dying, languid posture of her late so furious driver, who was stopp'd of a sudden, breathing short, panting, and, for that time, giving up the spirit of pleasure. As soon as he was dismounted, Louisa sprung up, shook her petticoats, and running up to me, gave me a

kiss and drew me to the side-board, to which she was herself handed by her gallant, where they made me pledge
them in a glass of wine, and toast a droll health of Louisa's
proposal in high frolic.

By this time the second couple was ready to enter the
lists: which were a young baronet, and that delicatest of
charmers, the winning, tender Harriet. My gentle esquire
came to acquaint me with it, and brought me back to the
scene of action.

And, surely, never did one of her profession accompany
her dispositions for the bare-faced part she was engaged
to play with such a peculiar grace of sweetness, modesty
and yielding coyness, as she did. All her air and motions
breath'd only unreserv'd, unlimited complaisance without the least mixture of impudence, or prostitution. But
what was yet more surprising, her spark-elect, in the
midst of the dissolution of a publick open enjoyment,
doted on her to distraction, and had, by dint of love and
sentiments, touched her heart, tho' for a while the restraint of their engagement to the house laid him under
a kind of necessity of complying with an institution which
himself had had the greatest share in establishing.

Harriet was then led to the vacant couch by her gallant,
blushing as she look'd at me, and with eyes made to justify any thing, tenderly bespeaking of me the most favourable construction of the step she was thus irresistibly
drawn into.

Her lover, for such he was, sat her down at the foot
of the couch, and passing his arm round her neck, prel-
uded with a kiss fervently applied to her lips, that visibly
gave her life and spirit to go thro' with the scene; and as
he kiss'd, he gently inclined her head, till it fell back on
a pillow disposed to receive it, and leaning himself down
all the way with her, at once countenanc'd and endear'd
her fall to her. There, as if he had guess'd our wishes, or
meant to gratify at once his pleasure and his pride, in
being the master, by the title of present possession, of
beauties delicate beyond imagination, he discovered her
breasts to his own touch, and our common view; but oh!
what delicious manuals of love devotion! how inimitable

fine moulded! small, round, firm, and excellently white: the grain of their skin, so soothing, so flattering to the touch! and their nipples, that crown'd them, the sweetest buds of beauty. When he had feasted his eyes with the touch and perusal, feasted his lips with kisses of the highest relish, imprinted on those all-delicious twin orbs, he proceeded downwards.

Her legs still kept the ground; and now, with the tenderest attention not to shock or alarm her too suddenly, he, by degrees, rather stole than rolled up her petticoats; at which, as if a signal had been given, Louisa and Emily took hold of her legs, in pure wantonness, and, in ease to her, kept them stretched wide abroad. Then lay exposed, or, to speak more properly, display'd the greatest parade in nature of female charms. The whole company, who, except myself, had often seen them, seemed as much dazzled, surpriz'd and delighted, as any one could be who had now beheld them for the first time. Beauties so excessive could not but enjoy the privileges of eternal novelty. Her thighs were so exquisitely fashioned, that either more in, or more out of flesh than they were, they would have declined from that point of perfection they presented. But what infinitely enrich'd and adorn'd them, was the sweet intersection formed, where they met, at the bottom of the smoothest, roundest, whitest belly, by that central furrow which nature had sunk there, between, the soft relieve of two pouting ridges, and which in this was in perfect symmetry of delicacy and miniature with the rest of her frame. No! nothing in nature could be of a beautifuller cut; then, the dark umbrage of the downy spring-moss that over-arched it bestowed, on the luxury of the landscape, a touching warmth, a tender finishing, beyond the expression of words, or even the paint of thought.

Her truly enamour'd gallant, who had stood absorbed and engrossed by the pleasure of the sight long enough to afford us time to feast ours (no fear of glutting!) addressed himself at length to the materials of enjoyment, and lifting the linen veil that hung between us and his master member of the revels, exhibited one whose emi-

nent size proclaimed the owner a true woman's hero. He
was, besides, in every other respect an accomplish'd gentleman, and in the bloom and vigour of youth. Standing
then between Harriet's legs, which were supported by
her two companions at their widest extension, with one
hand he gently disclosed the lips of that luscious mouth
of nature, whilst with the other, he stooped his mighty
machine to its lure, from the height of his stiff stand-up
towards his belly; the lips, kept open by his fingers, received its broad shelving head of coral hue: and when he
had nestled it in, he hovered there a little, and the girls
then deliver'd over to his hips the agreeable office of sup-
porting her thighs; and now, as if meant to spin out his
pleasure, and give it the more play for its life, he passed
up his instrument so slow that we lost sight of it inch
by inch, till at length it was wholly taken into the soft
laboratory of love, and the mossy mounts of each fairly
met together. In the mean time, we could plainly mark
the prodigious effect the progressions of this delightful
energy wrought in this delicious girl, gradually height-
ening her beauty as they heightened her pleasure. Her
countenance and whole frame grew more animated; the
faint blush of her cheeks, gaining ground on the white,
deepened into a florid vivid vermilion glow, her naturally
brilliant eyes now sparkled with ten-fold lustre; her languor was vanish'd, and she appeared, quick spirited, and
alive all over. He had now fixed, nailed, this tender creature with his home-driven wedge, so that she lay passive
by force, and unable to stir, till beginning to play a strain
of arms against this vein of delicacy, as he urged the to-
and-fro confriction, he awaken'd, rous'd, and touch'd her
so to the heart, that unable to contain herself, she could
not but reply to his motions as briskly as her nicety of
frame would admit of, till the raging stings of the pleasure
rising towards the point, made her wild with the intolerable sensations of it, and she now threw her legs and
arms about at random, as she lay lost in the sweet transport; which on his side declared itself by quicker, eager
thrusts, convulsive gasps, burning sighs, swift laborious
breathings, eyes darting humid fires: all faithful tokens of

the imminent approaches of the last gasp of joy. It came on at length: the baronet led the extasy, which she critically joined in, as she felt the melting symptoms from him, in the nick of which glewing more ardently than ever his lips to hers, he shewed all the signs of that agony of bliss being strong upon him, in which he gave her the finishing titillation; inly thrill'd with which, we saw plainly that she answered it down with all effusion of spirit and matter she was mistress of, whilst a general soft shudder ran through all her limbs, which she gave a stretch-out of, and lay motionless, breathless, dying with dear delight; and in the height of its expression, shewing, through the nearly closed lids of her eyes, just the edges of their black, the rest being rolled strongly upwards in their extasy; then her sweet mouth appear'd languishingly open, with the tip of her tongue leaning negligently towards the lower range of her white teeth, whilst the natural ruby colour of her lips glowed with heightened life. Was not this a subject to dwell upon? And accordingly her lover still kept on her, with an abiding delectation, till compressed, squeezed and distilled to the last drop, he took leave with one fervent kiss, expressing satisfy'd desires, but unextinguish'd love.

As soon as he was off, I ran to her, and sitting down on the couch by her, rais'd her head, which she declin'd gently, and hung on my bosom, to hide her blushes and confusion at what had pass'd, till by degree she recomposed herself and accepted of a restorative glass of wine from my spark, who had left me to fetch it her, whilst her own was re-adjusting his affairs and buttoning up; after which he led her, leaning languishingly upon him, to our stand of view round the couch.

And now Emily's partner had taken her out for her share in the dance, when this transcendently fair and sweet tempered creature readily stood up; and if a complexion to put the rose and lily out of countenance, extreme pretty features, and that florid health and bloom for which the country-girls are so lovely, might pass her for a beauty, this she certainly was, and one of the most striking of the fair ones.

Her gallant began first, as she stood, to disengage her breasts, and restore them to the liberty of nature, from the easy confinement of no more than a pair of jumps; but on their coming out to view, we thought a new light was added to the room, so superiourly shining was their whiteness; then they rose in so happy a swell as to compose her a well-formed fulness of bosom, that had such an effect on the eye as to seem flesh hardening into marble, of which it emulated the polished gloss, and far surpassed even the whitest, in the life and lustre of its colours, white veined with blue. Refrain who could from such provoking enticements to it in reach? He touched her breasts, first lightly, when the glossy smoothness of the skin eluded his hand, and made it slip along the surface; he press'd them, and the springy flesh that filled them thus pitted by force, rose again reboundingly with his hand, and on the instant effac'd the pressure: and alike indeed was the consistence of all those parts of her body throughout, where the fulness of flesh compacts and constitutes all that fine firmness which the touch is so highly attach'd to. When he had thus largely pleased himself with this branch of dalliance and delight, he truss'd up her petticoat and shift in a wisp to her waist, where being tuck'd in, she stood fairly naked on every side; a blush at this overspread her lovely face, and her eyes downcast to the ground seemed to be for quarter, when she had so great a right to triumph in all the treasures of youth and beauty that she now so victoriously display'd. Her legs were perfectly well shaped and her thighs, which she kept pretty close, shewed so white, so round, so substantial and abounding in firm flesh, that nothing could offer a stronger recommendation to the luxury of the touch, which he accordingly did not fail to indulge himself in. Then gently removing her hand, which in the first emotion of natural modesty she had carried thither, he gave us rather a glimpse than a view of that soft narrow chink running its little length downwards and hiding the remains of it between her thighs; but plain was to be seen the fringe of light-brown curls, in beauteous growth over it, that with their silky gloss created a

pleasing variety from the surrounding white, whose lustre
too, their gentle embrowning shade, considerably raised.
Her spark then endeavoured, as she stood, by disclosing
her thighs, to gain us a completer sight of that central
charm of attraction, but not obtaining it so conveniently
in that attitude, he led her to the foot of the couch, and
bringing to it one of the pillows, gently inclin'd her head
down, so that as she leaned with it over her crossed hands,
straddling with her thighs wide spread, and jutting her
body out, she presented a full back view of her person,
naked to her waist. Her posteriours, plump, smooth, and
prominent, form'd luxuriant tracts of animated snow, that
splendidly filled the eye, till it was commanded down the
parting or separation of those exquisitely white cliffs, by
their narrow vale, and was there stopt, and attracted by
the embowered bottom-cavity, that terminated this delightful vista and stood moderately gaping from the influence of her bended posture, so that the agreeable, interior
red of the sides of the orifice came into view, and with
respect to the white that dazzled round it, gave somewhat
the idea of a pink slash in the glossiest white satin. Her
gallant, who was a gentleman about thirty, somewhat
inclin'd to a fatness that was in no sort displeasing, improving the hint thus tendered him of this mode of enjoyment,
after settling her well in this posture, and encouraging her
with kisses and caresses to stand him through, drew out
his affair ready erected, and whose extreme length, rather
disproportion'd to its breadth, was the more surprizing,
as that excess is not often the case with those of his corpu-
lent habit; making then the right and direct application,
he drove it up to the guard, whilst the round bulge of
those Turkish beauties of her's tallying with the hollow
made with the bent of his belly and thighs, as they curved
inwards, brought all those parts, surely not undelightfully,
into warm touch, and close conjunction; his hands he kept
passing round her body, and employed in toying with her
enchanting breasts. As soon too as she felt him at home as
he could reach, she lifted her head a little from the pillow,
and turning her neck, without much straining, but her
cheeks glowing with the deepest scarlet, and a smile of

the tenderest satisfaction, met the kiss he press'd forward to give her as they were thus close joined together: when leaving him to pursue his delights, she hid again her face and blushes with her hands and pillow, and thus stood passively and as favourably too as she could, whilst he kept laying at her with repeated thrusts and making the meeting flesh on both sides resound again with the violence of them; then ever as he backen'd from her, we could see between them part of his long whitestaff foamingly in motion, till, as he went on again and closed with her, the interposing hillocks took it out of sight. Sometimes he took his hands from the semi-globes of her bosom, and transferred the pressure of them to those larger ones, the present subjects of his soft blockade, which he squeez'd, grasp'd and play'd with, till at length a pursuit of driving, so hotly urged, brought on the height of the fit, with such overpowering pleasure, that his fair partner became, now necessary to support him, panting, fainting and dying as he discharged; which she no sooner felt the killing sweetness of, than unable to keep her legs, and yielding to the mighty intoxication, she reeled, and falling forward on the couch, made it a necessity for him, if he would preserve the warm pleasure-hold, to fall upon her, where they perfected, in a continued conjunction of body and extatic flow, their scheme of joys for that time.

As soon as he had disengag'd, the charming Emily got up, and we crowded round her with congratulations and other officious little services; for it is to be noted, that though all modesty and reserve were banished from the transaction of these pleasures, good manners and politeness were inviolably observ'd: here was no gross ribaldry, no offensive or rude behaviour, or ungenerous reproaches to the girls for their compliance with the humours and desires of the men. On the contrary, nothing was wanting to soothe, encourage, and soften the sense of their condition to them. Men know not in general how much they destroy of their own pleasure, when they break through the respect and tenderness due to our sex, and even to those of it who live only by pleasing them. And this was a maxim perfectly well understood by these polite voluptuaries, these profound adepts in the great art and science of pleasure, who never shew'd these votaries of theirs a more tender respect than at the time of those exercises of their complaisance, when they unlock'd their treasures of concealed beauty, and shewed out in the pride of their native charms, ever-more touching surely than when they paraded it in the artificial ones of dress and ornament.

The frolick was now come round to me, and it being my turn of subscription to the will and pleasure of my particular elect, as well as to that of the company, he came to me, and saluting me very tenderly, with a flattering eagerness, put me in mind of the compliances my presence there authoriz'd the hopes of, and at the same time repeated to me that if all this force of example had not surmounted any repugnance I might have to concur with the humours and desires of the company, that though the play was bespoke for my benefit, and great as his own private disappointment might be, he would suffer any thing, sooner than be the instrument of imposing a disagreeable task on me.

To this I answered, without the least hesitation or mincing grimace, that had I not even contracted a kind of engagement to be at his disposal without the least reserve, the example of such agreeable companions would alone determine me and that I was in no pain about any thing but my appearing to so great a disadvantage after such superior beauties. And take notice that I thought as I spoke. The frankness of the answer pleas'd them all; my particular was complimented on his acquisition, and, by way of indirect flattery to me, openly envied.

Mrs. Cole, by the way, could not have given me a greater mark of her regard than in managing for me the choice of this young gentleman for my master of the ceremonies: for, independent of his noble birth and the great fortune he was heir to, his person was even uncommonly pleasing, well shaped and tall; his face mark'd with the small-pox, but no more than what added a grace of more manliness to features rather turned to softness and delicacy, was marvellously enliven'd by eyes which were of the clearest sparkling black; in short, he was one whom

any woman would, in the familiar style, readily call a
very pretty fellow.

I was now handed by him to the cock-pit of our match,
where, as I was dressed in nothing but a white morning
gown, he vouchsafed to play the male-Abigail on this
occasion, and spared me the confusion that would have
attended the forwardness of undressing myself: my gown
then was loosen'd in a trice, and I divested of it; my stay
next offered an obstacle which readily gave way, Louisa
very readily furnishing a pair of scissors to cut the lace;
off went that shell and dropping my upper-coat, I was
reduced to my under one and my shift, the open bosom
of which gave the hands and eyes all the liberty they
could wish. Here I imagin'd the stripping was to stop,
but I reckoned short: my spark, at the desire of the rest,
tenderly begged that I would not suffer the small remains
of a covering to rob them of a full view of my whole person; and for me, who was too flexibly obsequious to
dispute any point with them, and who considered the
little more that remain'd as very immaterial, I readily
assented to whatever he pleased. In an instant, then, my
under-petticoat was untied and at my feet, and my shift
drawn over my head, so that my cap, slightly fasten'd,
came off with it, and brought all my hair down (of which,
be it again remembered without vanity, that I had a very
fine head) in loose disorderly ringlets, over my neck and
shoulders, to the not unfavourable set-off of my skin.

I now stood before my judges in all the truth of nature,
to whom I could not appear a very disagreeable figure, if
you please to recollect what I have before said of my
person, which time, that at certain periods of life robs
us every instant of our charms, had, at that of mine, then
greatly improved into full and open bloom, for I wanted
some months of eighteen. My breasts, which in the state
of nudity are ever capital points, now in no more than in
graceful plenitude, maintained a firmness and steady independence of any stay or support that dared and invited
the test of the touch. Then I was as tall, as slim-shaped as
could be consistent with all that juicy plumpness of flesh,
ever the most grateful to the senses of sight and touch,

which I owed to the health and youth of my constitution. I had not, however, so thoroughly renounc'd all innate shame as not to suffer great confusion at the state I saw myself in; but the whole troop round me, men and women, relieved me with every mark of applause and satisfaction, every flattering attention to raise and inspire me with even sentiments of pride on the figure I made, which, my friend gallantly protested, infinitely out-shone all other *birthday* finery whatever; so that had I leave to set down, for sincere, all the compliments these connoisseurs overwhelmed me with upon this occasion, I might flatter myself with having pass'd my examination with the approbation of the learned.

My friend however, who for this time had alone the disposal of me, humoured their curiosity, and perhaps his own, so far that he placed me in all the variety of postures and lights imaginable, pointing out every beauty under every aspect of it, not without such parentheses of kisses, such inflammatory liberties of his roving hands, as made all shame fly before them, and a blushing glow give place to a warmer one of desire, which led me even to find some relish in the present scene.

But in this general survey, you may be sure, the most material spot of me was not excus'd the strictest visitation; nor was it but agreed, that I had not the least reason to be diffident of passing even for a maid, on occasion: so inconsiderable a flaw had my preceding adventures created there, and so soon had the blemish of an over-stretch been repaired and worn out at my age, and in my naturally small make in that part.

Now, whether my partner had exhausted all the modes of regaling the touch or sight, or whether he was now ungovernably wound up to strike, I know not; but briskly throwing off his clothes, the prodigious heat bred by a close room, a great fire, numerous candles, and even the inflammatory warmth of these scenes, induced him to lay aside his shirt too, when his breeches, before loosen'd, now gave up their contents to view, and shew'd in front the enemy I had to engage with, stiffly bearing up the port of its head unhooded, and glowing red. Then I

plainly saw what I had to trust to: it was one of those
just true-siz'd instruments, of which the masters have a
better command than the more unwieldy, inordinate siz'd
ones are generally under. Straining me then close to his
bosom, as he stood up fore-right against me and applying
to the obvious niche its peculiar idol, he aimed at inserting it, which, as I forwardly favoured, he effected at once
by canting up my thighs over his naked hips, and made
me receive every inch, and close home; so that stuck upon
the pleasure-pivot, and clinging round his neck, in which
and in his hair I hid my face, burningly flushing with my
present feelings as much as with shame, my bosom glew'd
to his; he carried me once round the couch, on which he
then, without quitting the middle-fastness, or dischan-
nelling, laid me down, and began the pleasure-grist. But
so provokingly predisposed and primed as we were, by
all the moving sights of the night, our imagination was
too much heated not to melt us of the soonest: and accordingly, I no sooner felt the warm spray darted up my
inwards from him, but I was punctually on flow, to share
the momentary extasy; but I had yet greater reason to
boast of our harmony: for finding that all the flames of
desire were not yet quench'd within me, but that rather,
like wetted coals, I glowed the fiercer for this sprinkling,
my hot-mettled spark, sympathizing with me, and loaded
for a double fire, recontinu'd the sweet battery with undy-
ing vigour; greatly pleas'd at which I gratefully endeavoured to accommodate all my motions to his best advantage and delight; kisses, squeezes, tender murmurs, all
came into play, till our joys, growing more turbulent and
riotous, threw us into a fond disorder, and as they raged
to a point, bore us far from ourselves into an ocean of
boundless pleasure, into which we both plunged together
in a transport of taste. Now all the impressions of burning
desire, from the lively scenes I had been spectatress of,
ripened by the heat of this exercise, and collecting to a
head, throbb'd and agitated me with insupportable irritations: I perfectly fevered and madden'd with their excess.
I did not now enjoy a calm of reason enough to perceive,
but I extatically, indeed, *felt* the power of such rare and

exquisite provocatives, as the examples of the night had proved towards thus exalting our pleasures: which, with great joy, I sensibly found my gallant shared in, by his nervous and home expressions of it: his eyes flashing eloquent flames, his action infuriated with the stings of it, all conspiring to rise my delight by assuring me of his. Lifted then to the utmost pitch of joy that human life can bear, undestroyed by excess, I touch'd that sweetly critical point, whence scarce prevented by the injection from my partner, I dissolved, and breaking out into a deep drawn sigh, sent my whole sensitive soul down to that passage where escape was denied it, by its being so deliciously plugged and chok'd up. Thus we lay a few blissful instants, overpowered, still, and languid; till, as the sense of pleasure stagnated, we recover'd from our trance, and he slipt out of me, not however before he had protested his extreme satisfaction by the tenderest kiss and embrace, as well as my the most cordial expressions.

The company, who had stood round us in a profound silence, when all was over, help'd me to hurry on my cloaths in an instant, and complimented me on the sincere homage they could not escape observing had been done (as they termed it) to the sovereignty of my charms, in my receiving a double payment of tribute at one juncture. But my partner, now dress'd again, signaliz'd, above all, a fondness unbated by the circumstance of recent enjoyment; the girls too kiss'd and embraced me, assuring me that for that time, or indeed any other, unless I pleased, I was to go thro' no farther publick trials, and that I was now consummatedly initiated, and one of them.

As it was an inviolable law for every gallant to keep to his partner, for the night especially, and even till he relinquish'd possession over to the community, in order to preserve a pleasing property and to avoid the disgusts and indelicacy of another arrangement, the company, after a short refection of biscuits and wine, tea and chocolate, served in at now about one in the morning, broke up, and went off in pairs. Mrs. Cole had prepared my spark and me an occasional field-bed, to which we retir'd, and there ended the night in one continued strain of pleasure, sprightly and uncloy'd enough for us not to have formed one wish for its ever knowing an end. In the morning, after a restorative breakfast in bed, he got up, and with very tender assurances of a particular regard for me, left me to the composure and refreshment of a sweet slumber; waking out of which, and getting up to dress before Mrs. Cole should come in, I found in one of my pockets a purse of guineas, which he had slipt there; and just as I was musing on a liberality I had certainly not expected, Mrs. Cole came in, to whom I immediately communicated the present, and naturally offered her whatever share she pleas'd: but assuring me that the gentelman had very nobly rewarded her, she would on no terms, no entreaties, no shape I could put it in, receive any part of it. Her denial, she observed, was not affectation of grimace, and proceeded to read me such admirable lessons on the economy of my person and my purse as I became amply paid for my *general* attention and conformity to in the course of my acquaintance with the town. After which, changing the discourse, she fell on the pleasures of the preceding night, where I learn'd, without much surprize, as I began to enter on her character, that she had seen every thing that had passed, from a convenient place managed solely for that purpose, and of which she readily made me the confidante.

She had scarce finish'd this, when the little troop of love, the girls my companions, broke in and renewed their compliments and caresses. I observed with pleasure that the fatigues and exercises of the night had not usurped in the least on the life of their complexion, or the freshness of their bloom: this I found, by their confession, was owing to the management and advice of our rare directress. They went down then to figure it, as usual, in the shop; whilst I repair'd to my lodgings, where I employed myself till I returned to dinner at Mrs. Cole's.

Here I staid in constant amusement, with one or other of these charming girls, till about five in the evening; when seiz'd with a sudden drowsy fit, I was prevailed in to go up and doze it off on Harriet's bed, who left me on it to my repose. There then I lay down in my cloaths and fell fast asleep, and had now enjoyed, by guess, about an hour's rest, when I was pleasingly disturbed by my new and favourite gallant, who, enquiring for me, was readily directed where to find me. Coming then into my chamber, and seeing me lie alone, with my face turn'd from the light towards the inside of the bed, he, without more ado, just slipped off his breeches, for the greater ease and enjoyment of the naked touch; and softly turning up my petticoat and shift behind, opened the prospect of the back avenue to the genial seat of pleasure; where, as I lay at my side length, inclining rather face downward, I appeared full fair, and liable to be entered. Laying himself then gently down by me, he invested me behind, and giving me to feel the warmth of his body as he applied his thighs and belly close to me, and the endeavours of that machine, whose touch has something so exquisitely singular in it, to make its way good into me. I wak'd pretty much startled at first, but seeing who it was, disposed myself to turn to him, when he gave me a kiss, and desiring me to keep my posture, just lifted up my upper thigh, and ascertaining the right opening, soon drove it up to the farthest: satisfied with which, and solacing himself with lying so close in those parts, he suspended motion, and thus steeped in pleasure, kept me lying on my side, into him, spoon-fashion, as he term'd it, from the snug indent of the back part of my thighs, and all upwards, into the space of the bending between his thighs and belly; till, after some time, that restless and turbulent inmate, impatient by nature of longer quiet, urg'd him to action, which now prosecuting with all the usual train of toying, kissing, and the like, ended at length in the liquid proof on both sides, that we had not exhausted, or at least were quickly recruited of last night's draughts of pleasure in us.

With this noble and agreeable youth liv'd I in perfect joy and constancy. He was full bent on keeping me to himself, for the honey-month at least; but his stay in *London* was not even so long, his father, who had a post in *Ireland*, taking him abruptly with him on his repairing thither. Yet even then I was near keeping hold of his affection and person, as he had propos'd, and I had consented to follow him in order to go to Ireland after him, as soon as he could be settled there; but meeting with an agreeable and advantageous match in that kingdom, he chose the wiser part, and forebore sending for me, but at the same time took care that I should receive a very magnificent present, which did not however compensate for all my deep regret on my loss of him.

This event also created a chasm in our little society, which Mrs. Cole, on the foot of her usual caution, was in no haste to fill up; but then it redoubled her attention to procure me, in the advantages of a traffic for a counterfeit maidenhead, some consolation for the sort of widowhood I had been left in; and this was a scheme she had never lost prospect of, and only waited for a proper person to bring it to bear with.

But I was, it seems, fated to be my own caterer in this, as I had been in my first trial of the market.

I had now pass'd near a month in the enjoyment of all the pleasure of familiarity and society with my companions, whose particular favourites (the baronet excepted, who soon after took Harriet home) had all, on the terms of community establish'd in the house, solicited the gratification of their taste for variety in my embraces; but I had with the utmost art and address, on various pretexts, eluded their pursuit, without giving them cause to complain; and this reserve I used neither out of dislike of them, or disgust of the thing, but my true reason was my attachment to my own, and my tenderness of invading the choice of my companions, who outwardly exempt, as they seem'd, from jealousy, could not but in secret like me the better for the regard I had for, without making a merit of it to them. Thus easy, and beloved by the whole family, did I go on; when one day, that, about five in the afternoon, I stepped over to a fruiterer's shop in *Covent Garden,* to pick some table fruit for myself and the young women, I met with the following adventure.

Whilst I was chaffering for the fruit I wanted, I observ'd myself follow'd by a young gentleman, whose rich dress first attracted my notice; for the rest, he had noth-

ing remarkable in his person, except that he was pale,
thin-made, and ventur'd himself upon legs rather of the
slenderest. Easy was it to perceive, without seeming to
perceive it, that it was me he wanted to be at; and keeping his eyes fixed on me, till he came to the same basket
that I stood at, and cheapening, or rather giving the first
price ask'd for the fruit, began his approaches. Now most
certainly I was not at all out of figure to pass for a modest
girl. I had neither the feathers nor *fumet* of a taudry
town-miss: a straw hat, a white gown, clean linen, and
above all, a certain natural and easy air of modesty
(which the appearances of never forsook me, even on
those occasions that I most broke in upon it, in practice)
were all signs that gave him no opening to conjecture
my condition. He spoke to me; and this address from a
stranger throwing a blush into my cheeks that still set
him wider off the truth, I answered him with an aukwardness and confusion the more apt to impose, as there
was really a mixture of the genuine in them. But when
proceeding, on the foot of having broken the ice, to join
discourse, he went into other leading questions, I put
so much innocence, simplicity, and even childishness into
my answers that on no better foundation, liking my person as he did, I will answer for it, he would have been
sworn for my modesty. There is, in short, in the men,
when once they are caught, by the eye especially, a fund
of cullibility that their lordly wisdom little dreams of, and
in virtue of which the most sagacious of them are seen so
often our dupes. Amongst other queries he put to me, one
was whether I was married. I replied that I was too young
to think of that this many a year. To that of my age, I answered, and sunk a year upon him, passing myself for not
seventeen. As to my way of life, I told him I had serv'd
an apprenticeship to a milliner in *Preston*, and was come
to town after a relation, that I had found, on my arrival,
was dead, and now liv'd journey-woman to a milliner in
town. That last article, indeed, was not much of the side
of what I pretended to pass for; but it did pass, under
favour of the growing passion I had inspir'd him with.
After he had next got out of me, very dextrously as he

thought, what I had no sort of design to make reserve of, my own, my mistress's name, and place of abode, he loaded me with fruit, all the rarest and dearest he could pick out, and sent me home, pondering on what might be the consequence of this adventure.

As soon then as I came to Mrs. Cole's, I related to her all that passed, on which she very judiciously concluded that if he did not come after me there was no harm done, and that, if he did, as her presage suggested to her he would, his character and his views should be well sifted, so as to know whether the game was worth the springs; that in the mean time nothing was easier than my part in it, since no more rested on me than to follow her cue and promptership throughout, to the last act.

The next morning, after an evening spent on his side, as we afterwards learnt, in perquisitions into Mrs. Cole's character in the neighbourhood (than which nothing could be more favourable to her design upon him), my gentleman came in his chariot to the shop, where Mrs. Cole alone had an inkling of his errand. Asking then for her, he easily made a beginning of acquaintance by be-speaking some millinery ware: when, as I sat without lifting up my eyes, and pursuing the hem of a ruffle with the utmost composure and simplicity of industry, Mrs. Cole took notice that the first impressions I made on him ran no risk of being destroyed by those of Louisa and Emily, who were then sitting at work by me. After vainly endeavouring to catch my eyes in re-encounter with his (as I held my head down, affecting a kind of conscious-ness of guilt for having, by speaking to him, given him encouragement and means of following me), and after giving Mrs. Cole direction when to bring the things home herself, and the time he should expect them, he went out, taking with him some goods that he paid for liberally, for the better grace of his introduction.

The girls all this time did not in the least smoke the mystery of this new customer; but Mrs. Cole, as soon as we were conveniently alone, insur'd me, in virtue of her long experience in these matters, that for this bout my charms had not miss'd fire; for that by his eagerness, his manner and looks, she was sure he had it: the only point now in doubt was his character and circumstances, which her knowledge of the town would soon gain her sufficient acquaintance with, to take her measures upon.

And effectively, in a few hours, her intelligence serv'd her so well that she learn'd that this conquest of mine was no other than *Mr. Norbert,* a gentleman originally of great fortune, which, with a constitution naturally not the best, he had vastly impaired by his over-violent pursuit of the vices of the town; in the course of which, having worn out and stal'd all the more common modes of debauchery, he had fallen into a taste of maiden-hunting; in which chase he had ruin'd a number of girls, sparing no expence to compass his ends, and generally using them well till tired, or cool'd by enjoyment, or springing a new face, he could with more ease disembarrass himself of the old ones, and resign them to their fate, as his sphere of achievements of that sort lay only amongst such as he could proceed with by way of bargain and sale.

Concluding from these premises, Mrs. Cole observ'd that a character of this sort was ever a lawful prize; that the sin would be, not to make the best of our market of him; and that she thought such a girl as I only too good for him at any rate, and on any terms.

She went then, at the hour appointed, to his lodgings in one of our inns of court, which were furnished in a taste of grandeur that had a special eye to all the conveniences of luxury and pleasure. Here she found him in ready waiting; and after finishing her pretence of business, and a long circuit of discussions concerning her trade, which she said was very bad, the qualities of her servants, 'prentices, journey-women, the discourse naturally landed at length on me, when Mrs. Cole, acting admirably the good old prating gossip, who lets every thing escape her when her tongue is set in motion, cooked him up a story so plausible of me, throwing in every now and then such strokes of art, with all the simplest air of nature, in praise of my person and temper, as finished him finely for her purpose, whilst nothing could be better counterfeited than her innocence of his. But when now fired and on edge, he proceeded to drop hints of his design and views upon me, after he had with much confusion and pains brought her to the point (she kept as long aloof from as she thought proper) of understanding him, without now affecting to pass for a dragoness of virtue, by flying out into those violent and ever suspicious passions, she stuck with the better grace and effect to the character of a plain, good sort of a woman, that knew no harm, and that getting her bread in an honest way, was made of stuff easy and flexible enough to be wrought upon to his ends, by his superior skill and address; but, however, she managed so artfully that three or four meetings took place before he could obtain the least favourable hope of her assistance; without which, he had, by a number of fruitless messages, letters, and other direct trials of my disposition, convinced himself there was no coming at me, all which too rais'd at once my character and price with him.

Regardful, however, of not carrying these difficulties to such a length as might afford time for starting discoveries, or incidents, unfavourable to her plan, she at last pretended to be won over by mere dint of entreaties, promises, and, above all, by the dazzling sum she took care to wind him up to the specification of, when it was now even a piece of art to feign, at once, a yielding to the allurements of a great interest, as a pretext for her yielding at all, and the manner of it such as might persuade him she had never dipp'd her virtuous fingers in an affair of that sort.

Thus she led him through all the gradations of difficulty, and obstacles, necessary to enhance the value of the prize he aim'd at; and in conclusion, he was so struck with the little beauty I was mistress of, and so eagerly bent on gaining his ends of me, that he left her even no room to boast of her management in bringing him up to her mark, he drove so plum of himself into every thing tending to make him swallow the bait. Not but, in other respect, Mr. Nobert was not clear sighted enough, or that he did not perfectly know the town, and even by experience, the very branch of imposition now in practice

upon him: but we had his passion our friend so much, he
was so blinded and hurried on by it, that he would have
thought any undeception a very ill office done to his pleasure. Thus concurring, even precipitately, to the point she
wanted him at, Mrs. Cole brought him at last to hug himself on the cheap bargain he consider'd the purchase of
my imaginary jewel was to him, at no more than three
hundred guineas to myself, and a hundred to the brok-
eress: being a slender recompense for all her pains, and all
the scruples of conscience she had now sacrificed to him
for this the first time of her life; which sums were to be
paid down on the nail, upon livery of my person, exclusive
of some no inconsiderable presents that had been made
in the course of the negociation: during which I had occasionally, but sparingly been introduc'd into his company,
at proper times and hours; in which it is incredible how
little it seem'd necessary to strain my natural disposition
to modesty higher, in order to pass it upon him for that of
a very maid: all my looks and gestures ever breathing
nothing but that innocence which the men so ardently
require in us, for no other end than to feast themselves
with the pleasures of destroying it, and which they are so
grievously, with all their skill, subject to mistakes in.

When the articles of the treaty had been full agreed
on, the stipulated payments duly secur'd, and nothing now
remained but the execution of the main point, which
center'd in the surrender of my person up to his free disposal and use, Mrs. Cole managed her objections, especially to his lodgings, and insinuations so nicely, that it
became his own mere notion and urgent request that this
copy of a wedding should be finish'd at her house: At
first, indeed, she did not care, said she, to have such doings in it . . . she would not for a thousand pounds have
any of the servants or 'prentices know it . . . her precious good name would be gone for ever—with the like
excuses. However, on superior objections to all other
expedients, whilst she took care to start none but those
which were most liable to them, it came round at last to
the necessity of her obliging him in that conveniency,

and of doing a little more where she had already done so much.

The night then was fix'd, with all possible respect to the eagerness of his impatience, and in the mean time Mrs. Cole had omitted no instructions, nor even neglected any preparation, that might enable me to come off with honour, in regard to the appearance of my virginity, except that, favour'd as I was by nature with all the narrowness of stricture in that part requisite to conduct my designs, I had no occasion to borrow those auxiliaries of art that create a momentary one, easily discover'd by the test of a warm bath; and as to the usual sanguinary symptoms of defloration, which, if not always, are generally attendants on it, Mrs. Cole had made me the mistress of an invention of her own which could hardly miss its effect, and of which more in its place.

Everything then being disposed and fix'd for Mr. Norbert's reception, he was, at the hour of eleven at night, with all the mysteries of silence and secrecy, let in by Mrs. Cole herself, and introduced into her bed-chamber, where, in an old-fashioned bed of her's, I lay, fully undressed, and panting, if not with the fears of a real maid, at least with those perhaps greater of a dissembled one which gave me an air of confusion and bashfulness that maiden-modesty had all the honour of, and was indeed scarce distinguishable from it, even by less partial eyes than those of my lover: so let me call him, for I ever thought the term *"cully"* too cruel a reproach to the men for their abused weakness for us.

As soon as Mrs. Cole, after the old gossipery, on these occasions, us'd to young women abandoned for the first time to the will of man, had left us alone in her room, which, by-the-bye, was well lighted up, at his previous desire, that seemed to bode a stricter examination than he afterwards made, Mr. Norbert, still dressed, sprung towards the bed, where I got my head under the cloaths, and defended them a good while before he could even get at my lips, to kiss them: so true it is, that a false virtue, on this occasion, even makes a greater rout and resistance than a true one. From thence he descended to my breasts, the feel I disputed tooth and nail with him till, tired with my resistance, and thinking probably to give a better account of me, when got into bed to me, he hurry'd his cloaths off in an instant, and came into bed.

Mean while, by the glimpse I stole of him, I could easily discover a person far from promising any such doughty performances as the storming of maidenheads generally requires, and whose flimsy consumptive texture gave him more the air of an invalid that was pressed, than of a volunteer, on such hot service.

At scarce thirty, he had already reduced his strength of appetite down to a wretched dependence on forc'd provocatives, very little seconded by the natural power of a body jaded and racked off to the lees by constant repeated overdraughts of pleasure, which had done the work of sixty winters on his springs of life: leaving him at the same time all the fire and heat of youth in his imagination, which served at once to torment and spur him down the precipice.

As soon as he was in bed, he threw off the bed-cloaths, which I suffered him to force from my hold, and I now lay as expos'd as he could wish, not only to his attacks, but his visitation of the sheets; where in the various agitations of the body, through my endeavours to defend myself, he could easily assure himself there was no preparation: though, to do him justice, he seem'd a less strict examinant than I had apprehended from so experienc'd a practitioner. My shift then he fairly tore open, finding I made too much use of it to barricade my breasts, as well as the more important avenue: yet in every thing else he proceeded with all the marks of tenderness and regard to me, whilst the art of my play was to shew none for him. I acted then all the niceties, apprehensions, and terrors supposable for a girl perfectly innocent to feel at so great a novelty as a naked man in bed with her for the first time. He scarce even obtained a kiss but what he ravished; I put his hand away twenty times from my breasts, where he had satisfied himself of their hardness and consistence, with passing for hitherto unhandled goods. But when grown impatient for the main point, he

now threw himself upon me, and first trying to examine
me with his finger, sought to make himself further way,
I complained of his usage bitterly: I thought he would
not have serv'd a body so . . . I was ruin'd . . . I did
not know what I had done . . . I would get up, so I
would . . . ; and at the same time kept my thighs so
fast locked, that it was not for strength like his to force
them open, or do any good. Finding thus my advantages,
and that I had both my own and his motions at command,
the deceiving him came to easy that it was perfectly playing upon velvet. In the mean time his machine, which
was one of those sizes that slip in and out without being
minded, kept pretty stiffly bearing against that part,
which the shutting my thighs barr'd access to; but finding,
at length, he could do no good by mere dint of bodily
strength, he resorted to entreaties and arguments: to
which I only answer'd with a tone of shame and timidity,
that I was afraid he would kill me . . . Lord! . . . , I
would not be served so . . . I was never so used in all
my born days . . . I wondered he was not ashamed of
himself, so I did . . . , with such silly infantile moods
of repulse and complaint as I judged best adapted to
express the character of innocence and affright. Pretending, however, to yield at length to the vehemence of his
insistence, in action and words, I sparingly disclosed my
thighs, so that he could just touch the cloven inlet with
the tip of his instrument: but as he fatigued and toil'd
to get it in, a twist of my body, so as to receive it
obliquely, not only thwarted his admission, but giving a
scream, as if he had pierced me to the heart, I shook him
off me with such violence that he could not with all his
might to it, keep the saddle: vex'd indeed at this he
seemed, but not in the style of any displeasure with me
for my skittishness; on the contrary, I dare swear he held
me the dearer, and hugged himself for the difficulties
that even hurt his instant pleasure. Fired, however, now
beyond all bearance of delay, he remounts and begg'd of
me to have patience, stroking and soothing me to it by
all the tenderest endearments and protestations of what
he would moreover do for me; at which, feigning to be

something softened, and abating of the anger that I had shewn at his hurting me so prodigiously, I suffered him to lay my thighs aside, and make way for a new trial; but I watched the directions and management of his point so well, that no sooner was the orifice in the least open to it, but I gave such a timely jerk as seemed to proceed not from the evasion of his entry, but from the pain his efforts at it put me to: a circumstance too that I did not fail to accompany with proper gestures, sighs and cries of complaint, of which that he had hurt me . . . he kill'd me . . . I should die . . . , were the most frequent interjections. But now, after repeated attempts, in which he had not made the least impression towards gaining his point, at least for that time, the pleasure rose so fast upon him that he could not check or delay it, and in the vigour and fury which the approaches of the height of it inspir'd him, he made one fierce thrust, that had almost put me by my guard, and lodged it so far that I could feel the warm inspersion just within the exterior orifice, which I had the cruelty not to let him finish there. but threw him out again, not without a most piercing loud exclamation, as if the pain had put me beyond all regard of being overheard. It was easy then to observe that he was more satisfy'd, more highly pleased with the supposed motives of his baulk of consummation, than he would have been at the full attainment of it. It was on this foot that I solved to myself all the falsity I employed to procure him that blissful pleasure in it, which most certainly he would not have tasted in the truth of things. Eas'd however, and relieved by one discharge, he now apply'd himself to sooth, encourage and to put me into humour and patience to bear his next attempt, which he began to prepare and gather force for, from all the incentives of the touch and sight which he could think of, by examining every individual part of my whole body, which he declared his satisfaction with in raptures of applauses, kisses universally imprinted, and sparing no part of me, in all the eagerest wantonness of feeling, seeing, and toying. His vigour however did not return so soon, and I felt him more than once pushing at the door, but so little in a condition to break in, that I question whether he had the power to enter, had I held it ever so open; but this he then thought me too little acquainted with the nature of things to have any regret or confusion about, and he kept fatiguing himself and me for a long time, before he was in any state to resume his attacks with any prospect of success; and then I breath'd him so warmly, and kept him so at bay, that before he had made any sensible progress in point of penetration, he was deliciously sweated, and weary'd out indeed: so that it was deep in the morning before he achieved his second let-go, about half way of entrance, I all the while crying and complaining of his prodigious vigour, and the immensity of what I appear'd to suffer splitting up with. Tired, however, at length, with such athletic drudgery, my champion began now to give out, and to gladly embrace the refreshment of some rest. Kissing me then with much affection, and recommending me to my repose, he presently fell fast asleep: which, as soon as I had well satisfy'd myself of, I with much composure of body, so as not to wake him by any motion, with much ease and safety too, played of Mrs. Cole's device for perfecting the signs of my virginity.

In each of the head bed-posts, just above where the bedsteads are inserted into them, there was a small drawer, so artfully adapted to the mouldings of the timber-work, that it might have escap'd even the most curious search: which drawers were easily open'd or shut by the touch of a spring, and were fitted each with a shallow glass tumbler, full of a prepared fluid blood, in which lay soak'd, for ready use, a sponge that required no more than gently reaching the hand to it, taking it out and properly squeezing between the thighs, when it yielded a great deal more of the red liquid than would save a girl's honour; after which, replacing it, and touching the spring, all possibility of discovery, or even of suspicion, was taken away; and all this was not the work of the fourth part of a minute, and on which ever side one lay, the thing was equally easy and practicable, by the double care taken to have each bed-post provided alike. True it is, that had he waked and caught me in the act, it would at least have covered me with shame and confusion; but then, that he did not, was, with the precautions I took, a risk of a thousand to one in my favour.

At ease now, and out of all fear of any doubt or suspicion on his side, I address'd myself in good earnest to my repose, but could obtain none; and in about half an hour's time my gentleman waked again, and turning towards me, I feigned a sound sleep, which he did not long respect; but girding himself again to renew the onset, he began to kiss and caress me, when now making as if I just wak'd, I complained of the disturbance, and of the cruel pain that this little rest had stole my senses from. Eager, however, for the pleasure, as well of consummating an entire triumph over my virginity, he said everything that could overcome my resistance, and bribe my patience to the end, which now I was ready to listen to, from being secure of the bloody proofs I had prepared of his victorious violence, though I still thought it good policy not to let him in yet a while. I answered then only to his importunities in sighs and moans that I was so hurt, I could not bear it . . . I was sure he had done me a mischief; that he had . . . he was such a sad man! At this, turning down the cloaths and viewing the field of battle by the glimmer of a dying taper, he saw plainly my thighs, shift, and sheets, all stained with what he readily took for a virgin effusion, proceeding from his last half-penetration: convinc'd, and transported at which, nothing could equal his joy and exultation. The illusion was complete, no other conception entered his head but that of his having been at work upon an unopen'd mine; which idea, upon so strong an evidence, redoubled at once his tenderness for me, and his ardour for breaking it wholly up. Kissing me then with the utmost rapture, he comforted me, and begg'd my pardon for the pain he had put me to: observing withal, that it was only a thing in course: but the worst was certainly past, and that with a little courage and constancy, I should get it once well over, and never after experience any thing but the greatest pleasure. By little and little I suffer'd myself to be prevailed on, and giving, as it were, up the point to him, I made my thighs, insensibly spreading them, yield him liberty of access, which improving, he got a little within me, when by a well managed reception I work'd the female screw so nicely, that I kept him from the easy mid-channel direction, and by dextrous wreathing and contortions, creating an artificial difficulty of entrance, made him win it inch by inch, with the most laborious struggles, I all the while sorely complaining: till at length, with might and main, winding his way in, he got it completely home, and giving my virginity, as he thought, the *coup de grâce*, furnished me with the cue of setting up a terrible outcry, whilst he, triumphant and like a cock clapping his wings over his down-trod mistress, pursu'd his pleasure: which presently rose, in virtue of this idea of a complete victory, to a pitch that made me soon sensible of his melting period; whilst I now lay acting the deep wounded, breathless, frighten'd, undone, no longer maid.

You would ask me, perhaps, whether all this time I enjoy'd any perception of pleasure? I assure you, little or none, till just towards the latter end, a faintish sense of it came on mechanically, from so long a struggle and frequent fret in that ever sensible part; but, in the first place, I had no taste for the person I was suffering the embraces of, on a pure mercenary account; and then, I was not entirely delighted with myself for the jade's part I was playing, whatever excuses I might have to plead for my being brought into it; but then this insensibility kept me so much the mistress of my mind and motions, that I could the better manage so close a counterfeit, through the whole scene of deception.

Recover'd at length to a more shew of life, by his tender condolences, kisses and embraces, I upbraided him, and reproach'd him with my ruin, in such natural terms as added to his satisfaction with himself for having accomplish'd it; and guessing, by certain observations of mine, that it would be rather favourable to him, to spare him, when he some time after, feebly enough, came on again to the assault, I resolutely withstood any further endeavours, on a pretext that flattered his prowess, of my being so violently hurt and sore that I could not possibly endure a fresh trial. He then graciously granted me a respite, and the next morning soon after advancing, I got rid of further importunity, till Mrs. Cole, being rang for by him, came in and was made acquainted, in terms of the utmost joy and rapture, with his triumphant certainty of my virtue, and the finishing stroke he had given it in the course of the night: of which, he added, she would see proof enough in bloody characters on the sheets.

You may guess how a woman of her turn ot address and experience humour'd the jest, and played him off with mixed exclamations of shame, anger, compassion for me, and of her being pleased that all was so well over: in which last, I believe, she was certainly sincere. And now, as the objection which she had represented as an invincible one, to my lying the first night at his lodgings (which were studiously calculated for freedom of intrigues), on the account of my maiden fears and terrors at the thoughts of going to a gentleman's chambers, and being alone with him in bed, was surmounted, she pretended to persuade me, in favour to him, that I should go there to him whenever he pleas'd, and still keep up all the necessary appearances of working with her, that I might not lose, with my character, the prospect of getting a good husband, and at the same time her house would be kept the safer from scandal. All this seem'd so reasonable, so considerate to Mr. Norbert, that he never once perceived that she did not want him to resort to her house, lest he might in time discover certain inconsistencies with the character she had set out with to him: besides that, this plan greatly flattered his own ease, and views of liberty.

Leaving me then to my much wanted rest, he got up, and Mrs. Cole, after settling with him all points relating to me, got him undiscovered out of the house. After which, as I was awake, she came in and gave me due praises for my success. Behaving too with her usual moderation and disinterestedness, she refus'd any share of the sum I had thus earned, and put me into such a secure and easy way of disposing of my affairs, which now amounted to a kind of little fortune, that a child of ten years old might have kept the account and property of them safe in its hands.

I was now restor'd again to my former state of a kept mistress, and used punctually to wait on Mr. Norbert at his chambers whenever he sent a messenger for me, which I constantly took care to be in the way of, and manag'd with so much caution that he never once penetrated the nature of my connections with Mrs. Cole; but indolently given up to ease and the town dissipations, the perpetual hurry of them hinder'd him from looking into his own affairs, much less to mine.

In the mean time, if I may judge from my own experience, none are better paid, or better treated, during their reign, than the mistresses of those who, enervate by nature, debaucheries, or age, have the least employment for the sex: sensible that a woman must be satisfy'd some way, they ply her with a thousand little tender attentions, presents, caresses, confidences, and exhaust their inventions in means and devices to make up for the capital deficiency; and even towards lessening that, what arts, what modes, what refinements of pleasure have they not recourse to, to raise their languid powers, and press nature into the service of their sensuality? But here is their misfortune, that when by a course of teasing, worrying, handling, wanton postures, lascivious motions, they have at length accomplish'd a flashy enervate enjoyment, they at the same time lighted up a flame in the object of their passion, that, not having the means themselves to quench, drives her for relief into the next person's arms, who can finish their work; and thus they become bawds to some favourite, tried and approv'd of, for a more vigorous and satisfactory execution; for with women, of our turn especially, however well our hearts may be dispos'd, there is a controlling part, or queen seat in us, that governs itself by its own maxims of state, amongst which not one is stronger, in practice with it, than, in the matter of its dues, never to accept the will for the deed.

Mr. Norbert, who was much in this ungracious case, though he profess'd to like me extremely, could but seldom consummate the main-joy itself with me, without such a length and variety of preparations, as were at once wearisome and inflammatory.

Sometimes he would strip me stark naked on a carpet, by a good fire, when he would contemplate me almost by the hour, disposing me in all the figures and attitudes of body that it was susceptible of being viewed in; kissing me in every part, the most secret and critical one so far from excepted that it received most of that branch of homage. Then his touches were so exquisitely wanton, so luxuriously diffus'd and penetrative at times, that he had made me perfectly rage with titillating fires, when, after all, and with much ado, he had gained a short-lived erection, he would perhaps melt it away in a washy sweat, or a premature abortive effusion that provokingly mock'd my eager desires: or, if carried home, how falter'd and unnervous the execution! how insufficient the sprinkle of a few heat-drops to extinguish all the flames he had kindled!

One evening, I cannot help remembering that returning home from him, with a spirit he had raised in a circle his wand had prov'd too weak to lay, as I turn'd the corner of a street, I was overtaken by a young sailor. I was then in that spruce, neat, plain dress which I ever affected, and perhaps might have, in my trip, a certain air of restlessness unknown to the composure of cooler thoughts. However, he seiz'd me as a prize, and without farther ceremony threw his arms round my neck and kiss'd me boisterously and sweetly. I looked at him with a beginning of anger and indignation at his rudeness, that softened away into other sentiments as I viewed him: for he was tall, manly carriaged, handsome of body and face, so that I ended my stare with asking him, in a tone turn'd to tenderness, what he meant; at which, with the same frankness and vivacity as he had begun with me, he proposed treating me with a glass of wine. Now, certain it is, that had I been in a calmer state of blood than I was, had I not been under the dominion of unappeas'd irritations and desires, I should have refused him without hesitation; but I do not know how it was, my pressing calls, his figure, the occasion, and if you will, the power-

ful combination of all these, with a start of curiosity to
see the end of an adventure, so novel too as being treated
like a common street-plyer, made me give a silent consent; in short, it was not my head that I now obeyed, I
suffered myself to be towed along as it were by this man-
of-war, who took me under his arm as familiarly as if he
had known me all his life-time, and led me into the next
convenient tavern, where we were shewn into a little
room on one side of the passage. Here, scarce allowing
himself patience till the waiter brought in the wine call'd
for, he fell directly on board me: when, untucking my
handkerchief, and giving me a snatching buss, he laid my
breasts bare at once, which he handled with that keenness
of lust that abridges a ceremonial ever more tiresome than
pleasing on such pressing occasions; and now, hurrying
towards the main point, we found no conveniency to our
purpose, two or three disabled chairs and a rickety table
composing the whole furniture of the room. Without
more ado, he plants me with my back standing against
the wall, and my petticoats up; and coming out with a
splitter indeed, made it shine, as he brandished it in my
eyes; and going to work with an impetuosity and eagerness, bred very likely by a long fast at sea, went to give
me a taste of it. I straddled, I humoured my posture, and
did my best in short to buckle to it; I took part of it in too,
but still things did not go to his thorough liking: changing then in a trice his system of battery, he leads me to
the table and with a master-hand lays my head down on
the edge of it, and, with the other canting up my petticoats and shift, bares my naked posteriours to his blind
and furious guide; it forces its way between them, and I
feeling pretty sensibly that it was not going by the right
door, and knocking desperately at the wrong one, I told
him of it:—"Pooh!" says he, "my dear, any port in a
storm." Altering, however, directly his course, and low-
ering his point, he fixed it right, and driving it up with a
delicious stiffness, made all foam again, and gave me the
tout with such fire and spirit, that in the fine disposition
I was in when I submitted to him, and stirr'd up so
fiercely as I was, I got the start of him, and went away

into the melting swoon, and squeezing him, whilst in the convulsive grasp of it, drew from him such a plenteous bedewal as, join'd to my own effusion, perfectly floated those parts, and drown'd in a deluge all my raging conflagration of desire.

When this was over, how to make my retreat was my concern; for, though I had been so extremely pleas'd with the difference between this warm broadside, pour'd so briskly into me, and the tiresome pawing and toying to which I had owed the unappeas'd flames that had driven me into this step, now I was grown cooler, I began to apprehend the danger of contracting an acquaintance with this, however agreeable, stranger; who, on his side, spoke of passing the evening with me and continuing our intimacy, with an air of determination that made me afraid of its being not so easy to get away from him as I could wish. In the mean time I carefully conceal'd my uneasiness, and readily pretended to consent to stay with him, telling him I should only step to my lodgings to leave a necessary direction, and then instantly return. This he very glibly swallowed, on the notion of my being one of those unhappy street-errants who devote themselves to the pleasure of the first ruffian that will stoop to pick them up, and of course, that I would scarce bilk myself of my hire, by my not returning to make the most of the job. Thus he parted with me, not before, however, he had order'd in my hearing a supper, which I had the barbarity to disappoint him of my company to.

But when I got home and told Mrs. Cole my adventure, she represented so strongly to me the nature and dangerous consequences of my folly, particularly the risks to my health, in being so open-legg'd and free, that I not only took resolutions never to venture so rashly again, which I inviolably preserv'd, but pass'd a good many days in continual uneasiness lest I should have met with other reasons, besides the pleasure of that encounter, to remember it; but these fears wronged my pretty sailor, for which I gladly make him this reparation.

I had now liv'd with Mr. Norbert near a quarter of a year, in which space I circulated my time very pleasantly between my amusements at Mrs. Cole's, and a proper attendance on that gentleman, who paid me profusely for the unlimited complaisance with which I passively humoured every caprice of pleasure, and which had won upon him so greatly, that finding, as he said, all that variety in me alone which he had sought for in a number of women, I had made him lose his taste for inconstancy, and new faces. But what was yet at least agreeable, as well as more flattering, the love I had inspir'd him with bred a deference to me that was of great service to his health: for having by degrees, and with most pathetic representations, brought him to some husbandry of it, and to insure the duration of his pleasures by moderating their use, and correcting those excesses in them he was so addicted to, and which had shatter'd his constitution and destroyed his powers of life in the very point for which he seemed chiefly desirous, to live, he was grown more delicate, more temperate, and in course more healthy; his gratitude for which was taking a turn very favourable for my fortune, when once more the caprice of it dash'd the cup from my lips.

His sister, Lady L . . . , for whom he had a great affection, desiring him to accompany her down to *Bath* for her health, he could not refuse her such a favour; and accordingly, though he counted on staying away from me no more than a week at farthest, he took his leave of me with an ominous heaviness of heart, and left me a sum far above the state of his fortune, and very inconsistent with the intended shortness of his journey; but it ended in the longest that can be, and is never but once taken: for, arriv'd at Bath, he was not there two days before he fell into a debauch of drinking with some gentlemen, that threw him into a high fever and carry'd him off in four days time, never once out of a delirium. Had he been in his senses to make a will, perhaps he might have made favourable mention of me in it. Thus, however, I lost him; and as no condition of life is more subject to revolutions than that of a woman of pleasure, I soon recover'd my cheerfulness, and now beheld myself once more struck off the list of kept-mistresses, and returned into the bosom of the community from which I had been in some manner taken.

Mrs. Cole still continuing her friendship, offered me her assistance and advice towards another choice; but I was now in ease and affluence enough to look about me at leisure; and as to any constitutional calls of pleasure, their pressure, or sensibility, was greatly lessen'd by a consciousness of the ease with which they were to be satisfy'd at Mrs. Cole's house, where Louisa and Emily still continu'd in the old way; and my great favourite Harriet used often to come and see me, and entertain me, with her head and heart full of the happiness she enjoy'd with her dear baronet, whom she loved with tenderness, and constancy, even though he was her keeper, and what is yet more, had made her independent, by a handsome provision for her and hers. I was then in this vacancy from any regular employ of my person, in my way of business, when one day, Mrs. Cole, in the course of the constant confidence we lived in, acquainted me that there was one *Mr. Barville*, who used her house, just come to town, whom she was not a little perplex'd about providing a suitable companion for; which was indeed a point of difficulty, as he was under the tyranny of a cruel taste: that of an ardent desire, not only of being unmercifully whipp'd himself, but of whipping others, in such sort, that tho' he paid extravagantly those who had the courage and complaisance to submit to his humour, there were few, delicate as he was in the choice of his subjects, who would exchange turns with him so terrible at the expense of their skin. But, what yet increased the oddity of this strange fancy was the gentleman being young; whereas it generally attacks, it seems, such as are, through age, obliged to have recourse to this experiment, for quickening the circulation of their sluggish juices, and determining a conflux of the spirits of pleasure towards those flagging, shrively parts, that rise to life only by virtue of those titillating ardours created by the discipline of their opposites, with which they have so surprising a consent.

This Mrs. Cole could not well acquaint me with, in any expectation of my offering my service: for, sufficiently easy as I was in my circumstances, it must have been the temptation of an immense interest indeed that could have induced me to embrace such a job; neither had I ever express'd, nor indeed felt, the least impulse or curiosity to know more of a taste that promis'd so much more pain than pleasure to those that stood in no need of such violent goads: what then should move me to subscribe myself voluntarily to a party of pain, foreknowing it such? Why, to tell the plain truth, it was a sudden caprice, a gust of fancy for trying a new experiment, mix'd with the vanity of proving my personal courage to Mrs. Cole, that determined me, at all risks, to propose myself to her, and relieve her from any farther lookout. Accordingly, I at once pleas'd and surpris'd her with a frank and unreserved tender of my person to her, and her friend's disposal on this occasion.

My good temporal mother was, however, so kind as to use all the arguments she could imagine to dissuade me: but, as I found they only turn'd on a motive of tenderness to me, I persisted in my resolution, and thereby acquitted my offer of any suspicion of its not having been sincerely made, or out of compliment only. Acquiescing then thankfully in it, Mrs. Cole assur'd me that bating the pain I should be put to, she had no scruple to engage me to this party, which she assur'd me I should be liberally paid for, and which, the secrecy of the transaction preserved safe from the ridicule that otherwise vulgarly attended it; that for her part, she considered pleasure, of one sort or other, as the universal port of destination, and every wind that blew thither a good one, provided it blew nobody any harm; that she rather compassionated, than blam'd, those unhappy persons who are under a subjection they cannot shake off, to those arbitrary tastes that rule their appetites of pleasures with an unaccountable control: tastes, too, as infinitely diversify'd, as superior to, and independent of, all reasoning as the different relishes or palates of mankind in their viands, some delicate stomachs nauseating plain meats, and finding no savour but in high-seasoned, luxurious dishes, whilst others again pique themselves upon detesting them.

I stood now in no need of this preamble of encouragement, of justification: my word was given, and I was determin'd to fulfil my engagements. Accordingly the night was set, and I had all the necessary previous instructions how to act and conduct myself. The dining-room was duly prepared and lighted up, and the young gentleman posted there in waiting, for my introduction to him.

I was then, by Mrs. Cole, brought in, and presented to him, in a loose dishabille fitted, by her direction, to the exercise I was to go through, all in the finest linen and a thorough white uniform: gown, petticoat, stockings, and satin slippers, like a victim led to sacrifice; whilst my dark auburn hair, falling in drop-curls over my neck, created a pleasing distinction of colour from the rest of my dress.

As soon as Mr. Barville saw me, he got up, with a visible air of pleasure and surprize, and saluting me, asked Mrs. Cole if it was possible that so fine and delicate a creature would voluntarily submit to such sufferings and rigours as were the subject of his assignation. She answer'd him properly, and now, reading in his eyes that she could not too soon leave us together, she went out, after recommending to him to use moderation with so tender a novice.

But whilst she was employing his attention, mine had been taken up with examining the figure and person of this unhappy young gentleman, who was thus unaccountably condemn'd to have his pleasure lashed into him, as boys have their learning.

He was exceedingly fair, and smooth complexion'd, and appeared to me no more than twenty at most, tho' he was three years older than what my conjectures gave him; but then he ow'd this favourable mistake to a habit of fatness, which spread through a short, squab stature, and a round, plump, fresh-coloured face gave him greatly the look of a *Bacchus,* had not an air of austerity, not to say sternness, very unsuitable even to his shape of face, dash'd that character of joy, necessary to complete the resemblance. His dress was extremely neat, but plain, and far inferior to the ample fortune he was in full possession of; this too was a taste in him, and not avarice.

As soon as Mrs. Cole was gone, he seated me near him, when now his face changed upon me into an expression of the most pleasing sweetness and good humour, the more remarkable for its sudden shift from the other extreme, which, I found afterwards, when I knew more of his character, was owing to a habitual state of conflict with, and dislike of himself, for being enslaved to so peculiar a gust, by the fatality of a constitutional ascendant, that render'd him incapable of receiving any pleasure till he submitted to these extraordinary means of procuring it at the hands of pain, whilst the constancy of this repining consciousness stamp'd at length that cast of sourness and severity on his features: which was, in fact, very foreign to the natural sweetness of his temper.

After a competent preparation by apologies, and encouragement to go through my part with spirit and constancy, he stood up near the fire, whilst I went to fetch the instruments of discipline out of a closet hard by: these were several rods, made each of two or three strong twigs of birch tied together, which he took, handled, and view'd with as much pleasure, as I did with a kind of shuddering presage.

Next we took from the side of the room a long broad bench, made easy to lie at length on by a soft cushion in a callico-cover; and every thing being now ready, he took his coat and waistcoat off; and at his motion and desire, I unbutton'd his breeches, and rolling up his shirt rather above his waist, tuck'd it in securely there: when directing naturally my eyes to that humoursome master-movement, in whose favour all these dispositions were making, it seemed almost shrunk into his body, scarce shewing its tip above the sprout of hairy curls that cloathed those parts, as you may have seen a wren peep its head out of the grass.

Stooping then to untie his garters, he gave them me for the use of tying him down to the legs of the bench: a circumstance no farther necessary than, as I suppose, it made part of the humour of the thing, since he prescribed it to himself, amongst the rest of the ceremonial.

I led him then to the bench, and according to my cue,

play'd at forcing him to lie down: which, after some little shew of reluctance, for form-sake, he submitted to; he was straightway extended flat upon his belly, on the bench, with a pillow under his face; and as he thus tamely lay, I tied him slightly hand and foot, to the legs of it; which done, his shirt remaining truss'd up over the small of his back, I drew his breeches quite down to his knees; and now he lay, in all the fairest, broadest display of that part of the back-view; in which a pair of chubby, smooth-cheek'd and passing white posteriours rose cushioning upwards from two stout, fleshful thighs, and ending their cleft, or separation by an union at the small of the back, presented a bold mark, that swell'd, as it were, to meet the scourge.

Seizing now one of the rods, I stood over him, and according to his direction, gave him in one breath, ten lashes with much good-will, and the utmost nerve and vigour of arm that I could put to them, so as to make those fleshy orbs quiver again under them; whilst he himself seem'd no more concern'd, or to mind them, than a lob-ster would a flea-bite. In the mean time, I viewed intently the effects of them, which to me at least appear'd surpris-ingly cruel: every lash had skimmed the surface of those white cliffs, which they deeply reddened, and lapping round the side of the furthermost from me, cut specially, into the dimple of it such livid weals, as the blood either spun out from, or stood in large drops on; and, from some of the cuts, I picked out even the splinters of the rod that had stuck in the skin. Nor was this raw work to be wonder'd at, considering the greenness of the twigs and the severity of the infliction, whilst the whole surface of his skin was so smooth-stretched over the hard and firm pulp of flesh that fill'd it, as to yield no play, or elusive swagging under the stroke: which thereby took place the more plum, and cut into the quick.

I was however already so mov'd at the piteous sight, that I from my heart repented the undertaking, and would willingly have given over, thinking he had full enough; but, he encouraging and beseeching me earnestly to pro-ceed, I gave him ten more lashes; and then resting, sur-

vey'd the increase of bloody appearances. And at length,
steel'd to the sight by his stoutness in suffering, I continued the discipline, by intervals, till I observ'd him wreathing and twisting his body, in a way that I could plainly
perceive was not the effect of pain, but of some new and
powerful sensation: curious to dive into the meaning of
which, in one of my pauses of intermission, I approached,
as he still kept working, and grinding his belly against the
cushion under him; and, first stroking the untouched and
unhurt side of the flesh-mount next me, then softly insinuating my hand under his thigh, felt the posture things
were in forwards, which was indeed surprizing: for that
machine of his. which I had, by its appearance, taken for
an impalpable. or at best a very diminutive subject, was
now, in virtue of all that smart and havoc of his skin behind, grown not only to a prodigious stiffness of erection,
but to a size that frighted even me: a non-pariel thickness
indeed! the head of it alone fill'd the utmost capacity of
my grasp. And when, as he heav'd and wriggled to and
fro, in the agitation of his strange pleasure, it came into
view, it had something of the air of a round fillet of the
whitest veal, and like its owner, squab, and short in proportion to its breadth; but when he felt my hand there, he
begg'd I would go on briskly with my jerking, or he
should never arrive at the last stage of pleasure.

Resuming then the rod and the exercise of it, I had
fairly worn out three bundles, when, after an increase of
struggles and motion, and a deep sigh or two, I saw him
lie still and motionless; and now he desir'd me to desist,
which I instantly did; and proceeding to untie him, I
could not but be amazed at his passive fortitude, on viewing the skin of his butcher'd. mangled posteriours, late so
white, smooth and polish'd, now all one side of them a
confused cut-work of weals, livid flesh, gashes and gore,
insomuch that when he stood up, he could scarce walk; in
short, he was in sweet-briars.

Then I plainly perceived, on the cushion, the marks
of a plenteous effusion, and already had his sluggard
member run up to its old nestling-place, and enforced
itself again, as if ashamed to shew its head; which noth-

ing, it seems, could raise but stripes inflicted on its opposite neighbours, who were thus constantly obliged to suffer for his caprice.

My gentleman had now put on his clothes and recomposed himself, when giving me a kiss, and placing me by
him, he sat himself down as gingerly as possible, with
one side off the cushion, which was too sore for him to
bear resting any part of his weight on.

Here he thank'd me for the extreme pleasure I had
procured him, and seeing, perhaps, some marks in my
countenance of terror and apprehension of retaliation on
my own skin, for what I had been the instrument of his
suffering in his, he assured me, that he was ready to give
up to me any engagement I might deem myself under to
stand him, as he had done me, but if that proceeded in
my consent to it, he would consider the difference of my
sex, its greater delicacy and incapacity to undergo pain.
Rehearten'd at which, and piqu'd in honour, as I
thought, not to flinch so near the trial, especially as I well
knew Mrs. Cole was an eye-witness, from her stand of
espial, to the whole of our transactions, I was now less
afraid of my skin than of his not furnishing me with an
opportunity of signalizing my resolution.

Consonant to this disposition was my answer, but my
courage was still more in my head, than in my heart; and
as cowards rush into the danger they fear, in order to be
the sooner rid of the pain of that sensation, I was entirely
pleas'd with his hastening matters into execution.

He had then little to do, but to unloose the strings of
my petticoats, and lift them, together with my shift, navel-
high, where he just tuck'd them up loosely girt, and might
be slipt up higher at pleasure. Then viewing me round
with great seeming delight, he laid me at length on my
face upon the bench, and when I expected he would tie
me, as I had done him, and held out my hands, not without fear and a little trembling, he told me he would by no
means terrify me unnecessarily with such a confinement;
for that though he meant to put my constancy to some
trial, the standing it was to be completely voluntary on
my side, and therefore I might be at full liberty to get up

whenever I found the pain too much for me. You cannot imagine how much I thought myself bound, by being thus allow'd to remain loose, and how much spirit this confidence in me gave me, so that I was even from my heart careless how much my flesh might suffer in honour of it.

All my back parts, naked half way up, were now fully at his mercy: and first, he stood at a convenient distance, delighting himself with a gloating survey of the attitude I lay in, and of all the secret stores I thus expos'd to him in fair display. Then, springing eagerly towards me, he cover'd all those naked parts with a fond profusion of kisses; and now, taking hold of the rod, rather waton'd with me, in gentle inflictions on those tender trembling masses of my flesh behind, than in any way hurt them, till by degrees, he began to tingle them with smarter lashes, so as to provoke a red colour into them, which I knew, as well by the flagrant glow I felt there, as by his telling me, they now emulated the native roses of my other cheeks When he had thus amus'd himself with admiring and toying with them, he went on to strike harder, and more hard: so that I needed all my patience not to cry out, or complain at least. At last, he twigg'd me so smartly as to fetch blood in more than one lash: at sight of which he flung down the rod, flew to me, kissed away the starting drops, and sucking the wounds eased a good deal of my pain But now raising me on my knees, and making me kneel with them straddling wide, that tender part of me naturally the province of pleasure, not of pain, came in for its share of suffering: for now, eyeing it wistfully, he directed the rod so that the sharp ends of the twigs lighted there, so sensibly, that I could not help wincing, and writhing my limbs with smart; so that my contortions of body must necessarily throw it into infinite variety of postures and points of view, fit to feast the luxury of the eye. But still I bore every thing without crying out: when presently giving me another pause, he rush'd, as it were, on that part whose lips, and round-about, had felt this cruelty, and by way of reparation, glews his own to them; then he opened, shut, squeez'd them, pluck'd softly the overgrowing moss, and all this in a style of wild passionate rapture and enthusiasm, that express'd excess of pleasure; till betaking himself to the rod again, encourag'd by my passiveness, and infuriated with this strange taste of delight, he made my poor posteriours pay for the ungovernableness of it; for now shewing them no quarter the traitor cut me so, that I wanted but little of fainting away, when he gave over. And yet I did not utter one groan, or angry expostulation; but in heart I resolv'd nothing so seriously, as never to expose myself again to the like severities.

You may guess then in what a curious pickle those soft flesh-cushions of mine were, all sore, raw, and in fine, terribly clawed off; but so far from feeling any pleasure in it, that the recent smart made me pout a little, and not with the greatest air of satisfaction receive the compliments, and after-caresses of the author of my pain.

As soon as my cloaths were huddled on in a little decency, a supper was brought in by the discreet Mrs. Cole herself which might have piqued the sensuality of a cardinal, accompanied with a choice of the richest wines: all which she set before us, and went out again, without having, by a word or even by a smile, given us the least interruption or confusion, in those moments of secrecy, that we were not yet ripe to the admission of a third to.

I sat down then, still scarce in charity with my butcher, for such I could not help considering him, and was moreover not a little piqued at the gay, satisfied air of his countenance, which I thought myself insulted by. But when the now necessary refreshment to me of a glass of wine, a little eating (all the time observing a profound silence) had somewhat cheer'd and restor'd me to spirits, and as the smart began to go off, my good humour return'd accordingly: which alteration not escaping him, he said and did everything that could confirm me in, and indeed exalt it.

But scarce was supper well over, before a change so incredible was wrought in me, such violent, yet pleasingly irksome sensations took possession of me that I scarce knew how to contain myself; the smart of the lashes was now converted into such a prickly heat, such fiery tin-

glings, as made me sigh, squeeze my thighs together, shift
and wriggle about my seat, with a furious restlessness;
whilst these itching ardours, thus excited in those parts
on which the storm of discipline had principally fallen,
detach'd legions of burning, subtile, stimulating spirits, to
their opposite spot and centre of assemblage, where their
titillation rag'd so furiously, that I was even stinging mad
with them. No wonder then, that in such a taking, and
devour'd by flames that licked up all modesty and reserve,
my eyes, now charg'd brimful of the most intense desire,
fired on my companion very intelligible signals of distress:
my companion, I say, who grew in them every instant
more amiable, and more necessary to my urgent wishes
and hopes of immediate ease.

Mr. Barville, no stranger by experience to these situations, soon knew the pass I was brought to, soon perceiv'd my extreme disorder; in favour of which, removing
the table out of the way, he began a prelude that flatter'd
me with instant relief, to which I was not, however, so
near as I imagin'd: for as he was unbuttoned to me, and
tried to provoke and rouse to action his unactive torpid
machine, he blushingly own'd that no good was to be expected from it unless I took it in hand to re-excite its
languid loitering powers, by just refreshing the smart of
the yet recent blood-raw cuts, seeing it could, no more
than a boy's top, keep up without lashing. Sensible then
that I should work as much for my own profit as his, I
hurried my compliance with his desire, and abridging the
ceremonial, whilst he lean'd his head against the back of
a chair, I had scarce gently made him feel the lash, before
I saw the object of my wishes give signs of life, and presently, as it were with a magic touch, it started up into a
noble size and distinction indeed! Hastening then to give
me the benefit of it, he threw me down on the bench; but
such was the refresh'd soreness of those parts behind, on
my leaning so hard on them, as became me to compass the
admission of that stupendous head of his machine, that I
could not possibly bear it. I got up then, and tried, by
leaning forwards and turning the crupper on my assailant,
to let him at the back avenue: but here it was likewise

impossible to stand his bearing so fiercely against me, in his agitations and endeavours to enter that way, whilst his belly battered directly against the recent sore. What should we do now? both intolerably heated; both in a fury; but pleasure is ever inventive for its own ends: he strips me in a trice, stark naked, and placing a broad settee-cushion on the carpet before the fire, oversets me gently, topsy-turvy, on it; and handling me only at the waist, whilst you may be sure I favour'd all my dispositions, brought my legs round his neck; so that my head was kept from the floor only by my hands and the velvet cushion, which was now bespread with my flowing hair: thus I stood on my head and hands, supported by him in such manner, that whilst my thighs clung round him, so as to expose to his sight all my back figure, including the theatre of his bloody pleasure, the centre of my fore part fairly bearded the object of its rage, that now stood in fine condition to give me satisfaction for the injuries of its neighbours. But as this posture was certainly not the easiest, and our imaginations, wound up to the height, could suffer no delay, he first, with the utmost eagerness and effort, just lip-lodg'd that broad acorn-fashion'd head of his instrument; and still frenzied by the fury with which he had made that impression, he soon stuffed in the rest; when now, with a pursuit of thrusts, fiercely urg'd, he absolutely overpower'd and absorb'd all sense of pain and uneasiness, whether from my wounds behind, my most untoward posture, or the oversize of his stretcher, in an infinitely predominant delight; when now all my whole spirits of life and sensation, rushing impetuously to the cock-pit, where the prize of pleasure was hotly in dispute and clustering to a point there, I soon receiv'd the dear relief of nature from these over-violent strains and provocations of it; harmonizing with which, my gallant spouted into me such a potent overflow of the balsamic injection, as soften'd and unedg'd all those irritating stings of a new species of titillation, which I had been so intolerably madden'd with, and restor'd the ferment of my senses to some degree of composure.

I had now achiev'd this rare adventure ultimately much

more to my satisfaction than I had bespoken the nature of it to turn out; nor was it much lessen'd, you may think, by my spark's lavish praises of my constancy and complaisance, which he gave weight to by a present that greatly surpassed my utmost expectation, besides his gratification to Mrs. Cole.

I was not, however, at any time, re-enticed to renew with him, or resort again to the violent expedient of lashing nature into more haste than good speed: which, by the way, I conceive acts somewhat in the manner of a dose of *Spanish* flies; with more pain perhaps, but less danger; and might be necessary to him, but was nothing less so than to me, whose appetite wanted the bridle more than the spur.

Mrs. Cole, to whom this adventurous exploit had more and more endear'd me, looked on me now as a girl after her own heart, afraid of nothing, and, on a good account, hardy enough to fight all the weapons of pleasure through. Attentive then, in consequence of these favourable conceptions, to promote either my profit or pleasure, she had special regard for the first, in a new gallant of a very singular turn, that she procur'd for and introduced to me.

This was a grave, staid, solemn, elderly gentleman whose peculiar humour was a delight in combing fine tresses of hair; and as I was perfectly headed to his taste, he us'd to come constantly at my toilette hours, when I let down my hair as loose as nature, and abandon'd it to him to do what he pleased with it; and accordingly he would keep me an hour or more in play with it, drawing the comb through it, winding the curls round his fingers, even kissing it as he smooth'd it; and all this led to no other use of my person, or any other liberties whatever, any more than if a distinction of sexes had not existed.

Another peculiarity of taste he had, which was to present me with a dozen pairs of the whitest kid gloves at a time: these he would divert himself with drawing on me, and then biting off the fingers' ends; all which fooleries of a sickly appetite, the old gentleman paid more liberally for than most others did for more essential

favours. This lasted till a violent cough, seizing and laying him up, deliver'd me from this most innocent and insipid trifler, for I never heard more of him after his first
retreat.

You may be sure a by-job of this sort interfer'd with no
other pursuit, or plan of life; which I led, in truth, with
a modesty and reserve that was less the work of virtue
than of exhausted novelty, a glut of pleasure, and easy
circumstances, that made me indifferent to any engagements in which pleasure and profit were not eminently
united; and such I could, with the less impatience, wait
for at the hands of time and fortune, as I was satisfy'd I
could never mend my pennyworths, having evidently
been serv'd at the top of market, and even been pam-
per'd with dainties: besides that, in the sacrifice of a few
momentary impulses, I found a secret satisfaction in respecting myself, as well as preserving the life and freshness of my complexion. Louisa and Emily did not carry
indeed their reserve so high as I did; but still they were
far from cheap or abandon'd tho' two of their adventures
seem'd to contradict this general character, which, for
their singularity, I shall give you in course, beginning first
with Emily's:

Louisa and she went one night to a ball, the first in the
habit of a shepherdess, Emily in that of a shepherd: I
saw them in their dresses before they went, and nothing
in nature could represent a prettier boy than this last did,
being so fair and well limbed. They had kept together for
some time, when Louisa, meeting an old acquaintance of
hers, very cordially gives her companion the drop, and
leaves her under the protection of her boy's habit, which
was not much, and of her discretion, which was, it seems,
still less. Emily, finding herself deserted, sauntered
thoughtless about a-while, and, as much for coolness and
air as anything else, at length pull'd off her mask and went
to the sideboard; where, eyed and mark'd out by a gentleman in a very handsome domino, she was accosted by,
and fell into chat with him. The domino, after a little discourse, in which Emily doubtless distinguish'd her good
nature and easiness more than her wit, began to make

violent love to her, and drawing her insensibly to some benches at the lower end of the masquerade room, for her to sit by him, where he squeez'd her hands, pinch'd her cheeks, prais'd and played with her fine hair, admired her complexion, and all in a style of courtship dash'd with a certain oddity, that not comprehending the mystery of, poor Emily attributed to his falling in with the humour of her disguise; and being naturally not the cruellest of her profession, began to incline to a parley on those essentials. But here was the stress of the joke: he took her really for what she appear'd to be, a smock-fac'd boy; and she, forgetting her dress, and of course ranging quite wide of his ideas, took all those addresses to be paid to herself as a woman, which she precisely owed to his not thinking her one. However, this double error was push'd to such a height on both sides, that Emily, who saw nothing in him but a gentleman of distinction by those points of dress to which his disguise did not extend, warmed too by the wine he had ply'd her with, and the caresses he had lavished upon her, suffered herself to be persuaded to go to a bagnio with him; and thus, losing sight of Mrs. Cole's cautions, with a blind confidence, put herself into his hands, to be carried wherever he pleased. For his part, equally blinded by his wishes, whilst her egregious simplicity favoured his deception more than the most exquisite art could have done, he supposed, no doubt, that he had lighted on some soft simpleton, fit for his purpose, or some kept minion broken to his hand, who understood him perfectly well and enter'd into his designs. But, be that as it would, he led her to a coach, went into it with her, and brought her to a very handsome apartment, with a bed in it; but whether it was a bagnio or not, she could not tell, having spoken to nobody but himself. But when they were alone together, and her *enamorato* began to proceed to those extremities which instantly discover the sex, she remark'd that no description could paint up to the life the mixture of pique, confusion and disappointment that appeared in his countenance, joined to the mournful exclamation: "By heavens, a woman!" This at once opened her eyes, which had hitherto been shut in down-right stupidity. However, as if he had meant to retrieve that escape, he still continu'd to toy with and fondle her, but with so staring an alteration from extreme warmth into a chill and forced civility, that even Emily herself could not but take notice of it, and now began to wish she had paid more regard to Mrs. Cole's premonitions against ever engaging with a stranger. And now an excess of timidity succeeded to an excess of confidence, and she thought herself so much at his mercy and discretion, that she stood passive throughout the whole progress of his prelude: for now, whether the impressions of so great a beauty had even made him forgive her her sex, or whether her appearance of figure in that dress still humour'd his first illusion, he recover'd by degrees a good part of his first warmth, and keeping Emily with her breeches still unbuttoned, stript them down to her knees, and gently impelling her to lean down, with her face against the bed-side, placed her so, that the double way, between the double rising behind, presented the choice fair to him, and he was so fairly set on a mis-direction, as to give the girl no small alarms for fear of losing a maidenhead she had not dreamt of. However, her complaints, and a resistance, gentle, but firm, check'd and brought him to himself again; so that turning his steed's head, he drove him at length in the right road, in which his imagination having probably made the most of those resemblances that flatter'd his taste, he got, with much ado, to his journey's end: after which, he led her out himself, and walking with her two or three streets' length, got her a chair, when making her a present not any thing inferior to what she could have expected, he left her, well recommended to the chairmen, who, on her directions, brought her home.

This she related to Mrs. Cole and me the same morning, not without the visible remains of the fear and confusion she had been in still stamp'd on her countenance. Mrs. Cole's remark was that her indiscretion proceeding from a constitutional facility, there were little hopes of any thing curing her of it, but repeated severe experience. Mine was that I could not conceive how it was pos-

sible for mankind to run into a taste, not only universally
odious, but absurd, and impossible to gratify; since, according to the notions and experience I had of things, it
was not in nature to force such immense disproportions.
Mrs. Cole only smil'd at my ignorance, and said nothing
towards my undeception, which was not affected but by
ocular demonstration, some months after, which a most
singular accident furnish'd me, and which I will here set
down, that I may not return again to so disagreeable a
subject.

I had, on a visit intended to Harriet, who had taken
lodgings at *Hampton-court*, hired a chariot to go out
thither, Mrs. Cole having prois'd to accompany me; but
some indispensable business intervening to detain her, I
was obliged to set out alone; and scarce had I got a third
of my way, before the axle-tree broke down, and I was
well off to get out, safe and unhurt, into a publick-house
of a tolerable handsome appearance, on the road. Here
the people told me that the stage would come by in a
couple of hours at farthest; upon which, determining to
wait for it, sooner than lose the jaunt I had got so far forward on, I was carried into a very clean decent room, up
one pair of stairs, which I took possession of for the time
I had to stay, in right of calling for sufficient to do the
house justice.

Here, whilst I was amusing myself with looking out of
the window, a single horse-chaise stopt at the door, out of
which lightly leap'd two gentlemen, for so they seem'd,
who came in only as it were to bait and refresh a little,
for they gave their horse to be held in readiness against
they came out. And presently I heard the door of the next
room, where they were let in, and call'd about them
briskly; and as soon as they were serv'd, I could just hear
that they shut and fastened the door on the inside.

A spirit of curiosity, far from sudden, since I do not
know when I was without it, prompted me, without any
particular suspicion, or other drift or view, to see what
they were, and examine their persons and behaviour. The
partition of our rooms was one of those moveable ones
that, when taken down, serv'd occasionally to lay them

into one, for the conveniency of a large company; and now, my nicest search could not shew me the shadow of a peep-hole, a circumstance which probably had not escap'd the review of the parties on the other side, whom much it stood upon not to be deceived in it; but at length I observed a paper patch of the same colour as the wainscot, which I took to conceal some flaw: but then it was so high, that I was obliged to stand upon a chair to reach it, which I did as softly as possibly, and, with a point of a bodkin, soon pierc'd it. And now, applying my eye close, I commanded the room perfectly, and could see my two young sparks romping and pulling one another about, entirely, to my imagination, in frolic and innocent play.

The eldest might be, on my nearest guess, towards nineteen, a tall comely young man, in a white fustian frock, with a green velvet cape, and a cut bob-wig.

The youngest could not be above seventeen, fair, ruddy, compleatly well made, and to say the truth, a sweet pretty stripling: he was—I fancy, too, a country-lad, by his dress, which was a green plush frock and breeches of the same, white waistcoat and stockings, a jockey cap, with his yellowish hair, long and loose, in natural curls.

But after a look of circumspection, which I saw the eldest cast every way round the room, probably in too much hurry and heat not to overlook the very small opening I was posted at, especially at the height it was, whilst my eye close to it kept the light from shining through and betraying it, he said something to his companion that presently chang'd the face of things.

For now the elder began to embrace, to press and kiss the younger, to put his hands into his bosom, and give him such manifest signs of an amorous intention, as made me conclude the other to be a girl in disguise: a mistake that nature kept me in countenance for, for she had certainly made one, when she gave him the male stamp.

In the rashness then of their age, and bent as they were to accomplish their project of preposterous pleasure, at the risk of the very worst of consequences, where a discovery was nothing less than improbable, they now proceeded to such lengths as soon satisfied me what they were.

The criminal scene they acted, I had the patience to see to an end, purely that I might gather more facts and certainty against them in my design to do their deserts instance justice; and accordingly, when they had re-adjusted themselves, and were preparing to go out, burning as I was with rage and indignation, I jumped down from the chair, in order to raise the house upon them, but with such an unlucky impetuosity, that some nail or ruggedness in the floor caught my foot, and flung me on my face with such violence that I fell senseless on the ground, and must have lain there some time e'er any one came to my relief: so that they, alarmed, I suppose, by the noise of my fall, had more than the necessary time to make a safe retreat. This they effected, as I learnt, with a precipitation nobody could account for, till, when come to myself, and compos'd enough to speak, I acquainted those of the house with the whole transaction I had been evidence to.

When I came home again, and told Mrs. Cole this adventure, she very sensibly observ'd to me that there was no doubt of due vengeance one time or other overtaking these miscreants, however they might escape for the present; and that, had I been the temporal instrument of it, I should have been at least put to a great deal more trouble and confusion than I imagined; that, as to the thing itself, the less said of it was the better; but that though she might be suspected of partiality, from its being the common cause of woman-kind, out of whose *mouths* this practice tended to take something more than bread, yet she protested against any mixture of passion, with a declaration extorted from her by pure regard to truth; which was that whatever effect this infamous passion had in other ages and other countries, it seem'd a peculiar blessing on our air and climate, that there was a plague-spot visibly imprinted on all that are tainted with it, in this nation at least; for that among numbers of that stamp whom she had known, or at least were universally under the scandalous suspicion of it, she would not name an exception hardly of one of them, whose character was not, in all other respects, the most worthless and despicable that could be, stript of all the manly virtues of their own sex, and fill'd up with only the worst vices and follies of ours: that, *in fine*, they were scarce less execrable than ridiculous in their monstrous inconsistence, of loathing and condemning women, and all at the same time apeing all their manners, airs, lips, skuttle, and, in general, all their little modes of affectation, which become them at least better than they do these unsex'd male-misses.

But here, washing my hands of them, I re-plunge into the stream of my history, into which I may very properly ingraft a terrible sally of Louisa's, since I had some share in it myself, and have besides engag'd myself to relate it, in point of countenance to poor Emily. It will add, too, one more example to thousands, in confirmation of the maxim that when women get once out of compass, there are no lengths of licentiousness that they are not capable of running.

One morning then, that both Mrs. Cole and Emily were gone out for the day, and only Louisa and I (not to mention the house-maid) were left in charge of the house, whilst we were loitering away the time in looking through the shop windows, the son of a poor woman, who earned very hard bread indeed by mending of stockings, in a stall in the neighbourhood, offer'd us some nosegays, ring'd round a small basket; by selling of which the poor boy eked out his mother's maintenance of them both: nor was he fit for any other way of livelihood, since he was not only a perfect changeling, or idiot, but stammer'd so that there was no understanding even those sounds his half-dozen, at most, animal ideas prompted him to utter.

The boys and servants in the neighbourhood had given him the nick-name of *Good-natured Dick*, from the soft simpleton's doing everything he was bid at the first word, and from his naturally having no turn to mischief; then, by the way, he was perfectly well made, stout, clean-limb'd, tall of his age, as strong as a horse and, withal, pretty featur'd; so that he was not, absolutely, such a figure to be snuffled at neither, if your nicety could, in favour of such essentials, have dispens'd with a face un-washed, hair tangled for want of combing, and so ragged a plight, that he might have disputed points of shew with e'er a heathen philosopher of them all.

This boy we had often seen, and bought his flowers, out of pure compassion, and nothing more; but just at this time as he stood presenting us his basket, a sudden whim, a start of wayward fancy, seiz'd Louisa; and, without con-sulting me, she calls him in, and beginning to examine his nosegays, culls out two, one for herself, another for me, and pulling out half a crown, very currently gives it him to change, as if she had really expected he could have changed it: but the boy, scratching his head, made his signs explaining his inability in place of words, which he could not, with all his struggling, articulate.

Louisa, at this, says: "Well, my lad, come up-stairs with me, and I will give you your due," winking at the same time to me, and beckoning me to accompany her, which I did, securing first the street-door, that by this means, together with the shop, became wholly the care of the faithful house-maid.

As we went up, Louisa whispered to me that she had conceiv'd a strange longing to be satisfy'd, whether the general rule held good with regard to this changeling, and how far nature had made him amends, in her best bodily gifts, for her denial of the sublimer intellectual ones; begging. at the same time, my assistance in procur-ing her this satisfaction. A want of complaisance was never my vice, and I was so far from opposing this extravagant frolic, that now, bit with the same maggot, and my curios-ity conspiring with hers, I enter'd plum into it, on my own account.

Consequently, as soon as we came into Louisa's bed-chamber, whilst she was amusing him with picking out his nosegays, I undertook the lead, and began the attack. As it was not then very material to keep much measures with a mere natural, I made presently very free with him, though at my first motion of meddling, his surprize and confusion made him receive my advances but aukwardly: nay, insomuch that he bashfully shy'd, and shy'd back a little; till encouraging him with my eyes, plucking him playfully by the hair, sleeking his cheeks, and forwarding my point by a number of little wantonness, I soon turn'd him familiar, and gave nature her sweetest alarm: so that arous'd, and beginning to feel himself, we could, amidst all the innocent laugh and grin I had provoked him into, perceive the fire lighting in his eyes, and, diffusing over his cheeks, blend its glow with that of his blushes. The emotion in short of animal pleasure glar'd distinctly in the simpleton's countenance; yet, struck with the novelty of the scene, he did not know which way to look or move; but tame, passive, simpering, with his mouth half open in stupid rapture, stood and tractably suffer'd me to do what I pleased with him. His basket was dropt out of his hands, which Louisa took care of.

I had now, through more than one rent, discovered and felt his thighs, the skin of which seemed the smoother and fairer for the coarseness, and even dirt of his dress, as the teeth of Negroes seem the whiter for the surrounding black; and poor indeed of habit, poor of understanding, he was, however, abundantly rich in personal treasures, such as flesh, firm, plump, and replete with the juices of youth, and robust well-knit limbs. My fingers too had now got within reach of the true, the genuine sensitive plant, which, instead of shrinking from the touch, joys to meet it, and swells and vegetates under it: mine pleasingly informed me that matters were so ripe for the discovery we meditated, that they were too mighty for the confinement they were ready to break. A waistband that I unskewer'd, and a rag of a shirt that I removed, and which could not have cover'd a quarter of it, revealed the whole of the idiot's standard of distinction, erect, in full pride and display: but such a one! it was positively of so tremendous a size, that prepared as we were to see something extraordinary, it still, out of measure, surpass'd our expectation, and astonish'd even me, who had not been used to trade in trifles. *In fine*, it might have answered very well the making a show of; its enormous head seemed, in hue and size, not unlike a common sheep's heart; then you might have troll'd dice securely along the broad back of the body of it; the length of it too was prodigious; then the rich appendage of the treasure-bag beneath, large in proportion, gather'd and crisp'd up round in shallow furrows, helped to fill the eye, and complete the proof of his being a natural, not quite in vain; since it was full manifest that he inherited, and largely too, the prerogative of majesty which distinguishes that otherwise most unfortunate condition, and gives rise to the vulgar saying *"A fool's bauble is a lady's play-fellow."* Not wholly without reason: for, generally speaking, it is in love as it is in war, where longest weapon carries it. Nature, in short, had done so much for him in those parts that she perhaps held herself acquitted in doing so little for his head.

For my part, who had sincerely no intention to push the joke further than simply satisfying my curiosity with the sight of it alone, I was content, in spite of the temptation that star'd me in the face, with having rais'd a Maypole for another to hang a garland on: for, by this time, easily reading Louisa's desires in her wishful eyes, I acted the commodious part and made her, who sought no better sport, significant terms of encouragement to go through-stitch with her adventure; intimating too that I would stay and see fair play: in which, indeed, I had in view to humour a new-born curiosity, to observe what appearances active nature would put on in a natural, in the course of this her darling operation.

Louisa, whose appetite was up, and who, like the industrious bee, was, it seems, not above gathering the sweets of so rare a flower, tho' she found it planted on a dunghill, was but too readily disposed to take the benefit of my cession. Urg'd then strongly by her own desires, and embolden'd by me, she presently determined to risk a trial of parts with the idiot, who was by this time nobly inflam'd for her purpose, by all the irritations we had used to put the principles of pleasure effectually into motion, and to wind up the springs of its organ to their supreme pitch; and it stood accordingly stiff and straining, ready to burst with the blood and spirits that swelled it . . . to a bulk! No! I shall never forget it.

Louisa then, taking and holding the fine handle that so invitingly offer'd itself, led the ductile youth by that master-tool of his, as she stept backward towards the bed; which he joyfully gave way to, under the incitations of instinct and palpably deliver'd up to the goad of desire.

Stopped then by the bed, she took the fall she lov'd, and lean'd to the most, gently backward upon it, still holding fast what she held, and taking care to give her cloaths a convenient toss up, so that her thighs duly disclos'd, and elevated, laid open all the outward prospect of the treasury of love: the rose-lipt overture presenting the cock-pit so fair, that it was not in nature even for a natural to miss it. Nor did he: for Louisa, fully bent on grappling with it, and impatient of dalliance or delay, directed faithfully the point of the battering-piece, and bounded up with a rage of so voracious appetite, to meet and favour the thrust of insertion, that the fierce activity on both sides effected it with such pain of distention, that Louisa cry'd out violently that she was hurt beyond bearing, that she was killed. But it was too late: the storm was up, and force was on her to give way to it; for now the man-machine, strongly work'd upon by the sensual passion, felt so manfully his advantages and superiority, felt withal the sting of pleasure so intolerable, that maddening with it, his joys began to assume a character of furiousness which made me tremble for the too tender Louisa. He seemed, at this juncture, greater than himself; his countenance, before so void of meaning, or expression, now grew big with the importance of the act he was upon. In short, it was not now that he was to be play'd the fool with. But, what is pleasant enough, I myself was aw'd into a sort of respect for him, by the comely terrors his motions dressed him in: his eyes shooting sparks of fire; his face glowing with ardours that gave another life to it; his teeth churning; his whole frame agitated with a raging ungovernable impetuosity: all sensibly betraying the formidable fierceness with which the genial instinct acted upon him. Butting then and goring all before him, and mad and wild like an over-driven steer, he ploughs up the tender furrow, all insensible to Louisa's complaints; nothing can stop, nothing can keep out a fury like his: with which, having once got its head in, its blind rage soon made way for the rest, piercing, rending. and breaking open all obstructions. The torn, split, wounded girl cries, struggles, invokes me to her rescue, and endeavours to get from under the young savage, or shake him off, but alas! in vain: her breath might as soon have still'd or stemm'd a storm in winter, as all her strength have quell'd his rough assault, or put him out of his course. And indeed, all her efforts and struggles were manag'd with such disorder, that they serv'd rather to entangle. and fold her the faster in the twine of his boisterous arms, so that she was tied to the stake, and oblig'd to fight the match out, if she died for it. For his part, instinct-ridder as he was, the expressions of his animal passion, partaking something of ferocity, were rather worrying than kisses. intermix'd with eager ravenous love-bites on her cheeks and neck, the prints of which did not wear out for some days after.

Poor Louisa. however, bore up at length better than could have been expected; and though she suffer'd, and greatly too, yet, ever true to the good old cause, she suffer'd with pleasure and enjoyed her pain. And soon now, by dint of an enrag'd enforcement, the brute-machine, driven like a whirl-wind, made all smoke again, and wedging its way up, to the utmost extremity. left her, in point of penetration, nothing to fear or to desire: and now,

> "Gorg'd with the dearest morsel of the earth,"
>   (SHAKESPEARE.)

Louisa lay, pleas'd to the heart, pleas'd to her utmost capacity of being so, with every fibre in those parts, stretched almost to breaking, on a rack of joy, whilst the instrument of all this overfulness searched her senses with its sweet excess, till the pleasure gained upon her so, its point stung her so home, that catching at length the rage from her furious driver and sharing the riot of his wild rapture. she went wholly out of her mind into that favourite part of her body, the whole intenseness of which was so fervously fill'd. and employ'd: there alone she existed, all lost in those delirious transports, those extasies of the senses, which her winking eyes, the brighten'd vermilion of her lips and cheeks, and sighs of pleasure deeply fetched, so pathetically express'd. In short, she was now as mere a machine as much wrought on, and had her motions as little at her own command as the natural himself, who thus broke in upon her, made her feel with a vengeance his tempestuous tenderness, and the force of the mettle he battered with; their active loins quivered again with the violence of their conflict, till the surge of pleasure, foaming and raging to a height, drew down the pearly shower that was to allay this hurricane. The purely sensitive idiot then first shed those tears of joy that attend its last moments, not without an agony of delight, and even almost a roar of rapture, as the gush escaped him; so sensibly too for Louisa, that she kept him faithful company, going off, in consent, with the old symptoms: a delicious delirium, a tremulous convulsive shudder, and the critical dying *Oh!* And now, on his getting off, she lay pleasure-drench'd, and re-gorging its essential sweets; but quite spent, and gasping for breath, without other sensation of life than in those exquisite vibrations that trembled yet on the strings of delight, which had been too intensively touched, and which nature had been so intensly stirred with, for the senses to be quickly at peace from.

As for the changeling, whose curious engine had been thus successfully played off, his shift of countenance and gesture had even something droll, or rather tragi-comic in it: there was now an air of sad repining foolishness, super-added to his natural one of no-meaning and idiotism, as he stood with his label of manhood, now lank, unstiffen'd, becalm'd and flapping against his thighs, down which it reach'd half-way, terrible even in its fall, whilst under the dejection of spirit and flesh, which naturally followed, his eyes, by turns, cast down towards his struck standard, or piteously lifted to Louisa, seemed to require at her hands what he had so sensibly parted from to her, and now ruefully miss'd. But the vigour of nature, soon returning, dissipated the blast of faintness which the common law of enjoyment had subjected him to; and now his basket re-became his main concern, which I look'd for, and brought him, whilst Louisa restor'd his dress to its usual condition, and afterwards pleased him perhaps more by taking all his flowers off his hands, and paying him, at his rate, for them, than if she had embarrass'd him by a present that he would have been puzzled to account for, and might have put others on tracing the motives of.

Whether she ever return'd to the attack I know not, and, to say the truth, I believe not. She had had her freak out, and had pretty plentifully drown'd her curiosity in a glut of pleasure, which, as it happened, had no other consequence than that the lad, who retain'd only a confused memory of the transaction, would, when he saw her, for some time after, express a grin of joy and familiarity, after his idiot manner, and soon forgot her in favour of the next woman, tempted, on the report of his parts, to take him in.

Louisa herself did not long outstay this adventure at Mrs. Cole's (to whom, by-the-bye, we took care not to boast of our exploit, till all fear of consequences were clearly over): for an occasion presenting itself of proving her passion for a young fellow, at the expense of her discretion, proceeding all in character, she pack'd up her toilet at half a day's warning and went with him abroad, since which I entirely lost sight of her, and it never fell in my way to hear what became of her.

But a few days after she had left us, two very pretty young gentlemen, who were Mrs. Cole's especial favourites, and free of her academy, easily obtain'd her consent for Emily's and my acceptance of a party of pleasure, at a little but agreeable house belonging to one of them, situated not far up the river *Thames*, on the *Surry* side.

Everything being settled, and it being a fine summer-day, but rather of the warmest, we set out after dinner, and got to our rendez-vous about four in the afternoon; where, landing at the foot of a neat, joyous pavilion, Emily and I were handed into it by our squires, and there drank tea with a cheerfulness and gaiety that the beauty of the prospect, the serenity of the weather, and the tender politeness of our sprightly gallants naturally led us into.

After tea, and taking a turn in the garden, my particu-

lar, who was the master of the house, and had in no sense
schem'd this party of pleasure for a dry one, propos'd to
us, with that frankness which his familiarity at Mrs.
Cole's entitled him to, as the weather was excessively hot,
to bathe together, under a commodious shelter that he
had prepared expressly for that purpose, in a creek of the
river, with which a side-door of the pavilion immediately
communicated, and where we might be sure of having
our diversion out, safe from interruption, and with the
utmost privacy.

Emily, who never refus'd anything, and I, who ever
delighted in bathing, and had no exception to the person
who propos'd it, or to those pleasures it was easy to guess
it implied, took care, on this occasion, not to wrong our
training at Mrs. Cole's, and agreed to it with as good a
grace as we could. Upon which, without loss of time, we
return'd instantly to the pavilion, one door of which open'd
into a tent, pitch'd before it, that with its marquise,
formed a pleasing defense against the sun, or the weather,
and was besides as private as we could wish. The lining
of it, imbossed cloth, represented a wild forest-foliage,
from the top down to the sides, which, in the same stuff,
were figur'd with fluted pilasters, with their spaces between fill'd with flower-vases, the whole having a gay
effect upon the eye, wherever you turn'd it.

Then it reached sufficiently into the water, yet contain'd convenient benches round it, on the dry ground,
either to kee our cloaths, or . . . , or . . . , in short,
for more uses than resting upon. There was a side-table
too, loaded with sweetmeats, jellies, and other eatables,
and bottles of wine and cordials, by the way of occasional
relief from any rawness, or chill of the water, or from any
faintness from whatever cause; and in fact, my gallant,
who understood *chère entière* perfectly, and who, for
taste (even if you would not approve this specimen of it)
might have been comptroller of pleasures to a *Roman* em-
peror, had left no requisite towards convenience or luxury
unprovided.

As soon as we had look'd round this inviting spot, and
every preliminary of privacy was duly settled, strip was
the word: when the young gentlemen soon dispatch'd the

undressing each his partner and reduced us to the naked
confession of all those secrets of person which dress generally hides, and which the discovery of was, naturally
speaking, not to our disadvantage. Our hands, indeed,
mechanically carried towards the most interesting part
of us, screened, at first, all from the tufted cliff downwards,
till we took them away at their desire, and employed them
in doing them and the same office, of helping off with their
cloaths; in the process of which, there pass'd all the little
wantonnesses and frolicks that you may easily imagine.

As for my spark, he was presently undressed, all to
his shirt, the fore-lappet of which as he lean'd languishingly on me, he smilingly pointed to me to observe, as it
bellied out, or rose and fell, according to the unruly starts
of the motion behind it; but it was soon fix'd, for now
taking off his shirt, and naked as a Cupid, he shew'd it
me at so upright a stand, as prepar'd me indeed for his
application to me for instant ease; but, tho' the sight of
its fine size was fit enough to fire me, the cooling air, as I
stood in this state of nature, joined to the desire I had of
bathing first, enabled me to put him off, and tranquillize
him, with the remark that a little suspense would only
set a keener edge on the pleasure. Leading then the way,
and shewing our friends an example of continency, which
they were giving signs of losing respect to, we went hand
in hand into the strem, till it took us up to our neck, where
the no more than grateful coolness of the water gave my
senses a delicious refreshment from the sultriness of the
season, and made more alive, more happy in myself, and,
in course, more alert, and open to voluptuous impressions.

Here I lav'd and wanton'd with the water, or sportively
play'd with my companion, leaving Emily to deal with
hers at discretion. Mine, at length, not content with making me take the plunge over head and ears, kept splashing
me, and provoking me with all the little playful tricks he
could devise, and which I strove not to remain in his debt
for. We gave, in short, a loose to mirth; and now, nothing
would serve him but giving his hands the regale of going
over every part of me, neck, breast, belly, thighs, and all
the *et cœtera*, so dear to the imagination, under the pretext of washing and rubbing them; as we both stood in

the water, no higher now than the pit of our stomachs, and which did not hinder him from feeling, and toying with that leak that distinguishes our sex, and it so wonderfully water-tight: for his fingers, in vain dilating and opening it, only let more flame than water into it, be it said without a figure. At the same time he made me feel his own engine, which was so well wound up, as to stand even the working in water, and he accordingly threw one around my neck, and was endeavouring to get the better of that harsher construction bred by the surrounding fluid; and had in effect won his way so far as to make me sensible of the pleasing stretch of those nether-lips, from the in-driving machine; when, independent of my not liking that aukward mode of enjoyment, I could not help interrupting him, in order to become joint spectators of a plan of joy, in hot operation between Emily and her partner; who impatient of the fooleries and dalliance of the bath, had led his nymph to one of the benches on the green bank, where he was very coridally proceeding to teach her the difference betwixt jest and earnest.

There, setting her on his knee, and gliding one hand over the surface of that smooth polish'd snow-white skin of hers, which now doubly shone with a dew-bright lustre, and presented to the touch something like what one would imagine of animated ivory, especially in those ruby-nippled globes, which the touch is so fond of and delights to make love to, with the other he was lusciously exploring the sweet secret of nature, in order to make room for a stately piece of machinery, that stood up-rear'd, between her thighs, as she continued sitting on his lap, and pressed hard for instant admission, which the tender Emily, in a fit of humour deliciously protracted, affecting to decline, and elude the very pleasure she sigh'd for, but in a style of waywardness so prettily put on, and managed, as to render it ten times more poignant; then her eyes, all amidst the softest dying languishment, express'd at once a mock denial and extreme desire, whilst her sweetness was zested with a coyness so pleasingly provoking, her moods of keeping him off were so attractive, that they redoubled the impetuous rage with which he cover'd her with kisses: and kisses that, whilst she seemed

to shy from or scuffle for, the cunning wanton contrived
such sly returns of, as were doubtless the sweeter for the
gust she gave them, of being stolen ravished.

Thus Emily, who knew no art but that which nature
itself, in favour of her principal end, pleasure, had inspir'd her with, the art of yielding, coy'd it indeed, but
coy'd it to the purpose; for with all her straining, her
wrestling, and striving to break from the clasp of his arms,
she was so far wiser yet than to mean it, that in her struggles, it was visible she aim'd at nothing more than multi-
plying points of touch with him, and drawing yet closer
the folds that held them every where entwined, like two
tendrils of a vine intercurling together: so that the same
effect, as when Louisa strove in good earnest to disengage
from the idiot, was now produced by different motives.

Mean while, their emersion out of the cold water had
caused a general glow, a tender suffusion of heighten'd
carnation over their bodies; both equally white and
smooth-skinned; so that as their limbs were thus amo-
rously interwoven, in sweet confusion, it was scarce possible to distinguish who they respectively belonged to,
but for the brawnier, bolder muscles of the stronger sex.

In a little time, however, the champion was fairly in
with her, and had tied at all points the true lover's knot;
when now, adieu all the little refinements of a finessed
reluctance; adieu the friendly feint! She was presently
driven forcibly out of the power of using any art; and indeed, what art must not give way, when nature, corre-
sponding with her assailant, invaded in the heart of her
capital and carried by storm, lay at the mercy of the proud
conqueror who had made his entry triumphantly and completely? Soon, however, to become a tributary: for the
engagement growing hotter and hotter, at close quarters,
she presently brought him to the pass of paying down the
dear debt to nature; which she had no sooner collected
in, but, like a duellist who has laid his antagonist at his
feet, when he has himself received a mortal wound, Emily
had scarce time to plume herself upon her victory, but,
shot with the same discharge, she, in a loud expiring sigh,
in the closure of her eyes, the stretch-out of her limbs,

and a remission of her whole frame, gave manifest signs that all was as it should be.

For my part, who had not with the calmest patience stood in the water all this time, to view this warm action, I lean'd tenderly on my gallant, and at the close of it, seemed'd to ask him with my eyes what he thought of it; but he, more eager to satisfy me by his actions than by words or looks, as we shoal'd the water towards the shore, shewed me the staff of love so intensely set up, that had not even charity beginning at home in this case, urged me to our mutual relief, it would have been cruel indeed to have suffered the youth to burst with straining, when the remedy was so obvious and so near at hand.

Accordingly we took to a bench, whilst Emily and her spark, who belonged it seems to the sea, stood at the sideboard, drinking to our good voyage: for, as the last observ'd, we were well under weigh, with a fair wind up channel, and full-freighted; nor indeed were we long before we finished our trip to Cythera, and unloaded in the old haven; but, as the circumstances did not admit of much variation. I shall spare you the description.

At the same time, allow me to place you here an excuse I am conscious of owing you, for having, perhaps, too much affected the figurative style; though surely, it can pass nowhere more allowably than in a subject which is so properly the province of poetry, nay, is poetry itself, pregnant with every flower of imagination and loving metaphors, even were not the natural expressions, for respects of fashion and sound, necessarily forbid it.

Resuming now my history, you may please to know that what with a competent number of repetitions, all in the same strain (and, by-the-bye, we have a certain natural sense that those repetitions are very much to the taste), what with a circle of pleasures delicately varied, there was not a moment lost to joy all the time we staid there, till late in the night we were re-escorted home by our 'squires, who delivered us safe to Mrs. Cole, with generous thanks for our company.

This too was Emily's last adventure in our way: for scarce a week after, she was, by an accident too trivial to detail to you the particulars, found out by her parents,

who were in good circumstances, and who had been pun-
ish'd for their partiality to their son, in the loss of him,
occasion'd by a circumstance of their over-indulgence to
his appetite; upon which the so long engross'd stream of
fondness, running violently in favour of this lost and in-
humanly abandon'd child whom if they had not neglected
enquiry about, they might long before have recovered.
They were now so overjoyed at the retrieval of her, that,
I presume, it made them much less strict in examining
the bottom of things: for they seem'd very glad to take for
granted, in the lump, everything that the grave and
decent Mrs. Cole was pleased to pass upon them; and
soon afterwards sent her, from the country, a handsome
acknowledgement.

But it was not so easy to replace to our community the
loss of so sweet a member of it: for, not to mention her
beauty, she was one of those mild, pliant characters that
if one does not entirely esteem, one can scarce help loving, which is not such a bad compensation neither. Owing all her weakness to good-nature, and an indolent
facility that kept her too much at the mercy of first impressions, she had just sense enough to know that she
wanted leading-strings, and thought herself so much
obliged to any who would take the pains to think for her,
and guide her, that with a very little management, she
was capable of being made a most agreeable, nay, a most
virtuous wife: for vice, it is probable, had never been her
choice, or her fate, if it had not been for occasion, or example, or had she not depended less upon herself than
upon her circumstances. This presumption her conduct
afterwards verified: for presently meeting with a match
that was ready cut and dry for her, with a neighbour's
son of her own rank, and a young man of sense and order,
who took her as the widow of one lost at sea (for so it
seems one of her gallants, whose name she had made free
with, really was), she naturally struck into all the duties
of their domestic life with as much simplicity of affection,
with as much constancy and regularity, as if she had never
swerv'd from a state of undebauch'd innocence from her
youth.

These desertions had, however, now so far thinned

Mrs. Cole's brood that she was left with only me like a hen with one chicken; but tho' she was earnestly entreated and encourag'd to recruit her *corps,* her growing infirmities, and, above all, the tortures of a stubborn hip-gout, which she found would yield to no remedy, determin'd her to break up her business and retire with a decent pittance into the country, where I promis'd myself nothing so sure, as my going down to live with her as soon as I had seen a little more of life and improv'd my small matters into a competency that would create in me an independence on the world: for I was, now, thanks to Mrs. Cole, wise enough to keep that essential in view.

Thus was I then to lose my faithful preceptress, as did the Philosophers of the town the White Crow of her profession. For besides that she never ransacked her customers, whose taste too she ever studiously consulted, besides that she never racked her pupils with unconscionable extortions, nor ever put their hard earnings, as she call'd them, under the contribution of poundage. She was a severe enemy to the seduction for innocence, and confin'd her acquisitions solely to those unfortunate young women, who, having lost it, were but the juster objects of compassion: among these, indeed, she pick'd but such as suited her views and taking them under her protection, rescu'd them from the danger of the publick sinks of ruin and misery, to place, or do for them, well or ill, in the manner you have seen. Having then settled her affairs, she set out on her journey, after taking the most tender leave of me, and at the end of some excellent instructions, recommending me to myself, with an anxiety perfectly maternal. In short, she affected me so much, that I was not presently reconcil'd to myself for suffering her at any rate to go without me; but fate had, it seems, otherwise dispos'd of me.

I had, on my separation from Mrs. Cole, taken a pleasant convenient house at *Marybone,* but easy to rent and manage from its smallness, which I furnish'd neatly and modestly. There, with a reserve of eight hundred pounds, the fruit of my deference to Mrs. Cole's counsels, exclusive of cloaths, some jewels, some plate, I saw myself in purse for a long time, to wait without impatience for what the chapter of accidents might produce in my favour.

Here, under the new character of a young gentlewoman whose husband was gone to sea, I had mark'd me out such lines of life and conduct, as leaving me at a competent liberty to pursue my views either out of pleasure or fortune, bounded me nevertheless strictly within the rules of decency and discretion: a disposition in which you cannot escape observing a true pupil of Mrs. Cole.

I was scarce, however, well warm in my new abode, when going out one morning pretty early to enjoy the freshness of it, in the pleasing outlet of the fields, accompanied only by a maid, whom I had newly hired, as we were carelessly walking among the trees we were alarmed with the noise of a violent coughing: turning our heads towards which, we distinguish'd a plain well-dressed elderly gentleman, who, attack'd with a sudden fit, was so much overcome as to be forc'd to give way to it and sit down at the foot of a tree, where he seemed suffocating with the severity of it, being perfectly black in the face: not less mov'd than frighten'd with which, I flew on the instant to his relief, and using the rote of practice I had observ'd on the like occasion, I loosened his cravat and clapped him on the back; but whether to any purpose, or whether the cough had had its course, I know not, but the fit immediately went off; and now recover'd to his speech and legs, he returned me thanks with as much emphasis as if I had sav'd his life. This naturally engaging a conversation, he acquainted me where he lived, which was at a considerable distance from where I met with him, and where he had stray'd insensibly on the same intention of a morning walk.

He was, as I afterwards learn'd in the course of the intimacy which this little accident gave birth to, an old bachelor, turn'd of sixty, but of a fresh vigorous complexion, insomuch that he scarce marked five and forty, having never rack'd his constitution by permitting his desires to overtax his ability.

As to his birth and condition, his parents, honest and fail'd mechanicks, had, by the best traces he could get of them, left him an infant orphan on the parish; so that it was from a charity-school, that, by honesty and industry, he made his way into a merchant's counting-house; from whence, being sent to a house in CADIZ, he there, by his talents and activity, acquired a fortune, but an immense one, with which he returned to his native country; where he could not, however, so much as fish out one single relation out of the obscurity he was born in. Taking then a taste for retirement, and pleas'd to enjoy life, like a mistress in the dark, he flowed his days in all the ease of opulence, without the least parade of it; and, rather studying the concealment than the shew of a fortune, looked down on a world he perfectly knew; himself, to his wish, unknown and unmarked by.

But, as I propose to devote a letter entirely to the pleasure of retracing to you all the particulars of my acquaintance with this ever, to me, memorable friend, I shall, in this, transiently touch on no more than may serve, as mortar to cement, to form the connection of my history, and to obviate your surprize that one of my high blood and relish of life should count a gallant of threescore such a catch.

Referring then to a more explicit narrative, to explain by what progressions our acquaintance, certainly innocent at first, insensibly changed nature, and ran into unplatonic lengths, as might well be expected from one of my condition of life, and above all, from that principle of electricity that scarce ever fails of producing fire when the sexes meet. I shall only here acquaint you, that as age had not subdued his tenderness for our sex, neither had it robbed him of the power of pleasing, since whatever he wanted in the bewitching charms of youth, he aton'd for, or supplemented with the advantages of experience, the sweetness of his manners, and above all, his flattering address in touching the heart, by an application to the understanding. From him it was I first learn'd, to any purpose, and not without infinite pleasure, that I had such a portion of me worth bestowing some regard on; from him I received my first essential encouragement, and instructions how to put it in that train of cultivation, which I have since pushed to the little degree of improvement you see it at; he it was, who first taught me to be sensible that the pleasures of the mind were superior to those of the body;

at the same time, that they were so far from obnoxious to, or incompatiable with each other, that, besides the sweetness in the variety and transition, the one serv'd to exalt and perfect the taste of the other to a degree that the senses alone can never arrive at.

Himself a rational pleasurist, as being much too wise to be asham'd of the pleasures of humanity, loved me indeed, but loved me with dignity; in a mean equally remov'd from the sourness, of forwardness, by which age is unpleasingly characteriz'd, and from that childish silly dotage that so often disgraces it, and which he himself used to turn into ridicule, and compare to an old goat affecting the frisk of a young kid.

In short, everything that is generally unamiable in his season of life was, in him, repair'd by so many advantages, that he existed a proof, manifest at least to me, that it is not out of the power of age to please, if it lays out to please, and if, making just allowances, those in that class do not forget that it must cost them more pains and attention than what youth, the natural spring-time of joy, stands in need of: as fruits out of season require proportionably more skill and cultivation, to force them.

With this gentleman then, who took me home soon after our acquaintance commenc'd, I lived near eight months; in which time, my constant complaisance and docility, my attention to deserve his confidence and love, and a conduct, in general, devoid of the least art and founded on my sincere regard and esteem for him, won and attach'd him so firmly to me, that, after having generously trusted me with a genteel, independent settlement, proceeding to heap marks of affection on me, he appointed me, by an authentick will, his sole heiress and executrix: a disposition which he did not outlive two months, being taken from me by a violent cold that he contracted as he unadvisedly ran to the window on an alarm of fire, at some streets distance, and stood there naked-breasted, and exposed to the fatal impressions of a damp night-air.

After acquitting myself of my duty towards my deceas'd benefactor, and paying him a tribute of unfeign'd sorrow, which a little time chang'd into a most tender, grateful memory of him that I shall ever retain, I grew somewhat comforted by the prospect that now open'd to me, if not of happiness at least of affluence and independence.

I saw myself then in the full bloom and pride of youth (for I was not yet nineteen) actually at the head of so large a fortune, as it would have been even the height of impudence in me to have raised my wishes, much more my hopes, to; and that this unexpected elevation did not turn my head, I ow'd to the pains my benefactor had taken to form and prepare me for it, as I ow'd his opinion of my management of the vast possessions he left me, to what he had observ'd of the prudential economy I had learned under Mrs. Cole, of which the reserve he saw I had made was a proof and encouragement to him.

But, alas! how easily is the enjoyment of the greatest sweets in life, in present possession, poisoned by the regret of an absent one! but my regret was a mighty and just one, since it had my only truly beloved *Charles* for its object.

Given him up I had, indeed, compleatly, having never once heard from him since our separation; which, as I found afterwards, had been my misfortune, and not his neglect, for he wrote me several letters which had all miscarried; but forgotten him I never had. Amidst all my personal infidelities, not one had made a pin's point impression on a heart impenetrable to the true love-passion, but for him.

As soon, however, as I was mistress of this unexpected fortune, I felt more than ever how dear he was to me, from its insufficiency to make me happy, whilst he was not to share it with me. My earliest care, consequently, was to endeavour at getting some account of him; but all my researches produc'd me no more light than that his father had been dead for some time, not so well as even with the world; and that Charles had reached his port of destination in the *South-Seas*, where, finding the estate he was sent to recover dwindled to a trifle, by the loss of two ships in which the bulk of his uncle's fortune lay, he was come away with the small remainder, and might, perhaps, according to the best advice, in a few months return to England, from whence he had, at the time of this my inquiry, been absent two years and seven months. A little eternity in love!

You cannot conceive with what joy I embraced the hopes thus given me of seeing the delight of my heart again. But, as the term of months was assigned it, in order to divert and amuse my impatience for his return, after settling my affairs with much ease and security, I set out on a journey for *Lancashire*, with an equipage suitable to my fortune, and with a design purely to revisit my place of nativity, for which I could not help retaining a great tenderness; and might naturally not be sorry to shew myself there, to the advantage I was now in pass to do, after the report *Esther Davis* had spread of my being spirited away to the plantations; for on no other supposition could she account for the suppression of myself to her, since her leaving me so abruptly at the inn. Another favourite intention I had, to look out for my relations, though I had none besides distant ones, and prove a benefactress to them. Then Mrs. Cole's place of retirement lying in my way, was not amongst the least of the pleasures I had proposed to myself in this expedition.

I had taken nobody with me but a discreet decent woman, to figure it as my companion, besides my servants, and was scarce got into an inn, about twenty miles from London, where I was to sup and pass the night, when such a storm of wind and rain sprang up as made me congratulate myself on having got under shelter before it began.

This had continu'd a good half hour, when bethinking me of some directions to be given to the coachman, I sent for him, and not caring that his shoes should soil the very clean parlour, in which the cloth was laid, I stept into the hall-kitchen, where he was, and where, whilst I was talking to him, I slantingly observ'd two horsemen driven in by the weather, and both wringing wet; one of whom was asking if they could not be assisted with a change, while their clothes were dried. But, heavens! who can express what I felt at the sound of a voice, ever present to my heart, and that is now rebounded at! or when pointing my eyes towards the person it came from, they confirm'd its information, in spite of so long an absence, and of a dress one would have imagin'd studied for a disguise: a horseman's great coat, with a stand-up cape, and his hat flapp'd . . . but what could escape the piercing alertness of a sense surely guided by love? A transport then like mine was above all consideration, or schemes of surprize; and I, that instant, with the rapidity of the emotions that I felt the spur of, shot into his arms, crying out, as I threw mine round his neck: "My life! . . . my soul! . . . my *Charles!* . . ." and without further power of speech, swoon'd away, under the pressing agitations of joy and surprize.

Recover'd out of my entrancement, I found myself in my charmer's arms, but in the parlour, surrounded by a croud which this event had gather'd round us, and which immediately, on a signal from the discreet landlady, who currently took him for my husband, clear'd the room, and desirably left us alone to the raptures of this reunion; my joy at which had like to have prov'd, at the expense of my life, power superior to that of grief at our fatal separation.

The first object then, that my eyes open'd on, was their supreme idol, and my supreme wish, Charles, on one knee, holding me fast by the hand and gazing on me with a transport of fondness. Observing my recovery, he attempted to speak, and give vent to his patience of hearing my voice again, to satisfy him once more that it was *me;* but the mightiness and suddenness of the surprize, continuing to stun him, choked his utterance: he could only stammer out a few broken, half formed, faltering accents, which my ears greedily drinking in, spelt, and put together, so as to make out their sense: "After so long! . . . so cruel . . . an absence! . . . my dearest *Fanny!* . . . can it? . . . can it be you? . . ." stifling me at the same time with kisses, that, stopping my mouth, at once prevented the answer that he panted for, and increas'd the delicious disorder in which all my senses were rapturously lost. Amidst however, this croud of ideas, and all blissful ones, there obtruded only one cruel doubt, that poison'd nearly all the transcendent happiness: and what was it, but my dread of its being too excessive to be real? I trembled now with the fear of its being no more than a dream, and of my waking out of it into the horrors of finding it

one. Under this fond apprehension, imagining I could
not make too much of the present prodigious joy, before
it should vanish and leave me in the desert again, nor
verify its reality too strongly, I clung to him, I clasp'd him
as if to hinder him from escaping me again: "Where have
you been? . . . how could you . . . could you leave
me? . . . Say you are still mine . . . that you still love
me . . . and thus! thus!" (kissing him as if I would con-
solidate lips with him!) "I forgive you . . . forgive my
hard fortune in favour of this restoration."

All these interjections breaking from me, in that wildness of expression that justly passes for eloquence in love,
drew from him all the returns my fond heart could wish
or require. Our caresses, our questions, our answers, for
some time observ'd no order; all crossing, or interrupting
one another in sweet confusion, whilst we exchang'd hearts
at our eyes, and renew'd the ratifications of a love unbated by time or absence: not a breath, not a motion, not
a gesture on either side, but what was strongly impressed
with it. Our hands, lock'd in each other, repeated the most
passionate squeezes, so that their fiery thrill went to the
heart again.

Thus absorbed, and concentre'd in this unutterable delight, I had not attended to the sweet author of it, being
thoroughly wet, and in danger of catching cold; when, in
good time, the landlady, whom the appearance of my
equipage (which, by-the-bye, Charles knew nothing
of) had gain'd me an interest in, for me and mine, interrupted us by bringing in a decent shift of linen and cloaths,
which now, somewhat recover'd into a calmer composure
by the coming in of a third person, I prest him to take the
benefit of, with a tender concern and anxiety that made me
tremble for his health.

The landlady leaving us again, he proceeded to shift;
in the act of which, tho' he proceeded with all that
modesty which became these first solemner instants of
our re-meeting after so long an absence, I could not contain certain snatches of my eyes, lured by the dazzling
discoveries of his naked skin, that escaped him as he
chang'd his linen, and which I could not observe the un-
faded life and complexion of without emotions of tender-

ness and joy, that had himself too purely for their object to partake of a loose or mistim'd desire.

He was soon drest in these temporary cloaths, which neither fitted him nor became the light my passion plac'd him in, to me at least; yet, as they were on him, they look'd extremely well, in virtue of that magic charm which love put into everything that he touch'd, or had relation to him: and where, indeed, was that dress that a figure like this would not give grace to? For now, as I ey'd him more in detail, I could not but observe the even favourable alteration which the time of his absence had produced in his person.

There were still the requisite lineaments, still the same vivid vermilion and bloom reigning in his face: but now the roses were more fully blown; the tan of his travels, and a beard somewhat more distinguishable, had, at the expense of no more delicacy than what he could well spare, given it an air of becoming manliness and maturity, that symmetriz'd nobly with that air of distinction and empire with which nature had stamp'd it, in a rare mixture with the sweetness of it; still nothing had he lost of that smooth plumpness of flesh, which, glowing with freshness, blooms florid to the eye, and delicious to the touch; then his shoulders were grown more square, his shape more form'd, more portly, but still free and airy. In short, his figure show'd riper, greater, and perfecter to the experienced eye than in his tender youth; and now he was not much more than two and twenty.

In this interval, however, I pick'd out of the broken, often pleasingly interrupted account of himself, that he was, at that instant, actually on his road to London, in not a very paramount plight or condition, having been wreck'd on the *Irish* coast for which he had prematurely embark'd, and lost the little all he had brought with him from the South Seas; so that he had not till after great shifts and hardships, in the company of his fellow-traveller, the captain, got so far on his journey; that so it was (having heard of his father's death and circumstances) he had now the world to begin again, on a new account: a situation which he assur'd me, in a vein of sincerity that, flowing from his heart, penetrated mine, gave him to farther pain, than that he had it not in his power to make me as happy as he could wish. My fortune, you will please to observe, I had not enter'd upon any overture of, reserving to feast myself with the surprize of it to him, in calmer instants. And, as to my dress, it could give him no idea of the truth, not only as it was mourning, but likewise in a style of plainness and simplicity that I had ever kept to with studied art. He press'd me indeed tenderly to satisfy his ardent curiosity, both with regard to my past and present state of life since his being torn away from me: but I had the address to elude his questions by answers that, shewing his satisfaction at no great distance, won upon him to waive his impatience, in favour of the thorough confidence he had in my not delying it, but for the respects I should in good time acquaint him with.

Charles, however, thus returned to my longing arms, tender, faithful, and in health, was already a blessing too mighty for my conception: but Charles in distress! . . . Charles reduc'd, and broken down to his naked personal merit, was such a circumstance, in favour of the sentiments I had for him, as exceeded my utmost desires; and accordingly I seemed so visibly charm'd, so out of time and measure pleas'd at his mention of his ruin'd fortune, that he could account for it no way, but that the joy of seeing him again had swallow'd up every other sense, or concern.

In the mean time, my woman had taken all possible care of Charles's travelling companion; and as supper was coming in, he was introduc'd to me, when I receiv'd him as became my regard for all of Charles's acquaintance or friends.

We four then supp'd together, in the style of joy, congratulation, and pleasing disorder that you may guess. For my part, though all these agitations had left me not the least stomach but for that uncloying feast, the sight of my ador'd youth, I endeavour'd to force it, by way of example for him, who I conjectur'd must want such a recruit after riding; and, indeed, he ate like a traveller, but gaz'd at, and addressed me all the time like a lover.

After the cloth was taken away, and the hour of repose came on, Charles and I were, without further ceremony, in quality of man and wife, shewn up together to a very handsome apartment, and, all in course, the bed, they said, the best in the inn.

And here, Decency, forgive me! if once more I violate thy laws and keeping the curtains undrawn, sacrifice thee for the last time to that confidence, without reserve, with which I engaged to recount to you the most striking circumstances of my youthful disorders.

As soon, then, as we were in the room together, left to ourselves, the sight of the bed starting the remembrance of our first joys, and the thought of my being instantly to share it with the dear possessor of my virgin heart, mov'd me so strongly, that it was well I lean'd upon him, or I must have fainted again under the overpowering sweet alarm. Charles saw into my confusion, and forgot his own, that was scarce less, to apply himself to the removal of mine.

But now the true refining passion had regain'd thorough possession of me, with all its train of symptoms: a sweet sensibility, a tender timidity, love-sick yearnings temper'd with diffidence and modesty, all held me in a subjection of soul, incomparably dearer to me than the liberty of heart which I had been long, too long! the mistress of, in the course of those grosser gallantries, the consciousness of which now made me sigh with a virtuous confusion and regret. No real virgin, in view of the nuptial bed, could give more bashful blushes to unblemish'd innocence than I did to a sense of guilt; and indeed I lov'd Charles too truly not to feel severely that I did not deserve him.

As I kept hesitating and disconcerted under this soft distraction, Charles, with a fond impatience, took the pains to undress me; and all I can remember amidst the flutter and discomposure of my senses was some flattering exclamations of joy and admiration, more specially at the feel of my breasts, now set at liberty from my stays, and which panting and rising in tumultuous throbs, swell'd upon his dear touch, and gave it the welcome pleasure of finding them well form'd, and unfail'd in firmness.

I was soon laid in bed, and scarce languish'd an instant for the darling partner of it, before he was undress'd and got between the sheets, with his arms clasp'd round me, giving and taking, with gust inexpressible, a kiss of welcome, that my heart rising to my lips stamp'd with its warmest impression, concurring to my bliss, with that delicate and voluptuous emotion which Charles alone had the secret to excite, and which constitutes the very life, the essence of pleasure.

Meanwhile, two candles lighted on a side-table near us, and a joyous wood-fire, threw a light into the bed that took from one sense, of great importance to our joys, all pretext for complaining of its being shut out of its share of them; and indeed, the sight of my idolized youth was alone, from the ardour with which I had wished for it, without other circumstance, a pleasure to die of.

But as action was now a necessity to desires so much on edge as ours, Charles, after a very short prelusive dalliance, lifting up my linen and his own, laid the broad treasures of his manly chest close to my bosom, both beating with the tenderest alarms: when now, the sense of his glowing body, in naked touch with mine, took all power over my thoughts out of my own disposal, and deliver'd up every faculty of the soul to the sensiblest of joys, that affecting me infinitely more with my distinction of the person than of the sex, now brought my conscious heart deliciously into play: my heart, which eternally constant to Charles, had never taken any part in my occasional sacrifices to the calls of constitution, complaisance, or interest. But ah! what became of me, when as the powers of solid pleasure thickened upon me, I could not help feeling the stiff stake that had been adorn'd with the trophies of my despoil'd virginity, bearing hard and inflexible against one of my thighs, which I had not yet opened, from a true principle of modesty, reviv'd by a passion too sincere to suffer any aiming at the false merit of difficulty, or my putting on an impertinent mock coyness.

I have, I believe, somewhere before remark'd, that the feel of that favourite piece of manhood has, in the very nature of it, something inimitably pathetic. Nothing can be dearer to the touch, nor can affect it with a more delicious sensation. Think then! as a love thinks, what must be the consummate transport of that quickest of our senses,

in their central seat too! when, after so long a deprival, it
felt itself re-inflam'd under the pressure of that peculiar
scepter-member which commands us all: but especially
my darling, elect from the face of the whole earth. And
now, at its mightiest point of stiffness, it felt to me something so subduing, so active, so solid and agreeable, that I
know not what name to give its singular impression: but
the sentiment of consciousness of its belonging to my su-
premely beloved youth, gave me so pleasing an agitation,
and work'd so strongly on my soul, that it sent all its sensitive spirits to that organ of bliss in me, dedicated to its reception. There, concentreing to a point, like rays in a
burning glass, they glow'd, they burnt with the intensest
heat; the springs of pleasure were, in short, wound up to
such a pitch, I panted now, with so exquisitely keen an
appetite for the eminent enjoyment that I was even sick
with desire, and unequal to support the combination of
two distinct ideas, that delightfully distracted me: for all
the thought I was capable of, was that I was now in touch,
at once, with the instrument of pleasure, and the great-
seal of love. Ideas that, mingling streams, pour'd such an
ocean of intoxicating bliss on a weak vessel, all too narrow
to contain it, that I lay overwhelm'd, absorbed, lost in an
abyss of joy, and dying of nothing but immoderate delight.

Charles then rous'd me somewhat out of this extatic
distraction with a complaint softly murmured, amidst a
croud of kisses, at the position, not so favourable to his
desires, in which I receiv'd his urgent insistance for admission, where that insistance was alone so engrossing a
pleasure that it made me inconsistently suffer a much
dearer one to be kept out; but how sweet to correct such
a mistake! My thighs, now obedient to the intimations of
love and nature, gladly disclose, and with a ready submission, resign up the soft gateway to the entrance of pleasure: I see, I feel the delicious velvet tip! . . . he enters
me might and main, with . . . oh! my pen drops from
me here in the extasy now present to my faithful memory! Description too deserts me, and delivers over a task,
above its strength of wing, to the imagination: but it must
be an imagination exalted by such a flame as mine that
can do justice to that sweetest, noblest of all sensations,

that hailed and accompany'd the stiff insinuation all the way up, till it was at the end of its penetration, sending up, through my eyes, the sparks of the love-fire that ran all over me and blaz'd in every vein and every pore of me: a system incarnate of joy all over.

I had now totally taken in love's true arrow from the point up to the feather, in that part, where making no new wound, the lips of the original one of nature, which had owed its first breathing to this dear instrument, clung, as if sensible of gratitude, in eager suction round it, whilst all its inwards embrac'd it tenderly with a warmth of gust, a compressive energy, that gave it, in its way, the heartiest welcome in nature; every fibre there gathering tight round it, and straining ambitiously to come in for its share of the blissful touch.

As we were giving them a few moments of pause to the delectation of the senses, in dwelling with the highest relish on this intimatest point of re-union, and chewing the cud of enjoyment, the impatience natural to the pleasure soon drove us into action. Then began the driving tumult on his side, and the responsive heaves on mine which kept me up to him; whilst, as our joys grew too great for utterance, the organs of our voices, voluptuously intermixing, became organs of the touch . . . and oh that touch! how delicious! . . . how poignantly luscious! . . . And now! now I felt to the heart of me! I felt the prodigious keen edge with which love, presiding over this act, points the pleasure: love! that may be styled the Attic salt of enjoyment; and indeed, without it, the joy, great as it is, is still a vulgar one, whether in a king or a beggar; for it is, undoubtedly, love alone that refines, ennobles and exalts it.

Thus happy, then, by the heart, happy by the senses, it was beyond all power, even of thought, to form the conception of a greater delight than what I was now consummating the fruition of.

Charles, whose whole frame was convulsed with the agitation of his rapture, whilst the tenderest fires trembled in his eyes, all assured me of a perfect concord of joy, penetrated me so profoundly, touch'd me so vitally, took me so much out of my own possession, whilst he seem'd himself so much in mine, that in a delicious enthusiasm, I imagin'd such a transfusion of heart and spirit, as that coalescing, and making one body and soul with him, I was he, and he, me.

But all this pleasure tending, like life from its first instants, towards its own dissolution, liv'd too fast not to bring on upon the spur its delicious moment of mortality; for presently the approach of the tender agony discover'd itself by its usual signals, that were quickly follow'd by my dear love's emanation of himself that spun out, and shot, feelingly indeed! up the ravish'd in-draught: where the sweetly soothing balmy titillation opened all the juices of joy on my side, which extatically in flow, help'd to allay the prurient glow, and drown'd our pleasure for a while. Soon, however, to be on float again! For Charles, true to nature's laws, in one breath expiring and ejaculating, languish'd not long in the dissolving trance, but recovering spirit again, soon gave me to feel that the true-mettle springs of his instrument of pleasure were, by love, and perhaps by a long vacation, wound up too high to be let down by a single explosion: his stiffness still stood my friend. Resuming then the action afresh, without dislodging, or giving me the trouble of parting from my sweet tenant, we play'd over again the same opera, with the same delightful harmony and concert: our ardours, like our love, knew no remission; and, all as the tide serv'd my lover, lavish of his stores, and pleasure milked, overflowed me once more from the fulness of his oval reservoirs of the genial emulsion: whilst, on my side, a convulsing grasp, in the instant of my giving down the liquid contribution, render'd me sweetly subservient at once to the increase of his joy, and of its effusions: moving me so, as to make me exert all those springs of the compressive exsuction with which the sensitive mechanism of that part thirstily draws and drains the nipple of Love; with much such an instinctive eagerness and attachment as, to compare great with less, kind nature engages infants at the breast by the pleasure they find in the motion of their little mouths and cheeks, to extract the milky stream prepar'd for their nourishment.

But still there was no end of his vigour: this double

discharge had so far from extinguish'd his desires, for that time, that it had not even calm'd them; and at his age, desires are power. He was proceeding then amazingly to push it to a third triumph, still without uncasing, if a tenderness, natural to true love, had not inspir'd me with self-denial enough to spare, and not overstrain him: and accordingly, entreating him to give himself and me quarter, I obtain'd, at length, a short suspension of arms, but not before he had exultingly satisfy'd me that he gave out standing.

The remainder of the night, with what we borrow'd upon the day, we employ'd with unweary'd fervour in celebrating thus the festival of our re-meeting; and got up pretty late in the morning, gay, brisk and alert, though rest had been a stranger to us: but the pleasures of love had been to us, what the joy of victory is to an army: repose, refreshment, everything.

The journey into the country being now entirely out of the question, and orders having been given over-night for turning the horses' heads towards London, we left the inn as soon as we had breakfasted, not without a liberal distribution of the tokens of my grateful sense of the happiness I had met with in it.

Charles and I were in my coach; the captain and my companion in a chasie hir'd purposely for them, to leave us the conveniency of a *tête-à-tête*.

Here, on the road, as the tumult of my senses was tolerably compos'd, I had command enough of head to break properly to him the course of life that the consequence of my separation from him had driven me into: which, at the same time that he tenderly deplor'd with me, he was the less shocked at; as, on reflecting how he had left me circumstanc'd, he could not be entirely unprepar'd for it.

But when I opened the state of my fortune to him, and with that sincerity which, from me to him, was so much a nature in me, I begg'd of him his acceptance of it, on his own terms. I should appear to you perhaps too partial to my passion, were I to attempt the doing his delicacy justice. I shall content myself then with assuring you, that after his flatly refusing the unreserv'd, unconditional donation that I long persecuted him in vain to accept, it was at length, in obedience to his serious commands (for I stood out unaffectedly, till he exerted the sovereign authority which love had given him over me), that I yielded my consent to waive the remonstrance I did not fail of making strongly to him, against his degrading himself, and incurring the reflection, however unjust, of having, for respects of fortune, barter'd his honour for infamy and prostitution, in making one his wife, who thought herself too much honour'd in being but his mistress.

The plea of love then over-ruling all objections, Charles, entirely won with the merit of my sentiments for him, which he could not but read the sincerity of in a heart ever open to him, oblig'd me to receive his hand, by which means I was in pass, among other innumerable blessings, to bestow a legal parentage on those fine children you have seen by this happiest of matches.

Thus, at length, I got snug into port, where, in the bosom of virtue, I gather'd the only uncorrupt sweets: where, looking back on the course of vice I had run, and comparing its infamous blandishments with the infinitely superior joys of innocence, I could not help pitying, even in point of taste, those who, immers'd in gross sensuality, are insensible to the so delicate charms of VIRTUE, than which even PLEASURE has not a greater friend, nor than VICE a greater enemy. Thus temperance makes men lords over those pleasures that intemperance enslaves them to: the one, parent of health, vigour, fertility, cheerfulness, and every other desirable good of life; the other, of diseases, debility, barrenness, self-loathing, with only every evil incident to human nature.

You laugh, perhaps, at this tail-piece of morality, extracted from me by the force of truth, resulting from compar'd experiences: you think it, no doubt, out of place, out of character; possibly too you may look on it as the paltry finesse of one who seeks to mask a devotee to Vice under a rag of a veil, impudently smuggled from the shrine of Virtue: just as if one was to fancy one's self compleatly disguised at a masquerade, with no other change of dress than turning one's shoes into slippers; or, as if a writer should think to shield a treasonable libel, by concluding it with a formal prayer for the King. But, independent of my flattering myself that you have a juster opinion of my sense and sincerity, give me leave to represent to you, that such a supposition is even more injurious to Virtue than to me: since, consistently with candour and good-nature, it can have no foundation but in the falsest of fears, that its pleasures cannot stand in comparison with those of Vice; but let truth dare to hold it up in its most alluring light: then mark, how spurious, how low of taste, how comparatively inferior its joys are to those which Virtue gives sanction to, and whose sentiments are not above making even a sauce for the senses, but a sauce of the highest relish; whilst Vices are the harpies that infect and foul the feast. The paths of Vice are sometimes strew'd with roses, but then they are for ever infamous for many a thorn, for many a cankerworm: those of Virtue are strew'd with roses purely, and those eternally unfading ones.

If you do me then justice, you will esteem me perfectly consistent in the incense I burn to Virtue. If I have painted Vice in all its gayest colours, if I have deck'd it with flowers, it has been solely in order to make the worthier, the solemner sacrifice of it, to Virtue.

You know Mr. C° ° * O° ° °, you know his estate, his worth, and good sense: can you, will you pronounce it ill meant, at least of him, when anxious for his son's morals, with a view to form him to virtue, and inspire him with a fix'd, a rational contempt for vice, he condescended to be his master of the ceremonies, and led him by the hand thro' the most noted bawdy-houses in town, where he took care he should be familiarized with all those scenes of debauchery, so fit to nauseate a good taste? The experiment, you will cry, is dangerous. True, on a fool: but are fools worth so much attention?

I shall see you soon, and in the mean time think candidly of me, and believe me ever,

MADAM,

Yours, etc., etc., etc.

THE END

Appendix

It is unlikely that a complete bibliography of *Memoirs of a Woman of Pleasure* will ever be compiled, so many and varied have been the editions printed in most countries of the western world. As an indication of the range of such editions, however, the best guide remains, as it has for the past seventy-five years, a curious work published in London in 1885 by a prominent English bibliophile, Henry Spencer Ashbee, who with fine Victorian dissemblance hid his identity as author behind the *nom de plume* Pisanus Fraxi, and titled his work

CATENA
LIBRORUM TECENDORUM:
Being
Notes
Bio- Biblio- Icono-graphical and Critical
on
Curious and Uncommon Books

On the following pages the complete bibliographic record of John Cleland's master work is reproduced as it appeared in the *Catena*.

THE PUBLISHER

MEMOIRS OF A WOMAN OF PLEASURE *from the Original Corrected Edition with a Set of Elegant Engravings.*

8vo.; without place or date; 2 vols.; pp. 152 and 167.
Although undoubtedly old, this is evidently not the *editio princeps;* it is however complete, and contains an episode which is not to be found in the editions of 1749 or 1784, or indeed in any subsequent issue which I have had the opportunity of examining. The passage occurs in the latter part of the work, and contains the details of a scene which Fanny witnessed on her trip to Hampton Court. Its exact place in the volume is between two paragraphs—the first ending with the words: "they now proceeded to such lengths as soon satisfied me what they were."—the latter beginning: "The criminal scene they acted I had the patience to see to the end," &c.

(There follows the text of the expurgated passage, which text has been omitted here. [Pub.])

The bibliography of this best known of all English erotic novels is, as M. FERNAN DRUJON justly remarks, "le (*sic*) plus obscure." [1] In spite of every possible research, I have never been able to meet with a copy of the first edition. I have been told by those who said they had seen the volume that one did exist in the library of the British Museum, but it is certainly not there now. JAMES CAMPBELL, an indefatigable student of erotic literature, told me that he had never had the good fortune to encounter a copy of the original edition, which must certainly be of great rarity.

The precise date of the first appearance of this work is indeed involved in doubt. The year 1750 has been adopted by the English bibliographers,[2] but it must certainly have been issued earlier, probably in 1747 or 1748, and the edition given by GAY[3] as the original: "G. FENTON 1747-50, 2 vols." may possibly be correct.[4] In 1750 GRIFFITHS brought out an emasculated version in *one* volume, which he caused to be favourably noticed in his own review, and which is "said to be taken from a very loose work, printed *about two years ago* in *two* volumes." Further, in COPIES TAKEN FROM THE RECORDS we find, under date Nov. 8, 1749, a warrant for the seizure of "a most obscene and infamous book entitled the *Memoirs of a Woman of Pleasure*," and a second warrant, dated March 15, 1749-50, against "*Memoirs of Fanny Hill*." The former of these I take to be the original edition of 1747, or latest early in 1749, while the *Memoirs of Fanny Hill* is in all probably the very book noticed in *The Monthly Review*, especially as the reviewer makes mention of "the step lately taken to suppress this book." The article in question appeared in the No. for April, 1750, and as it is in many respects curious and interesting, I give it place in extenso:

Memoirs of Fanny Hill. One volume 12 mo. Price bound in Calf 3s. This is a work of the Novel kind, thrown into the form of letters, from a reformed woman of the town to her friend, containing memoirs of her past life, and de-

---

[1] CAT. DES OUVRAGES &C. CONDAMNÉS, p. 163.
[2] BIBLIOGRAPHER'S MANUAL, vol. 1, p. 477.
[3] BIBLIOGRAPHIE, vol. 5, p. 50.
[4] The date 1742, as given by COHEN, at col. 78 of his GUIDE, edit. 1876, is probably an error. F. DRUJON gives 1745-50, which appears also to be a mistake.

scribing the steps by which she was led into the paths of vice and infamy.

Though this book is said to be taken from a very loose work, printed about two years ago, in two volumes, and on that account a strong prejudice has arisen against it, yet it does not appear to us that this performance, whatever the two volumes might be, (for we have not seen them) has anything in it more offensive to decency, or delicacy of sentiment and expression, than our novels and books of entertainment in general have: For, in truth, they are most of them (especially our comedies, and not a few of our tragedies) but too faulty in this respect.

The author of Fanny Hill does not seem to have expressed any thing with a view to countenance the practice of any immoralities but merely to exhibit truth and nature to the world, and to lay open those mysteries of iniquity that, in our opinion, need only to be exposed to view, in order to their being abhorred and shunned by those who might otherwise unwarily fall into them. The stile has a peculiar neatness, and the characters are naturally drawn. Vice has indeed fair quarter allowed it; and after painting whatever charms it may pretend to boast, with the fairest impartiality, the supposed female writer concludes with a lively declaration in favour of sobriety, temperance and virtue, on even the mere considerations of a life of *true taste*, and happiness in *this world;* considerations which are often more impartially attended to (especially by our modern free-thinkers) than the more solemn declamations of a sermon; and which are, in truth, no improper groundwork for a reformation, and considerations of a more weighty and serious nature.

As to the step lately taken to suppress this book, we really are at a loss to account for it; yet, perhaps, all wonder on this head will cease, when we consider how liable great men are to be misinformed, how frequently obliged to see with other men's eyes, and hear with other people's ears.

•• The news-papers inform us, that the celebrated history of *Tom Jones* has been suppressed in France, as an immoral work.

I am unable then to offer any description of the original edition, and shall confine myself, as is my invariable custom, to noting such editions as I have myself examined, none of which, as I before observed, includes the passage above cited. As all these reprints contain omissions and variations, more or less important, either in the words or punctuation, due to the slovenliness of the irresponsible printers through whose hands they have passed, it is the more to be regretted that the original reading as approved by the author cannot be established. I endeavour to notice the different issues as nearly as possible in chronological order.

[5]1. MEMOIRS OF A WOMAN OF PLEASURE. *London: Printed for G. Fenton in the Strand MDCCXLIX.*

Large 12mo.; 8 vols.; pp. 228 including title-page, and 250; a small fleuron on the title-page; no bastard title; large type; 12 mezzotinto engravings. Although this edition dates one year earlier than that given by Lowndes as the original, I am, for reasons already advanced, doubtful whether it is really the first issue of the work. It figures among the books of which the circulation was forbidden in Belgium.[6]

2. MEMOIRS OF A WOMAN OF PLEASURE. *London: Printed in the Year M. DCC. LXXVII.*

12mo. (counts 6); size of letter-press 4⅜ by 2¾ inches; two lines on title-page between the words "Pleasure" and "London"; the half-title reads *Memoirs of a ***** of ********;* 2 vols.; paging runs through; pp. 307 including title-page; vol. 1. ends at p. 146. I do not know whether this edition was illustrated; there are no plates in the copy before me.

3. MEMOIRS OF A WOMAN OF PLEASURE. *London: Printed for G. Fenton in the Strand M.DCC.LXXXI.*

12mo.; 2 vols.; pp. 172 and 187; no plates in the copy I have examined.

4. MEMOIRS OF A WOMAN OF PLEASURE. *London: Printed for G. Fenton in the Strand 1784.*

12mo; 2 vols.; pp. 154 and 168; 12(?) engravings. A. S. L. BÉRARD possessed a copy of this edition, which he imagined to be the original; he remarks: "Les nombreuses figures qui accompagnent ce livre sont aussi mauvaises sous le rapport du dessin que sous celui de la gravure.

[5] I am not quite certain as to the punctuation of the title-pages of Nos. 1, 2, 4, 10, 20, although the wording may be relied upon.
[6] CAT. DES LIBRES DÉFENDUS par la Commission Impériale et Royale, p. 55.

Cette édition est d'une extrême rareté, même en Angle-
terre." [7]

5. Memoirs of F****** H***. *Vol. I. London: Printed
for G. Fenton, in the Strand. M.DCC.LXXXIV.*

12mo. (counts 6); size of paper 7¼ by 4¾, of letterpress
5⅝ by 3⅛ inches; 2 vols.; pp. 132 and 144 ex titles; on
title-page a figure between two double lines; the half-title
reads *Memoirs of F**** H****. I have before me a copy
of this same edition with a title-page bearing date
MDCCLXXIX, and with four stars instead of six after the
letter "F"; as on the half-title of the 1784 edition there
are only four stars, whereas there are six in the title-page,
I suspect this title-page to be spurious. There are no plates
in either copy.

6. Memoirs of ************************* *Vol. I.
London: Printed for G. Fenton in the Strand.*

12mo.; 2 vols.; pp. 228 and 252 in all; 11 mezzotinto
engravings, coloured, of which six are in the first, and five
in the second volume; although without date. this is evidently of the last century. The late Mr. F. Hankey, of
Paris, possessed a fine copy of this edition.

7. There is an edition of 1829, in 12mo., 2 vols., pp. 159
and 176, with 18 plates, but I am not certain of the wording of the title.

8. Memoirs of a Woman of Pleasure: *Written by
Herself Embellished with Numerous Copper Plate Engravings Vol. I. London: Printed for the Proprietors. 1831*

12mo.; size of letter-press 3¾ by 2⅔ inches; 2 vols.; pp.
131 and 144; two lines on the printed title-pages; in addition to the engravings, of the number of which I am not
certain, there are two obscene, emblematical, engraved
title-pages; type small and indistinct. The second volume
concludes with: "Madam, Yours, &c. * * Finis."

9. I have before me another copy of this edition, or
what would at first sight appear to be the same. It has,
however, the following curious variation: At the end of
the second volume "Yours &c." are omitted, and inverted
initials are added, thus: "Madam, * * F— H— Finis."

10. Memoirs of a Woman of Pleasure or *the Life
of Miss Fanny Hill In two Volumes From the Original*

[7] Catalogue, MS.

*Quarto Edition of the Author John Cleland Esq. Illustrated
with Twenty-five Original Engravings. London Printed by
John Jones, Whitefriars 1832 Price Three Guineas.*

Large 12mo.; pp. 120 and 135; published by W. Dugdale; the twenty-five engravings are coloured, well done,
and consist of 12 small inserted in the text, and 13 large,
including an engraved title-page, with: Memoirs of Miss
Fanny Hill *a Woman of Pleasure.*

11. This edition was reprinted without date, the same
plates, price three guineas.

12. The Life and Adventures of Fanny Hill, *A Fair
Cyprian, By John Cleland, Esq.*

A lithographed and coloured title-page, with obscene
subjects, without place or date; no printed title-page; the
half-title reads: *Memoirs of a Woman of Pleasure; or, the
Life of Fanny Hill;* 8vo.; size of paper 6¾ by 4⅛; of letter-
press 5⅜ by 3¼ inches; 2 vols. in one; the paging runs
through, but is irregular, that of the first volume terminates
at page 80, while that of vol. II begins with p. 97, and
concludes with p. 173; 20 coloured lithographs, obscene
and badly done; published by W. Dugdale, about 1850.

13 and 14. I have before me two distinct reprints of
this edition; the title-pages are similar, except that "Esq."
is omitted, and on the more modern issue the "J" in the
word "John" is turned; the lithographs are also turned; the
paging, with its irregularity, is the same in all three issues.

15. Memoirs of the Life of the Celebrated Miss
Fanny Hill, *Detailing, in glowing language, her Adventures as a Courtezan and Kept-Mistress; her strange vicissitudes and happy end. Illustrated by numerous elegant
amorous engravings. Reprinted from the original Quarto
Edition of John Cleland. "If I have painted vice in its gayest colours, if I have decked it with flowers, it has been
solely in order to make the worthier, the solemner sacrifice
of it, to virtue." London: Printed by H. Smith, 37, Holy-
well Street, Strand. 1841.*

12mo (counts 6); size of letter-press 4⅜ by 2¾ inches;
pp. 207, with 4 of title and contents; 8 coloured engravings, free but not obscene; 5 lines on title-page; divided
into 11 letters, with headings; W. Dugdale was the publisher. This is a castrated edition, and is probably a reprint
of the work noticed in the *Monthly Review.*

16. MEMOIRS OF THE LIFE OF FANNY HILL, or *the career of a Woman of Pleasure. Illustrated with Coloured Plates. London:—Printed for the Booksellers*

8vo.; size of letter-press 4¼ by 2¾ inches; two double lines on title-page; 2 vols. in one; paging runs through both vols.; 120 pages in all; a portrait of *Fanny Hill* as frontispiece, and 7 badly done lithographs, 8 illustrations in all, coloured, not indecent. This is another castrated edition, which, however, differs somewhat from that noted immediately above; it is worthless.

17. The above edition was again issued, identical in every respect, but without the portrait, and with a fresh set of woodcuts, eight in number, badly done, free, but not obscene.

18. Original Edition. MEMOIRS OF THE LIFE OF MISS FANNY HILL. *Illustrated with beautifully Coloured Plates. Price One Guinea.*

Title on outer board in which it is bound; a half-title, but no title-page; 8vo.; no signatures; size of paper 6½ by 4, of letter-press 4⅝ by 2⅜ inches; 2 vols. in one; paging runs through; pp. 144 in all; 8 wretched woodcuts, coloured, not indecent. This is the same version, with slight alterations, as No. 16; it is of no value.

19. THE SINGULAR LIFE AND ADVENTURES OF MISS FANNY HILL. *A Fair Cyprian, Many Years Resident in Russell Street, Covent Garden, Originally Written by John Cleland Esquire. First Published by R. Griffith, at the Dunciad, in St. Paul's Church Yard. London: Re-Printed by Turner, 23 Russell Court, Drury Lane.*

Engraved title, with a well-drawn vignette, free but not obscene, representing Mr. H. surprising Fanny with her footman Will. This edition, of which I have seen the title-page only, is 12mo. size, and was published by W. DUGDALE, about 1830; it was sold openly, and is consequently a castrated version; there were probably plates, not obscene.

20. MEMOIRS OF A WOMAN OF PLEASURE *written by herself. London.*

There is a lithographed frontispiece with: *The Life and Adventures of Fanny Hill, a Fair Cyprian by* JOHN CLELAND.

12mo.; 2 vols.; paging runs through both vols.; pp. 284; lithographed plates; published in New York, about 1845.

Justice has been rendered abroad to the undoubted merits of Cleland's novel by the numerous translations through which it has passed. I am not aware that it has been done into Spanish, but it may be read, in a more or less curtailed form, in most of the other leading languages of Europe. I will begin with the French renderings, which are the most numerous; none of those, however, which I have seen is complete, and none contains the passage above quoted.

1. LA FILLE DE JOYE. *Ouvrage quintessencié de l'Anglois. A. Lampsaque, 1751.*

8vo.; size of paper 6⅝ by 4, of letter-press 5 by 2⅝ inches; pp. 172 ex title; monogram on the title-page, which is printed in red and black; no plates. This version is much curtailed. It begins with: "Tu veux ma chère Amie, que je retrace à tes Yeux les égarements de ma première jeunesse," &c., and ends thus: "Adieu ma chère, ce qui (*sic*) j'exige de ton amitié, c'est de ne point divulguer mes égarements & de me croire, &c. Fin." This is no doubt, as GAY indicates, the first French edition. He adds that the translator's name is LAMBERT, son of a Paris Banker.[8]

2. This rendering was reprinted, about 1860, by FISCHABER of Stuttgart, without date, wording of title-page the same, except that the impress was changed nto *Cologne, Chez PIERRE MARTEAU.* 12mo.; size of paper 5⅛ by 3¼, of letter press 4¹⁄₁₆ by 2¾ inches; pp. 108; on title-page are a fancy line and a geometrical figure; no plates.

This translation, divided into two parts, or volumes, is the same as in the following Nos. 3, 4, 5, 6, 7, 8, 9.

3. NOUVELLE TRADUCTION DE WOMAN OF PLEASUR (sic), *ou Fille de Joie. Par M. Cleland, Contenant les Mémoires de Mademoiselle Fanny, écrits par elle-même. Avec Figures. Premiere Partie. A Londres, Chez G. Fenton, dans le Strand. M.DCC.LXXVI.*

12mo.; size of letter-press 3⅝ by 2 inches; pp. 119 and 132 in all; two single lines, one double line, and a small

[8] BIBLIOGRAPHIE, vol. 5, p. 50. In the CATALOGUE DES LIVRES DÉFENDUS, p. 29, already referred to, a copy is noted with date 1709, evidently in error.

fleuron on title-page; a bastard-title with the first six words of the title-page; and a half-title: *Mémoires de Miss Fanny, écrits par elle-même;* 15 engravings, unsigned, of which one only, that which serves as frontispiece, has an inscription, and refers to part I, p. 55. This is the most desirable of all the French editions, and was published at Paris by CAZIN. No mention is however made of it in CAZIN SA VIE ET SES ÉDITIONS. H. COHEN describes it correctly, and adds: "Les figures de cette édition très-rare comptent au nombre des plus belles de BOREL et d'ELUIN." [9] ÉDOUARD TRICOTEL has also noted this edition.[10]

4. LA FILLE DE JOIE, *Par M. Cleland, Contenant les Mémoires de Mademoiselle Fanny, écrits par elle-même. Avec Figures. Tome Premier. A Londres. M.DCC.LXXVI.*

12mo. (counts 6); size of letter-press 4 by 2¼ inches; 2 vols.; pp. 111 and 128; two single and one double line on title-page; 15 engravings similar to those in the Cazin edition, they do not correspond with the English text, but the French text has been made to suit them. The half-title reads *Mémoires de Miss Fanny, &c.*

5. Title-page, and size as above; pp. 107 and 116; eight engravings copied from above.

6. As No. 5, except that on title-page "Mademoiselle" is contracted into "Mlle," and the title does not head the pages as in Nos. 4 and 5.

7. Title-page as No. 4; pp. 107 and 115; two (?) engravings (one to each vol.), entirely different from those above mentioned.

8. NOUVELLE TRADUCTION DE LA FILLE DE JOYE. *Par Mr. Cleland, Contenant Les Mémoires de Mlle. Fanny, écrite* (sic) *par elle-même. Avec Figures. Premiere Partie. Londres, M.DCC.LXXVI.*

12mo.; size of letter-press 4¼ by 2¼ inches; pp. 101 and 116; the title-page is enframed, and has three fancy lines and a small fleuron; a frontispiece and three engravings roughly done, but curious, quite different from those above noticed; they all belong to the first part, and are detailed in the *Avis au Relieur* on last page.

[9] GUIDE DE L'AMATEUR, 1876, col. 78.
[10] BIBLIOGRAPHIE ÉROTIQUE, MS.

9. La Fille de Joie, *ou Mémoires de Mademoiselle Fanny, Ecrits par elle-même. Nouvelle Edition. Avec Figures. Tome Premier. A Londres, 1790.*

12mo. (counts 6); size of letter-press 3¾ by 2 inches; pp. 143 and 142 ex titles; one graduated and one plain line on title page; engravings as in No. 4, of which there appear to be fifteen only, although the last is numbered 16; the volumes are differently divided, the second beginning at "Ayant déjà passé," &c., instead of at "Tandis que j'étois," &c., as in Nos. 4 to 8.

10. Nouvelle Traduction de Woman of Pleasur (sic) *ou Fille de Joye de M. Cleland Contenant Les Memoires de Mlle. Fanny écrits par Elle-meme Avec xv Planches en taille douce Partie I. Londres Chez G. Fenton dans le Strand MDCGLXX.*

8vo.; size of paper 8⅝ by 5¼, of letter-press 6¼ by 3¼ inches; 2 parts; pp. 170 ex titles, the paging continued through both parts; the title-pages are engraved and surrounded with a fancy border, at the bottom of which, under the frame, is a 2; they are alike with exception of I or II to indicate the respective part, under which is a double line; to each part there is a frontispiece (both identical in every respect) representing a naked woman standing in the middle of an apartment before a pedestal, out of which protrudes a phallus; the design is enframed, outside the frame there is (at the top) I, and (at the bottom) the inscription *Voeux de Chasteté à la Moderne;* the engravings are in reality only 13 in number, the title and frontispiece of the first part being counted as two, they are all numbered, some at the top, some at the bottom, and some in the design; they are not enframed, they are specified in the *Avis au Relieur* which concludes the second part; they are weak in design and poor in execution; to each part there is a second half-title: *Mémoires de Miss. Fanny, écrits par elle-même.*, but there is neither printed nor bastard title.

Of this version the first part begins: "Je vais te donner, ma chère Amie, une preuve indubitable" &c., and ends: "qui tenoit une bonne hôtellerie, l'épousa." The second part begins: "Tandis que j'étois embarrassée de ce que je deviendrois, &c." and concludes with: "c'est de ne point divulguer mes égarements, & de me croire, &c."

11. La Fille de Joie, *ou Mèmoires de Miss Fanny, Écrits par Elle-Même. A Paris, Chez Madame Gourdan. M.DCC.LXXXVI.*

Large 8vo.; size of letter-press 5¾ by 3 inches; 2 parts;
the paging runs through both parts; pp. 235 ex titles: on
the printed title-page there is a vignette of two cupids
seated round a basket of flowers; there is no printed title
to the second part; both parts have half titles: *Mémoires
de Miss Fanny, écrits par Elle-Même;* one bastard-title at
the beginning of the volume: *La Fille de Joie;* there are
two engraved title-pages, one for each part, worded:
NOUVELLE TRADUCTION DE WOMAN OF PLEASUR (*sic*) *ou
Fille de Joye de M. Cleland Contenant Les Memoires
de Melle Fanny écrits par Elle-même Avec des Planches
en taille douce P^re Partie. A Londres. M.DCCLXXVII,*
with a vignette of a cupid, his penis erect, grinding a
knife at a grindstone, while a female cupid is pissing
upon it; the engraved title-page for the second part differs
in the form of the letters, and slightly in the wording,
"de M. Cleland" becomes "Par Mr Cleland," "Seconde
Partie" is given in full, the vignette here represents seven
naked children, the males with cloven hoofs and erect
members, dancing round an altar on which is an erect
phallus; both engraved title-pages are surrounded by two
lines, and in that to the first part, immediately under
"P^re Partie" are two lines, which are omitted in the engraved title-page to the second part; to the first part there
is an engraved frontispiece enframed, representing a
woman holding up her shift, and admiring her backside
in an oval mirror, while a cupid opens a door through
which fly winged hearts; there is a statue, with erect member, in a niche, over which is written, "Priappe"; the
word "Fanny" is inscribed over the door, and above the
whole design "Frontispiece."; to each part there is an
engraved full page tail-piece, enframed, that terminating
the first part represents Mercury copulating with Venus,
surrounded with flowers and clouds, and is inscribed
within the design (above) "Les Joies Célestes," (below)
"Fin de la Premiere Partie"; that at the end of the volume portrays another naked couple, possible Jupiter
and Juno, in a similar attitude, and on clouds, it is desig-
nated within the design (above) "Charme des Yeux,"
(below) "Fin de la Deuxieme & Derniere Partie"; there
are besides 31 engravings, all obscene excpt Nos. 1, 2, 10,
14, 15, 16, 21, 31, 32, all enframed; in the volume (both
parts), there are then 33 plates (including the two tail-
pieces) all numbered, 1 frontispiece, and 2 engraved and
illustrated title-pages, or 36 engravings in all; the engravings in this edition are certainly not by Borel and

Eluin;[11] they are in the same style, and possibly by the same artist as those in *Therese Philosophe* the large 8vo. edition without date, in *L'Academie des Dames. Venise chez* PIERRE ARETIN, no date, and as those in *Le Portier, Grenoble de l'Imprimerie de la Grande Chartreuse.* This is by far the most luxurious of all the French editions of *La Fille de Joye.* The text is the same as No. 10.

12. The above edition was reprinted in 1881, at Brussels, by MM. GAY and DOUCÉ; title-page similarly worded with impress altered into: *Boston Chez* WILLIAM MORNING; 8vo.; size of paper 6⅝ by 4 inches; pp. vi and 157; small geometrical figure on title-page; the plate of No. 11 reproduced. An *Avant-Propos* of two pages is added.

13. LA FILLE DE JOIE *ou Mémoires de Miss Fanny écrits par elle-même. Tome I. A. Londres, Chez Les Marchands de Nouveautés. MDCCXXXVI.*

Large 12mo. (counts 6); size of paper 7¼ by 4⅜, of letter-press 5⅜ by 3¼ inches; 2 vols.; pp. 92 and 84; on the title-pages are two short lines and a small scroll; this is a Brussels edition of about 1860; there are 15 engravings from the same copper-plates as done for the edition of 1776, No. 4; the half-title reads: *Mémoires de Miss Fanny, &c.*

14. LA FILLE DE JOIE *ou Mémoires de Miss Fanny écrits par elle-même. Tome Premier. Amsterdam et Paris. 1788.*

Small 8vo.; size of paper 6¼ by 4⅛, of letter-press 4⅜ by 2¾ inches; pp. 98 and 100; two graduated and one plain line on title-pages. This is a Brussels reprint, 1872 or 73, of the edition immediately before mentioned, and contains a reproduction in bistre, and by photography, of the same 15 plates; price 20 frcs.; the bastard title reads: *Miss Fanny.*

To recapitaulate the peculiarities of the various French translations: The edition of 1751, No. 1, is very much abridged; those of 1770 and (1777) 1786, Nos. 10 and 11, though following the previous one as far as it goes, are considerably more ample; and the subsequent editions, with some slight variations, follow the text of 1770. Two of the plates in the editions with 8 and 15 figures do not correspond with the English text, and there are some slight changes made in the text of the French translation

[11] As GAY affirms, nor are they taken from any English edition, but are in every respect French.

of 1776, No. 4, in order to make it tally with the engravings. But in the Brussels edition, dated 1736, No. 13, the text of the 1770 edition, No. 10, is followed, while the plates used are those belonging to the edition of 1776, so that text and illustrations do not correspond. The Stuttgart edition without date, No. 2, follows the text of the edition of 1751, as before mentioned.

A complete translation, from the pen of M. JOSEPH DE CHAIGNOLLES, has been promised for several years, and is, I believe, already in manuscript.[12]

Another version will be found in LA BRUNETTE, *ou Adventures d'une Demoiselle*. A Amsterdam 1761. 8vo., pp. 96. It forms the second tale, pp. 25 to 96, in LA FILLE SANS FEINTIZE.[13] In the MÉMOIRES D'UNE CÉLÈBRE COURTISANNE DES ENVIRONS DU PALAIS ROYAL, *ou vie et aventures de M.lle Pauline surnommée la veuve de la Grande Armée. Paris*, TERRY, 1833, 8vo.,[14] with folding, lithographed frontispiece, bearing three subjects, is reproduced, pp. 178 to 189, the latter part of Cleland's novel, from the bathing episode to the end of the book, but castrated and otherwise altered. The Barville flagellation incident is given in *La Lettre*, p. 67 to the end of CHÉRUBIN, *ou l'Heureux libertin, suivi d'une lettre de Julie à Pauline sur quelques goûts bizarres de certains hommes avec lesquels elle s'est trouvée, illustré de 4 gravures sur acier. Amsterdam, 1796.*

It is known in Germany as DAS FRAUENZIMMER VON VERGNÜGEN, and occupies the first volume of the PRIAPISCHE ROMANE. The German translation is complete, and contains the suppressed passage.[15]

There are two Italian renderings, one of which is said to be by Count CARLO GOZZI.[16] Both have passed through several editions. I have seen only:

LA MERETRICE INGLESE *o Avventure di Fanny Will Parigi* 1861.

[12] LE BIOGRAPHE, year 1873-4, p. 191.
[13] This volume resembles in appearance LES FOLLES AMOURS DES DAMES. *Cette présente Année.* Both were probably published in Holland.
[14] DICT. DES OUVRAGES ANONYMES, vol. 3, col. 191.
[15] I suspect therefore that Herr HAYN is in error when he says that it is a translation from the French. He has certainly drawn on his own imagination for the English title given by him at p. 115 of BIBLOTHECA GERMANORUM EROTICA, as "The Girl of Pleasure."
[16] *Avant Propos* to the Brussels reprint of LA FILLE DE JOIE, No. 12, ante.

8vo.; size of letter-press 5 by 2¾ inches; pp. 95; 4 bad woodcuts. This version is translated from the French, and abbreviated even from that. It is no doubt a reprint.

Finally, there is a Portuguese translation:

O Vôo da Innocencia ao auge da Prostituição, ou Memoiras de Miss Fanny, escriptos por ella mesma, 2 tomos em 1 volume, com 7 estampas.[17]

Few works have been more frequently illustrated than the *Memoirs of a Woman of Pleasure*, but really good artists have not, as a rule, exercised their talents on its adornment. The two best sets of plates are: firstly, those by Borel and Eluin, already mentioned; and secondly, a series by George Cruikshank; they are unsigned, but there can be no doubt that they were designed and etched by the great artist; their size would admit of their insertion into an 8vo. volume, but I know neither the edition for which they were done, nor their exact number; they are extremely rare.

(*There follows a list of mezzotints, which has been omitted here.* [*Pub.*])

The procuress, Mrs. Cole, is supposed to be Mother Douglas, of the Piazza, the same woman that Hogarth introduced into his *March to Finchley, Industry and Idleness*, plate xi., and in *Enthusiasm Delineated*. Foote, in his comedy of *The Mirror*, brings her on the stage as Mrs. Cole, a character he used to play himself. Joseph Reid's Mrs. Snarewell, in his farce of *The Register Office*, is intended for the same person.[18]

The name of Cleland's heroine has been frequently used to render attractive catchpenny publications, which have no connection with his work, other than a similarity of title. Such are: The Pathetic Life of the Beautiful Fanny Hill, *Showing how she was seduced, &c.*; and The Last Legacy of Miss Fanny Hill, *a Woman of Pleasure, Containing Useful Instructions for Young Men and Women, &c.* Such pernicious, deceptive garbage, not unfrequently issued by psuedo-pious people, should be avoided. The fraud which aids in palming it on the public must defeat the objects of its promulgators.

[17] I have not seen this volume, but extract the title from a catalogue at the end of *O Cherubim*, noticed at p. 160 of the Index Librorum Prohibitorum.

[18] The Whore's Rhetorick, 1836, p. xii.; Hogarth's Works, series 1; p. 289, and series 2, p. 132, note.